GLENN TRUST
THE GHOST

BOOKS

By Glenn Trust

Sole Justice

Sole Survivor
Road to Justice
Target Down
The Ghost
Dark Winter
Shadow Man

Vinci Books

vinci-books.com

Published by Vinci Books Ltd in 2025

1

Copyright © Glenn Trust 2021

The author has asserted their moral right to be identified as the author of this work in accordance with the Copyright, Designs and Patents Act 1988. This work is a work of fiction. Names, characters, places and incidents are the product of the author's imagination or are used fictitiously. Any resemblance to actual persons, living or dead, places and incidents is entirely coincidental.
All rights reserved. No part of this publication may be copied, reproduced, distributed, stored in any retrieval system, or transmitted in any form or by any means, including photocopying, recording, or other electronic or mechanical methods, nor used as a source for any form of machine learning including AI datasets, without the prior written permission of the publisher.
The publisher and the author have made every effort to obtain permissions for any third party material used in this book and to comply with copyright law. Any queries in this respect should be brought to the attention of the publisher and any omissions will be corrected in future editions.
A CIP catalogue record for this book is available from the British Library.
Paperback ISBN: 9781036704377

Printed and bound in Great Britain by Clays Ltd, Elcograf S.p.A.

ONE

Damned If I Know

"There she is."

"You sure it's her?"

"Goddammit, Chester. You always askin' questions like you think I'm some kind of fool?"

"Sorry, Cope. I didn't mean nothing by it. Just wanted to be sure." Chester nodded. "You're right. You been doing this sorta thing a lot longer than me. I guess that's why I'm nervous about getting it right. Never done anything like this before."

"Here." Cope held out the binoculars. "See for yourself."

"Thanks." Chester took the binoculars, leaned against the truck bed's side to steady himself, and peered through the lenses. After a minute, he nodded. "Yeah, it's her Jeep. Gotta be her."

"It is," Cope snapped and snatched the binoculars back to give the pickup on the road below a last look. "I'd say she's doing about twenty, maybe twenty-five miles an hour. That gives us plenty of time."

Copeland Plunkett and Chester Welch leaned against the rusty fenders of a nondescript, beat-up four-wheel-drive pickup on a rocky promontory overlooking the canyon road. A winding switchback dirt trail climbed the mountainside to their observation point. It would take at least ten minutes to ease the pickup down the trail, over boulders and ruts.

That was no worry. From their vantage point, they could see the Jeep still had a good five miles of twisting turns and creek beds to navigate before it reached the bottom of their mountain. They had more than enough time to descend and set up before the Jeep rounded the last bend and found them waiting.

Cope pulled a ski mask from his back pocket. "Put your mask on and let's go."

Amelia Downes took the turns on the winding canyon road cautiously but with confidence. She'd driven it a thousand times before, had learned to drive long before the legal driving age on this very road in her father's old truck, him seated at her side, clutching the handhold on the doorframe when she took a turn too fast, but generally letting her figure things out without saying too much.

She rounded a bend and swerved expertly thirty yards up the mountainside to the right to detour around a boulder in the road. As big as a house, the boulder had been there as long as she could remember. For all she knew, it could have been deposited there ten thousand years ago, or a million. It didn't matter. The people who used the road accepted the boulder's presence the way they accepted the surrounding mountains, a permanent part of their landscape. The boulder belonged there as much as the mountains, so they detoured around it and kept going.

The first two hours of the trip to Elko to pick up supplies wound through the northern Nevada mountains, across creek fords, and around more boulders even larger than the one at the bend. It was a desolate country, and the isolated stretch of road could have been the model for all the lonesome roads sung about by everyone from Sinatra to Yoakam.

Amelia loved the desolation and loneliness of it. Hours, and sometimes days, could go by without ever seeing another vehicle. That suited her. She was at peace with the solitude.

Nestled along a small river in the northern Nevada mountains, the tiny town of Turnbridge was home. She had no desire to leave for the big city like most of the young people had. Still, she looked forward to the monthly run for supplies and made a day of each visit, picking up essentials and socializing for a few hours.

She spent her days helping her father and Uncle Ron Benson run the D&B Mine operation, which meant she spent most her of time with older men, some very old. The visits to Elko gave her a chance to catch up on news, chat with friends her own age, flirt with the taphouse bartender, sip a beer, and down a burger she hadn't cooked herself. Cal Jackson should be working the bar today, and Cal filled out those Wranglers just right.

She smiled and settled back. The day was dry and clear, the gravel road in reasonably good condition. What the hell. She knew this road like the back of her hand. Her foot pressed harder on the accelerator.

The old pickup made the final switchback turn a couple of hundred feet above the canyon road. Below them, the Jeep was in sight, much closer than they expected.

"Shit!" Cope sat in the passenger seat, pistol in hand, ready to carry out their orders. "We're gonna miss her. Step on it!"

"Step on it?" Wide-eyed, Chester turned his head.

"Faster! Gotta get there before her!"

Chester jerked his head back around to focus on the dirt trail, his knuckles turning white as he gripped the wheel and his foot stomped on the accelerator. The canyon road rose to meet them like a concrete wall. The pickup hit a dirt mound at the point where the mountain trail came out onto the road. The front end lifted a couple of feet and the truck's underframe bellied out as it came back down before sliding into the roadway without slowing.

"Nooo!" Chester yelled and closed his eyes.

Amelia looked up to the right in time to see the pickup come flying at her over the dirt mound. Then the world went dark.

Amazingly, the old truck's suspension held. The Jeep wasn't so fortunate. The cattle pusher mounted over the truck's grille cut a deep jagged V in the passenger side and pushed the Jeep across the road, slamming it into a rock wall.

Cope and Chester sat stunned for nearly a minute as the dust settled. The only sound was the popping and creaking of cooling metal.

Then Cope looked at Chester. "What in the fuck did you do!"

"You said go faster," Chester mumbled, still dazed.

"I didn't say kill her!"

"Kill her?" Chester's eyes were wider than ever now. "Did I … You don't think she's … Do you?"

"How the fuck do I know?" Cope pushed his door open and stepped out, rubbing his right knee. "You busted my knee up, dammit!" He limped around, working the knee up and down and wincing with the pain.

"I didn't mean to, Cope. Really, I didn't" Chester got out of the driver's side patting himself up and down to make sure he was all in one piece. "That's alright, Cope. I ain't hurt,"

"Well, that's just fucking great for you, ain't it."

"All I mean is, I can do what you want," Chester said meekly. "Just tell me what and you set back and rest up some. Only …" A worried look came across his face. "Only don't tell me to … you know …"

"What? Don't kill her?" Cope sneered. "It's likely you already done that."

"Don't say that, Cope." Chester followed his partner to the Jeep.

Peering through the Jeep's caved in passenger side, they could see Amelia Downes laying against the driver's door, her head against the cracked window, bleeding. She wasn't moving, and the driver's side was lodged against the rocks.

"Shit," Cope muttered and walked around to the front of the Jeep. He turned, surveyed the ground around the rock wall, and pointed. "There, pick up that rock."

Chester paled. "Wh-what you want me to do with it?"

"Pick up the damned rock!" Cope's voice echoed off the mountain slope and rock wall.

"No." Chester shook his head solemnly, terrified that Cope's next order would be to smash the girl's skull with the rock. "Not 'til you tell me what for."

"So's we can break out the damned windshield and pull

her out." Cope shook his head in disgust. "You really are a moron, aren't you?"

"Don't say that," Chester said and bent over. "See I'm getting the rock."

It weighed about twenty-five pounds. Chester lifted it and banged it against the windshield. Nothing happened.

"Harder," Cope said.

Chester lifted the rock and hit the windshield harder. A spider web crack opened up in the glass.

"Again!" Cope shouted.

Chester repeated the process, and the safety glass shattered into thousands of pieces.

It took fifteen minutes to cut the seat belt off and work Amelia away from the door, over the steering wheel, and out through the shattered windshield. They laid her in the dirt beside the Jeep, catching their breath. She was alive but bleeding from the wound in her scalp and unconscious.

Chester said nothing and stood gawking at her. Cope rubbed his sore knee, thinking.

"What now?" Chester finally asked.

"Damned if I know."

TWO

Where to Now?

Where to now? It was the question he asked himself a thousand times a day.

Sole gave himself the usual answer. I have no idea.

It had become his routine. Each day, he pointed the old pickup toward the sun, or away from it, randomly moving from state to state, from coast to coast, guided by instinct, or by chance. He wasn't really sure which.

He hoped the winding path he'd followed would be impossible to track. In the last year, he'd put ten thousand miles between himself and the confrontation in the Mexican desert with the *Los Salvajes* cartel.

On the surface, there seemed to be no reason to continue running. *Los Salvajes* had gone silent after he eliminated their leader, Bebé Elizondo, along with Alejandro Garza, the man who murdered his wife and children. John Sole had hoped that would be enough to kill the pain and fill the black hole sucking away his reason to exist.

It was not. The pain remained, just under the surface, a

wound scabbed over but not fully healed. The slightest thought, a brief memory of a smile or laugh ripped the scab away, and the wound bled.

Part of him was grateful for that. Healing and deliverance meant that the memories would fade away, that he would forget. He couldn't allow himself to do that.

So now what? The answer was simple—now nothing. Nothing was easy. Nothing was safer for everyone. There were no commitments, no attachments, no responsibilities. Without commitment, there could be no guilt. Without attachment there could be no loss. And without responsibility, he could not hurt others.

So, he kept moving, remaining anonymous. He stopped here and there to work some odd job and put a few dollars away in his pack. Then he moved on again.

He was moving now along a two-lane highway in northern Nevada, generally pointed toward Idaho but with no particular destination in mind. He'd driven all night and a couple of hundred more miles since daybreak. It was time to rest.

A sign up ahead hanging at an intersection with a gravel road read, *Turnbridge - 22 miles*. Riddled with bullet holes, the sign hung precariously from a rusted metal pole.

He slowed, yawned, and stretched in the seat, then nodded and turned the pickup off the asphalt onto the gravel. "Looks like you're not going to make Idaho today, John-boy," he muttered.

The first few miles ran through ranch land, and he considered pulling off into one of the pasture entrances and sleeping in the pickup, but he'd done that three nights in a row, and besides the ache in his back, he was bone tired. Just twenty miles or so, and there will be some sort of bed and maybe something to eat besides convenience store snacks.

The Ghost

The ranch country disappeared. Mountains closed in around the road, in places rising vertically from the shoulder for thousands of feet.

After a few miles, he came to a stream crossing the road. Another sign warned, *Dickinson Ford—Danger—Do Not Cross During High Water.* He slowed and poked his head out the driver's window. The stream trickle pleasantly enough and he could see the gravel bottom. To be safe, he engaged the pickup's four-wheel-drive and rolled slowly into the water. He could hear a waterfall somewhere up the canyon. No doubt the spring melt would turn the stream into a torrent.

He crossed without a problem and accelerated as much as he dared in the dwindling light on an unfamiliar road. Ahead there was a fork, one branch taking a sharp bend to the right and the other heading off straight ahead, up a mountain ravine.

Which way now. Straight ahead or to the right. He looked around for another sign to guide him to Turnbridge, but whoever was in charge of signs must have figured that if you made it this far, you knew where Turnbridge was. If not, you were on your own.

The road heading up the mountain ravine seemed an unlikely place for a town to be situated. He opted for the bend to the right.

Fifteen miles more to Turnbridge, he reckoned. The thought occurred to him that the town might be nothing more than one of the old mining ghost towns scattered around the Nevada backcountry.

"Well, you're committed now," he whispered.

Sleeping with ghosts didn't seem so bad. Ghosts were quiet and didn't shoot at you.

No, but they haunt. They bring back memories and that's not good. He shook his head. Stop thinking and drive.

Hunched over the wheel, he focused on the road to Turnbridge.

THREE

They Blew It

The phone chimed once. Peter Jenks answered immediately.

"Yes."

"We took her."

"Say that again."

Cope Plunkett swallowed and repeated his announcement, unable to conceal the tremor in his voice. "We took her ... I mean, things happened and ... we had no choice, so ..." He paused and swallowed again. "We took her."

"What in the fuck are you talking about!" Jenks was shouting now. "Taking her was not in the plan. What *things* happened?"

"W-well, we w-was coming down the trail to cut her off, like we p-planned," he stammered. "And then there she was."

"There she was? What the hell does that mean. Of course, there she was. That was the plan!"

"Right, exactly. I mean that was the plan, and we were there like we planned except ..."

"Except what!" Jenks took a breath to calm himself. He

knew Plunkett was terrified of him. Jenks liked it that way, usually. Now, he wanted the facts and wanted them quickly, but Plunkett sounded like he was about to shit himself and stroke out on the other end of the line.

"Well, she sort of got there first."

"Sort of? What's that mean?" Jenks managed to say without shouting.

"Well, I mean she got there first … surprised us and all, and …"

"And?"

"Yeah … I mean we was coming down the trail to cut her off like we planned, but she must have been going faster than we thought she could go, so she got there first and we …"

"You're not making sense!"

Jenks was shouting again. Plunkett started to stammer again.

"I-I'm not? I mean, don't you see if …"

"If she got there first, how did you happen to take her?"

"Oh, that."

He could almost see Plunkett nodding his head as the lightbulb flicked on, and he understood the question. Plunkett continued while Jenks resisted the urge to throw the phone through the window.

"So, what we did was speed up, you know, so we could get there ahead of her like we planned. Except we didn't get there first. We sort of got there at the same time."

Jenks remained silent now, visualizing the scene in his mind. The pickup careening down the switchback trail. The Jeep approaching on the canyon road. And then …

"That is to say," Plunkett said in conclusion. "We plowed into the Jeep."

"You crashed into her!"

"Yes, but don't worry," Plunkett added quickly. "Didn't hurt the pickup much at all. That old truck is tough, and that cattle bumper caved in the whole side of the Jeep."

"The girl! What happened to the girl?"

"Right, the girl." Plunkett nodded at Chester Welch. "She was unconscious. Got knocked around pretty good, so we figured the best thing was to take her with us and call you, so that's just exactly what we're doing now," Plunkett concluded, seemingly proud that they had come up with an alternate plan on their own.

"You took her," Jenks said, shaking his head in disgust. "You thought that was a good idea ... all on your own, without contacting me."

"Well, you know how phone service is down on that canyon road. No signal, so we couldn't really contact you without just leaving her there."

"Has she seen your faces?" Jenks seethed.

"Has she ..." Plunkett's face paled.

"What?" Chester Welch leaned forward, concerned by the sudden fear on his partner's face, eyes wide, mouth frozen half open. "What did he say, Cope?"

"Quiet," Plunkett managed to squeak out.

"What," Jenks snapped back.

"No sir, not you. I was talking to Welch." He took a deep breath, then mumbled. "She might have seen us. I mean, just for a second. Like I say she's been in and out a lot, knocked out of things by the crash and all."

"Dammit!" Jenks shouted. "Get some masks and put them on. Make sure she doesn't see your faces."

"Right, we got masks," Plunkett said proudly. "So, we could do the plan and all."

"Well, put them on! Do not let her see your faces." Jenks

thought things through for a second and added, "And don't talk to her."

"Right, masks," Plunkett said. "We'll get right on that, Mr. Jenks, and no talking to her."

"And no names! Not yours, not mine, no names period. Use your heads for once." Jenks paused for a moment, considering Plunkett's mental acuity and added quietly, "Are we on speaker?"

"No sir! I figured you would want this to be a sort of private talk."

"Good thinking."

Plunkett missed the sarcasm in Jenks' tone and answered appreciatively, "Thanks Mr. J… I mean thanks. Don't worry about a thing."

"I'm already worried." He wanted to add, 'you moron', but didn't want to rattle Plunkett any more than he already was. "Where are you?"

"We brought her to the cabin. Figured that was a good spot. No one knows about it."

Jenks thought about that for a second and nodded. "Alright. Keep her there, and both of you stay put until you hear from me. Is that clear?"

"Yessir."

"Good."

Jenks disconnected. Plunkett looked at Chester Welch, seated in a plastic chair on the other side of the small room. He leaned forward like a man expecting bad news.

"So how was he?" Welch asked. "How bad a trouble are we in?"

"It wasn't good, but all in all he took things about as good as you might expect." Plunkett nodded at the dusty, moldy mattress on the floor beside Welch. Amelia Downes lay on top, eyes closed and apparently unconscious, her hands and feet bound with rope, and a torn sheet wrapped around her head to bandage the wound in her scalp. "We stay here with her until he calls back."

"Okay." Welch nodded. "That's all?"

"Put your mask on and don't talk to her."

"Okay, Cope."

"And no names!" Plunkett looked hard at Welch. "Use your head for once."

"Right." Welch reached for the ski mask shoved in his back pocket, relieved that Jenks hadn't given them an order to do away with the girl, or for Plunkett to do away with him. He pulled the mask over his head and the thought occurred to him—or maybe Plunkett received the order to do away with both of them, but wasn't going to share it with him. Chester Welch backed his chair into a corner where he could watch the girl with one eye and Plunkett with the other.

Peter Jenks sat for a minute behind the desk. The plan had turned to shit. He had no choice but to own that. Plunkett and Welch were his recruits. He had assured everyone that they could execute the simple plan he put together.

He pushed himself up from the desk and walked into the tiny hallway of an old house on one of the 'Tree Streets' in Elko, Nevada. The house was one of the oldest structures in the city, had once been a fashionable home on the fringes. Now it was just off the main drag, Idaho Street, and was one of the last remaining vintage structures in the neighborhood surrounded by the shops, offices, casinos, motels, and gas stations that crowded in around it as Elko grew and the gold mining industry boomed.

Gold mining opportunities were the reason Entente Mining Corporation, known as EMC in the industry, purchased the house and turned it into its local start-up office. Start-up meant Jenks was one of two occupants. He held the title of Chief of Special Operations, but his responsibilities were far less benign than the euphemistic job title implied.

In Entente's world of acquisitions, hostile takeovers, and third-world despots, Special Operations had many meanings. Operating primarily in countries where it was common practice to play loose with the rules, Jenks' Special Operations plans often involved, bribery, extortion, veiled threats, and open intimidation, all to meet Entente's goals of dominating the global mineral mining market.

In the furtherance of those goals, he and Turner Bates, Senior Vice President and Head of Business Development, had come to Elko and set up shop. The first order of business was the acquisition of a small gold mining operation in the northern mountains near the Idaho state line.

The owners of the D&B Mine, Jake Downes and Ron Benson refused to sell. After twenty years working for one of the big corporate mines in the area, they pooled their resources and put a down payment on an old mine near the township of Turnbridge. For that, they got everything, the mine, the mineral rights, and the aging equipment left behind by the previous owners. They went to work hiring miners and equipment operators, offering shares in the mine to offset the low wages they could provide. Most of the applicants were like them, people tired of working for the big corporates and willing to take a chance, strike out on their own, and just maybe strike it rich.

It was risky, but risk had always been part of mining. The only certainty was that there was, in fact, gold in the mountains. Northern Nevada had become one of the largest gold mining centers in the world, and that was why Entente Mining Corporation showed up in the little-known, backwater city of Elko.

Jenks' plan was simple enough, and by Entente's customary methods in more remote parts of the globe, it was fairly innocuous. Entente made them an offer. Downes and Benson refused to sell. Entente sweetened the offer three times, throwing a little more cash at them. They still refused, so the decision was made to move on to a tactic that had always worked in the past—intimidation.

One night after an evening of socializing with locals, the partners walked out to their pickups to discover their front tires slashed. Another time, someone left dead cats on their porches. Ron Benson's house was vandalized inside while he was away visiting family in Colorado. A fire started from unknown causes in Downes' backyard, burning down a shed where he stored his tools.

There were no suspects, and no one from Entente took responsibility for these acts, or even acknowledged that they occurred. They never issued a warning to Downes and Benson. That would have been foolhardy and would have connected Entente to the crimes and landed someone in prison.

Instead, each act of intimidation was preceded a day before by a phone call from Turner Bates in which he made a slightly better offer than before. Downes and Benson always refused the offer. Bates never mentioned the attempts at intimidation, and they could prove no connection between the strictly business phone calls and the incidents, but Downes and Bates understood completely and held their ground. This was their mine, and they were by-God going to mine it.

Unaccustomed to delays in such dealings, the Entente Board of Directors put pressure on the Chairman-CEO, Owen Syndall, to get the deal done. In turn, Syndall, in his most genteel Ivy League manner, applied pressure on Bates to get the deal done. Genteel or not, Bates understood that his multi-seven-figure job depended on acquiring the mine and turned to his right-hand man, Peter Jenks.

The simple plan, the one Plunkett and Welch botched, was to pressure Downes, and by extension Benson, where he was most vulnerable. They would focus on his daughter, Amelia.

It was supposed to be a simple matter of intimidation. Stop her on the deserted canyon road. Shout and point their pistols at her. Shoot some bullet holes in the Jeep. Do their best to frighten her. They were never to mention Entente or the mine acquisition, but they were to give her a message in these exact words—*It will get worse.*

There would be no connection to Entente, Bates, or Jenks. The men involved would disappear and never be seen again or identified. The same tactics had successfully concluded deals many times before. There was no doubt they would succeed again.

After all, Downes loved his daughter and was highly protective of her, the way any father is of a young woman thrown in the midst of a testosterone-driven, predominantly male culture. Since his wife's death eight years earlier, Amelia had become his partner and confidante. His smile was always broadest when Amelia was in the room.

Ron Benson was equally protective of her. She looked at him as a favorite uncle. He'd known her almost since birth and regarded her as a surrogate daughter, the one he never had. Surely, when the intimidation was directed at Amelia, the men would take their generous payoff and move away.

The Ghost

The botched execution of the simple plan changed everything. Plunkett and Welch kidnapped her, an act that escalated things far beyond their clumsy abilities to pull it off without being caught. When law enforcement became involved, they would be tracked down. The finger would eventually be pointed at Entente, Syndall, Bates, and Jenks.

He'd erred in relying on Plunkett and Welch, but Entente's time constraints forced him to put a team together more quickly than usual. He found the two out-of-work drifters hanging out in a bar in Carlin. After drinks and a promise of a hefty bonus, they agreed to go to work for him and then disappear quietly.

They handled the preliminary, smaller acts of intimidation well enough. Jenks thought they could handle Amelia Downes, threaten her, give her the message that things were about to get worse, and then leave Nevada with their pockets lined.

No connection with Entente would be left behind, but Downes and Benson would know where the threat to Amelia came from and could not, would not, ignore it. Except Plunkett and Welch were idiots, and they blew it.

Shit! Jenks tapped on Turner Bates' door. "We need to talk."

FOUR

Not Looking for Trouble

The surprise was complete. He hadn't seen another vehicle or person on the road in the hour since taking the turnoff to Turnbridge. Now there were three, two pickups and a banged-up Jeep against the canyon's rock wall.

Sole slowed, scanning the vehicles and surrounding rocks for the drivers. No one was in sight, and the little warning alarm in his head went off. In fact, it wailed like a tornado siren before the F5 hits.

Three abandoned vehicles, one crashed, and no one in sight. The back of his neck tingled with tension. His brain shouted—Danger!

Maybe going to Turnbridge wasn't such a good idea. He'd been caught in enough ambushes, had even organized a few, to recognize this one. He had three options—Get the hell out of there, exit the truck to investigate and take the fight directly to whoever had the road blocked, or sit there and wait to see what happened next.

He discarded the idea of sitting and waiting. Inaction was not in his makeup.

That left investigating and possibly fighting it out or getting the hell away from the area—his preferred option.

He craned his head to scan the high rocks surrounding the canyon. A hundred pairs of eyes could be watching and waiting to see what he would do. Out in the open, he would be an easy target, and without more information about the intent of those unseen eyes, standing in the open seemed foolhardy.

The pickup provided little cover, and whoever was watching could shoot it up anyway and take him out without ever confronting him. They hadn't done that … yet. Maybe that meant they were waiting for him to choose the third option—get out of the area and mind your own business.

"Alright, you win … whoever you are," he muttered. "No sudden moves. I'll just ease my ass back out the way I came in."

He shifted the gears to reverse, lifted his foot from the brake, and pressed ever so lightly on the accelerator while looking through the rearview mirror to navigate around the rocks and bend in the road.

"Hold it!" The shouted command came from in front.

Sole rocked the pickup to a stop, but kept the engine running and the gears in reverse. He swiveled his head around to look out the windshield.

The muzzle of the Browning hunting rifle in 7mm magnum caliber yawned at him from ten yards. The man glaring at him over the sights held it with an easy familiarity that told Sole he knew how to use the rifle.

At this range, the magnum rounds could punch a hole in the windshield, in John Sole, exit through the back of the truck cab, and continue on another couple hundred yards. As a demonstration in the physics of ballistics, it would be interesting to watch. As the subject of the demonstration, Sole had no desire to take part.

He looked into the eyes of the man holding the rifle and waited. His right hand moved toward the .45 caliber Colt 1911 tucked into the seat beside him. He could still survive, but the odds were diminishing as the seconds passed and the man with the rifle took control of the situation within the enclosed area that would become their battlefield.

Better to go down with a fight if it came to that, he decided. His hand touched the butt of the pistol. The time to act had come—then it passed just as quickly.

"Take that hand out from between the seats!" a voice shouted to his left.

He had come from the rocks on the driver's side while Sole focused on the man with the Browning. Armed with a Winchester .30-30, the second man looked into Sole's eyes and nodded as if to say, you have a choice to make, so make it. Something in his eyes told Sole he hoped he would pull the Colt so he could pour .30 caliber slugs into him until he was a bloody hunk of Swiss cheese.

Sole slid his hand away from the pistol and slowly raised both hands over the steering wheel. He chanced turning his head to the left.

The man there took a step forward. The muzzle of the .30-30 inched closer, pointed directly between his eyes.

He was fiftyish, wearing blue jeans, denim work shirt, and a faded red, threadbare ball cap with a *D&B Mining* patch sewn to the front covering iron-gray hair. Like a good cop, Sole registered all of this instinctively.

"Turn it off," the man barked.

Sole nodded and lowered his right hand.

"Slow. Stay away from whatever gun you got down there

by the seat." The man leaned forward, the Winchester at his shoulder, finger on the trigger.

"Right," Sole said. "Slow. Like molasses."

Keeping his left hand elevated over the wheel, he allowed his right to creep down toward the ignition switch. He gave it a turn. The pickup's engine died, and he raised his hand again.

Gravel crunched, and Sole turned his head toward the front of the pickup. The man with the Browning approached until he stood at the truck's bumper, the rifle extended toward him over the hood until it was less than four feet from Sole's nose. He was black, dressed in the same fashion as his companion, with the same battered ball cap on his head, and the same hard look in his eyes.

"Where is she?" the man with the .30-030 hissed between clenched teeth, his gray eyes boring into Sole.

"I don't know who you're talking about, friend."

"I'm not your friend," .30-30-man said and leaned the muzzle a little closer to Sole's face. "You believe that?"

"I believe it," Sole said. "That rifle in my face is pretty convincing."

"Then I'll ask it one more time. Where is she?"

"Mister, if I knew, believe me, I would tell you. Hell, I'd lead you to her, whoever she is." Sole shook his head. "But I don't know, and that's the truth of it."

"You expect me to believe that you just happen to come along on the road to Turnbridge the same day my daughter gets wrecked and kidnapped." He spat to the side as if the idea was so incredulous the words tasted bad. "There aren't ten cars a week on this road, and you just come passing by, today, at this exact moment. That's what you want me to believe?"

"Believe what you want, but it's the truth," Sole replied,

his eyes focused on the man's hand and trigger finger. "Coincidences do happen, and I am just passing through."

"Get out." .30-30-man took a step out and motioned with the rifle's muzzle.

Sole pushed the door open and stepped out, hands in the air.

"Over there. Put your back against that boulder and don't move."

Sole moved to the edge of the canyon wall and put his back against the rock.

"Check the truck, Ron."

Magnum-man nodded, leaned his rifle against the pickup's fender, and pulled the door open. He rummaged around the driver's side for a minute, held up the Colt 1911 for his companion to see, laid it on the pickup's hood, then moved to the passenger side.

One by one, he pulled Sole's weapons from behind the seats, a Glock and two rifles. He placed the weapons alongside the Colt and turned to face Sole.

"You go well-armed for a man not looking for any trouble and just here by coincidence."

"So do you," Sole said and nodded at the rifle.

"Who said we're not looking for trouble?" .30-30-man growled. "I want my daughter back or I promise you, there'll be trouble you can't even imagine."

"I've seen trouble." Sole nodded. "I can imagine."

"Just so you know we aren't playing around here," .30-30-man snapped.

Magnum-man gathered up Sole's weapons and took them to one of the pickups parked beside the smashed Jeep. When he came back, he had a bundle of electrical wiring zip-ties in his hand.

"Turn around."

The Ghost

Sole complied and with the skill of someone who worked with his hands, Magnum-man pulled the ties around his wrists and secured them behind his back. He spun Sole around so that they were standing nose to nose.

"Can you tell me what all this is about?" Sole asked.

.30-30-man lowered his rifle and stepped forward, clamping a burly fist over Sole's arm. "You're coming with us."

FIVE

Plausible Deniability

Turner Bates swiveled his chair to face the computer screen and camera on his desk, took a deep breath, clicked on the icon that activated Entente's intra-company video conference system, and waited. A chime sounded and an instant later Owen Syndall's face filled the screen. He did not look happy.

"I've been expecting your call," Syndall said sharply. "The board meets in half an hour, and they expect our report." He paused. "A positive report."

"Sorry," Bates said with a deferential nod. "There have been a few delays."

"Delays? What sort of delays." Syndall's brow furrowed. "You assured me the Nevada project was moving forward."

"It is. Nothing to worry about. There are always delays," Bates said quickly and raised his palm in a way that was supposed to reassure his boss, but which only aggravated him all the more.

"Stop the bullshit!" Syndall snarled. "Low hanging fruit! That's what you said we were going after. Buy out a small-

The Ghost

time operation. Build it until we had a strong foothold in the Nevada market. Then we go after the big boys."

The big boys were two global mining enterprises that had beaten Entente to the Nevada gold rush by a couple of decades. Trivial details like that had never stopped Entente in the past, and Bates had assured Syndall that he could push things forward according to schedule. What he hadn't counted on were two intractable old-timers who would just as soon go back to the old days of pulling a burro along and hacking the gold from the mountains with a pick and shovel before selling out their entrepreneurial dream to a global conglomerate with a New York Stock Exchange ticker symbol.

"Sorry," Bates began again. "What I mean is that they are playing hardball. Nothing we haven't dealt with before."

"Hardball?" Syndall's tone became sarcastic. "Two backcountry gold miners playing hardball with Turner Bates and Entente Mining Corporation? That seems a little hard to believe."

"As I say, nothing we haven't dealt with before. They turned down our initial offer. That was to be expected."

"What about the others?"

"Turned down," Bates said and braced himself.

"Turned down?" Syndall leaned across his desk toward the computer screen until the camera lens fishbowl effect turned his face into an angry, elongated mask. "All four of them? Turned down!" he shook his head. "That is not a report I can make to the Board."

"You don't have to," Bates said calmly, trying to reassure his boss. "Tell them we are making progress and will have the deal closed within the month."

"And the hardball game?" Syndall leaned even closer to the screen. "What if they continue to pass on the deal?"

"We are taking steps to … motivate them." Bates nodded reassuringly. "I am confident when we …"

"Stop!" Syndall raised a hand and leaned as far away from the screen as possible. "I don't want to know."

Bates smiled. Plausible deniability—Syndall's standard response when it was time to play rough. Kennedy used it when the CIA planned to assassinate Castro. Johnson and his entire administration used it to fund and escalate a war that their own Defense Department said officially, but secretly, was unwinnable. Nixon used it when, on his behalf, E. Howard Hunt's operatives broke into DNC offices at the Watergate.

Owen Syndall used it to position Entente into one of the largest and most powerful mining conglomerates in the world. Nothing was off-limits. Threats, intimidation, coercion were all tools to be used to further Entente's reach. And Turner Bates was his E. Howard Hunt, free to do what was necessary to move the company closer to global domination of the mining industry — as long as Owen Syndall had no direct knowledge of the tactics he employed.

"Fair enough," Bates said and managed not to smirk. "You can report that negotiations are tougher than we expected but we are confident of success."

"Are we?"

"I wouldn't say it if I didn't believe it," Bates said with bravado. "There is always a price, and it's only a matter of time before we find that price and take control of the D&B Mine."

"How much time?"

"Not much." Bates was thinking fast. How much time would they need to do what was necessary? "Like I said, a month."

"A month," Syndall said doubtfully then nodded.

"Alright. You have a month. I'll try to hold the Board off that long, but their patience is running out. There's talk about making changes ... at the top."

"Understood." Bates nodded. "We are fast-tracking negotiations today."

"Good." Syndall leaned forward again, his eyes boring into the camera. "This is important, Bates ... for both of us. I serve at the discretion of the Board, and you serve at my discretion. You would do well to keep that and the prospect of losing your multimillion-dollar stock options in mind. Now get it done."

Syndall tapped his mouse, and the video call ended. Bates looked across his desk. Peter Jenks had listened to the conversation without revealing his presence. If Bates was Entente's Howard Hunt, Jenks was his G. Gordon Liddy, an operative, ready, willing, and capable of doing whatever was required to move the mission forward.

"You heard," Bates said. "Fast-track. How do we clean up the mess your boys made on the canyon road?"

"We leverage it."

Bates thought about it then nodded. "I suppose you're right."

"It's messier than we wanted," Jenks admitted. "But whether we intended it or not, we now have the sort of leverage they can't ignore."

"Repercussions?"

"Don't worry about that." Jenks smiled. "There won't be any. Not for you or anyone else."

Bates nodded and asked no more questions. If Owen Syndall craved plausible deniability to save his skin, Turner Bates cherished it.

SIX

The Ghost

They were angry, frustrated, desperate even, and without any plan at all. That made them dangerous. John Sole had seen it before, had lived it, and he knew the darkness that could descend over decent men driven by desperation.

Bound hand and foot in the back crew cab of one of the pickups, he bounced along, listening to his captors speak over the portable radios they carried. Mostly they asked questions of each other, trying to come up with a plan, but from the snippets of radio conversation, he could piece together what had happened.

The daughter of one of them, the one driving the pickup carrying Sole, was missing, her car left wrecked and abandoned on the side of the road. It took little investigative skill to see that another vehicle struck the Jeep and rammed it violently against the rock wall. He'd taken all that in before they bound him and shoved him into the back of the pickup.

That she was missing from the scene indicated that there was more to this than a standard hit and run. No one had reported the accident. Listening to their nervous chatter, he gathered more facts. The daughter—Amelia, he'd heard one of them call her—was experienced in living in the backcountry, and she would have stayed with the Jeep or walked back along the road to Turnbridge. She definitely would not head out into the wilderness in search of help or a shortcut.

"I'm gonna kill that fucking Bates," the one driving Sole said into the radio. "I swear to God, Ron, if they harm one hair on her head, I will kill him with my bare hands."

"Not if I get to him first, Jake," the reply crackled over the radio.

Another piece of information. The man driving him was Jake. Ron followed in the second pickup.

The conversation died away. The pickups bounced along the dirt road for another hour before slowing. Sole managed to raise his head enough to peer out the window.

The road they were on was still gravel, but improved somewhat as it passed through the center of a small town—Turnbridge, Sole assumed. The pickups passed down the quarter-mile length of the main street and slowed enough so the dust plume behind them would not coat everything in town. When they reached the end of the row of buildings, they increased speed again.

Fifteen minutes later, they veered to the right and took another road up a steep incline for half a mile, then leveled out and rocked to a stop in a dirt clearing cut out of the side of a mountain. Jake, the driver, waited a few seconds to let the dust settle, then got out and pulled open the rear door. He reached in with a burly hand, dragged Sole out by the collar, and dumped him in the dirt.

"Let's go." Jake bent down and grabbed him by an arm.

The second man, Ron, came up and took him by the

other arm. They were big men, muscled from years of work in the mines, and had no trouble holding him between them, his toes dragging in the dirt, as they walked to a nearby doublewide. They mounted the wooden steps, with his feet dangling in the air, and pushed the door open.

Tossed inside like a sack of potatoes, Sole hit the floor hard. Jake and Ron followed him in. Jake kicked the door closed with the back of his boot, and they stepped forward together, standing over him, glaring down.

"Start talking," Jake said through clenched teeth, the words clipped and tight from the pent-up rage he was working hard to control.

Lying on his side, trussed like a hog, Sole felt as helpless as a catfish in the bottom of a johnboat about to be brained and fileted. He twisted so he could look into their faces. "What do you want to know?"

"Where's my daughter?" Jake said, his voice rising now. "That's what I goddamn want to know!"

"You want the truth, or you want me to make something up?" Sole said, trying to find a way to reason with them.

"You say anything except the truth, and I will kill you where you lie. Plenty of places up here to dump a shitbag like you where no one will ever find the body except the coyotes and the crows." Jake pulled a nine-millimeter pistol from his waistband, worked the slide, and racked a shell into the chamber. "Now start talking. Where did Bates take my daughter?"

"My name is John Sole. I don't know this Bates person." He tensed and prepared himself for what was to come. "That's the truth."

Jake's boot lashed out and caught Sole in the gut. He lowered the pistol so that the muzzle pointed directly into

Sole's face, and for a moment, Sole thought he might pull the trigger.

"I was a police officer back in Atlanta a few years back." He was speaking faster now, figuring he only had seconds to convince Jake to slow down and think things through. "A drug cartel murdered my family ... wife and children." His voice broke as he dredged up the memory. An odd sense of guilt overwhelmed him. It felt wrong to bring up their memory like this, even to save his skin, but he added, "I found the ones who did it. They'll never do anything like that again."

Jake hesitated and after a few seconds lowered the pistol by his side so that it pointed at the floor. "So now you work for Bates ... that it? You've gone rogue."

"No." Sole shook his head. "Now, I don't do much of anything."

"A drifter then. The kind of person Bates would use to do his dirty work," Ron said and shook his head. "How do we know anything you're saying is true?"

"Check it out. You have internet up here?"

"We have a satellite connection for the mine business," Ron said and looked at Jake. "Maybe we should check it out before we make a decision on him."

"Alright." Jake took a deep breath. "We'll check it out, but it's still not enough to change things between us."

Sole nodded and lay back on the floor to relieve the ache in his neck from looking up at the two men. Ron disappeared into an adjacent room. Jake stood quietly, waiting, the pistol still in his hand. Sounds of keyboard clicks let Sole know that Ron was searching the internet, and he prayed the search engine would provide enough information to at least make them stop and think before they did something undoable.

Several minutes passed, and Ron came back into the room. He held up a paper. It was a grainy printout of a photo from a newspaper article several years before.

"That's him," he said, handing the printout to Jake and nodding at Sole. "Picture's not the best, and he looks a lot scruffier now, but I'd say that's him. John Sole, Atlanta detective … wife and children murdered … suspected that a drug cartel was responsible but never proved and there were no arrests for the murder."

"They did it," Sole said from the floor.

"Sole disappeared a few years back," Ron continued. "Dropped off the radar according to a couple of follow-up stories." He shrugged, and that's it.

"Alright." Jake looked it over and nodded. "But it's thin. You might be an ex-cop, but not anymore. You could be working for Bates … gone off the deep end after your family was murdered."

Sole's face twitched as if he'd been slapped. "Don't talk about them."

"You brought them up," Jake snapped back.

"It's my memory, not yours," Sole said, his voice tinged with anger. "Do what you want, but don't talk about my family."

The emotion on Sole's face was obvious. The first hints of doubt crept into Jake's voice. "Alright, you tell us about it."

Sole did. He recounted the hunt for the cartel, Elizondo and Garza, and the battle in the desert that found some justice for his family. The two miners could hear the pain in every word, see it on his face. He never mentioned names but made it clear that there were others he protected and who would remain protected, regardless of what Jake and Ron decided to do to him.

They listened intently to every word. When he finished, the two miners stood silently over him, assessing, processing the story he told them.

Finally, Ron said, "You're a ghost."

"Never heard it put that way," Sole replied. "But true enough, I suppose."

"Must have seemed that way to those cartel people. Leading them around, disappearing, out of sight then showing up to haunt them when the time was right, letting them see you when you wanted them to, then vanishing again."

"I suppose you could look at it that way." Sole squirmed around and sat up as best he could. "Now are you going to cut me loose or do away with me? Whichever it is, let's get it done. My arms and legs are killing me."

"I believe him." Ron looked at Jake. "What he says jives with the newspaper reports. After what happened to his family, I don't think he'd have anything to do with hurting Amelia. It's written all over his face."

"Maybe," Jake said with a look that seemed almost disappointed that he couldn't shoot holes in the man on the floor. "Still seems like a big coincidence, him showing up just when Amelia goes missing."

"Or providence." Ron pulled a lock-blade knife from the sheath on his belt, bent over, and cut the zip-ties.

Jake thumbed the safety on the pistol and slid it back under his waistband.

Sole sat up, rubbing the life back into his wrists and ankles. He looked up at the two men standing over him. "You know my name. How about sharing yours with me?"

"I reckon that's only fair," Jake said. "The way we kidnapped you, I suppose you'll want to report us to the sheriff in Elko. Only thing I ask is that you wait until we figure a way to get my daughter back."

"I'll wait," Sole said.

"Thank you." Jake nodded. "I'm Jake Downes. Ron Benson here is my partner. We own the D&B Mining Company."

"Alright." Sole rose from the floor and stretched, lifting his knees up and down to get the circulation flowing. "And who is this Bates you keep talking about?"

"An asshole," Ron said.

"An asshole with money," Jake added. "He's been trying to buy us out so a big conglomerate can take over our claim, except we aren't selling."

"Until now, anyway," Ron chimed in. "With Amelia at risk, we may have to give them what they want and pack it up."

"You're telling me that Bates and this conglomerate have kidnapped your daughter?" Sole looked from one to the other, trying to wrap his mind around what they said. "You have to go to the sheriff and report it."

"Can't." Jake shook his head. "This isn't about ransom, exchanging money for my daughter. If it was, it would make sense to call in the law. I haven't got it all figured out yet, but this is something else, about getting the mine from us."

"You mean exchange your daughter for the mine?" Sole shook his head. "I don't see how that works. They'd be guilty of kidnapping and never be able to claim title to the mine."

"Like I said, I don't have it all figured out. They must have some sort of plan to keep us quiet and eliminate any ties back to Bates or the company he works for. Besides, even if the sheriff looked at things, there won't be any proof."

The Ghost

"You can't be certain of that. I was a cop, remember. There are always clues, evidence, things they forget, mistakes they make, something that leads back to those responsible."

"And while the sheriff looks around and tries to stir up this evidence, they have my daughter. What do you think happens if they think he is on their trail?"

"You actually think they would harm her?"

"Don't think it. I know it. Anyway, I'm not taking chances with her life," Jake said, a hard edge to his voice. "As soon as they think he is getting close, she will disappear for good. These people play rough. It's the way they've been doing business around the world for years. Everyone in the industry knows it. Rumors been flying around for years about the way they get things done."

"If that's true, how do they get away with it? Why aren't they in prison?"

"Because until now they've kept the dirty work away from here," Ron said. "Expanded their operations to places where the rules are gray at best ... if there are any rules at all."

"But this isn't some third-world banana republic." Sole shook his head. "They can't operate like that here."

"Can't they?" Jake raised an eyebrow. "They've had lots of practice, learned all the tricks and they've been using them on us."

"How?"

"They started little," Ron said. "Made us offers for the mine ... good offers ... the kind of offers that we'd be crazy to turn down." He smiled and shrugged. "I guess we're crazy, so we said no. Couple of days later things start happening. Little things at first. dead cat on the porch, windows broken out, vehicles vandalized, tires slashed.

Then another offer and we say no again. More things happen, more vandalism, small fires start in places they should never start. Not enough to destroy much, but enough to get our attention. They keep making offers and we keep saying no, and the little suspicious events turn into bigger ones each time."

"And you reported these suspicious events to the sheriff."

"We did," Jake said. "He sent a deputy to investigate. I suppose they did the best they could, but like we were saying, these people are pros. They've had lots of practice around the world, plenty of time to get good at what they do. They don't leave evidence behind, and the sheriff said without some probable cause, some link back to Bates there was no legal recourse. He said it could all just be coincidence."

"It could be, you know," Sole said. "I showed up. That was a coincidence. You said it yourself."

"If it's a coincidence like you say …" Jake's brow furrowed and his square jaw trembled for a moment. "Then where is Amelia?"

"That's right," Ron broke in. "Where is she? Look, the last offer was big … way more than anyone else would turn down. Hell, when we were younger, we would have taken the money and run off to a Caribbean island." He exchanged a nod with Jake. "We talked about it, thought about it. I mean it was a helluva lot of money." He shook his head. "But this mine is our dream. It belongs to us, so, we said no again and told them to stop wasting their time. We aren't selling. That was three days ago. Today … well, you saw what happened. Amelia's gone."

"And you're sure that no one else would target you for

the vandalism incidents ... disgruntled employee ... a creditor, maybe?"

"We're positive." Jake was adamant. "We don't have any disgruntled employees. They get a share of the mine profits as part of their pay, so they all work hard, and there are no shady backroom credit deals with loan sharks. We mortgaged everything legally to put up the down payment on the operation, and we are up to date with our creditors."

Sole wasn't convinced. A global mining conglomerate using strong-arm tactics against a tiny operation hidden away in the Nevada mountains, the idea seemed farfetched. This was the United States after all, not some underdeveloped, economically challenged dictator-state where the chief potentate and his underlings could be bribed to look the other way.

He thought about what they told him and it all came back to the one certainty—Amelia Downes was missing. It didn't really matter if Bates and his mining conglomerate were responsible. Sole made up his mind and for once the little voice in his head did not urge him to cut ties and get the hell out of Dodge.

He nodded and said, "Alright. I'll do it."

"Do what?" the two men said simultaneously.

"I'll help you find your daughter."

"You?" Jake shook his head. "We're not asking you to do that. Just stay out of our way and don't call the sheriff until we settle things with Bates and get Amelia back."

"How do you propose to do that?"

Their furrowed brows and silence showed that they had no idea how to do that.

"You need someone they don't know to poke around and find out what's going on and where she is and do it quietly ... invisibly. You said it yourself. I'm a ghost, unseen and unknown, especially around here. Plus, I'm an ex-cop. I know what to look for." Sole's expression hardened, and they saw the man that hunted down the killers who took his family away. "I can do this. I've done it."

Ron and Jake exchanged glances. Ron nodded and said, "He's right. We'd be two bulls in a china shop, as likely to get Amelia hurt as to find her."

"Alright." Jake took a breath and looked at Sole. "It makes sense. Just one thing."

"What?"

"We don't go to the sheriff with this."

"I wouldn't think of it."

SEVEN

Not the Sharpest Tacks

"What do we do now, Cope?"

They stood outside the cabin, looking up at the mountain slopes rising above. The trees on the peaks swayed in the wind, but at this distance appeared to be no more than feathers fluttering in a summer breeze. Plunkett pulled a pack of smokes from his shirt pocket, leaned against a pine, and lit up, inhaling deeply before responding.

"We wait," he said in between puffs. "Like Mr. Jenks said. He's sending someone up to help us out with her."

"What's that mean?" Welch's brow furrowed, considering the words. "Help us out ... how?"

"I dunno ... help." Plunkett shrugged. "The plan got blown, so now we got to do something with her."

"The plan got blown because we blew it, Cope." Welch leaned toward Plunkett, his stubbled face a mask of concern. "You ever think of that? We blew it!"

The cigarette between Plunket's fingers paused in midair. Welch was right. They blew it. What did that mean to a man like Peter Jenks? He stood poised like that, leaning against the tree, hand suspended in the air, cigarette dangling between his fingers for several seconds. As he considered the answer to that question, the concern on Welch's face deepened into something close to fear. Finally, Plunkett nodded, and the cigarette continued its journey to his mouth.

"What?" Welch asked. "C'mon, Cope. What do you think? We're in trouble, right?" He smacked a fist into a palm, shook his head, and gritted his teeth. "I knew it. We're deep in some shit now. I mean dead cats and starting fires is one thing, but this ... taking the girl. That's something else. That's the kind of thing people like us get disappeared over."

"Calm down," Plunkett said mildly. "You asked what I think, so here it is."

He dropped the cigarette to the ground, stepped on it with his boot heel, and looked up. "Yeah, the plan got blown, and yeah, we blew it, sort of, but it wasn't our fault and it was his plan, and she was coming faster than anyone woulda thought, and it couldn't be helped." Plunkett sounded like he was trying to convince himself as much as Welch.

"Jenks is a smart man," he continued rationalizing. "And he gets all that. He ain't happy, but he gets it. So, he's gonna send us someone to take over ... make a new plan. That's okay. Big businesses, they do that ... always making new plans ... you know, to get things done. But this company he works for, they're legit. Hell, they got offices in New York ... listed on the stock exchange and all that shit. No way they're gonna get their hands dirty taking out a couple of drifters if that's what you're thinking." Plunkett shook his head. "No way."

"You sure, Cope?" Welch worked hard at trying to absorb his partner's confidence.

"I'm sure of it." Plunkett patted his shirt pocket for another cigarette. "Hell, he's probably gonna pay us off and send us on our way ... tell us what assholes we are for blowing it, but who cares. We get our money, and we'll have enough to take us anywhere."

"Anywhere?"

"Most anywhere," Plunket said with a confident nod.

"Anywhere?" Welch repeated.

"Well, there's gotta be limits, but that money will get us far enough we won't have to think about Mr. Peter Jenks no more."

Amelia Downes lay on the moldy mattress listening to every word, the blood from her scalp wound dried to a crusty brown down the side of her face. The pine where Plunkett leaned stood five feet from the thin plank wall of the shack. It didn't take long for her to realize that her kidnappers were not the sharpest tacks in the box of thugs their boss employed.

Their conversation revealed much but didn't answer all of her questions. The impact with the truck and the rock wall had rendered her unconscious for a time, but she became aware of her surroundings a short while after they bound her with a couple of pieces of old rope and tossed her into the back of their pickup. One of them sat in the truck bed with her as a guard while the other drove. With her eyelids slightly parted, she managed to see him clearly enough hunkered down, leaning against the truck sidewall, smoking, unaware that she had regained consciousness.

He was thin, with short-cropped, graying hair and a stubble of beard. His clothes were like those of thousands of other miners in northern Nevada—a threadbare work shirt, dusty blue jeans, steel-toed work boots with the leather worn off the toes to reveal a shiny glint of metal beneath, all of it topped off with a battered ball cap.

She watched him for a while but said nothing. Confident that she was trussed up and unconscious, he ignored her and smoked one cigarette after another. Amelia decided to let them think she was unconscious for the time being. If she had to make a move, their surprise might give her a slight advantage, and she could use all the advantage she could get.

Once they got her to the cabin and tossed her on the mattress, she listed to the talk and learned that the one in the truck bed with her was Cope. The other was Chester.

She chanced a peek through slitted eyelids to examine her surroundings. Chester was dressed like Cope in typical miner work clothes, but he stood a good six inches taller than his partner in crime and probably weighed in thirty pounds heavier.

Soon after arrival, and after some nervous conversation, Cope made the call to someone they referred to as Mr. Jenks. From the one-sided phone conversation, she gleaned that Jenks was none too happy with his hired thugs, told them to put on masks around her, and not to use names. Too late for that, she thought and held back the smile that threatened to spread across her supposedly unconscious face.

After that, they went outside to have their *private* conversation—the one she listened to through the cabin wall. It was clear Chester was concerned about having failed in their mission to intimidate, threaten, or whatever Jenks had sent them to do to her. Whatever it was, kidnapping was not in the plan. That might be another advantage. Her brow wrinkled, considering how she could use that information, and also realized it might put her in greater danger.

Cope had reassured Chester that all was well. They would collect their pay and get the hell out of Nevada. That sounded good, except Amelia shared Chester's fears. Whether it was intended or not, the kidnapping happened. There were unintended consequences accompanying that fact. As Chester said, it was the kind of thing that got people *disappeared*.

While they talked outside, she examined her surroundings. It was typical of the old cabins and lean-tos that dotted the hidden mountain ravines. This one wasn't much more than a hut. The wood plank floor was an afterthought and sat directly on the dirt. Not more than ten feet by ten feet in size, nearly half the space was taken up by stacks of one-gallon water jugs bought at a discount store in Elko and crates of canned and dried foods. Several moldy mattresses were stacked haphazardly in one corner, four white plastic chairs made up the furnishings, and a Coleman stove on the floor in the center appeared to be the kitchen.

She knew it was the type of cabin hunters had probably used for several years, but hunting season was two months away. No hunters would pass this way anytime soon, and even if they did, in the era of recreational vehicles, most had better accommodations hooked to their pickup's trailer hitch than this cold, damp hideaway.

The conversation outside died away. She decided it was time to make her presence known.

"Hey! Anyone! I need to pee!"

A few seconds later, the door opened and closed again abruptly.

"The masks! Put your mask on!" She recognized the voice as Cope's.

"Oh, yeah. Right," Chester mumbled, and a few more seconds passed.

"I said I need to pee!" she shouted.

The door burst open, and the two men stumbled into each other as they pushed through, pulling the ski masks down over their faces.

Nope. Definitely not the sharpest tacks in the box. Good.

EIGHT

Crime Scene

Jake Downes slowed as they approached his daughter's smashed Jeep, then reversed and backed around so they could tow the car away.

"Stop here," Sole said and pushed open the passenger door.

"Here?" Ron Benson was already out of the rear seat, rigging the tow strap to the truck's hitch.

"Wait," Sole ordered. "This is a crime scene. You want my help, let me look around first."

"Alright, look around," Jake said, and got out of the truck to follow.

"Stay behind me," Sole said, walking slowly toward the Jeep, eyes fixed on the ground.

"What are you looking for?" Ron asked.

"Don't know … yet." Sole continued his slow walk toward the Jeep lodged against the rock wall.

When he got within a few yards, he stopped. Tire tracks crossed the road from the other side. He followed them to the point where they came down a dirt trail running up the mountainside. Jake and Ron followed behind, watching and listening.

"They were moving fast." He pointed at the spot where the tracks ended in the road and then picked up again several feet up the mountainside trail. "Looks like they hopped this little embankment on the side of the road. See how the dirt is dug up here where they hit. They came down hard, then must have smashed into your daughter."

"Sons of bitches," Jake muttered. "You think they tried to kill her in the crash, hitting her that hard?"

Sole ignored the question. "Where does this lead?" He pointed up the mountainside trail.

"Don't know. Never been up this one," Ron said. "There're hundreds of these little switchback trails all over these mountains. Some not much more than game paths cut by deer, elk, mountain goats. Others made by hunters using their four-wheelers to go after the game. Hell, some were probably made by prospectors in the old days, climbing around with their burros."

"Let's see where it leads." Sole started up the trail. Jake and Ron exchanged a look, shrugged, and followed.

Fifteen minutes later they climbed the last incline and emerged onto a prominence. The trail continued around the backside of the mountain, but the tire tracks ended there.

"They watched her approach from here." Sole pointed to the spot in the distance where Amelia would have come around the bend in her Jeep, and added, "When they saw her, they headed back down the trail to the road to intercept her."

"We know they intercepted her. What else does it tell you?" Jake snapped. He was desperate for some good news about his daughter.

The Ghost

Sole didn't have any. He looked at Jake and answered honestly, "Tells me they watched and intended to intercept her. It wasn't a random accident with some lost hunters who got spooked when they crashed into her. You were right. It was intentional."

Jake's jaw tightened. "So, all of this, just to tell me I'm right about Amelia being taken. Goddammit, I already knew that."

"You suspected it, but you didn't know. Now you do," Sole said and started back down the trail. "It's a start."

As they descended the trail, Ron walked beside his friend, put a hand on his shoulder, and said, "Give him a chance, Jake. We're no worse off with him helping than before, and he might come up with something we wouldn't. He took out the cartel, remember."

"So, he says," Jake grumbled. "What proof do we have of that?"

"I don't know." Ron shrugged. "I believe him, I guess, and it doesn't make any sense that someone working for Bates would come along the road after they took Amelia."

They reached the bottom of the trail where it ended at the road. Sole pointed down. "See those two deep gouges on the road about three feet apart."

"I see them," Jake said.

"Probably made by a bull-bar bumper over the grill when their vehicle bottomed after coming over the embankment. Had to be a heavy-duty truck."

"So what?"

"So, that tells us they had a heavy-duty truck with a bull-bar bumper on the front, and we can keep an eye out for one."

"Lots of those around," Jake said.

"Yep, and one of them took your daughter. We just need to find it."

Sole stooped, pulled out his cell phone, and took several pictures of the gouge marks in the dirt. "Ron, come stand beside the marks. Put your boot between them so we get some scale in the picture."

"Scale?" Jake frowned. "You want scale like these are official crime scene pictures?"

"Not official," Sole said, moving to get the gouge marks and Ron's boot in the frame. "For the record."

"For the record? So, you are going to the sheriff with this, after you promised not to." Jake's frown turned to an angry scowl. "Thought we had an agreement."

"We do, and I'm not going to the sheriff." Sole finished taking the picture and turned to face Jake. "But if we find who did this to your daughter, and we get her back safely, you might want to report it and have them prosecute those responsible. Right?"

"I suppose so," Jake said, the anger fading.

"These pictures aren't exactly CSI-type evidence but they can help the investigators make a case against those responsible."

"Sorry." Jake nodded, duly chastised. "So, you're saying someone in a heavy-duty truck rammed into my daughter and tried to kill her."

"No, I'm not saying that." Sole turned, his eyes following the trail up the mountainside to the lookout point, then back down across the road to the crash site. He approached the Jeep for the first time.

The phone was out again, the camera taking pictures of the Jeep from every possible angle. Close-ups of the wheels, the side wedged against the rocks, the interior. He leaned in to examine the blood on the steering wheel and seat.

The Ghost

"Not too much blood," he said. "Can't be positive, and there could be internal injuries, but from the small amount of blood I'd say her injuries were not life-threatening." He looked over his shoulder at Jake. "I don't think they were trying to kill her."

"Then why take the chance of wrecking her like that?" Ron asked. "Impact like that could have killed her."

"Good question." Sole nodded. "Let's think it through."

He turned and looked up the mountain again. "Okay. They started up there watching, waiting for her to come down the road. When they saw her, they came back down ... in a hurry." He turned back to the Jeep and thought for a second, then he nodded. "That's it."

"What's it?" Jake said. "Explain."

"She got here first. They didn't expect that. They rushed, maybe panicked a little because they were under orders to do something."

"Do what?"

"I don't know. Harass her, threaten her, frighten her. You said that after every offer they did something a little more violent with no proof that they were responsible. Something to encourage you to sell. Maybe they figured that threatening Amelia was the one thing that might make you agree to sell."

"I swear to God, I am going to kill that son of a bitch, Bates," Jake said for the hundredth time in the hours since Sole encountered him.

Sole shook his head. "I don't think he's who you want, at least not the only one."

"He's the son of a bitch we been talking to," Ron said, his voice rising.

"That's why I doubt he would have any connection to

something like this, not overtly at least. There must be someone else he relies on to do the dirty work."

"Jenks," Jake and Ron said in unison.

"Who?"

"A guy named Peter Jenks," Ron said. "Bates calls him his assistant. Took a lot of notes in the first couple of meetings we had with him."

"Where'd you meet?"

"Entente rents a little house in Elko as their start-up headquarters."

"Address?"

Jake gave him the address and Sole jotted it down. "You have his phone number?"

"Why? You gonna call the bastard and ask him to bring my daughter back?"

"No. Just covering all the bases. We don't know where this is all leading and a way to contact them in a hurry might come in handy."

"Right." Jake gave him Turner Bates' number.

Sole added it to the notes on his pad, then asked, "After you met with Bates and his assistant, Jenks, took his notes, what happened next?"

"Nothing, except for the harassment and vandalism," Jake said. "We said no to the deal. There wasn't any reason to meet. Every other contact with Bates has been by phone."

"Tell me about Jenks." Sole held the pen over the notepad.

Jake thought for a second and said, "Didn't speak much, or at all. Very intent listener though. Like we said, he took a lot of notes." His eyes narrowed. "Like you, on a pad of paper."

"Could he have been ex-law enforcement?"

The Ghost

"Maybe." Ron nodded. "Or could be ex-military. Very squared away, if you know what I mean. Wore the suit like it was a uniform, very neat, creases where they're supposed to be, clean-cut and no scruffy beard or mustache like lots of guys wear today. Looked fit too, not some musclebound hulk, but in shape ... like he could run a marathon and then go ten rounds in the ring if he had to."

"Good." Sole nodded, scribbling on the pad. "Height, weight, hair color?"

"About six feet, give or take an inch. Like I said, trim, so probably not over one seventy-five. Brown hair."

"And the other, the one you talked to, Bates?"

"Different," Jake said. "Soft, gray hair, round face. If you saw them together, you'd know who was who."

"Okay then." Sole tucked the notebook in the back pocket of his jeans. "That's where I start."

"You're gonna go talk to them." Jake shook his head. "They'll just say they don't know anything."

"Not talk." Sole smiled. "But if they are behind what happened to Amelia ..."

"They are," Jake interrupted.

"Then one of them ... I'm betting on Jenks ... will know where she is. That's the link. I just have to find a way to get him to lead me to her."

"How are you going to do that?" Ron asked.

"I wish I knew," Sole answered honestly. "But there is always a way if I can get close enough."

"That's it? You try to get Jenks to lead you to her?" Jake's frown was back.

"No. There's something you two can do."

"What?"

"I don't think they would have taken Amelia back to Elko. Too many witnesses."

"True enough." Jake nodded. "Amelia has a lot of friends in Elko, people who would recognize her if they saw her."

"Right. I think they are probably holding her somewhere up here in the mountains. Makes sense if you think about it. Whoever is working for Jenks, or Bates or both of them, would need a place to lie low when not doing their dirty work. If Jenks is a professional, as I suspect he is, he would not want to be seen with them unless necessary."

"So, you think he's got them stashed away somewhere in the mountains."

"That's my guess, and wherever the people are who did this …" He nodded at the wrecked Jeep. "That's where they'll have Amelia."

"Lot of territory up here … thousands of square miles." Ron looked around at the surrounding peaks. "They could be anywhere, holed up in one of the old cabins hidden away in the valleys and ravines."

"That's your job, then. Start scouring the area, looking for signs of people, vehicles passing through places where no one should be. You know the area, the places they'd most likely try to hide out. My guess is it'll be someplace secluded but not too far off the beaten path. A place they can get back and forth from quickly to do Jenks' dirty work and still stay hidden."

"We'll get on it." Jake nodded. "Can I ask a question?"

"Sure. Ask away."

"If they took Amelia, and didn't mean to hurt or kill her, that means she's safe, right?"

It was the question Sole was afraid he might ask. Jake Downes deserved an honest answer. "No, I think she is in serious danger and we need to find her."

NINE

I'm Hungry

"We're here." Freddy Yang stood on the curb outside the Elko Regional Airport terminal, a roller bag on the pavement beside him, his cell phone at his ear.

"Good." Peter Jenks sat behind the desk in his office a mile away. "Took long enough." A day had already passed since Plunkett and Welch came up with the bright idea to kidnap Amelia Downes. Jenks was anxious get things resolved.

"Got the first flight out we could," Yang said. "Should we come there?"

"No, not here," Jenks said quickly. Letting Turner Bates see Yang and Sink would only complicate things. "I'll meet you."

"Low profile ... understood." Low profile was code for:

We want you to do something heavy-handed, dirty, and illegal, and we want to keep you as far away as possible from our sparkling corporate image.

Virtually every assignment they received from Jenks fit

that description. It didn't matter. They'd received the urgent message that there was a problem in Elko requiring immediate attention, and Jenks paid well. They hopped the first flight to Elko.

"Get a car … four-wheel-drive type," Jenks continued. "Use one of your other identities."

"I know the drill," Yang said, slightly annoyed that Jenks felt he had to remind him of protocols.

"Good," Jenks said. "Write down this address. I'll meet you there in half an hour."

Jenks gave him the name and address of a small bar in Carlin, Finn's Lounge. It was an after-shift hangout for miners, which meant it was open twenty-four hours a day, making it a convenient spot to use as their meeting place. Located twenty-five miles from Elko, they could speak there, away from the prying eyes of the local sheriff's department, or anyone wondering about the two new strangers in town.

"We'll be there," Yang said and disconnected.

"I'm hungry." Carl Sink stood quietly at Yang's side, waiting until the call ended. A large duffle gripped firmly in his fist, he stood with his head tilted up, watching airplanes take off over the terminal building, climbing to rise over the surrounding mountains.

He paid little attention to Yang's conversation with Jenks. Yang would fill him in on the details later and let him know his role. For now, he repeated the only thing of real importance to him. "I said, I'm hungry."

"I heard you," Yang snapped, rolling his bag back through the terminal to the rental car kiosks. "We'll get some food after we pick up a car."

That was enough explanation for Sink, and he nodded. "Okay."

Yang went to three rental car desks before he found one

The Ghost

with a four-wheel-drive vehicle available. Sink tagged along, standing just behind his shoulder at each stop.

"Yes, sir, we have a four-wheel-drive available. Just one." The rental agent flashed her best customer service smile at Yang. "I'm afraid it's an economy size pickup, not a full size."

"That'll do," Yang said without returning the smile.

"Great!" the agent exclaimed as if she had just scored twenty bucks on a scratch-off ticket. "I'll just need to see your driver's license."

Yang pulled out the fake ID of the day and handed it over. The agent smiled, propped it beside her keyboard, and began typing. After a minute she looked up and asked, "Would you like the Loss Damage Waiver coverage."

"No, thanks."

"Alright, but I must warn you that if the vehicle is damaged, you will be responsible for the damage." She said it with a doubtful look as if he must not have understood the question. To show she truly cared, she flashed the smile again, the way she might for someone with a learning disability, and added, "You should also consider the liability, personal injury protection, and personal possessions loss coverage. In the event of ..."

"Listen," Yang interrupted. "I don't want the extra insurance coverage. Are you going to rent me the pickup or are you going to keep wasting our time?"

"Oh." The smile disappeared, replaced by a look approaching disgust, the kind of look she would shoot at someone who hated children and drowned puppies in his spare time. "Fine then. Is this ... gentleman ... going to be driving the vehicle at all." She jerked her head in Carl Sink's direction.

"No."

"You're sure. He's traveling with you, right? So, if he's going to drive, I will need his …"

"Look …" Yang looked down at her name badge, strategically positioned at the apex of her breast, just above the place where her nipple would be so that customers … mostly male … had a reason to stare at her tits while they reconsidered the whole insurance thing. "Look, Kathy, I'm the only one driving. Now, rent me the pickup or I'll put in a call to your home office and explain how we spent twenty-four hours flying in from Thailand, and your delays made us miss out on a million-dollar deal because you wouldn't shut up about the damned insurance."

"A-a million dollars." Kathy's face flushed, then paled. "I'm very sorry …" She looked hard at the rental application for an instant. "Mr. Phuong. I'll have you taken care of in just a moment."

Kathy was the model of efficiency for the next two minutes, putting together the paperwork, folding it neatly in a little cardboard folder, and taking the keys from the rack behind her to lay them on top of the rental agreement. She flashed the smile again. "Once again, Mr. Phuong, I apologize for any delay. You can pick up your rental in aisle three, space nine."

"Thank you." Yang snatched the keys and paperwork from the counter and turned to leave. Carl Sink trailed along behind with his enormous duffel bag, seemingly unconcerned about anything except the fact that he was hungry.

"Have a pleasant stay in Elko, Mr. Phuong."

Yang ignored her and left through the side door to the rental car lot. He found the pickup and tossed his bag behind the driver's seat. Sink's duffel was too large to fit and had to go in the truck bed behind the cab.

The Ghost

They were pulling from the terminal lot onto Mountain City Highway headed toward the interstate when Carl Sink said his first words since landing that had nothing to do with his appetite. "Why'd you say that?"

"What?" Yang said, negotiating the surprisingly heavy traffic around Elko's airport and shopping district.

"About coming in from Thailand," Sink said. "We flew here from Cleveland."

"For effect," Yang said with a sigh. "To make a point and get her ass moving so we could leave."

That was enough, Yang decided. Keep it short and simple. It was just one of a million such questions he'd answered for his partner over the years. No doubt, there would be a million more.

While Yang kept his answer short and simple, there was nothing simple about Carl Sink. He was complex, maybe the most complex person Yang had ever known. Some mistook his differentness for a slowness of the mind, but it wasn't. Sink was not stupid.

Sink perceived the world on a different wavelength than most people, through a different lens, examining the most nondescript of everyday events with an amazing, sometimes frightening intensity while completely missing the obvious. A blue October sky or dazzling Maui sunset would completely escape his attention as insignificant. At the same time, the discarded plastic bag along the interstate, caught up by the wind of passing cars, or an ant crawling along a crack in the sidewalk, could hold his attention for hours.

It was just a matter of understanding how Sink's brain processed information, Yang decided after working with him on a few jobs. Tactically, his thinking was sound. Some might even call him a genius in their line of work. He was efficient, thorough, and when necessary, brutal. Operating from a worldview that was unfettered by the usual emotions and concepts of morality, Sink was untroubled by conscience and never hesitated when harshness was required, qualities that made him a valuable asset to Yang and Peter Jenks over the years.

"To get her ass moving," Sink muttered to himself as he considered Yang's response. Why telling her that they flew in from Thailand would make her move her ass remained a puzzle, but Carl Sink was accustomed to such puzzles. He nodded and filed it away as just another curious idiosyncrasy of these other humans who inhabited the planet with him.

The twenty-minute drive along I-80 to Carlin took them past the point where the old Hastings Cutoff came through a gap in the mountains into the valley and surrounding ranch lands. The ill-fated Donner Party had used the cutoff route because of the promise that it would cut three hundred miles from their journey to California. Whoever made them the promise didn't know what the hell they were talking about. The Hastings Cutoff actually added a hundred miles to the trip, a minor detail that left them stranded in the Sierra Nevada Mountains when the snows came. The rest is history.

Yang and Sink were unaware of any of this. They passed through the Carlin Tunnels, bored through one of the mountains the Donner party had to circumnavigate. A few miles farther, they took the exit to Carlin. Unlike the Donner Party, Freddy Yang had the luxury of relying on his phone's map app. They found their destination easily and wheeled into the lot of Finn's Lounge. It was a dingy place, on a side street, the parking lot half rutted dirt and half-broken asphalt.

The Ghost

Sink led the way across the lot to the door, holding his oversized duffel high enough that it did not drag on the ground. "They got food here?" he asked over his shoulder.

"Pretty sure they do," Yang replied.

"Good." Sink gave a satisfied nod. "I'm hungry."

TEN

Messing With Their Minds

"You know he's going to kill you." Huddled in the corner of the cabin, Amelia looked up from the can of baked beans they'd given her, the plastic spoon halfway to her mouth as if the thought had just occurred to her. She shoveled the beans into her mouth, chewed, swallowed, and then nodded as if she had made up her mind about it. "Yeah, he's going to kill you."

They stood over her, watching her eat, the ski masks pulled down over their faces. One of them, the bigger one, Chester she had learned, moved nervously from one foot to the other. Good.

"Shut up," Plunkett said. "You don't talk. You understand? And we don't talk to you."

"Little late for that, wouldn't you say?" She smiled and spooned in another mouthful of beans. "Heard you guys talking outside. These walls are thin. Some guy … you called him Jenks."

"C'mon, let her talk," Welch said. "She heard us outside, so might as well. Just one more thing we fucked up, and too late to change it now." He turned to Amelia. "Why'd you say that? He's gonna kill us? He could just pay us off, and we get out of the state. Hell, with the money he owes us, we could get out of the country and disappear. Right Cope?"

"Right," Plunkett growled, annoyed. "And we're not supposed to be using names."

"Too late for that too," Amelia chimed in, looking up from the floor where she sat cross-legged, holding the can of beans in her lap. She decided it was time to seriously mess with their heads. She grinned at Plunkett. "You're Cope, and your friend here is Chester. Did I get it right?"

Plunkett frowned. Welch nodded and cast a nervous look in Amelia's direction.

"She knows who we are, Cope."

"She might know our first names, but that don't mean nothing. She don't know us, where we come from, where we go after Jenks ..." Plunkett shook his head and snarled, angry that he'd slipped up and used the name. "After we get paid off."

"You really believe all that crap about getting paid off?" Amelia laughed. "You seem pretty smart," she lied. "You must realize that when your boss, Jenks, gets here we are all going to disappear, dumped in some ravine or down an old mine shaft."

"Why would he do that?" Welch said. The desperate look on his face told her she'd touched a nerve. He might be a dull tack in the box, but he suspected that their boss, Jenks, was going to do exactly what she said. Kill them all.

"Yeah, why?" Plunkett threw at her, still pissed that Welch wouldn't stop talking to her, but equally curious, if not quite as desperate, to hear her take on the situation. "We did what he wanted."

"I don't think so." Amelia shook her head. "I'm pretty sure he didn't want you to ram your truck into my Jeep, smash me into the rocks, and almost kill me. An accident like that leaves too much evidence behind. Your truck might have been disabled and got you stuck there, and if you killed me, he loses all leverage over my father. It doesn't make sense. You definitely did not do what he wanted."

She paused and looked up, thinking for a few seconds before continuing. "No, I think you were supposed to cut me off, wave your guns in my face, fire off some rounds, maybe shoot some holes in my Jeep, and then take off. All of that was supposed to be an anonymous warning to my father and Uncle Ron with no ties back to your boss, but a warning just the same to accept the deal and sell out."

"So, what if that was the plan?" Plunkett asked. "We did the next best thing."

"No, you did the worst thing." Amelia gave him a sad smile. "Even after crashing into me, you could have left me there. That would have done about the same thing ... served as an anonymous warning to my father." She shook her head. "But you didn't. You came up with the brilliant idea to take me with you." She stopped and gave them a curious look. "Whose idea was that? Yours Cope? You seem to be the one with the ideas."

Welch glared at his partner. "I told you it was a bad idea bringing her along."

Plunkett shook his head. "Still don't mean he's going to kill anybody, not you or us."

"Of course, it does!" Amelia laughed out loud. "He might not want to, but he has no choice now. Let me lay it all out for you." She leaned forward and started ticking off the points one by one.

"The warning ... cutting me off, waving your guns

around, firing off a few rounds ... all of that would have been illegal, but with no way to identify you, you would probably have gotten away with it, and there would be no link back to your boss. I don't think my father would sell anyway, but you would have gotten away, maybe even collected your pay and headed out while Jenks tried to think of another way to get the mine."

She sighed. "Kidnapping, that's another matter. With a kidnapping there's evidence ... me. He can't leave me around to talk about what happened or his entire operation goes to hell. So, he has to get rid of me, and we all know theirs is only one way to do that permanently." She leaned forward and looked into the eyeholes of Plunkett's ski mask. "And if he has to get rid of me, he has to get rid of you, because now you aren't just kidnappers, but accomplices and witnesses to a murder ... mine."

"Bullshit," Plunkett said, trying to sound convincing, but failing.

"No, not bullshit," Welch said, shaking his head. "It's what I been trying to tell you, Cope. Jenks ain't got no choice now."

"That's right," Amelia threw in quickly, to keep the momentum of doubt going her way. "It's not bullshit. It's logic. Let me ask you a question? Does your boss, Jenks, seem like the kind of man who overlooks little details ... details that could send him and the people he works for to prison?"

"What's your point?" Plunkett said, snarling like a trapped animal, the tough-guy demeanor fading.

"Simply this." She pointed at them, then tapped her chest. "You and me ... we are details he cannot overlook, not if he wants to stay out of prison. Kidnapping wasn't in the plan, but now that it happened, the plan has to change, and the details have to disappear ... permanently."

"I think she's right," Welch said softly, a noticeable tremor in his voice.

"Shut up. I got to think about things," Plunkett snapped back.

"Don't think too long," Amelia said. "I'm pretty sure a man like your boss is going to take care of the *details* sooner rather than later. We might have a little time to figure a way out of this, but not much."

"I said, shut up."

"Okay." Amelia placed the can of beans on the floor. "Now I have to go to the bathroom again. You keep feeding me beans and I'll be shitting every hour."

Both men straightened momentarily at the vulgarity coming from a woman who seemed to be more in control than they were. Plunkett nodded at Welch, and he unknotted the rope around her ankles.

They escorted her outside to the slit trench that served as the cabin's toilet. A tarp thrown over a rope provided some privacy while she did her business.

On the other side, she could hear them whispering, but they made a point of keeping their voices muted. She couldn't make out what they said, but one thing was certain. Her effort to mess with their minds was working. They had doubts. That was a start.

Amelia, on the other hand, had no doubts. She believed everything she said. Jenks had only one solution to the problem these dimwits had created. Time was running out, and she had to convince them that there was another way ... a way to survive.

ELEVEN

Keep Carl Happy

Peter Jenks looked up from a table in the corner of Finn's Lounge and lifted a hand. Freddy Yang nodded and led the way through the dimly lit, smoke-filled room with Carl Sink on his heels.

Yang pulled a chair out and sat across from Jenks. Sink lifted his oversized duffel over the table and dropped it in a safe spot against the wall, then pulled a chair beside the duffel and sat so that no one could approach it without going through him.

"What the hell is that?" Jenks said, staring at the duffel. "You didn't bring weapons on the flight, did you?"

Sink ignored the question and looked toward the bar. "They got food here? I'm hungry."

Jenks looked at Yang. "What's in the bag?"

"Not weapons." Yang shook his head.

"Then what? Damn thing is big enough to carry a body." Jenks' eyes narrowed. "Tell me there's not a body in that thing."

"Nope, not a body." The usually unreadable Yang let out a chuckle and sighed. "Carl is in love."

"In love?" Jenks' eyes flashed from Yang to Sink to the duffel and back to Yang.

"It's his girlfriend," Yang said and grinned. "Inflatable kind. He found it … I mean her … in a pawnshop in Cleveland. They've become quite the couple. Inseparable you might say."

"You're shitting me."

"Nope, not even a little bit."

"Does he …" Jenks leaned closer over the table and lowered his voice. "I mean, does he actually do it with it … her. I mean, for God's sake, he found it … her … in a pawnshop. That means someone else …" A look approaching horror mixed with disgust crossed Jenks' face.

"Tell you the truth," Yang said, shaking his head. "I don't know, and I'm not asking. He carries her around deflated in the bag. Fills her with air at night. I visited his room once, and he had her sitting in a chair, hotel bathrobe draped around her, for modesty's sake. I have no idea if he talks to her or …" Yang shrugged. "Well, I have no idea, and like I said, I don't want to know."

"Damn it, Freddy. You guys are my A-Team. I have to be able to rely on you, especially on this one. Tell me we aren't going to have any distractions with this girlfriend in a bag thing. I need you two focused on the job."

"As long as Carl has the duffel, we're focused," Yang said. "Don't worry about the job. We'll take care of it."

"Alright." Jenks nodded and cast a final doubtful look at the duffel. "Let's talk business."

"Carl needs food first," Yang said. He looked toward the bar. "What's on the menu."

"Never eaten here, but not much. Bar food."

"I'll be right back."

Yang left and went to the bar. Jenks sat staring at Sink and his duffel. There was no point trying to strike up a conversation with Sink. Jenks had tried that before only to have Sink stare at him like he was from another planet, and for all he knew, that was what Carl Sink thought. It was a strange phenomenon. Sink's utter indifference to the world around him had a way of making others feel as if they were ones out of place.

Yang returned with a styrofoam tray full of greasy, cheesy nachos and a paper-wrapped burrito all heated in the microwave behind the bar. He set them in front of Sink and went back to the bar to retrieve a beer for himself.

When he returned, his partner was munching on nachos, staring intensely at a moth fluttering against a neon beer sign in the window. "Okay," Yang said, taking a long sip from the bottle. "Tell us what you need."

Jenks spoke in low tones, barely above a whisper, outlining the issue. He'd hired a couple of local drifter types who seemed capable of doing what was necessary. Low key stuff—harassment, intimidation, nothing too heavy.

The targets of the operation were hard-headed, wouldn't make a deal, and couldn't be reasoned with, so he escalated matters.

"You should have called us," Yang interjected, the beer in one hand as leaned forward over the table to hear Jenks' explanation of events.

"I know." Jenks nodded. "Ordinarily I would have. You know that, but this time there were time constraints, and you were tied up on another project."

It was true. Specialists in the field of cleaning up other people's messes, Yang and Sink were in high demand. Governments, foreign and domestic, corporations, high-profile celebrities, mobsters, and anyone else with money to pay and a problem to solve, made use of their services. Yang and Sink were not squeamish or particular about anything except their fee. Public knowledge of their client lists would have caused red-faced embarrassment in very unexpected places. Jenks knew not to ask what project had them engaged when he needed them.

"So, you escalated matters, to speed up the … negotiation." Yang smiled. "And things turned to shit."

"That's a somewhat harsh assessment," Jenks said, frowning and then shrugged. "But I suppose it's accurate."

"How do you want us to handle it?"

"As I said, there are time constraints, so we need to expedite things. It has to happen as quickly as possible and no one can know that we are involved. That means …"

Yang lifted a hand to indicate he understood. "No witnesses. The usual treatment."

"Right." Jenks nodded. "The usual."

"And the usual fee," Yang said. "Plus, an additional ten percent for expediting to meet your time constraints."

"Done." Jenks was not about to argue over the surcharge. "Hell, get this done and I'll gladly pay the additional fee and buy your partner a dozen more girlfriends on top of it."

"Just the fee." Yang smiled. "Carl is a one girlfriend man. He is quite attached to Lola."

"Lola?" Jenks threw a curious glance at Sink, eating his nachos and burrito while watching the moth by the window. "He named his plastic …"

Yang put a finger to his lips and shook his head. "We don't get into that. Suffice it to say that he and Lola have an arrangement that works for them. Carl is happy, and I haven't heard Lola complain."

"You haven't heard Lola complain?" Jenks leaned back and shook his head. "You're worrying me, Freddy."

"I'm fucking with you." Yang laughed out loud. "We'll get it done. Just pay our fee plus ten percent and we're good." He looked at Sink. "Right, Carl?"

"I'm thirsty," Sink said, ignoring his partner's question. The tray of nachos and burrito wrapper were empty.

"I'll get some beers." Jenks stood. "We definitely want to keep Carl happy."

Yang and Jenks laughed. Carl Sink stared at the moth.

TWELVE

He Knew Who to Follow

He was feeling guilty. Who are you kidding? He shook his head, chewing nervously at the inside of his cheek.

After retrieving his pickup and going over the crime scene the afternoon before, Sole had driven back to Elko and located the Entente offices. It was evening by then and they were closed, so he checked into a budget hotel on Idaho Street, grabbed some fast food, slept a few hours, and then spent the rest of the night, pacing and trying to come up with some sort of plan to find Jake's daughter.

He'd thrown a lot of confident words at Jake Downes and Ron Benson—I was a cop; I know what to do; you need me to find your daughter—but the truth was John Sole knew the odds of finding Amelia alive decreased with every passing hour. And the hours were passing with alarming regularity and no news.

He was out early, before sunup, and sat all day in an apartment complex parking lot across from a historic old house in Elko watching and doing nothing more. The house wasn't much to speak of, a one-story, rock-walled building that had once been the home of some prominent Elko citizen, and which, over the years had been converted into a dentist's office, a floral shop, and most recently into the offices of Entente Mining Corporation.

He'd briefly considered going to the sheriff with the information he had, but he'd promised not to, and the truth was that Jake and Ron were right. If Bates and Jenks were willing to go to extremes like kidnapping, intentional or not, they were willing to do much more to stay out of prison and to protect themselves and the interests of Entente. Sending the sheriff on their trail would only push them to act rashly if they hadn't already.

If Amelia was already dead, reporting it now would change nothing. If she lived, he had a chance to find her.

His analysis of the crash site on Turnbridge Road told the story. The kidnapping was an accident, the result of poor planning and execution. Jenks would want to eliminate all the witnesses, Amelia and her accidental abductors, and he wouldn't take chances again. He'd do it himself or bring in someone he trusted to take care of the dirty work.

With no other options, Sole sat through the day, staking out the Entente offices, waiting for ... what? He had no idea.

The only hope they had was that Jenks or the people who worked for him would lead them to Amelia. Finding the cabin hidden in the mountains was a longshot, an assignment he had given to Jake and Ron mostly to keep them out of the way while he snooped around.

With no idea when the Entente office opened up, he'd been in the parking lot, watching the house before five in the morning. Clean-cut and squared away, just as Jake had described him, Peter Jenks showed up at six-thirty. Round-faced Turner Bates came in at nine.

After that ... nothing. Hours passed, and no one entered or left the house.

Time was running out. The clock in his mind ticked off the minutes, and still, nothing happened. An innocent life hung in the balance, and there he sat doing exactly ... nothing.

Then something happened. A side door opened and Jenks walked outside, climbed into the Audi he had parked there at six-thirty in the morning, and sped away.

Sole gave him a half-block lead before pulling from the apartment complex. It was late afternoon, and traffic around Elko was busy with miners going to and from the lots where buses picked them up to take them to the mines while dropping off those just finishing their shifts. Jenks bypassed the bus lots and took Idaho Street out of town to the westbound entrance onto I-80.

Sole backed off until the Audi disappeared up the ramp, then accelerated until he could see it half a mile ahead. The twenty-minute ride to Carlin, Nevada was uneventful. Jenks didn't seem to be in any particular hurry, cruising along at the speed limit, using his signals when passing other vehicles, and stopping carefully at the top of the exit ramp. Sole allowed two other cars to go up the ramp before following the Audi, then trailed it at a distance as Jenks drove a few blocks to a dingy bar off the small city's main drag.

Jenks parked near the building and went inside while Sole passed, circled the block, and returned to park at the opposite end of the deteriorating parking lot. He thought about going to the Audi and giving it a quick once over, peering inside for anything that might be useful, but decided not to push his luck. Jenks had to be at a place like this to meet someone, and that someone might show up at any moment and find him snooping.

The Ghost

Sole went inside and made his way through the smoky room to the bar. A heavyset man in a denim shirt and ball cap ambled over and ran a dirty rag over the bar top.

"What'll you have?"

"Beer."

"Yeah, what flavor?" the bartender barked at him, his lips twisted up in an annoyed smirk. "We got more than one."

"Miller Lite," Sole said and pulled out a stack of bills that lit up the bartender's eyes. He placed a five on the bar top. "This cover it?"

"Yeah, that'll cover it. Three-fifty for the beer." The bartender smiled for the first time. "Want me to keep the change?"

"We'll see." Sole was not about to perpetuate this surly asshole's poor service by offering up a tip. He tapped the bar top. "Put it here."

"Right." The bartender kept the forced smile on his face and dropped the change on the bar. His eyes went to the pocket where Sole had stuffed the wad of bills. "Let me know if you need anything else."

Sole nodded and sipped his beer. The bartender retreated.

The mirror behind the bar provided a good view of the room and of Jenks seated by himself at a table in the far corner. Now what?

Sole sipped his beer, finished it, and looked up to see the bartender, all smiles now, with another in his hand. He placed it in front of Sole.

"Figured you was thirsty. Want a chilled glass with that?"

Sole eyed the bartender's grimy fingernails and the

sweat stains under his armpits, wondering who washed the glasses. "Bottle's fine."

He threw another five on the bar. The bartender brought the change back and placed it carefully with what he'd brought earlier.

Sole sipped more slowly this time, and the bartender kept his distance. Half an hour passed and Sole was beginning to think he was wasting time. Then the door opened and two men entered.

One was of medium build, trim and fit like Jenks, and appeared to be Asian or Asian American. The other, also fit and trim but taller, carried an oversized duffel bag. Clearly not miners, they had Sole's attention immediately.

Sole stared into the fly-specked mirror and watched them take a seat at Jenks' table. The distance was too great to hear their conversation, and they leaned forward, speaking in low tones so that he probably would have heard nothing if he'd been sitting three feet away at the next table.

They spoke for almost an hour, at least the Asian and Jenks huddled together speaking. The man with the duffel devoured a plate of nachos and a nasty-looking microwaved burrito, seemingly oblivious to what they were discussing, focused on the food and the duffle that he kept close at hand.

Weapons? Bringing weapons into a bar without a reason was not the brightest move, but experience had taught Sole that if the bad guys were all geniuses, the police wouldn't catch so many of them. Still, these guys were probably pros, and it was unlikely Jenks would hire someone who walked around with a big bag of guns.

The conversation ended. The burrito and nachos were gone. Jenks bought another round of beers for the table, then left while they finished the beers.

Sole stood, scooped up the change, leaving two quarters on the bar, and walked out.

"Son of a bitch," the bartender muttered. "You call that a tip?"

Sole turned back. "Here's a tip for you, sport. Change shirts, clean the shit out from under your fingernails, and this next one might harder but …" Sole leaned toward the bartender. "Don't be a prick."

Outside, Sole waited in his truck. Jenks was gone, but it didn't matter. He knew who to follow now.

THIRTEEN

A Simple Plan

Sticky grit coated her eyelashes. Amelia lifted her bound hands to her face and rubbed her knuckles over her eyes to clear it away so she could open them. The cabin was dark. From the opposite side, she heard her captors snoring.

Good. She needed some time to think.

Convinced that everything she said to Cope and Chester the day before was true, she knew it was only a matter of time, no more than a few hours she was certain, before Jenks got his shit together and eliminated the problem the boys had created for him. If they stayed in the cabin, they'd all be at the bottom of some hidden ravine with bullet holes through their skulls by the end of the day.

They had to do something, and they had to do it quickly. She wanted to shout at the two sleeping beauties on the other side of the cabin, tell them to get their dumb asses up and get moving, but that hadn't worked yesterday. There had to be a way to get through and motivate them to get the hell away from the cabin. She forced herself to lie quietly and think things through.

The Ghost

They'd grabbed her from the Turnbridge Road the afternoon she headed into Elko. Then a night in the cabin and orders from their boss, Jenks, to stay put. No doubt he needed time to figure out how to handle things. He would want to keep his hands clean, so he had to find someone to do the dirty work. How long would that take? Not long, she decided. Entente had plenty of money, and money made things happen fast.

Now they were spending a second night in the cabin. If Jenks spent yesterday figuring out what to do about the kidnapping, calling in someone to take care of things, he would want it done quickly. Wait too long and the boys here might get jumpy and take matters into their own hands and disappear, and no doubt, they would be sloppy about it. She knew Chester had no desire to add murder to their crime, but Cope would do whatever he thought would save his ass, and with what she had learned about him, he would make a mess of it. Jenks would know that too.

No, Jenks wouldn't wait, because he couldn't. Loose ends were dangerous for him, and Cope and Chester were the loosest of ends. He had to do something, and he would do it today. She was sure of it.

Take a deep breath, girl, she thought. Let's look at the other side of things. Maybe you're getting yourself worked up over nothing. Maybe you've been reading too many murder mysteries. It's a pretty big jump from trying to intimidate a couple of old-timers into selling their mine to murder. No, it's a huge jump.

It is possible Jenks will pay off the boys and send them on their way, then claim he had nothing to do with her kidnapping. Don't let your imagination run away with you.

Okay, she reasoned. Going from intimidation tactics to murder *is* a big jump, but that was before kidnapping entered the picture. What about that? Would that force Jenks to escalate the tactics?

Damned good question. She lay like that, arguing with herself back and forth while the boys snored. The arguments always circled back to the accidental kidnapping. One way or another, Jenks had to do something about that or face prison time along with his hired hands. She made up her mind.

"Hey!" She squirmed around on the floor as far as she could to face the two sleeping men. "Wake up!"

Cope grunted, "Hold it. We'll take you to the shitter later."

"It's not that." She pointed at the cabin's door. "There … I heard something out there."

"Just an animal … deer or something," he mumbled. "Go back to sleep."

"Deer don't talk," she said. "I heard a voice."

"A voice?" Chester sat up, rubbing his eyes. "Whose voice?"

"How the hell do I know? A damned voice, somewhere out there in the woods."

"Cope?" Chester looked at his partner. "She heard a voice. Maybe Jenks is out there to take care of things like he said."

"Or maybe she's hearing things," Cope said but sat up on his mattress.

"I know what I heard," Amelia said.

Cope pulled his pistol from under the mattress and stood. Turning the bolt on the door lock, he opened it an inch to peer outside.

"Dark out there. Can't see shit."

"Well, whoever it is, can see this cabin pretty plain." Amelia was committed now, working on them for all she was worth. "They're probably waiting for daylight ... for us to come out in the open."

Cope closed the door and turned the bolt in the lock again. "You're full of shit."

"Are you willing to take that chance ... wait until daylight so they can pick us off?"

"I don't want to get picked off, Cope." Chester was standing now, his pistol in his hand.

"Shut up, you idiot. She's fucking with you."

"I'm not fucking with you," Amelia said. "Like I said yesterday. Your boss has to do something about the kidnapping and that means no witnesses." She looked through the gloom to the place where Chester's face was. "You know I'm right."

"She is right." Chester looked at Cope, his voice pleading. "It makes sense, Cope, and I don't want to get picked off come daylight."

"Even if she is right, not much we can do right now. Pitch black and can't see shit right now. We'll just have to wait until daylight." He scowled at Amelia. "If she even heard anything out there."

"Oh, I heard it ... voices, talking low out in the woods," she lied, and then told the truth, "But I have a plan."

"A plan?" Chester said, his voice tinged with childlike hope. "What's your plan?"

"Damn it, Chester, she's fucking with you!" Cope took a step across the cabin toward Amelia and pointed the pistol at her. "Shut your fucking mouth or I'll shut it for you."

"No." Amelia shook her head, looking into the pistol's barrel. It was time to go for broke. "You can shoot me if you want, but I figure that's what's going to happen when Jenks or whoever he sends gets here. So do what you want, but I have a plan."

Her eyes bored into his over the pistol. For the first time, Cope Plunkett wavered. He lowered the pistol. "Alright. What's your damned plan?"

She explained. It was a simple plan, which was a good thing, considering the combined lack of brainpower her captors possessed.

When she finished, she said, "See, it's easy. Nothing changes if Jenks is not planning to get rid of us, but if he is, we might just survive."

"I think we should do it," Chester said hopefully. "It makes sense, Cope. You know it does."

Seconds passed before Cope nodded. "Alright. I still don't think you heard shit out there, but I don't suppose it'll make a difference." The pistol was up again, pointing into her face. "But if you try anything, I'll put a bullet in you. You understand?"

"I understand." Amelia nodded, and for the first time since the kidnapping, had a glimmer of hope that she might survive.

FOURTEEN

Protecting Their Own

"Feel like something's gonna bust inside." Jake sat glaring out into the night through the truck's windshield, arms folded over his chest as if they were straight-jacketed. "I've got to do something."

"We are doing something," Ron answered. "We're looking for some sign of where they might have taken Amelia like that John Sole fella asked us to do."

"It's not enough." Jake shook his head, and his arms tightened more over his chest. "I feel like a damned fool."

"Been saying that for years," Ron said with a chuckle. "What made you finally agree?"

"Sitting out here in the dark while Amelia is …" Jake's voice trailed off, and he leaned forward, peering into the blackness of a moonless night in the mountain backcountry. "It's a fool's errand, wandering around these mountains like this in the dark."

"Seemed like a good idea when we set out to do it." Ron nodded. "Made sense that they would have her holed up out here somewhere, and we know these mountains."

"And now here we sit, stuck until daybreak." Jake shook his head in disgust. "Damned foolish thing to do when she needs us."

"We agreed it was the right thing to do," Ron said and turned to his friend, speaking softly. "It was the only thing for us to do, unless you want to go to the sheriff. You know he'd have a hundred deputies out here banging around into each other, and whoever took Amelia would be long gone and she'd be …" He didn't finish the sentence.

"Just the same. Sitting here in the dark, trapped on this summit is making me crazy."

"I know. I know," Ron said because there wasn't anything else to say.

After taking Sole back to his truck and the crash site the day before, they towed Amelia's Jeep back to Turnbridge, threw some supplies into their packs and drove up into the mountains in Jake's pickup, searching for some sign, some trace of a trail that would lead them to Amelia. When night came on, it was too dangerous to climb along the ridges and trails that crisscrossed the slopes, so they moved at a snail's pace along the bottom of ravines and washes, looking for signs of Amelia or her abductors.

When daylight came, they agreed they had wasted the night. Down in the ravines, visibility was limited to a few yards around them.

In the morning, they slept for a while in the pickup's bed. Then in the afternoon, Ron came up with a change in strategy as they sat munching jerky and drinking bottled water for lunch.

"This prowling along the canyons and dead-end ravines, looking for Amelia is about as like to turn her up as bumping into an honest man in Congress. We might run across her, but the odds are definitely stacked against us."

The Ghost

"What are you suggesting?" Jake asked.

"We get up to a high point and watch. If we see some suspicious movement, we mark the position on the map and head out to check it. If it's nothing, then we go high again and keep looking. At least we'll have visibility. Hell, down here in these valleys and hollows she could be on the other side of the ridge and we'd never know it."

"Shit, there's a thousand places they could hide out."

"More like a million," Ron said. "But you got a better idea?"

"No, I don't." Jake shook his head. "Alright, let's do it."

They began climbing up the narrow switchback trails to a summit that gave them a good three-hundred-sixty-degree view of the surrounding country. While Nevada is known for its deserts, it also has more mountain peaks over ten thousand feet than any other state and over three hundred mountain ranges. Mountain vistas fill the landscape in every direction. Being up high at least gave them a chance to see movement in the distance without having to stumble across it.

They'd spent most of the afternoon on the summit, using binoculars to scan the mountains and valleys. From their vantage point they had a view of the surrounding country for a hundred miles in every direction but limited their search to the trails, ridges, passes, and dry washes that served as roads in the backcountry. The theory was that whoever had Amelia hadn't gone too far, and had wanted to get out of sight quickly.

Night settled around them as they sat on the summit. Navigating the dangerous switchback trail in the dark was out of the question unless they wanted to risk rolling off the side of the mountain, which would have ended their search for Amelia. So, they sat through the night in the truck's cab, looking out into the dark.

Once, Ron said, "I smell smoke."

Jake rolled his window down and sniffed the night air. He shrugged. "Maybe, but up this high, it could drift here from a hundred miles away. See any light … a fire … flame … anything?"

Ron was silent for a few minutes, scanning the surrounding area with the binoculars. "No, nothing."

They settled in again, Jake becoming edgier as the night wore on. Around eleven, his phone chimed. At least up high they had a good cell signal. He put it on speaker and answered.

"Wondering if we were ever going to hear from you again," he said bluntly.

"Been a productive day, I think," Sole answered.

"That mean you know where my daughter is?"

"No, but I think I know who will lead us to her."

He reviewed the stakeout at the Entente offices and Jenks' meeting with the two men at Finn's Lounge in Carlin.

"So, what now?" Jake asked.

"I'll be on their tail in the morning. Where are you right now?"

"We're sitting at the top of a damned mountain. Thought it might make a good lookout point, but now we're trapped up here until daylight. Fool's errand wandering around these mountains. We should have been there with you."

"No," Sole said bluntly. "You should not have. They would have made you in a second and we'd never see your daughter again."

"That's what you say." Jake's voice rose, annoyed and frustrated.

The Ghost

"Easy now, Jake," Ron broke in. "He's right. Bates and Jenks know us. We don't know anything about stakeouts and they would have spotted us for sure." He spoke in the direction of the phone. "Sorry, Mr. Sole. Jake's just a little frustrated up here, having to wait out the night. Things will look different in the morning when we can move around some. What's next? Same plan tomorrow? Scout around for the hideout?"

"Call me John, and no need to apologize. I get it." He paused, then added, "No, tomorrow, you stay up on your mountain until you hear from me. I'll be following Jenks' boys, but I might need more eyes so I don't blow my cover. You may be able to keep an eye on things if I have to drop back and lose sight of them on the back roads."

"Right," Ron said. "Sounds like a good plan, doesn't it, Jake?"

"I suppose so," Jake mumbled.

"Alright, then. I'll call you when we're on the move in the morning. Get some rest."

The call disconnected.

"Well, at least that's something, don't you think?" Ron said, trying to ease Jake out of his funk.

"You trust that Sole fella, don't you?" Jake asked, ignoring Ron's question.

"Feel like we have to trust him, Jake." Ron thought for a second and nodded. "And yes, I trust him. That newspaper article laid it all out ... family murdered by a cartel ... he disappears. Yeah, I believe he did what he said ... took care of the ones who killed his family."

"What proof do you have of that?" Jake snapped.

"He called us, didn't he? Told us about the men Jenks brought in. He didn't have to do that, did he?"

"Or maybe it's a trap ... a way for Bates and Jenks to

get rid of us too." Jake shook his head. "All that bullshit about it was an accidental kidnapping ... that they didn't mean to do it. Could be just bullshit to set us up."

"No." Ron shook his head. "I believe him. You saw the scene, the way the Jeep was, the way they rammed it. Looked more like an accident to me than something intentional." He shrugged. "Anyway, I believe him."

"Tomorrow will tell." Jake turned toward Ron, his eyes narrow and burning with pent-up frustration and worry about his daughter. "Anything goes wrong tomorrow and I'm going to do to Bates what they did to Amelia."

"What's that mean?" Ron's eyes widened. "Not ..."

Jake nodded. "Kidnap him. Take him somewhere private and make him tell us where she is."

"You mean to torture him?"

"I mean do what we gotta do."

"And then we'll go to prison. Think about what you're saying."

"I have thought about it. She's my daughter ..."

"And she's like a daughter to me," Ron interrupted. "We have to be there for her, not sitting in prison for the next thirty years."

"You saying you're not in with me if I have to do it ... take Bates."

"You know I'm with you, Jake." Ron took a deep breath. "I'm just saying let's give Sole a chance to work this through."

Outside, an owl swooped silently past the truck windows. A few seconds later, a rabbit let out an eerie, pain-filled squeal. Nature followed its course. The rabbit searched for food. The owl did the same. Just like people, Jake thought, listening to the life and death struggle, each doing what they had to for survival, to protect their own.

The Ghost

"I'll give him a chance." Jake nodded. "After that, I'll do things my way."

FIFTEEN

Negotiating with Idiots

"Quiet!" Amelia hissed dramatically, leaning toward Chester, prying at the wall planks with the blade end of a shovel they found in the cabin. "Told you I heard voices out there. We don't want to draw their attention."

There were no voices, but having convinced them earlier that Jenks was sending people to finish the job they botched, she had to continue the ruse. The plan was to pry away a couple of planks from the cabin's back wall and squeeze out without being seen. Then they would climb the mountain behind them to a ridge above and watch for Jenks or whoever he sent.

After that ... after that, she would be flying by the seat of her pants. Somehow, she had to convince them to get as far away from the cabin as possible so she could ditch them in the backcountry and make her escape. If Jenks sent someone to finish them off, as she was certain he would, it would be a simple matter to convince them to get the hell away from the cabin. If no one showed up, then she'd have to do some quick thinking, but at least she'd be out of the cabin with her hands and feet free to run or defend herself if necessary.

Getting them to untie her had turned into another mind-numbing exercise. At Chester's urging, Cope agreed to take the rope off her legs and feet. She stood, extended her hands toward them, and said, "I'll need my hands too."

Cope's eyes narrowed, but he said nothing. Amelia remained silent, hands extended, waiting to be released. Chester looked from Cope to Amelia and then back at his partner. It was a standoff. Cope didn't trust her. Amelia asserted what little control she could over the situation in an effort to save her skin and theirs.

Chester broke the silence. "Say why."

"Say why?"

"Yeah, just so Cope gets it."

"I get it," Cope growled.

"Right, Cope gets it," Chester backpedaled. "But say it to me. Why should we untie your hands?"

Amelia shook her head, as if in disbelief at the question. "Because I can't lead us out of here through these mountains without my hands."

"You ain't leadin' nobody," Cope snarled.

"Fine. Then let's forget it all and sit here and wait until someone comes along to shoot holes in us."

"Maybe I got another plan," Cope said. "We talked about getting out of the cabin, but I been thinking we could just drive back to Elko, cut you loose somewhere, and hit the road out of the state. Hop on the interstate there and we'd be gone."

"How many roads are there that come up here?" Amelia asked.

"You know how many. There's one."

"Right. Just one." She spoke like a teacher explaining a

math problem to an exceptionally slow student. "So, you see …"

"Right, one road." Chester chimed in and nodded, the light brightening in his eyes. "Means one way out."

Maybe Chester was the bright one. That was a scary thought. She nodded and said, "Right, one road. If you try to drive down it, you're sure to run into Jenks or whoever he sends up here to take care of things."

"Get it, Cope?" Chester turned a hopeful eye on his partner. "We can't drive out, so she's gotta be able to walk."

"More like hike and climb," Amelia threw in.

"You expect us to just let you take off into these mountains?" Cope shook his head. "If we did that, Jenks would kill us for sure, and it'd be our fault he did."

"No offense," Amelia said and smiled. "But he probably will kill us all, and it's already your fault. It was your fault the second you came up with the bright idea to kidnap me instead of just scare the shit out of me with those guns."

"Still." Cope snarled. "We're not letting you loose."

"Not asking you to. You have the guns, we'll be on foot, and I am not faster than a bullet."

Cope thought for a second and then grinned. "'Course, we could just head out on foot and leave you here for Jenks."

"Yes, you could." Amelia nodded. "And Jenks would still kill you. Might take a little longer than getting rid of me, but he can't let you get away." Her brow wrinkled. "I can't believe you don't understand that."

"She's right, Cope."

"Shut up, Chester." Cope was angry, but he didn't throw up an argument. With all the power he could muster in his feeble imagination, he wanted to believe that Jenks was going to do what he said, pay them off and send them on their drifting way, but somewhere under all the hopeful stubbornness, he knew it wasn't true.

"I won't shut up," Chester said after a few indecisive seconds. "Not this time. It's both our lives." He nodded at Amelia. "All our lives. I know it wasn't supposed to be that way, but it is. She's got the plan to get out of it. We got no choice but to do it."

"That's right. I have the plan." Amelia waited, her hands raised for them to unknot the rope. "Once we get the hell out of this cabin, I know these mountains … grew up out here exploring them, hunting with my father. There're a million places we can hide out until my father comes to find me … trails and passes that you'd only know about if you'd traveled them before. Places you don't know about … places Jenks would never know about."

"And if he isn't sending someone to …" Cope paused, not wanting to say the words and admit to the possibility.

"To kill all of us?" Amelia gave a confident smile. "That's easy. We'll be up high watching the cabin from a place where they won't be able to see us. You'll be able to tell pretty quick what they plan on doing when they get there. Then you make up your mind, but if it looks like they plan on doing what I said, we head out over the mountains and hide out until help comes. When my father comes, you release me to him. We'll go to the sheriff, Jenks will go to prison, and you two cut out in any direction you choose and disappear."

"I think it's a good plan, Cope," Chester said hopefully. "Don't you think it's a good plan, Cope?"

"Where do we watch the cabin from?" Cope asked.

"There's a rocky ridge covered with cedars about a quarter mile up the slope behind the cabin. I saw it when you took me to the latrine." She raised her hands higher.

"But I need my hands free to climb without falling off the mountain."

"Or we could leave you here, climb the ridge ourselves and wait and see," Cope said with a clever grin as if he had outsmarted her.

"Yep, you could do that. And then what? Where will you go?" She sighed. "We've been through this. You don't know these mountains like I do. I know where the safe places are, other cabins hidden away, streams for drinking water. Wandering around up here, I'd say you'd be dead in a week, coyotes and buzzards picking at your bones."

"Don't want no coyotes eating my bones," Chester said, shaking his head.

Several more seconds passed, the wheels spinning furiously in Cope's brain before he said, "Just so, we're clear. If we watch from up on that ridge like you say, and it looks like Jenks is on the up and up with us, we're taking you down to him, getting our money and leaving." The childishly clever grin was back on his face. "You willing to risk your ass on that deal?"

"That's the deal," Amelia said with a somber nod, wondering if he was going to ask her to pinky swear or spit and shake on it. "Now untie my hands and let's get moving. Daylight's coming, and I expect your boss will want to wrap things up quick."

Cope nodded. Chester bent over and untied her.

She rubbed her wrists and said, "Let's go."

They left a lantern burning in the cabin to give the appearance that it was occupied and squeezed through the opening in the planks. Amelia stopped and looked up the mountain slope. There had to be a game trail or some path that led up the mountainside. She scanned the slope until

The Ghost

she found a bare patch of dirt on the slope fifty feet from the cabin. She led the way toward it.

"This is it," she said, pointing at the depression in the ground.

"This is what?" Cope leaned forward and peered at the spot.

"The path up to the ridge."

"That ain't no path."

"It's all the path we got," she said and started climbing. "Get moving. It'll be getting light soon."

It took thirty minutes to clamber up the rocky, twisting game trail along the rock cliffs. Plunkett and Welch stayed on her heels, their pistols in their belts and their hands busy grabbing handholds to secure themselves as they climbed.

By the time they reached the ridge, the predawn sky was turning gray. They concealed themselves in the cedars, the men lying prone on either side of her to keep her boxed in. Then they waited, peering down at the cabin.

Amelia breathed deeply to catch her breath. It had been a long and trying night, and she wasn't sure which was more tiring—the climb or negotiating with idiots.

SIXTEEN

Rookie Mistake

The door to the motel room popped open at five-forty-five. Sole watched from a strip shopping center across the street, sipping a cup of gas station coffee. The shopping center was closed and had anyone noticed the pickup, they might have wondered about the lone man drinking coffee, staring across the street.

He wasn't too concerned about that. Parked in the shadows of a billboard sign, he was as hidden as he could be, given the circumstances. Leaning back in the seat with his head low, it would be difficult to spot him even if someone was looking for him, and he was fairly certain the men Jenks brought in were more accustomed to hunting than being hunted. Predators, even human ones, tended not to be as wary as their prey, especially when they are focused on the scent of their victims.

The two men he'd followed from Finn's Lounge the night before walked from the room. He'd given them nicknames for his own amusement, a habit he'd developed working stakeouts with his partner, Detective Randy Travis.

The Ghost

That was another life, one he'd lived eons ago, but the habit remained.

Now, Secret Asian Man walked from the room to the rental pickup parked in the space outside the room. Bag Man followed him out, still carrying the oversized duffel. Sole watched him pull on the room door to make sure it was locked, then follow his partner to their pickup. Bag Man threw the duffel in the back and exchanged words with Secret Asian Man as he pulled open the passenger door. The conversation did not last long, and while Sole couldn't hear what they said, he sensed it had something to do with the duffel.

When Secret Asian Man finished saying whatever was on his mind, Bag Man gave a brief reply and then sat in the passenger seat. The pickup pulled away from the motel. Sole waited until they passed the first traffic signal before pulling out of the shopping center.

Despite the early hour, there was already a fair amount of traffic on Idaho Street. Not too concerned about detection, Sole closed up the distance a bit. Miners started early and worked long hours, and the cars and buses already making their morning runs provided excellent cover. Following his targets once they hit the backcountry roads would be more problematic, but he'd cross that bridge when he got to it.

He expected them to head for Mountain City Highway and then north toward the cutoff to Turnbridge. Instead, they made a turn off Idaho Street and headed toward the Entente Mining offices.

"Okay, so what are you boys up to now?" Sole muttered and started searching ahead for a place to pull off and watch without being seen.

Freddy Yang walked from the room to the pickup without looking back. It had been a long night. The motel was booked solid and without a reservation they'd been forced to share a room. For Yang, that was about as restful as sleeping in the basement of a whorehouse with the walls thumping and beds squeaking overhead.

At least Sink waited until Yang turned off the bedside lamp, but that wasn't much consolation. He was drifting off to sleep when he heard the first sounds.

Sink was inflating his girlfriend, Lola.

Yang was not a praying man, but he couldn't help muttering, "No, God please, not that."

Sink ignored him, concentrating on Lola. More sounds drifted over from the other side of the room. Whispers, rustling under the covers, calloused hands stroking vinyl. Yang shuddered and tried folding the pillow around his head. It didn't help.

Half the night passed before the sounds faded away, and Sink, his passions sated, began snoring. Yang welcomed the snoring and managed to grab a few hours of sleep before it was time to get to work on Jenks' project.

In the morning, he showered and dressed quickly, eager to get the hell out of the room. Sharing a room on occasion, had never been an issue before Lola entered the picture. Now, Yang was seriously considering whether he should make this a solo act.

Working with Sink had certain requirements, the first being to keep him focused on the mission. When Sink dragged the duffel from the room, Lola now deflated and folded carefully inside, Yang's exasperation boiled to the surface.

The Ghost

"Dammit, Carl. We're working today. You don't need to bring her along. She'll be safe. Trust me, just leave the bag in the room and no one will bother her."

Sink stood by the passenger door looking from the duffel in the pickup bed to Yang and back. Then he nodded and said, "No, she can come."

"Fuck it," Yang muttered as Sink sat down and closed the door. "Fuck it all to hell."

He wheeled from the motel lot, annoyed and telling himself to cut Sink loose after this job. No more babysitting a grown man who was more interested in staring dreamily at the taco crumbs on a fast-food restaurant table than he was in the job they were doing. Most of all, no more Lola.

Five minutes after leaving the motel, they pulled into the lot at the Entente Offices. Peter Jenks came out as Yang cut the truck's ignition.

"Here." Jenks passed a bag, considerably smaller than Lola's, through the window to Yang. "Your tools for the day." He reached in a pocket and retrieved a slip of paper and handed it to Yang. "Directions to the cabin. Cell service and GPS are spotty up in those mountains. If you need to call, you'll have to get up high somewhere for a signal."

"We won't need to call," Yang said.

Jenks stepped back. Yang backed the pickup away from the building and pulled back out onto the street. The meeting had lasted less than two minutes.

They were a couple of hundred yards ahead when they pulled into the lot at Entente. Sole passed the building, noticed that Jenks' Audi was in the lot, and searched for a place to park and watch. The apartment complex across the street he'd used the day before was too obvious as he passed them, so as a precaution, he drove by and pulled into the driveway of a house a block away.

Secret Asian Man and Bag Man seemed oblivious to his presence. Cars moved steadily by on the street in both directions, people going to or returning from work. If they noticed him at all, he was just another miner returning home after a night shift.

Binoculars screwed to his eyes, he watched from the cab of his truck as Jenks came outside, handed them a bag. Guns or money or both, Sole thought. Probably guns. Money wouldn't be paid until the job was done. If they were smart it would go to an offshore account in the Cayman Islands or Antigua.

So now they had weapons for sure. That left the question about the oversized duffel, but whatever was in it seemed less important than the bag Jenks delivered to them.

Sole squinted as Jenks handed over the slip of paper. Instructions, directions, contact information, or all of the above. Jenks said something. Secret Asian Man said something back then pulled their pickup back out onto the street.

The rap on the passenger window startled Sole. Staring through the binoculars, he'd lost his situational awareness.

"You need something?" The man glaring at him through the window was in his sixties, probably retired, and up before daylight after a lifetime of rising early to head to the mines.

"No. Sorry," Sole said and threw the pickup up into gear.

"Wait a minute, fella!" The old man banged on the window harder. "What call do you have to come set in my driveway like you own the place? Hey, there. Hold on!"

Sole punched the accelerator and left him standing

beside the drive, hands on his hips, an angry look on his face. The interaction only lasted a few seconds, but it was enough time for Secret Asian Man to reach the stop sign at the next intersection and turn back toward Idaho Street. Sole roared down the block and followed and just glimpsed them before disappearing around the corner, turning back onto Idaho Street. Where they were headed after that, he couldn't be certain, but he had an idea.

Guessing was never the best way to conduct an investigation, but he guessed that Jenks' boys would head toward the Turnbridge Road. It only made sense.

While looking for a place to watch the Entente offices the day before, he'd become a little familiar with the area and knew that the side streets crisscrossed and cut through to Mountain City Highway, the road leading north out of town. He jerked the wheel to the right, raced to the next stop sign, turned right, and then left at the next intersection. Driving as fast as he dared without drawing attention to himself, he came to a stop at the highway and waited.

The top of the large duffel was visible in the bed of their truck as they passed by a minute later. Sole breathed a sigh of relief, gave them some space, then pulled out to follow. That was a damned rookie mistake, he thought, angry at himself. That cannot happen again, John-boy.

SEVENTEEN

Waiting Game

Sunrise came early at the summit. Jake and Ron spent the night dozing and watching the surrounding valleys and ravines from high on the mountain ridge they'd selected as their lookout point. Overhead, the stars faded. Blackness morphed into brightening shades of gray until the night sky took on a deep blue tint. The swollen, orange-red ball of the sun edged above the distant peaks, until, with a last lunge upward, it leaped above the horizon. Shrinking as it climbed into the sky, its intensity grew ever brighter.

They squinted into the brightening day and scanned the surrounding mountains. Only the peaks were visible. Darkness still cloaked what lay below. Hours would pass before it fully lit up the landscape. Some of the more hidden ravines would not see daylight until noon when the sun passed almost directly overhead, and then the shadows would change direction as the early sunset approached.

In the distance, a narrow ribbon of dirt, a road, curled around the base of one mountain, and just caught a bit of

The Ghost

sunlight. The section of Turnbridge Road stood out starkly white against the dark backdrop of the slopes.

"See that stretch out there," Ron pointed off toward the road, peering through his binoculars. "That's where we'll see them."

"If they're coming," Jake grumbled, but he held his binoculars to his eyes and watched the road.

"Gotta think positive," Ron said.

"I am positive ... positive that if they hurt a hair on my daughter's head, I will kill them all ... starting with that son of a bitch Bates."

"If we knew where they had her, I'd be right there with you, but we don't know where they are. That's why we're sitting here, keeping watch, on the lookout for them."

"That's the problem. Sitting here, doing nothing, is making me crazy. She's my baby girl. I have to do something or go out of my mind."

"We are doing something. You heard Sole. He'll be following but staying back out of sight. We're his eyes. We spot them, follow them to their hideout and then we get Amelia back."

Ron kept it simple. In painting his picture of the situation, he avoided all the other potential outcomes, most of which involved never seeing Amelia again.

Jake was no fool. He didn't require a detailed drawing of the possibilities. Like a kettle boiling over, he hissed out a final seething, ear-scorching stream of profanities, accompanied by graphic threats of violence, mutilation, and slow death aimed at Bates, Jenks, and anyone else who might touch his daughter.

Then he settled back to wait and watch because Ron was right. It was the only thing they could do.

Following the rental pickup out of Elko was a simple matter... at first. An experienced undercover investigator, Sole had no problem maintaining a discreet distance while keeping Secret Asian Man and Bag Man in sight, moving along with the stream of miners and contractors heading to and from the mines north of the city.

After traveling the first ten miles north of Elko on the main two-lane highway that cut through northern Nevada toward the Idaho state line, tailing his subjects got trickier. Sole backed off until the rental pickup was nearly a mile ahead. While he couldn't be certain, he suspected he knew their destination—the Turnbridge Road. Arriving at that belief required no great investigative expertise. Amelia Jakes had been waylaid and abducted there. Whoever took her had to be somewhere in the surrounding mountains since he had passed no other vehicles on the road before his encounter with Jake and Ron.

If, as he also suspected, Jenks' men were going to clean up affairs, they would lead him to Amelia and the kidnappers. It all added up to a lot of suspicions and way too many ifs, but it was the best plan he could devise and it relied on remaining undetected until they arrived at Amelia's location.

The highway made a series of curves through a pass in the mountains. He accelerated to close up the distance with a minivan he'd been following to use as cover. When they emerged from the pass, Wildhorse Lake spread out to his left. To the right, ranch land extended a couple of miles toward the mountains. The rental pickup ahead slowed as if they were searching for something. Sole maintained his speed, just another driver headed up to Idaho.

The Ghost

By the time they made the turn onto the Turnbridge Road, Sole and the minivan in front were only a couple of hundred yards behind. The rental pickup stopped as they passed the turnoff.

Sole followed the minivan into a lakeside campground a half-mile beyond the Turnbridge Road. He waited a minute and then circled through the campground back onto the highway. By the time he made it back to Turnbridge Road, the rental pickup was a good three-quarters of a mile ahead, trailing a rooster tail of dust. Good. The dust would screen him as he followed. He picked up his cell phone.

Jake answered immediately. "Thought you would never call."

"They're coming your way. Do you have a view of the road?"

"We can see a section, probably about a quarter-mile of it. Before and after that, it disappears behind the mountains. If they are coming to where Amelia disappeared, they'll have to pass by where we can see."

"Alright." It was another if, but they had no choice. Sole thought for a moment and said, "Do you have time to get in position closer before they get to the spot where they'll pass."

"Yeah. If they just turned onto the road, it'll take them about an hour to reach the section we're watching. Give us half an hour and we'll be in position close enough to throw rocks at them."

"Don't do that," Sole said, unamused.

"Just a figure of speech," Jake came back. "They won't see us."

"Alright. Make sure they don't. Everything depends on them leading us to Amelia."

"We know that," Jake snapped back. "She's my daughter, remember."

Tempers were short. Everyone was on edge, and understandably, Jake was the edgiest. They had one chance to do this right without killing Amelia in the process.

"We're not pros at this like you." Ron came on the line before Jake could respond, speaking mildly, trying to ease the tension. "But we'll do our best. You just tell us where and when."

"Fair enough." Sole didn't feel much like a pro right now. There were too many unknowns. "For now, just keep an eye on them. We need them to lead us to Amelia."

"Right," Ron said. "We'll stay out of sight but close."

"Alright. You have a charger for your phone?"

"It's plugged in right now."

"Good. Keep it plugged in and don't disconnect the call. We may need to communicate quickly. You keep me advised of everything you are doing, and I'll do the same."

He settled in, watching the dust cloud ahead. There was nothing to do now except for the hardest part of undercover work—wait.

Freddy Yang watched the rearview mirror as he drove, more out of habit than concern that someone might be following. They had arrived in Elko, unknown to anyone except Peter Jenks. Even his boss, Turner Bates, did not know them. No one would be looking for them. Still, watching his trail was programmed into him, a survival instinct, the way a mountain lion will double back on his trail to see the hunter following.

The line of vehicles behind them on the road thinned as

The Ghost

they drove. Some turned on well-improved gravel roads marked by signs to the big-name corporate mines. Others pulled onto dirt paths that weren't much more than tire tracks through the sage left by workers heading to the smaller mining operations.

As they approached the pass that led into the valley by Wildhorse Lake, a half dozen vehicles remained behind them stretched out for a mile. Checking the mirror after leaving the winding pass road, Yang saw that all but two had turned off toward the last mine—a minivan and an older pickup.

He turned onto Turnbridge Road and slowed, checking his mirror for the vehicles. Both passed the turnoff, the pickup trailing the minivan. A half-mile farther on, they pulled off the road into a campground. Yang relaxed.

He glanced down at the directions Jenks had given them, spread on the console between the seats, and gunned the engine. Until they reached the turnoff up a dry wash that led to the hidden cabin, the route was pretty simple. Jenks had warned them to make sure they paid attention to the directions and landmarks. A wrong turn and they could end up wedged in some forgotten ravine, without cell service, and a long hike out.

Yang focused on his driving, the toughest part of this assignment for him. The mission itself was straightforward. It always was. Find the problem. Eliminate the problem. Get paid and wait for the next assignment.

He glanced at Carl Sink. His partner stared up at the passing hillsides, seemingly oblivious to the world. The only sign of his connection to what was happening was to turn and check on Lola's comfort in the duffel whenever the truck bounced over a hole or rut. Then he would turn back to stare out the window, waiting for Yang to tell him to go to work.

"What do you hear?" Turner Bates stood in the door to Peter Jenks' office.

"Things are underway," Jenks said, looking up from the stack of papers he was pretending to read.

It was always like this when a mission was in progress. Waiting for the report that all had gone as planned was the hardest part. He would have greatly preferred to be out in the mountains taking care of things himself, or at least leading Yang and Sink to their target, but that was unthinkable. There could be no hint of a connection to Jenks, Bates, or Entente Mining.

"Are they going to …?" Bates started without finishing.

"You really want to know?" Jenks smiled. Bates never wanted to know the details of the operations he conducted on his behalf. That he almost asked, demonstrated an unusual level of concern.

"No." Bates shook his head quickly and raised a hand as if to ward off evil. "No details. You handle things like always."

"That's what I'm doing." Jenks leaned back in his chair, running a cold eye over the man he called boss.

"And this will solve our problem?" Bates continued nervously. "The one that …"

"You mean what happened on the road?" Jenks' brow furrowed. Bates seemed unusually concerned about things today. He nodded. "It will resolve that problem, yes."

"And the other?" Bates shifted nervously from one foot to the other. "The …uh … acquisition of the mine?"

The Ghost

"No," Jenks shook his head and frowned. "But you already know this. We will have to come up with other solutions for that."

"Such as? Do you have any thoughts on that?"

"None that you want to hear," Jenks said bluntly.

"But …" Bates began and stopped. Jenks was right. He didn't want to hear, but he already knew.

If Downes and Benson dug in and still wouldn't sell, the only option left was to remove them from the picture. They had no survivors other than Downes' daughter, and with her gone, if something happened to them, the mine and assets would go to probate. There would be a bidding war, but Entente had the funds to outbid everyone else and acquire the mine, probably for less than they were offering Downes and Benson.

Removed from the picture. Those were the words he used to himself because other words—murder, assassination, killing—those words were too ugly and too bluntly accurate.

It was one thing to eliminate a village elder, or several village elders, in some far-off jungle. But *removing* two stubborn mine owners—American mine owners—was something else again. It was like shitting in your own backyard and then walking around barefoot. It was too close to home.

He tried to shake the worry away. It didn't matter, he told himself. They had to do what was necessary, and besides, he wasn't eliminating anyone. Whatever happened would happen under Jenks' orders. That thought made him feel better about things.

He returned to the matter at hand. "So, what do we do now?"

"We wait," Jenks replied bluntly and nodded at the chair across from his desk. "Want to join me?"

"This is bullshit." Cope Plunkett shifted on the ground beside Amelia, put down the binoculars, and rubbed his elbows. "Ain't nobody coming."

"You heard Jenks," Chester said across her back from the other side. "He's sending someone today."

"Yeah. He said to help straighten things out."

"So, he's sending someone," Chester repeated. "We wait here until we see how they're planning to straighten things out."

"Fuck it." Cope sat up. "I got half a mind to go back down there and wait for them."

"You're right about one thing," Amelia said, lying prone on the ridge between the two men. "You've got half a mind if you go back down there."

"Hah!" Chester laughed. "That's good, Cope. Half a mind … hah!"

"You best shut up or I'm liable to toss you off this ridge." Cope glared at Amelia. "That'll solve part of the problem."

"You ain't tossing nobody off." Chester sat up now and faced Cope. "We got in this together. She's part of it now. So, we see it through together."

"Yeah, and how long we gotta wait to see things through like you say?" Cope looked at the sky. "Sun's been up a while now."

"Up here on the ridge it is. Not down there," Amelia said and nodded at the cabin below. "Still gray dawn down low. I expect they are taking their time picking their way along the trails in the dim light."

"Makes sense," Chester said, trying to reason with his

partner. "Don't it make sense, Cope? Not full daylight down there so they got to move slow in this country."

"Sense or not, I still say this waiting game is bullshit," Cope said, rolled over on his belly, and picked up the binoculars.

Chester relaxed and did the same. "That's good, Cope. Let's just keep a lookout and we'll see what happens."

Amelia watched the interaction between them with interest. As time passed, Chester was asserting himself more, making his opinions heard. Cope didn't like it, and while for now, he didn't fight against it either, the tension was growing between them.

She considered how that might be useful to her at some point. The moment would come when she might find a way to leverage that tension to her benefit. For now, though, she had to agree with Cope on one point. This waiting game was bullshit.

EIGHTEEN

A Very Bad Idea

"There." Ron Benson pointed into the distance with one hand, the other holding the binoculars to his eyes. "That's got to be them."

"Yeah." Jake Downes nodded, peering through his lenses. "No one else would be on the road this time of day and this far out." He picked up the cell phone. "We got them spotted."

"Cop... at," Sole responded.

"Say that again," Jake said, speaking louder than necessary into the phone. "This damned connection is going in and out."

"Copy that," Sole repeated, and the signal cleared momentarily enough for them to understand.

Then it crapped out again on him as he said, "I'm about half a mile behind them, following their dust trail. I'll let you know where they turn off and you can head in that direction to pick them up."

High above on their ridge, Jake and Ron stared at the phone, eyes narrowed, trying to piece together what he said from the snippets they heard. "Cop tha ... half ... mile behi ... follow ... back ..."

"Did you get that?" Jake asked.

"Think he said he copied, but after that, all I could make out for sure was something about *follow*."

"Yeah." Jake nodded. "I heard that too."

"You think he wants us to follow them?" Ron asked.

"Can't be sure." Jake picked up the binoculars again and scanned the portion of road visible from their ridge. The pickup was already around the bend that took it out of their line of vision. As he searched below, he saw Sole's pickup come into view on the road.

"Okay." He nodded. "There he is, coming around the bend. I'd say he's about half a mile behind them following their dust trail."

"Smart," Ron said. "What do you think we should do?"

"Not sure." Jake lowered the binoculars. "But I'll be damned if I'm gonna just sit here and wait anymore."

"I'm with you." Ron turned and pulled open the passenger door. "Let's go."

Jake climbed behind the wheel, reversed, and turned the truck to follow the narrow switchback trail down the mountainside. "If we can get to the old Bureau of Land Management cut through, we should be able to spot them and see where they're headed."

"Right." Ron picked up the cell phone and spoke into the speaker. The call had disconnected. He punched in Sole's number again and heard an annoying three-note screech followed by a voice saying, *"We're sorry. Your call cannot be completed at this time."*

He looked at Jake. "Looks like we're on our own for now."

"Doesn't matter." Jake leaned over the wheel, focusing

on the trail, pushing the truck as fast as he dared on the narrow trail. "We know what they plan on doing. We just have to get ahead of them and stop it from happening."

"Be better to have Sole with us," Ron said, staring at the phone that for the moment was nothing more than a useless chunk of plastic, silicon chips, and wire.

"It would," Jake agreed. "And if we can get hold of him good, but I'm not letting those bastards get near Amelia."

"Like I said, I'm with you." Ron punched Sole's number into the phone again and got the same annoying message from the same annoying automated voice. He tried again a minute later and got nothing.

He put the phone down on the console. There was no point trying again. The lower they descended behind the mountain ridges, the weaker the signal would be.

Several miles away on the Turnbridge Road, Sole stared at the useless phone in his hand. He'd known that cell communications would be spotty in the mountains, but he had hoped they could hear enough to coordinate their movements.

The dust trail ahead was holding, guiding him along behind the rental truck. He decided to take a chance.

A clearing ahead at one of the dry creek crossings offered an opportunity to reestablish communications. With one eye on the dust trail ahead, he stopped on the road, jumped from the truck, and scrambled up the adjacent ridge. After climbing a couple of hundred feet, he faced the general direction of the ridge Jake and Ron had used to watch the road. He checked his phone. He had a signal and dialed up Jake's phone ... and got the same automated message Ron received earlier from the annoying voice that said they were sorry the call didn't go through, but that really meant, *"Go somewhere where you have a signal, dumbass."*

"Shit!" he shouted, and hurried back down the ridge, mostly on his ass. In the distance, the dust trail was settling back to earth, and without it, his chances of following were slim to none. He started the truck and gunned the engine, fishtailing as he crossed the dry creek and tried to gain on the rental pickup.

In disgust, he tossed the cell phone onto the dashboard. Jake and Ron must be moving down below the ridges. That could only mean one thing. They were going to try to intercept Secret Asian Man and Bag Man alone, and that, Sole knew, was a very bad idea.

NINETEEN

Don't Ever Do That Again

At exactly twenty-five and three-quarters miles along the Turnbridge Road, just as Jenks' directions stated, Freddy Yang spotted the bend in the road marked by an immense and unique, teardrop-shaped rock formation, pointed at the top and then swelling out toward the ground before narrowing and rounding off at the bottom. It looked as if it might topple over in the slightest breeze or by the pressure of a single fingertip against its side, but appearances are deceiving. Weighing several hundred tons and anchored twenty feet beneath the soil, the rock formation wasn't going anywhere. Melting snows cascading down the mountainsides and the occasional torrents that overflowed the adjacent streambed through the millennia had carved it into a piece of mind-boggling natural artwork.

Yang had no interest in art or the rock's geologic history. Carl Sink, staring at a speck of dirt on the window for the last ten miles, had less interest. He was lost in the small corner of the world he occupied at present, oblivious to everything else.

The Ghost

Yang nodded, relieved that the rock was where it was supposed to be. This was unfamiliar territory, and Jenks had emphasized that there was no time for the usual preparation and exploration customary before carrying out one of his assignments.

Yang slowed to a complete stop beside the rock, looked down at the paper Jenks had provided, then turned the wheel to the left, shifted into four-wheel-drive, and eased the rental pickup forward into the dry streambed. The rock marked the turnoff that would lead them eventually to the cabin where they would take care of business for Jenks and his Entente bosses.

He let the truck bounce and crawl over the rock-strewn streambed for a half-mile, then stopped again to check the directions. Sure enough, there was a place where the four-foot-high banks had been eroded down, probably from a combination of floods and hunters crossing the stream on ATVs. He turned the pickup and climbed out of the streambed and checked the directions once more.

Follow the ATV tracks up the bald ridge leading away from the stream for two miles. Turn left again into another streambed, this one higher up and smaller, for another half mile. Right onto an old dirt trail, probably cut by some unknown miner a hundred years earlier. Then around the base of a large rocky bluff and follow the trail to the cabin. Yang noted the position of the last bend before arriving at the cabin and decided that was where he and Sink would go to work.

Alright, let's do it. He increased speed slightly, driving up the bald ridge, and breathed a sigh, relieved that the directions were accurate. The one thing he did not want to do was to call Jenks and tell him they were lost and could not locate their objective.

"You see them?" Jake gripped the wheel, letting the truck careen down a rocky ravine. He jammed the brakes, skidded to the left and swerved around a boulder, then hit the accelerator again.

"N-no I d-d-don't s-s-see them," Ron said through teeth vibrating and chattering with every lurch and bump of the truck. The front end went down into a deep hole and then bounced up so hard his jaws slammed shut with enough force that he thought he broke a tooth, or several teeth.

"S-slow d-down, d-dammit!" he managed to stutter at Jake after a particularly jarring bounce. "You break an axle and we aren't going to be any help to Sole or Amelia."

"Sorry. Can't help it." Jake took his foot off the accelerator and let the truck slow. "You're right. Not thinking too straight, I guess. I can't bear the thought of those assholes going after my daughter."

"I feel the same," Ron said. "So, let's get there in one piece and do what we have to do."

"Right."

They drove another mile down the ravine, Jake slowing and easing the truck over the bigger rocks and holes. At a low point, where several ravines separated by the mountain ridges dropped into a small valley, he stopped to consider options. "What do you think?"

Ron scanned the slopes and ridges rising around them, nodded, and said, "We know the general direction they were heading," he said, reasoning things out. "We don't know where they turned off but, we have to be a lot closer to them than we were." He pointed up a slope. "This ridge rises and meets that shoulder on the mountain up there. That's generally in the line of the direction they were headed on the Turnbridge Road when we saw them. The other slopes head away from their line of travel." He nodded. "I'd say we go up that shoulder and see if we can spot them again, or some sign of them passing."

Jake nodded without speaking and turned up the slope. They hadn't gone a quarter-mile before their way was blocked by massive boulders and rocks impassable even for the four-wheel-drive. Above the rocks, pines and cedar grew in abundance, further hindering passage.

"Shit!" Ron said. "Not such a good idea, after all."

"Look." Jake pointed down the slope.

"That's got to be them," Ron said.

A half mile away and several hundred feet below them they could make out the roof of a smaller pickup. It was moving away from them along a switchback trail.

"Hold on!" Jake released the brake, jerked the wheel to the right, and stomped on the gas.

A game trail, no more than a foot or so wide, wound around the side of a boulder. Jake headed for it, increasing speed.

"Not a good idea!" Ron shouted. "Jake ... no!"

Jake ignored him.

They careened around the boulder, the left tires on the narrow path made by deer and elk, the right tires spinning for traction on the downward slope, the entire truck tilted to the side at forty-five degrees. Jake managed to fishtail it around the boulder until the front end pointed uphill. Only their speed and forward momentum had prevented them from rolling sideways down the mountainside back into the ravine, dead or mangled, with no hope of ever being discovered or any way to call for help.

With the front end pointed uphill now, Jake gunned the engine. The truck began moving up the slope, bouncing over rocks and mowing down saplings with the front bumper. The tires began losing traction in the loose shale covering the slope, and it seemed they would start rolling back down the mountainside, four-wheel-drive or not.

Jake gripped the wheel until his knuckles were white. Ron did the same to the sides of the seat. They were barely moving now, the rear wheels digging deep to push them forward. The front end of the truck rose, the wheels spinning in the air. Jake punched the accelerator. It was a do or die move, and dying was a distinct possibility.

The front end swung precariously back. The men held their breath, expecting at any moment for it to flop back on its roof and plummet down the slope.

Then, slowly … ponderously slowly … achingly, the front end came down and the spinning wheels dragged them up onto the shoulder of the mountain slope where it met the ridge.

They sat for a minute without speaking, breathing deeply, each still gripping the wheel and the seat so that the other would not see their trembling hands.

When his heart rate had slowed enough that he could speak without panting, Ron said, "Don't ever do that again."

"I won't," Jake said solemnly, then turned the wheel and let the truck roll forward, following the shoulder around the side of the mountain where the ground was bare, kept clear by snow slides and winter winds.

"I mean it," Ron said. "You at least talk things over with me before you pull some boneheaded stunt like that."

"I heard you," Jake said. "I said I won't."

"Because if you do …" Ron paused. What would he do? They were partners. More than that, they were like broth-

The Ghost

ers. "Because if you do, I'll tell Amelia and she will beat the living shit out of you."

Jake had to brake and hold on to the wheel, his body rocking as he laughed. It was contagious, and a second later, Ron was laughing. They laughed for a minute, tears rolling down their faces, the kind of insane laughter that comes after an extremely close encounter with the grim reaper, knowing that you cheated him ... for now.

Ron caught his breath and said, "Alright. Let's get this done."

TWENTY

It Has to Be This Way

"What the fuck?" Freddy Yang slowed the rental pickup as it came around a bend in the trail. Ahead, a much larger truck had pulled across the trail. Two men stood in front of it, glaring at them over the sights of rifles held to their shoulders.

"Get out!" Jake Downes ordered.

Yang lifted his hands above the steering wheel so they were visible through the windshield and leaned his head out the side window. "What's this all about?"

"Get out!" Jake repeated. "Now!"

"Do it!" Ron Benson shouted. He stood a good eight feet to the side, toward the rear of the truck they had positioned across the trail to block it.

"Trouble," Yang whispered.

Without moving his head, Carl Sink's eyes dropped from the speck of dirt on the passenger window that held him fixated for the past hour to gaze at the two men blocking their way. He gave no sign that he understood the situation.

The Ghost

Nothing about him changed, except for the movement of his eyes. That was enough for Yang.

"Okay, okay," Yang called out through the passenger window. "I'm getting out. Just be careful with those guns."

Keeping both hands where they could see them, he reached through the open window and pulled the handle, pushed the door open, and stepped out, his hands raised in front at chest level. "Can I ask what the problem is?" Yang said, his tone showing the right amount of deference, concern mingled with curiosity and a disarming smile on his face. "There must be some mistake."

"Maybe," Jake grunted. "We'll see." He waved the rifle's muzzle toward Sink. "Tell your friend to get out."

"Well, you see, that's the problem," Yang said, shrugging his shoulders.

"It's gonna be a problem if he doesn't get his ass out here now."

"You don't understand." Hands still raised in front, Yang turned his palms up and let the smile widen, one man trying to reason with another. "My friend's name is Carl and he ... well, he isn't quite right."

"What the hell does that mean?"

"Carl is different."

"Different how? You mean slow?"

"Something like that." Yang nodded. "But not slow. He sees the world differently. That's all."

"Sees the world different?" Jake shook his head to remind himself to get back to business. "Doesn't matter. Get his ass out here now, and you better have a good reason for being up here."

"You see," Yang continued, acknowledging nothing Jake said. "Carl is different and his doctor ... psychologist really ... thought it would be good to get him away ... up in the mountains or somewhere away from the city and people, so we came out here to Nevada to explore. By the way, my name is Freddy, and I'm really sorry if we stumbled on the wrong road. We didn't mean to trespass."

Yang yammered on with no sign of fear or appreciation for the guns pointed at his face. More experienced men—men experienced in dealing with killers—might have taken this as a sign of impending danger, of lightning about to strike where it was least expected. Jake and Ron were not those men. They had no idea of the danger they faced at that moment.

A few seconds later, they learned. Yang took a step forward, still smiling. He reached into his shirt pocket and pulled out a slip of paper. "Here. This is the written recommendation from Carl's doctor. It says to take him out and expose him to fresh sights and sounds." He took another step forward, holding out the paper that was nothing more than a receipt for gas and a bag of donuts from a convenience store in Elko. "Just look it over and you'll understand."

"Hold it!" Jake shouted. "You stay right there."

At Jake's shout, Ron swiveled to point his rifle directly at Yang. Their lesson in dealing with killers was short and brutal.

As Ron swiveled to support Jake, Carl pushed open the passenger door and calmly stepped out. Ron heard and started to turn back toward him.

Four shots cracked in rapid succession. The acrid smell of burnt powder wafted from the pistol in Carl's hand.

Two of the nine-millimeter rounds struck Jake, and he went down with a hard thud at the front of their truck.

The other two rounds caught Ron as he swiveled. He fell sideways, rolling down the slope into a cedar that prevented him from plunging another thousand feet down the mountainside.

Carl turned and sat back down in the passenger seat to gaze once more at the speck of dirt on the window. Yang walked over to Jake, gave him a kick in the side, then looked down the slope at Ron. Satisfied that they were no longer a threat, he climbed behind the wheel of their truck, started the engine, and drove it as far up the slope as he could. It wasn't very far, only a few feet, but it gave them enough room to drive their rental pickup around it on the narrow trail. A minute later, they disappeared around the next bend.

Sole was still fifteen minutes away when he heard the shots echo down the mountain. After leaving the road to try and get a cell phone signal, the rental pickup's dust plume he'd been following had nearly dissipated. A few miles farther on, he lost it completely. That could only mean one thing. Secret Asian Man had turned the rental off the road onto some mountain trail that Sole missed.

He attempted another call to Jake and Ron and got the same annoying *"Sorry, there is no signal"* message. No shit.

He stopped on the road, cursing himself for yet one more rookie mistake, turned around, and backtracked. Returning to a point on the Turnbridge Road where he was sure he had seen the dust trail ahead, he reversed again and drove forward slowly, searching for a turnoff that headed up into the mountains.

At the base of a huge, odd-shaped rock, he found what he was looking for. The crumbled bank of a dry streambed showed the tire marks where a vehicle recently left the road.

Sole told himself that it had to be rental pickup and hoped he was right.

He'd only been following the path up the mountain a few minutes when he heard the shots. That confirmed that he was on the right trail. It also meant that Jake and Ron had confronted the men in the rental. He pushed forward as fast as he could until, coming around a bend in the trail, he spotted Jake's truck, partially off the trail with its nose pointing up the mountain. Jake lay motionless on the ground.

Sole braked, jumped from the pickup, and ran to Jake. There was no need to check for a pulse or breathing. He looked into the open eyes and knew he was dead. Bullet holes in the center of his chest and one in his head confirmed that fact.

Sole pounded a fist against his leg. You did this, he thought. You stupid son of a bitch. You did this.

Is it ever going to end? The pain and blood and destruction. No, never, not as long as you are around. It's what you do. It's your legacy.

One more person paid the price for your pride and your stupidity. There was another. Where was Ron?

He stood and began searching around the truck, looking up the mountainside, then looking down the slope. … and saw him. Ron lay motionless, wedged against a tree.

Sole scrambled, sliding on his ass down to him. As he reached out to check for a pulse, Ron's eyes opened. Thank God.

"Hold on. I'll get you out of here." Sole put his arms around Ron's chest and from his sitting position, used his feet to push them both up the slope to the trail.

"Jake? Where's Jake?" Ron asked through gritted teeth.

The Ghost

Sole shook his head. "I'm sorry. I was too late to save him, or you, if we don't get you out of here."

"No." Ron tried to pull away. "You have to get them ... stop them."

"I will." Sole held him tight under the arms and pushed hard with his feet. "First, I have to get you some help."

"No." Ron shook his head. "No time."

"Yes," Sole said and with a final push of his legs they came up onto the trail, falling backward and panting, Sole from the exertion and Ron in pain.

They lay side by side on their backs for a few seconds, catching their breath, then Sole turned to examine Ron's wounds. Like Jake, he had one bullet hole in his chest. It had entered at an angle as Ron turned, punched through ribs and a lung, turned internal organs into jelly, and sliced off a piece of spleen as it exited. The resulting internal bleeding was massive. The second bullet, aimed at his head, knocked a chunk of skull off the side of his head as he pivoted, but the bullet did not penetrate the brain and Ron still managed to cling to life.

"I have to get you some help." Sole reached for his phone.

"No." Ron lifted a hand and grabbed him by the wrist. "No time ... follow them before they get to Amelia."

"No. You first." Sole shook his head and lifted the phone, then threw it in the dirt. There was no signal.

"Get to Amelia," Ron whispered. "Jake died for her. Don't make it for nothing. You find her, get her away from them, protect her."

"I can't leave you." Sole's voice was pleading, a man begging for the burden of guilt to be lifted from his shoulders.

"Listen to me." Ron's grip on his wrist tightened.

"Nothing has changed. They will kill her. If you stay with me, she has no chance. You have to stop them. Jake's already dead." He blinked and nodded. "I will be too ... not long, now," he wheezed between rapid, shallow breaths. "You can't save me, but you can save her save her. It has to be this way."

He was right. Sole knew it. Nothing had changed. They were going to kill her, if they hadn't already.

He looked down at Ron. Either way, he had to find out and do what he could ... for Jake and for Ron.

"Alright." Sole nodded. "I'll find her."

Ron didn't hear. His tenuous hold on life evaporated in the mountain breeze like a dandelion puff before a spring storm.

TWENTY-ONE

Who Sent You?

Freddy Yang stopped the rental pickup, pushed the door open, and stepped out without saying a word. There wasn't any reason to speak. For all of his oddities, personality quirks, and downright borderline schizophrenic behavior, Carl Sink did not require direction when it was time to go to work. Whatever the gods had withheld in the ability to interact in the real world—the world experienced through the eyes of everyone else—they had made up for with an instinctive ability to understand the nature of his work and the most efficient methods for accomplishing it.

At a point just short of the spot where the trail ahead the trail took a sharp bend to the right, Yang stopped. If Jenks' directions were correct—and they always had been in the past—the cabin would sit around the bend, backed up near a pile of rocks on the mountain slope.

He moved into the trees on the left. Sink went to the right and disappeared behind the boulders lining the trail.

They moved as a team, advancing on the cabin with military precision, each aware of the other's position. Yang paused as he came to the clearing ahead. Sink watched from the opposite side, waiting for him to get into position.

He took a deep breath. This was the tricky part. The space between him and the cabin was relatively open. No one was stirring around outside, but that didn't mean that they wouldn't notice him advancing from the single window in the front wall. If he was spotted, their plan would change. The result would be the same, but the execution would be much messier. And there was the risk that he or Carl might be injured in the process.

Well, that's why Jenks pays you the big bucks, he told himself and darted from behind a tree, running in a low crouch. He covered the space to the cabin's side wall in seconds. No shouts of alarm emanated from inside. There was no sound at all from the cabin.

Assholes must still be asleep. No one was watching. Yang shook his head, smirking. These clowns were definitely not pros. He wondered how Jenks tied up with them. He was usually more selective about the people he brought into a job. Entente must really be putting pressure on them to get this done in a hurry.

That they were dealing with amateurs worked to their benefit and eased Yang's concerns. Taking out pros made things trickier. Popping a couple of good old boys too lazy to stand watch would have them back in Elko and on a plane back to civilization by the afternoon.

He edged around the side of the cabin. Without seeing, he knew that Sink was making his way to the front. Neither spoke. No signal, audible or otherwise, was necessary. They relied on perfect timing and an intimate understanding of how the other would react in any situation, born out of years of working together.

In position now, both men waited and listened, ready to

The Ghost

back up the other if there was some sign that the occupants had detected their presence. The cabin remained silent.

Yang could almost count off the seconds in his head until Sink made his entry into the cabin. At the exact moment his mental countdown ended, he heard the front door crash open. He tensed, waiting for sounds of gunfire or for someone to attempt an exit through the loose planks in the back wall.

The only sounds were the birds waking and calling to each other in the trees. He moved to the loose planks and peered through a crack. Sink moved carefully around the interior, checking in every dark corner for the occupants. Then he turned and stepped out the door into the clearing.

Yang trotted around to the front, and both men began a deliberate search of the surrounding rocks and trees. They moved carefully, although Yang did not expect to find anyone hiding there. If they had run because they suspected a trap, they were already long gone.

A deafening explosion echoed off the surrounding rock walls, and he whirled, dropping to a knee with his pistol extended toward the sound. "What the fuck are you shooting at?"

Sink stood at the edge of the clearing, firing up at a rock-lined ridge. His brain accustomed to focusing on the most minute details in his surroundings, Sink had spotted an arm moving and pointing in their direction. It was just a brief flittering movement, but it was enough. He began throwing rounds up at the spot.

"Oh." Yang nodded, pointed his pistol at the ridge, and began firing.

They had little chance of hitting anyone, but they might be able to injure or slow them down. Both men emptied their magazines, reloaded, and assessed the situation above.

The movement had ceased. There had definitely been someone up there watching, but that someone had pulled back away from the edge as the bullets started banging off the rocks.

"Shit," Yang said.

"Follow," Sink said, uncharacteristically throwing out an opinion about their next course of action.

"Not yet." Yang shook his head and pulled out his phone. At least this high up they had a signal. He punched in a number, and waited. When it connected, he said simply, "'They're gone."

"What do you mean, gone?" Peter Jenks snapped back.

"I mean, they aren't here," Yang replied calmly.

"They heard you coming."

"No way." Yang shook his head as he spoke on the phone. "No way. They were already gone, hiding up on a ridge above. Even if they heard us coming … which they did not … but even so, they couldn't have made it up there in the time it took us to make our way to the cabin from our truck."

"Shit."

"Yeah," Yang said. "What's next."

"We go after them." Jenks was silent for a minute, trying to come up with a plan. "Alright. You wait there. I'll put together some gear and meet you on the trail. Then we'll go after them."

"You too?"

"Me too," Jenks replied. "Don't worry. You still get paid."

"I'm not worried," Yang said. "Just surprised. You always leave the dirty work to us."

"Just be ready when I get there," Jenks said, annoyed. "Might take a while. I'm going to pull the satellite and topo-

The Ghost

graphic maps. That's rough country and the terrain will tell us which way they have to travel. We'll figure out where they're headed and be there waiting."

"We'll be here."

The call ended. Yang started down the trail. Carl called out behind him again and nodded at the ridge above, "Follow."

"Later," Yang said.

"Okay," Sink muttered, lowered his head, and offered no further opinion. He followed Yang down the trail.

Sole's heart raced as he rounded a bend and found himself fifty yards from the rental pickup stopped in the middle of the trail. Figuring they had him in their crosshairs, he jammed on the brakes and pulled on the door handle, leaning low, ready to roll out onto the ground and take evasive action. He braced himself for the fusillade of bullets that would come tearing at him at any moment, punching holes in his truck and him.

Winding and bouncing along the mountain trail, he knew he was going too fast to conceal his movements from anybody who might be watching, but he had no choice. Jake and Ron died trying to save Amelia. He barely knew them, but he understood their sacrifice, would have made the same sacrifice for his family. He would not allow it to be wasted. So, he drove like a wild man, taking chances he would ordinarily avoid.

The truck slid to a stop. He rolled out onto the ground, then scurried around to the rear and crouched behind a fender. Seconds passed without the sound of gunfire and bullets slamming through the pickup's sheet metal sides.

Alright. You got lucky, John-boy. Now keep your head down.

Pistol out in front, he approached the rental he'd been following. Crouching as he walked around it, he checked the interior. It was empty. The oversized duffel was still in the bed. He pulled it over the side and knelt beside the truck to examine it.

"You have got to be shitting me," he muttered, opening the flap and peering inside.

A pair of green painted eyes stared up at him from a deflated plastic face. He almost laughed out loud, then caught himself and looked around. This had to be a trap of some sort. A sex doll in the bed of a pickup. He'd seen some weird shit in his days, but this was among the weirdest.

Gunfire erupted up the trail, around the bend. He crouched lower until he was certain it was not aimed at him.

The realization hit him square in the face that he was late … once again … and somebody else was paying the price. He moved forward, knowing that he was too late to change what had happened, but determined to even things up for Jake and Ron.

He'd only gone a few yards when he heard voices, just a few words, and then silence. The killers were coming back for their vehicle. A second later, they rounded the bend in the trail.

Sole didn't hesitate. These were the men who had killed Jake, left Ron for dead, and for all he knew, had just killed Amelia. All of his planning had turned to shit, his big words, telling Jake and Ron they needed him, that he had done this before. All of it turned to nothing more than an arrogant lie. But he could make this part right.

As the surprise registered on Secret Asian Man's face,

The Ghost

Sole raised his arm and fired. The killer went down, clutching his gut.

There was no surprise on Bag Man's face, only an odd, preoccupied look as if he were pondering some unseen puzzle, but his reaction was immediate. His expression never changed as he raised his arm and fire three rounds at Sole, who dove for cover beside the rental. Two rounds slammed into the rental's side. The third shattered the side window, peppering Sole's face with glass. Bagman kept firing, bursts of three, walking the rounds toward Sole as he scrambled along the side of the rental.

He was a sitting duck. Exposed on the ground beside the truck, with no time to return fire without stopping and being hit by the barrage Bag Man fired at him, he looked for the only concealment he could find—the oversized duffel. It wasn't much, but doubling the bag over and using it as a shield, he pulled it close and scrambled away, trying to bring his pistol up to bear on his attacker.

Bag Man's face froze in horror. Inexplicably, he did not continue to fire and finish Sole. Instead, he walked forward, his gun at his side, crying out, "Lola!"

Who the hell is Lola? Bag Man came on, increasing pace to a gallop, and it dawned on Sole that Lola was in the bag. Bag Man was almost on him now, his gun still at his side reaching with the other hand for Sole, or Lola in the duffel, or both.

"Fuck you," Sole said through gritted teeth.

He made it to the edge of the trail, pushed the duffel over the side of the trail and down the rocky slope. The bag tumbled and rolled, bouncing over rocks and scrub trees clinging to the slope.

Sole raised his pistol as Bag Man came on, centering it on his chest.

"No!" Bag Man screamed and went down the slope after the duffel.

Sole watched in amazement as he plunged after the duffel, somersaulting head-over-heels down the mountainside, banging into trees and rocks. He came to rest close to the spot where the duffel had lodged against a pine, blood soaking into the ground around his head. Sole watched for movement, but if Bag Man was alive, he showed no sign of it.

Sole stood and leaned against the side of the rental truck, breathing hard and surprised that he was still alive. He wiped his hand across his face. Blood trickled from the cuts left by the shattered glass, but nothing serious. No doubt Bag Man had intended for the bullet to plow through his skull. Sole figured that considering how fast he was moving to get out of the line of fire, it was a damned good shot, and he would not have wanted to face Bag Man in anything close to a fair fight.

The cuts and scratches stung, but it was time to move. He peered over the hood of the rental truck.

Secret Asian Man lay fifty feet away on the side of the trail. Sole approached him slowly, arm out, the pistol pointed into his face. He was alive, his strangled breaths sending bloody foam into the air, but he was dying, and Sole wasted no time. "Who sent you?"

A grin split Freddy Yang's face in two, like a bloody gaping wound. He moved his head slightly from side to side but said nothing.

"Was it Jenks?" Sole asked.

"You some kind of cop?" Yang whispered.

"Some kind," Sole said and then decided the dying man deserved a little truth, so he gave him a little. "Used to be a cop."

"Figures." Yang's brow furrowed for a moment. A pained grimace tightened his face. He sputtered and coughed blood. Then he spoke in a whisper. "What about Carl?"

"Who?"

"Carl ... my partner."

"Oh." Sole nodded. Bag Man had a name. "He took a header down the mountain going after the bag."

"Dumb fucker." Yang coughed up more blood and shook his head. "I was going to dump him, anyway."

"Why the hell was he worried about the bag?"

"Dumb fucker," Yang repeated and shook his head, ignoring the question.

Fair enough. Carl was a dumb fucker. No argument. Sole repeated his first question. "Did Jenks send you?"

"You going to kill me if I don't tell you?" Yang let out a bloody, gurgling chuckle, then stopped and took a wheezing breath. "I'm dead, anyway." His eyes met Sole's. "Besides, you know the answer. Question is ... who sent you?"

It was true. He knew the answer.

He stared at Secret Asian Man for several seconds. Dying or not, there was a chance he might survive long enough to mention the man who killed him and Bag Man. If Sole was going to keep his promise to Jake and Ron, he had to remain unknown and unseen.

Sole lifted the pistol. Yang closed his eyes. A final clap of thunder filled the air. A hundred and fifteen grains of copper-jacketed lead plowed through Yang's skull before the sound registered in his brain.

TWENTY-TWO

He Didn't Argue

It was unmistakable. No thunder, sonic booms, fireworks, or backfiring vehicles were responsible for the four distant but distinct cracking explosions. The gunshots echoed crisply in the mountain air, rebounding off the slopes and down the rocky canyons.

Four shots, then nothing. The deafening silence that followed had an ominous finality to it, a signal that whatever confrontation had occurred, started suddenly and ended as quickly with a definite winner and loser.

Amelia didn't want to think about who the loser might be. A protracted firefight would have been preferable to the silence. Would have signaled that all was not lost. That there was hope. That the fight continued. That her father was pushing forward somehow to find her.

To her left, Chester jumped to his knees as the shots rang out.

"Get down, you idiot," Cope hissed.

Amelia remained prone between them, praying and peering down from the ridge at the cabin below.

The Ghost

"What was that?" Chester asked, trying to control the trembling in his voice, and then more firmly added, "And don't call me an idiot."

"You serious?" Cope looked at him across Amelia's back. "Gunshots, that's what." He noted the look of warning in Chester's eye and refrained from calling his partner an idiot this time.

"Yeah, but who was shooting?" Chester continued. "You think it was Jenks, come looking for us?"

"Dunno." Cope put the binoculars to his eyes and scanned the terrain below, wishing Chester would shut the hell up. Who else but Jenks, or someone he sent, would be up here shooting?

"But why would he shoot?" Chester persisted, his concern rising with every unanswered question he threw out. "Ain't no one up here to shoot at, is there? Who would he be shooting at?"

"How the hell do I know who he's shooting at, or if it's even Jenks. Maybe it was hunters or someone taking some target practice, or someone just plunking at pine cones."

"You really think it was hunters or someone shooting at stuff for practice?" Chester asked with pathetic hopefulness. A few seconds passed and then he shook his head, his brain processing that possibility. The hopefulness vanished. "No, I don't think hunters would shoot like that and it didn't sound like a rifle someone would hunt with." Having reasoned that much out, Chester was back to his original question. "Who do you think was doing that shooting down there?"

Cope ignored him and stared through the binoculars. Chester looked at Amelia. "What about you? What do you think about that shooting?"

As much as she hated to admit it, Chester was right about one thing. The shots did not carry the deep-throated reverberation of a high caliber hunting rifle, the type of firearm her father and Ron Benson would carry with them. Handguns meant that someone else did the shooting. That meant … She shook her head, trying to push out the thought of what that might mean for her father and Ron, and blinked away the tears that welled up in her eyes.

"I think we should get the hell out of here." She turned toward Cope. "We should leave now."

"Not yet." He adjusted the lens pieces against his eyes. "Not until we see who it is."

"We do that and they might see us and pick up our trail," Amelia said.

"I said not yet," Cope said with his usual stubborn surliness, grinding his teeth as he said it. "We don't know they're coming after us. We only know Jenks said he would send someone to take care of you."

"We've been through this already. How are you going to find out if it's me or all of us they're after? Just walk up to Jenks and ask him if he plans to kill you?" Amelia shook her head and smirked. "That's one hell of a brilliant plan. Stand there while he puts a bullet between your eyes?"

"We just …" Cope began and then closed his mouth. He didn't have a good answer, so he said the only thing he could think of, the reason they'd gotten involved in this to begin with. "He owes us money."

"Dead men don't spend money," Amelia snapped back. "I can't believe I'm sitting here arguing with a dead man."

"Look, we took a job. Jenks owes us money … a lot of it. He paid us for the other jobs, and before I hightail it into the mountains on your say-so, I want to know there's a reason to run, and I'm not …"

"Look," Chester whispered, lowering his head behind a

rock and pointing down to the clearing where the cabin sat against the rocks.

"What?" Cope whispered and then shut his mouth.

A man darted from behind a tree to a rock and then to another rock closer to the cabin. He stood with his back against it, out of sight from anyone in the cabin, and remained motionless. A minute passed, and he looked around the rock and nodded.

Amelia followed the direction of his gaze across the clearing. "He's got a partner." A second man stood behind a tree on the opposite side of the cabin.

"Why are they on foot?" Despite the question, the look of terror on Chester's face showed that he already knew the answer.

"Must have left their vehicle down the trail out of sight. Trying to sneak up on us," Amelia said. "They would have done it too if we stayed down there." She turned to Chester. "Let me borrow your binoculars."

He handed them over, and she peered through the lenses, spinning the focus dial for a few seconds. "They've got guns in their hands."

"Jenks is after us," Chester whispered. "Oh, God. He sent them after us."

Cope stared at the men below without speaking, watching them run in a low crouch toward the cabin. One went to the rear. The other approached the door. It was clear they had done this before. Their movements were timed and coordinated. After the man at the rear had time to get into position there, the man crouching by the door rose suddenly, kicked it open, and entered, the gun in his hand pushed forward.

A minute later, he came back out into the clearing and stood waiting for the man in the rear to join him. They exchanged words briefly. Both men surveyed the surrounding woods and rocks for a few seconds, then without speaking, the man who had entered the cabin lifted his arms, holding his handgun in front in a combat stance, pointed it directly at the ledge where they hid, and fired a round, then another, and another.

The bullets pinged and skittered off the rocks. The distance was too great for an aimed shot from a handgun to hit them, but a ricochet could kill just as well as a direct hit. They scrambled away from the edge, staying low.

"Shit," Cope muttered as he put distance between himself and the volley of bullets still hitting the rocks.

"I think I'm shot," Chester said and wiped at a trickle of blood flowing down the side of his face.

Amelia stopped to examine the wound. "Just a scratch, probably from a rock splinter knocked off by one of the bullets. You'll live."

"You sure?" Chester asked, unconvinced that it wasn't more serious.

"I'm sure. You'll be fine unless we stand here and talk about it. We have to get out of her now."

Amelia glanced at Cope, his face a mixture of fear and confusion, but for once, he didn't argue. She turned and led the way along the switchback trail that led around the other side of the mountain and away from the gunfire.

TWENTY-THREE

Not Smart Enough

Cope Plunkett and Chester Welch did not answer their phones. If Peter Jenks was planning their demise before, now he wanted them drawn, quartered, and their twitching limbs fed to rats while they watched.

"Where the hell are you? I told you to stay in the cabin until I sent you help. You motherfuckers better call!"

Peter Jenks was shouting so loudly into the cell phone that Turner Bates came from his office to stand in the doorway. Without speaking, he peered in at his fuming Chief of Special Operations, waiting for the flush in his face to subside.

Jenks slammed the phone down on his desk, saw him standing there, and barked, "What!"

They had what many would consider an unconventional relationship. Bates was his titular boss, the man who made sure he was well paid for his services, and who laid out the projects and goals.

The bossing ended there. Bates needed Jenks, and Jenks

knew it, and he never let Bates forget it. Bates was the pretty-boy, the polished corporate executive who made the reports, had drinks with the chairman and Board of Directors, played tennis and golf with them, got invited to all the swank soirees.

Jenks remained in the background, his face unseen and his true role unknown to Entente's higher-up mucky-mucks, but he was crucial to his boss' success. That gave him significant power over Bates, who, thanks to Jenks, pulled in a seven-figure salary plus several hundred thousand more in bonuses when the deals went through.

Then there were the stock options, corporate junkets, lavish expense accounts, invitations to presidentially hosted dinners, free tickets to the Super Bowl, and a never-ending list of perks and benefits that made his wife and children think he was the greatest provider, most loving husband, and best dad in the world. But it was Jenks who made it all happen.

Bates stood in the doorway, hands folded before him, waiting like a schoolboy for permission to enter the principal's office.

"What do you want, Turner?" Jenks repeated without inviting him in.

"Just heard the noise," Bates offered. "Thought I would see if ... if there was anything I can do."

"Anything you can do?" Jenks' lips twisted into a wry smirk as if the question was the dumbest thing he'd heard all day, which it was. "What did you have in mind, Turner? Maybe I should brief you on what's happening, give you all the dirty details so that you are fully up to speed. That way you can give me the benefit of your vast experience in handling field operations." His tone dripped venom. "Or maybe you'd like to get down in the trenches with me, get your hands dirty, do something useful. You know, dispose of a body."

"A body?" Bates' eyebrows lifted in a wide-open, comical way that made him look like he just stepped out of an old Tom and Jerry cartoon.

"A figure of speech," Jenks lied, shaking his head, knowing that once Yang and Sink did their work, there would, indeed, be bodies needing disposal, or at least hiding. He sighed. "If you're so concerned, come in and sit down. I'll brief you in detail."

Bates lifted a hand. "No, no … unnecessary. I don't need the details. Just checking in to make sure you were alright."

"I'm just dandy," Jenks shot back and stared without saying anything further.

Several uncomfortable seconds passed before Bates shuffled from one foot to the other and said, "Well, I better go check in with Owen Syndall."

"Yes, you better do that."

"Board meeting coming up, you know," Bates offered, knowing it sounded lame. He shifted his eyes to the window behind Jenks' head so he wouldn't have to look him in the eyes.

"Yeah, I know." Jenks didn't try to hide the disgust on his face and dismissed Bates with a nod. "You can go now. I have work to do."

"Right." Bates turned away from the door. "I'll leave you to it."

Jenks shook his head, picked up the phone again, and punched in Yang's number this time. He let it ring for a minute and then tossed it back on the desk. Shit.

They'd probably gone back to their vehicle and lost the cell signal. He wanted to modify their plan, but they were out of contact. After thinking things through, he realized meeting them at the mountain cabin would waste time. Better to have them meet him somewhere central along the Turnbridge Road. The topographic maps and satellite images showed that the passes and ravines leading away from the cabin all led back down to the road at various points along its length. If they took up a central position along the road, found some high ground, stayed concealed, they should be able to spot them … eventually … maybe.

Shit. Problem was that eventually was not part of Entente's timeline, and now he would have to waste more time going up the trail to the cabin to contact Yang and Sink and let them know.

Fuck it. It was the best he could do, and he was damn-well going to make it happen. Like Bates, Peter Jenks had a lot riding on bringing this deal to a close. The kidnapping of Amelia Downes had reinforced a rule he had always lived by—never deal with amateurs.

For the thousandth time in the last few days, he made a mental promise to never again violate that rule, but for now, he had to put that mistake behind him. The best way to do that was to make it disappear, and that meant intercepting them when they came down out of the mountains. It wasn't as clean a plan as having Yang and Sink take care of things at the secluded cabin, but he could still salvage things, he told himself.

Jenks stood, gathered up the maps and satellite images, and headed for the door. Plunkett and Welch were gone and apparently in hiding, suspicious of his promise to *send help* and the order to remain in the cabin. He'd underestimated them. Incredibly, the two bumbling drifters figured out what he had planned for them, and headed for the hills.

"But not smart enough," he muttered, heading out and slamming the door behind with enough force that it rattled the windows in Turner Bates' office. "I'm going to end this clusterfuck today."

TWENTY-FOUR

You Sonsabitches Hold On

The sound was faint but distinct. They froze in their tracks. Amelia turned her head up, listening, testing the wind like an animal sensing danger. The crack of gunfire echoed off the rock walls and canyons, repeating back and forth until it faded away in the distance.

"Someone's shooting again. Who you think it is?" Chester asked, his eyes wide and worried. "They following us, you think?"

"How the hell do I know?" Cope snapped back.

The last reverberation of gunfire ended, and they stood silently on the trail waiting, listening. A minute later, another shot rang out.

"I think we should go back," Amelia said.

"What?" Chester's eyes widened. "Why? That's shooting back there. Already been shot at today and don't want no more of it."

"You're the one who told us we had to get away from there," Cope said. "You're crazy as a loon if you think we're going back."

"Right. I did." Amelia nodded and then explained. "But my father and Ron Benson will be out looking for me ... for us. If they found those men who were shooting at us, they might have taken them out. So, we go back to the ledge and see what's happening. If it's my father and Ron, you can turn me over to them, and we all get out of this."

"You get out of this," Cope said. "We go to prison."

"No." Amelia shook her head. "My father will offer you a reward for bringing me back. I'll make sure of it."

"A reward?" Chester's eyes brightened. "You hear that, Cope? A reward."

"I hear." Cope's eyes narrowed. "How much?"

"A lot," Amelia said. "I'm his only daughter, so probably as much as Jenks was going to pay you. And after the reward, I'll tell him you helped me escape, that your boss Jenks is behind everything. He'll listen to me, and you boys will be on your way to spend the reward money."

"That's just all talk," Cope growled.

"I think we should do it," Chester said. "We go back to the ledge, like she says, and see what's happening. If it's her father, this whole thing could be over."

"And if it's not?" Cope frowned, trying to come up with a reason to disagree.

"Then we do like we agreed," Amelia said. "We get back on this trail and put distance between us and them."

"*Agreed*." Cope spat the word out. "You make it sound like you're some kind of partner in this."

"I guess I am, in a way," Amelia said. "That's your fault. You dragged me into it."

"No partner of mine." Cope's eyes narrowed. "Not now. Not never."

"Fine. We're not partners." She shrugged. "No loss to me, but you could still have the reward my father will pay.

The only way to know is to go back and see if he shows up at that cabin."

"Right, we won't know if we don't go back," Chester parroted.

"No." Cope shook his head, glaring at Amelia. "Not playing your games anymore."

"I'm not playing games. If that shooting was my father taking out the men who came to the cabin, we have a chance to get out of this now."

"No." Cope shook his head again.

It was a stalemate. Then Chester said, "Yes."

"What?" Cope's eyes raised in surprise.

"We're going back." Chester leaned toward his partner. "You don't get to make all the decisions anymore. It's 'cause of you we're in this fix."

"Me?" Cope tapped his chest and shook his head in protest. "But I ..."

"It was you that picked the spot to watch for her on the road. You who said to speed up coming down that mountainside so we could cut her off ... so fast we ran into her. You who said we take her with us and got Jenks pissed at us. You called all those shots." Chester raised his arms and looked around at the mountains. "And look where we are now."

"I never said ..." Cope began, but Chester interrupted.

"Don't care about what you never said." Chester was adamant. "We're going back to see who did that last shooting we heard. We'll figure things out after that." He looked at Amelia. "You lead the way."

Walking single file on the narrow trail, they made their way back around the side of the mountain to the ledge they'd left a few minutes earlier. Belly-down, they got as low as they could and scooted forward to peer over the edge at the clearing below.

Within seconds, they saw a man working his way through the trees and boulders below, his features indistinguishable in the shadows. He moved carefully, like a cat testing his footing, then darting from the trees to the rocks, waiting a minute, listening, watching. Then moving again closer to the cabin. His weapon was out, held in a low ready position, prepared to take on anyone he encountered in the cabin. He made the last final rush to the side of the cabin, working his way along the side toward the front door.

"Who is that?" Chester whispered.

"Don't know," Amelia said. "Can't make him out." She didn't add that his agility made it unlikely that he was her father or Ron Benson.

"What do you think?" Chester whispered again. "Go down and do like you said? Turn you over to him?"

"No." Amelia shook her head, her eyes focused on the man below. "Not yet. Not until we know for sure who he is. Now keep quiet and watch."

The man below disappeared inside. A minute passed, the only sound the distant screech of a hawk. The trees surrounding the cabin swayed in the breeze, their shadows undulating across the clearing like ripples on water.

"What the hell is he doing in there?" Cope hissed. "I think ..."

"Shut up," Amelia hissed back. "He's being careful. Just wait."

A few seconds later, the man stepped from the cabin and walked out of the shadows into the sunlit clearing. One thing became certain. Whoever he was, he was not her father or Ron Benson.

"I think we should just go down and turn her over,"

Cope said. "Whoever it is, we just get it over with." He looked at Chester. "C'mon. I still say Jenks is going to pay us off and send us on our way."

"They were shooting at us. You forget that already?" Their whispers were increasing in volume as the disagreement deepened.

"Hold it down," Amelia said, "or that man down there will decide for you." She looked at Cope, shaking her head in disgust. "First, you want to go down and turn me in. Then the shooting starts and you want to head for the hills. Now you want to go down again. My daddy would say you can't decide whether to check your ass and scratch your watch or the other way around."

Cope stiffened and snarled back, "They were shooting, but we don't know it was at us." He gave her a sour sneer, the kind a kid on a playground uses trying to one-up an antagonist. "Maybe they thought they was just shooting at you."

"That's right," Chester interrupted. "And what about her?" He stared at his partner, his eyes narrow and hard. "Even if he lets us go, what about her? You gonna let them shoot her?" He shook his head. "I didn't get into this to do no killing."

"We aren't killing anybody."

"We turn her over and it's the same thing." Chester shook his head. "You know that's what they probably gonna do to her. It's the reason Jenks sent those men up here, sneaking up on the cabin, shooting at us up here."

"You say probably, and that means we don't know … not for sure. Maybe he'll just send her home."

"You really think that?" Chester was incredulous. "No, too chancy. I'm not gonna have her on my conscience the rest of my life."

The Ghost

"You two, shut up." Amelia motioned to the clearing below. "Look."

The man walked in circles, searching the ground. He stopped, knelt down, picked something up, and then looked up at the surrounding rocks and mountainside until his eyes rested almost exactly on the spot where they lay watching. He held his weapon up, sighting along the barrel toward their ridge.

"Let's go," Amelia said, moving. "Before bullets start banging off these rocks again."

"Right." Chester nodded and started scooting on his belly backward away from the ledge. "You can stay, Cope, but we're leaving. You wanna go down and talk to him, have at it. I've seen enough."

"Shit," Cope snorted, staring down at the man in the clearing who had lowered his gun but was still surveying the ledge where they watched. "Fuck it." He pushed himself back from the edge and crawled after the others. "You sons-abitches hold on. I'm coming."

TWENTY-FIVE

Amelia Was Alive

He wound his way through the trees and rocks, choosing each step with care, examining the place where his foot would fall. Moving from tree to tree, rock to rock, and then again to the next tree, he stopped at each to watch and listen before moving forward moving again.

When he reached the edge of the clearing, fifty feet from the cabin, he knelt and waited, hoping for some noise, some movement inside that would signal life, a survivor. There was nothing. No noise from inside. No movement visible through the single window. No one coming outside to relieve themselves in the slit-trench latrine.

The ominous silence chilled Sole. Secret Asian Man and Bag Man had done their job. The shooting he'd heard and their unconcerned, almost nonchalant, ambling down the middle of the trail toward him afterward, signaled that they'd done what Jenks sent them to do. Sole was too late … once again.

"Shake it off," he muttered to himself. You don't know

The Ghost

anything yet, not for certain. Do what you came here to do. Keep your promise.

Steeling himself for what he would find inside, he made the last dash across the clearing to the cabin. He leaned against the side wall for a moment, catching his breath, then moved to the door, kicking it open and rushing in, weapon in front, ready to take on Amelia's kidnappers if they still lived.

That was a big *if*. The cabin was empty. Relieved and frustrated at the same time, it took less than a minute to make the circuit of the tiny interior.

No dead bodies littered the floor. Good.

Amelia remained missing. Bad.

He walked out the door into the clearing, searching for some clue to what happened. The gunshots from Secret Asian Man and Bag Man had been unmistakable. That raised an important question. Who were they shooting at?

He began making a circuit of the clearing, scanning for some sign that Amelia and her kidnappers had been there. He reached the point where he had come from the trees to cross to the cabin and turned, eyes searching for something, anything, that might tell him what had happened.

It wasn't much. Just a ray of reflected sunlight. If it had been earlier in the day, before full sunrise, or later after the sun lowered behind the peaks, he would have never seen it.

But he did see it, an unmistakable glint off a metallic object, shining on the bare ground. He strode across the clearing, eyes focused on the bit of reflected light.

The shell casing was on its end, with the percussion cap facing up. He picked it up, raised the open end to his nose, and sniffed. The scent of burnt propellant was unmistakable. The nine-millimeter round had been fired recently.

A semicircle of similar shell casings littered the

surrounding ground. A few feet away, more shell casings lay in the dirt. Of all of them, only the one in his hand had been on its end and positioned to catch the sunlight in just the right way to reflect it into his eyes. What were the odds of that?

Finally, a good omen. He shook that thought away quickly as if to ward off bad luck, telling himself there are no omens, good or otherwise. There is only what you do, or don't do, John-boy, so do something right for once.

He turned in a three-hundred-sixty-degree circle, searching the surrounding rocks and trees. They were close, too close for Secret Asian Man and Bag Man to just stand in the open and fire off an entire magazine of rounds, not if the kidnappers hid in the trees and rocks with weapons of their own to return fire, and Sole was reasonably certain they would have weapons of their own.

The killers must have had a more distant target. He pieced things together as his eyes scanned for clues. A distant target explains why they had emptied the magazines in their pistols, firing from one fixed position, standing in the open in the clearing. They were not concerned about return fire.

He swiveled to peer across the clearing at the rocks and slope leading up the mountainside. If Amelia and her kidnappers suspected some sort of trap, it would make sense to leave the cabin, hide in the rocks and trees, and try to escape. But where? Heading back down the trail was a bad idea. The old pickup with a bull catcher bumper still parked to the side of the cabin must belong to the kidnappers. That meant they were on foot.

"Where did you go, Amelia?" he whispered.

His eyes searched systematically over the far side of the clearing. He began low, moving his head slowly, scanning, then raising his eyes a bit higher, and then still higher up the slope.

He stopped, his eyes fixed on a barely perceptible line of bare dirt at a point where the rocks ended and gave way to trees clinging to the slope. It was a game trail, cut by deer, elk, and mountain goats. He knew game trails. Most were nothing more than a slight depression on the earth, often barely passable and sometimes hazardous for humans to use. But if you were desperate, if two killers were headed your way, you might decide that the possibility of falling down the mountain was preferable to the certainty of a bullet through the brain.

Sole lifted the pistol in his hand and sighted along the barrel, moving it up, trying to visualize what the killers saw when they started firing. At a point a couple of hundred feet above the clearing, the game trail became indistinguishable on the mountain slope. He continued tracking with his pistol and then stopped.

A rocky ledge overlooked the clearing. There. Could they have been shooting at someone up there?

Arm still raised, he looked down at the shell casings on the ground and stood at roughly the spot nearby where a round fired from a semiautomatic pistol would send the shell casing out the ejection port to land with the others on the ground. Then he looked along the pistol barrel again.

He saw nothing but rocks, but the more he stood there weighing it all, the more convinced he was that they had been up there. The game trail led almost to that point. The rocks provided excellent cover. If they hid there, the odds were better than even that Amelia was still alive, or probably so... hopefully so.

Don't overthink it, he told himself. You've got the beginning of a plan. Get moving.

He needed the gear from his truck. Turning, he jogged back down the trail, making no effort to conceal his movements. There wasn't time for that.

Around the bend he passed the body of Secret Asian Man, staring blindly at the sky. As he passed the rental pickup they'd been driving, he heard the scrambling sound of someone coming up the slope. Sole turned, stunned to find Bag Man, still alive, breathing hard, blood running down his face, pushing himself up onto the trail with his feet while he clutched the oversized duffel to his chest.

Their eyes met. Bag Man, nodded, knowing what to expect, and said simply, "Don't hurt Lola."

"I won't," Sole replied, lifted the pistol in his hand, and sent a bullet through Bag Man's brain.

Carl Sink dropped to the trail with a thud, the duffel still in his arms. Sole turned and continued jogging back down the trail to his truck without a backward glance and no crisis of conscience. The life issues that caused Bag Man to cling to his plastic girlfriend would have been an interesting puzzle to unravel at another time, in another place, but not now. Jenks sent him there to kill Amelia. He and his partner had killed Jake and Ron. His fetish attachment to Lola the blow-up doll would have been good for a laugh over beers at the end of a long stakeout, but now they were irrelevant.

Bag Man could rot where he fell. Amelia was alive, at least there was a chance she was, and he intended to keep his promise to her father.

TWENTY-SIX

Pine Nuts Is Good

"How much farther?" Chester plodded behind Amelia, puffing and wheezing in the thin air.

"A ways," she said. "Altogether I figure about ten miles as the crow flies."

"We ain't crows," Chester managed to get out between pants.

"No, we aren't. So, double it to account for winding around in these mountains."

"Twenty miles. Damn, that's a long way."

"It is. I figure we've gone about five today."

"Only five miles? Hell, we'll never make it today."

"Nope. We won't."

"And where is it that we get out of these mountains?"

"Little town on the Idaho line ... Merchantville. Not much there, but there are people and shelter. I figure we can get food there too, and I'll contact my father."

"And what the fuck about us?" Cope asked in his usual surly way, catching up from behind. Unlike Chester, who tended to chatter along as they walked, he had said nothing since leaving the ledge over the cabin.

"You boys can do what you want," Amelia said over her shoulder, watching her feet and where she placed them at a spot where the trail narrowed to inches, not much more than a shallow cut in the mountainside. "Personally, I'd recommend you get the hell out of Nevada."

"You said there'd be a reward for us," Cope threw back. "Not leaving without that."

"Of course not." Amelia shook her head and smirked. "My dad will be happy to pay you once I'm safe. I promise you that, but we have to get there first." She moved to the upside of a boulder resting precariously on the slope and scrambled around it, bent over so her hands supported her on the ground. On the other side, the trail opened up, and the ground leveled out some.

She turned and surveyed the area for a few seconds as the others made their way around the boulder. When they were all on the trail again, she plopped down on a rock in the shade of a pinyon pine and said, "Let's take a break."

"Good." Chester nodded and dropped to the ground, leaning back against a boulder on the other side of the trail. "So, if we won't make it to this Merchant ... whatever the hell it is ... today, what do we do? Walk all night?" He nodded toward the slope on the downside of the trail. "It's pretty steep. One wrong step in the dark and it's a hell of a long ways down."

"No. We'll stop before it's full dark." She looked around and nodded up the slope toward the summit of the mountain they'd been switch-backing around for several hours. "This is the Mahogany Range and that peak above us is Merritt Mountain, highest point in the range."

"What the hell's that got to do with how far we have to

walk today?" Cope grumbled and looked up, eyeing the summit above. "You sayin' we gonna climb this mountain."

"No. I'm saying I know where we are. I've hunted around here with my father. There's another cabin down in the ravine on the other side of the mountain. We can rest there tonight, get up early and walk out to Merchantville by the end of the day tomorrow."

She didn't mention that it had been years since she spent a frosty October night there with her father when they stayed out later than they should have, field dressing an elk he'd killed. The cabin might be there or might not. Winter snows, avalanches, flash floods, wind, and just plain decay had a way of wearing things down or washing them away up here. Still, it was the best she could come up with. Besides, it wasn't her fault they were in this predicament. They were the kidnappers, after all. She didn't really give a damn if they had to spend an uncomfortable night propped against a tree on the mountain slope. In fact, it would be a pleasure to see Cope, clinging to the mountainside, trying to keep warm.

"What about food? What we gonna eat?" Cope scowled at her, sounding like a whining child. "We had food back at the cabin where we were. You're so smart, why didn't you think to bring some along?"

"If you had listened to me from the start, we could have talked things over like adults, packed up some food from the cabin, and been ready for this." She shook her head in disgust. "But since it took me all day and half the night to convince you that someone wanted to put a bullet in your ass, we left in kind of a hurry. Or did you forget that?"

"You need to mind how you talk to me, you little bitch." Cope leaned over, sneering into her face, close enough for her to smell his rancid breath and see the angry spit fly out in little drops as he talked. "I could still make things right with Jenks ... put a bullet in you and show him we did what he wanted done and he didn't need to send anyone after us. What about that?" He smirked. "Problem solved and then we really could get our pay."

"I can't believe Chester lets you do the thinking." She shook her head. "Put a bullet in me and what then? Carry my dead body fifteen miles out of here to show it to Jenks?"

"I'd just leave you layin' there and bring him back to see." Cope straightened up and gave a mean grin. "See. I bet he'd get a fuckin' kick out of that."

"Bring him back where?" Amelia said calmly, looking up from the rock where she sat while Cope stood over her. The open-mouthed, puzzled look on his face made her laugh. "You have no idea where we are or how to get out of these mountains. You get rid of me and you'll be coyote shit in two days." She shook her head, laughing harder. "You really must be the dummy of your mama's litter. I'm surprised she didn't drown you to strengthen the gene pool."

It was a mistake, and she knew it as the words left her mouth. She was angry, frustrated, tired, and worried sick about her father and Ron. Most of all, she was worn out by Cope's nasty, argumentative, bullshit response to everything. But she knew better than to poke sleeping dogs ... or morons with guns.

Red-faced and furious, Cope reached out with one hand and grabbed her by the throat, and with the other, banged the barrel of his pistol into her forehead hard enough to raise a lump.

"That's it! I'm gonna put a fuckin' bullet in you now, bitch. We're probably all dead anyway, and I'll be goddammed if I'll let a smart-mouthed piece of ass like you talk to me like that. You fucking bi..."

The Ghost

Chester's ham-like fist caught him on the side of the head and sent him sprawling on the ground. Cope rolled over and lay still, his eyes wide and stunned. Chester reached down and picked up his pistol, and waggled it in Cope's face like a scolding finger.

"We ain't shootin' nobody. I said that already and you better remember it. We didn't get into this for no killin'." He leaned closer and waited a few seconds while the fog cleared from Cope's eyes. "You get it?"

Cope just stared back.

"Do you?" Chester's voice rose.

Cope nodded.

"Say it."

"I get it."

"Good." Chester tucked the pistol in his belt and went back to his seat on the ground across from Amelia. "So, like Cope was sayin, what are we gonna eat?"

She didn't know whether to laugh or cry but decided that she'd pushed her luck far enough with Cope, and didn't much feel like crying now. That would come later.

She turned on the rock and picked up a couple of pine cones, recently dropped and just beginning to open. With a dirty fingernail, she pulled back several woody scales and plucked out the seeds hidden inside. She held out her hand. "Here. Eat these."

Chester let her dump them in his hand, then sat there staring at his open palm. "What are they?"

"Pine nuts." Amelia broke a few more out of another pine cone and plopped them in her mouth, munching them and nodding. "Good food, and all we're likely to find around here."

Chester looked doubtful for a moment, then shrugged

and tossed the seeds in his mouth, chewing with gusto. He smiled. "They *are* good."

"Yep." She looked around at the ground under the pinyon. Pine cones were scattered in a wide circle, some already open, their seeds gone. "We better gather up as many as we can here, and anywhere we see them from now on. Looks like the squirrels and chipmunks have already started on them, so look for the ones that aren't open. We'll need as many pine nuts as we can get to keep us going the rest of today and tomorrow."

"Right." Chester hopped up and took off his outer shirt, buttoned it up, and tied the shirttail in a knot to make a bundle to carry them. He began gathering pine cones and called over to Cope, who was just sitting up, holding a hand to the lump on the side of his face. "C'mon, Cope. Help me gather up these pine cones. Pine nuts is good!"

TWENTY-SEVEN

He Made Up His Mind

Sole grabbed what little gear he had from his truck and headed back up the trail toward the cabin. He traveled light. The .30-06 rifle Monty Sole once used to save his son's life, a couple of pistols, including his Colt 1911 .45ACP, a .40 caliber Glock from his police days, and three twelve-ounce bottles of water.

He tucked the 1911 in his waistband and put the Glock, water, and extra ammo in a hiker's backpack he'd been carrying around for emergencies. Then he slung the rifle over his shoulder and trotted back up the trail.

He didn't have much of a plan. Follow the game trail up to the ledge overlooking the cabin. See if he could figure out what direction they had taken. Track them down. Rescue Amelia from her kidnappers. Simple.

Simple, except it was a shit plan with too many variables to make it more than a hopeful attempt to find Amelia. He was a cop, not Daniel Boone. He knew from experience that tracking someone in rough country was not as easy as movies made it look. Picking up signs and determining that the person you were tracking made them was a chancy thing. Hollywood always showed the tracker pointing at a telltale displaced twig or rock to indicate the passage of the people he was after. But those twigs and rocks could just as easily be moved by an animal, and Sole doubted he was expert enough to tell the difference, and the rocky ground was not likely to offer up tracks to follow. Once he was in the mountain backcountry, he knew there would be other game trails moving in different directions. How would he know which one Amelia and the kidnappers had taken?

The answer was, he wouldn't. He figured his chances of picking up their trail and staying on it until he caught up with them was only about thirty percent, if that. Not great odds, but it was the best plan he could come up with on short notice. Loaded with his gear now, he jogged back up the trail toward the cabin.

Attracted by the aroma of fresh meat, crows had come to investigate the bodies of Secret Asian Man and Bag Man. A few were already pecking inquisitively at their clothes and bits of exposed skin. Cawing and flapping their wings, senior birds, pushed the juveniles away so they could claim the best morsels, exercising the first rule of scavenging—size matters. The larger and stronger the animal, the more it could claim for its share. But the second rule sometimes overrode all others—first come, first served, and the little beasts tended to be first on the scene.

Sole watched for a moment, trying not to think of the bodies of Jake and Ron, probably undergoing similar treatment at that exact moment. The crows were hard at work. The faces would go first, the soft and accessible tissues of the mouth, the tongue, and eyes would be claimed by the early diners. Later, when decay or larger animals split open the corpses, the inner organs would go. Bone and muscle would be claimed by the larger predators—coyotes, mountain lions, bobcats. The crows were just the first arrivals to the banquet. By nightfall, the place would be crawling with scavengers looking for a free meal.

Eventually, what remained of the bodies would be dragged off into the brush until barely a trace remained of the men who died there. He picked up a stone to toss it at the crows, but his arm froze in midair, the stone clenched in his fist as if he'd stumbled on a gold nugget.

Unless someone came to claim them. The thought hovered in his mind.

As he stared at the bodies, another plan began taking form. Someone *would be coming along* to claim the bodies. Peter Jenks would want to know what happened to the killers he sent to clean up the mess. When he didn't hear from them, he would have to find out what happened ... maybe. Or maybe he would just sit back and let things take their course.

No, Sole decided. Too much was at stake, including going to prison for the rest of his life for accessory to murder and kidnapping. Jenks would have to find out and then clean up the mess himself if necessary. A man who handled problems the way Jenks did would not trust to chance to protect him. There had been too many mistakes. When he saw the bodies of his killers sprawled out on the road, he would go after the kidnappers and Amelia himself to make certain that they disappeared.

It was not a certainty by any means, but it seemed highly probable. Sole had no idea where the kidnappers had taken Amelia, and the decision to play mountain man and go wandering about in the backcountry looking for them was made out of desperation to do something, anything, to keep his promise. Jenks also might not know where they went, but he had a connection to them that Sole lacked. He must have had a way to contact them, give them their assignments, some way of interacting with them, and that might be all Sole needed.

He stood there watching the crows get down to serious business, working on the killers' bodies, while he thought things through. They might be on the run from Jenks, but he, at least, had some connection to them, and a better idea of what they would do next. Sole had no connection and no ideas.

As if to confirm his change of plans, a metallic ringing filled the air. The crows looked up, squawked, flapped, and then settled back down on the bodies. Sole walked over to the rental truck and peered inside.

A cell phone on the console lit up as the phone chimed. Sole picked it up. He didn't recognize the number, but it could only be one person.

He made up his mind, put the phone back on the console, and tossed a stone at the crows. They flapped and squawked and lifted off the ground, leaving the musty scent of feathers in the air. Some flew away to the rocks on the side of the next mountain in the range. The senior birds settled nearby in the pines and rocks, leaning over the trail, turning their heads this way and that, watching and waiting for the human to get the hell out of their domain.

Sole glanced at them and several of the larger birds stared back defiantly, squawking. "Don't worry. I'm leaving."

He turned to jog back down the trail to his pickup with the uneasy sense that the crows were watching him, considering whether he might be another meal in their future. "Not today," he called over his shoulder, then glanced back.

The crows weren't watching him, after all. They were busily dividing up the best parts of Secret Asian Man and Bag Man.

TWENTY-EIGHT

Worried

"Are we alone?" Owen Syndall, CEO and Chairman of the Board of Entente Mining Corporation, gazed into the computer screen from his glass-walled penthouse office. Beyond the windows, Wall Street towers rose like fortresses, each protecting the financial turf they claimed as theirs.

"We are." Turner Bates took note that Syndall was calling from his office, not from one of his palatial homes nestled on a mountainside or overlooking a white sand beach, or from his yacht, or the Gulfstream G-700 jet that the Entente board had approved for his personal use.

It was a lifestyle that had attracted Bates from his earliest years in school. Unlike Syndall, who was born to wealth, Bates came from a middle-class family and worked his way through Harvard Business School. After graduating Cum Laude, he spent several years jumping from job to job seeking just the right opportunity to climb the corporate ladder but always found himself looking up at so many asses clinging to the ladder above him, blocking his way, that he was becoming disillusioned.

A dedicated free-market capitalist, he discovered that the free-market system he deeply believed in had morphed into something else. Corporatism had replaced capitalism.

The entrepreneurial spirit—ingenuity, innovation, hard work—and the opportunity for success offered to anyone willing to put in the hours had always appealed to him. But corporatism was not that.

These days, relationships mattered more than ability. Government connections, regulatory oversight designed and manipulated by the corporations that were being regulated, along with a large dose of political quid pro quo often determined corporate success or failure.

With no prospects or connections, it seemed his climb up the corporate ladder would probably only take him high enough to land him in some mid-level job in an office in Topeka or some other place equally distant from the shining center of the financial universe. There he would be doomed to biding his time until retirement. It was then, at his point of greatest disillusionment, that he reconnected with Owen Syndall, a Harvard classmate.

Syndall's career began high on the ladder to success. After graduating with mediocre grades and in the bottom third of his class, his father's connections landed him a director-level position with Entente Mining Corporation as the head of Emerging Markets. The position required no extensive knowledge of mining, and despite the job title, marketing skills were not required. What was required was the ability to schmooze it up with dignitaries, corporate executives, and third-world potentates, skills that were right up Syndall's frat-boy alley. He'd been schmoozing since he was old enough to accompany his father on rounds of golf at the country club. Free market capitalism meant virtually nothing to Syndall, who knew from watching his father's dealings for decades that relationships were the key to corporate success.

While going through resumes to flesh out his newly formed department at Entente, he came across one with a vaguely familiar name. He and Bates had not been close in college, had hardly known each other, but Syndall knew Bates had excelled as a student while he coasted through on his family name. Having an actual marketing and business expert on his team would be helpful.

So, the relationship began, and with Bates' business acumen at his disposal, Syndall advanced up the ladder of success, taking Bates along with him, at a respectful distance, of course. Entente grew into one of the largest international mining concerns on the globe, but their development of the U.S. market lagged. That had to change.

Bates drew up the plans. Syndall pitched them to the Board of Directors, and before they had time to finalize all the details, Bates and his assistant, Peter Jenks, were in Elko, trying to persuade Jake Downes and Ron Benson to sell them their mining operation.

Now was the time to make their move. The board wanted action. Syndall wanted action.

None of that mattered. All of their planning went out the window, stymied by Downes' and Benson's stubborn refusals to sell, and that was unacceptable. The symbiotic relationship between Bates and Syndall fed on success. Failure was not an option.

"Let me see," Syndall said, wanting proof that Bates was indeed alone in his office.

Bates turned the camera to pan his office, got up and closed the door, and then returned to his computer. "As you can see, we're alone," Bates said stiffly, more than a little annoyed that Syndall doubted his word.

"Don't sulk. Just being careful," Syndall replied. "Maybe if you had been a bit more careful, we wouldn't be in this fix now."

Bates' teeth clenched and ground together, but he remained silent.

"So where are we?" Syndall asked, reclining back in his leather chair as an executive helicopter flew by his window close enough for Bates to see the tail number on his screen.

"It's being taken care of today," Bates said.

"Damage?"

"It will be messy," Bates replied honestly. "Nothing we can't handle, and we'll make sure there is no linkage back to us or Entente, but ..." He paused, hesitating.

"What?" Syndall sat up a little straighter in his chair.

"It would be helpful if you could buy us a little more time with the board."

"You just said that there will be no links back to you or your man, Jenks. If that's true, then why more time?"

Bates found it amazing and disconcerting that he had to explain. It was clear from the start of their relationship that he, not Syndall, was the brains behind their success, but certainly, Syndall was smart enough to figure that out for himself. Bates explained anyway. "Nothing points back to us or Entente… directly. That could change if we move too fast, start trying to push things too soon, it may raise suspicions, and even if there is no proof of any criminal activity, the suspicions themselves could be enough for regulators to scrutinize everything we've been doing." To make sure Syndall understood his point, he added, "Not just here, but in other areas."

"Right …other areas" Syndall intoned the words, chewing them over, digesting them, trying to get all the meaning out and what they implied. A minute passed before he said, "Alright. I'll work with the board and get us a little more time, but it won't be much. We're at the bottom of a rising market right now, perfect timing for a move like this, but that won't last forever. They will want things wrapped up before the pricing cycle turns on us."

"Understood." Bates nodded. "Thank you, Owen." He used his boss' name to emphasize the bond between them.

"Don't thank me," Syndall replied without using his first name. "There isn't much time. Just get it done."

The call ended. The computer screen went momentarily blank and then returned to Bates' desktop display. He sat quietly, replaying the call in his mind. What was that all about?

Syndall had been briefed, knew the problem they faced and what they were doing about it. So why the call? Why the warning that there isn't much time? And as he asked himself the questions, the answer became obvious. Because Syndall was worried about something else … something bigger.

They'd been handling problems for him for years. Southeast Asia, South America, the Middle East. The string of successes during Entente's rise in stature was impressive. Wherever the problem arose, Bates and Jenks resolved it or eliminated it. Syndall had never batted a concerned eye over it before, but this time, he was worried. Why?

Over the years, Bates had taken a back seat, watched Syndall smile his smooth, handsome smile and rise through the corporate ranks on the shoulders of the work Bates did for him. He accepted that arrangement because Syndall was generous about sharing the wealth, and there was a lot of it to share. But now, Syndall was clearly worried, and that had Bates worried.

His wagon was hitched to Syndall's rising, privileged star, but there was always danger in approaching stars too closely. When they go supernova, they incinerate everything in their path.

Maybe it was nothing. Maybe he was overthinking, but Turner Bates did not want to become a cinder left behind by Syndall's exploding star.

TWENTY-NINE

A Good Day, My Ass

The first order of business was to ditch the Audi and grab a four-wheel-drive rental at the airport. Jenks was careful to use a different car rental agency than Yang and Sink had, and he kept Entente out of the transaction by paying with his personal credit card. He drove out with a Chevy pickup, bigger than he wanted, but the best they had available on the lot.

Next, he drove to the house he rented on the hillside rising to the north of Elko. The neighborhood was fashionable, befitting a senior executive with a global mining company. Turner Bates' house was farther up the hillside, where the neighborhood transitioned into a gated and far more exclusive community.

Wheeling into the circular drive in front, he hopped out and headed for the front door. That was a mistake.

"Mr. Jenks! Oh, Mr. Jeeennnkks!" Across the street, eighty-six-year-old Sally Gascon sat on her front porch, rocking and taking in the morning sun. She waved her hand high. "Mr. Jenks!"

The Ghost

Shit. Where the fuck is your brain, Jenks thought, and turned, smiling. "Hi, Mrs. Gascon. Nice day, isn't it?"

"It is, indeed," Mrs. Gascon exclaimed with the sort of childlike enthusiasm senior citizens sometimes have about the most mundane things. "And please call me Sally. No one calls me Mrs. Gascon except the paperboy."

"Will do, Sally. You enjoy the day now," Jenks said and started toward the front door.

"Is that a new truck you have there?" Mrs. Gascon shouted. "It looks new! Is it?"

"Just giving it a test drive," Jenks called back and gave a quick glance up and down the street. Just fucking great. Soon, the whole fucking neighborhood would be in on the conversation, wanting to know all about the vehicle he intended to use to find and murder Amelia Downes and the idiots who took her.

"Oh, that's nice!" Mrs. Gascon called back. "My son, Robert, is thinking about buying a new truck. He would be interested in what you think about that one."

"I'll let you know what I think," Jenks called back. "Now I have to get to work."

He turned for the door. Mrs. Gascon wasn't finished.

"I thought you must be off today, test driving a new truck and all, and home at this time of day. Gracious, it seems you never get home before dark!" She raised a hand to the side of her mouth to make sure her voice carried across the street. "You must be the hardest working person I know around here!"

This just kept getting worse. At this rate, she'd be wanting to know his plans for the afternoon. He figured it would go something like this.

Well, Sally, it's like this. First, I'm going to find the killers I sent out to do a job but who, for some mysterious reason, are incommuni-

cado. Then we're going to find the two jerk-offs I sent out to do a simpler job and who decided it would be a wonderful idea to kidnap Amelia Downes. After that, I plan to find a spot way back in the mountains; you know, someplace far away from prying eyes, where I will put a bullet in each of their heads and dump them in a hidden ravine. Then I'll send the killers on their way, wire the money to their account in Cayman, and, with a little luck, I'll be back home by midnight. Oh, and if I think you might repeat a bit of this to anyone, I will be visiting you tonight to eliminate that possibility. Clear enough?

Instead, Jenks sighed, turned, and smiled widely. "That's really nice of you to say, Sally. I try to work hard and set a good example." He grinned at her. "When the boss is looking, anyway."

"When the boss is looking! Hah!" She laughed and slapped her knee. "That's a good one ... when the boss is looking!"

Jenks made it to the front door, unlocked it, and got inside before she stopped laughing and asked another question. He flipped on a light. Heavy drapes shrouded the interior and kept anyone outside from seeing in, night or day. The atmosphere was heavy and gloomy even with the lights on. Jenks preferred it that way. Prying eyes and nosey neighbors had ruined the plans of less cautious men.

The sparse furnishings included two chairs and a sofa rented from a pay-as-you-go furniture store in Elko. A widescreen television, bought at one of the big box stores, hung from a wall across from the chairs. Other than a bed, a nightstand, and four cheap tv trays that served as side tables, coffee table, and dining table, the place was bare.

Some might have called it oppressively austere, but for Jenks, it was home, or at least as much home as he had. One day he planned to settle down, but not until his bank account had grown to the point that he could make that *somewhere* a small island he'd purchased a few years earlier with a bonus check from Entente for a job well-done in an obscure southeast Asian nation-state. Off the coast of Belize, the island was also off the beaten tourist path.

A small house sat in the center of the island, not much more than a shack really, and with minimal amenities. Once that would have been enough for him, but his ideas of comfort had escalated since beginning his relationship with Turner Bates. By his calculations, a few more years of putting away the funds that flowed his way from Entente and he could build a more suitable home.

He walked to a back bedroom and pushed the door open. This side of the house was even darker than the front, and he turned on another light. Two trunks stood against a wall. He opened one and stood contemplating the contents for a few seconds.

Then he reached down and retrieved a Heckler & Koch MP5 submachine gun, ideal for ending close-range encounters quickly. With the possibility that he might have to take a distance shot across a mountain valley, he grabbed a custom .308 caliber rifle. A gunsmith in Zurich spent three months fabricating and assembling the pieces. The result was a rifle that would have made any sniper in any army in the world drool with envy. At the time, he'd spent more than he ever thought he would for a weapon, but it had repaid him handsomely over the years. More than a few of Entente's problems had been resolved by the .308. Those on the receiving end never heard the distant crack of the rifle or the buzz-humming of the bullet before it plowed through their brains.

From the second trunk, he retrieved several burner phones still in their plastic cases and an army-style rucksack.

He put the weapons and phones inside the rucksack, turned off the light, and walked back through the house.

Parting the drapes, he peeked outside. Shit. Sally Gascon was still sitting in her rocker on the porch, waiting for him to come back out. Fuck it. He walked outside, locking the door behind him.

"Off again, are you!" Sally called from across the street.

He ignored her and tossed the rucksack onto the passenger seat as he climbed behind the Chevy's wheel.

"Have a good day!" Sally called as he started the engine, pulled around the circular drive onto the street, and gunned the engine.

"A good day, my ass," he mumbled.

THIRTY

Let's Do This

The hardest part was waiting.

The dead bodies were simple. He left them where they lay, Secret Asian Man and Bag Man down the trail around the bend from the cabin, Jake and Ron farther back down the trail where they'd met the killers. The only thing he really had to do to prepare for Jenks' arrival was to figure out what to do with his truck.

He thought about rolling it to the edge and letting it careen down the mountainside. Then he could use the killers' rental, but that was too chancy. Jenks might notice the keys were missing and if he left them in the ignition, Jenks might take them with him. Besides, he was attached to the old beater. It was home.

Instead, he drove it up to the clearing. The kidnappers' truck was parked to one side, backed in with its rear up against the rock wall. There was enough space beside it for Sole to back in his pickup. Once he had it parked, he walked into the clearing to give things a look over.

The extra truck looked innocuous enough. Maybe Jenks

wouldn't notice it. If he did, maybe he didn't know that the kidnappers only used one truck. Maybe he would just assume they brought a second vehicle to the cabin hideout. Maybe was the best that Sole could do.

With the backpack over one should and the rifle over the other, he began moving up the game trail. Most of the climb was a scramble over the loose shale and gravel covering the slope. At times, it reduced him to crawling, hands clutching at roots and rocks to keep from sliding back down. Aware that Amelia had already made the climb, he gained a new respect for the woman. Clinging to the same rocks she must have used to make her way up, he felt a different connection, a closer one than the mere promise made to her father. More than a name now, she became a living, breathing, struggling, person—someone worth saving if he could.

A couple of hundred feet above the cabin, the trail disappeared into a tumbled pile of rocks. He climbed up and over and came out onto the ledge that overlooked the cabin. Ragged chips and scars pockmarked the rock, bright yellow-white splotches that showed where the bullets fired by the killers impacted. The absence of blood trails showed that the firing had been ineffective.

A trail led away from the ledge around the side of the mountain. He followed it for a hundred yards to see what he could and knew he'd made the right decision. Ten thousand square miles of mountain wilderness stretched out before him. Even with a good trail to follow, it would have been nearly impossible to track Amelia and her kidnappers without some idea about where they were headed, and he was all out of ideas. Convinced that the decision to let Jenks lead him to Amelia was his best chance to find her, he returned to the ledge.

He stood for a moment surveying the clearing and cabin below, then knelt and retrieved one deformed bullet from the rocks and held it to his nose. The fresh metallic odor of the copper jacket mingled with lead confirmed that someone had recently fired it. He looked around and found a pile of rocks near the edge and lay down behind it.

She might have lain in that exact spot, he realized, watching the cabin, waiting to see if killers were coming after all. They did come, and he wondered if she had known they would or if her kidnappers decided to play things safe after botching their assignment.

Every indication was that her kidnappers were not much more than bumbling amateurs. They crashed their truck into her. They kidnapped her when all they had to do was threaten her. He was certain the decision to watch from the ledge must have been her idea. She had known the killers would come, had figured it out, then probably had to convince her abductors to hide out with her just to be safe. Once again, his respect for her grew.

He hunkered down behind the pile of rocks to watch the clearing below, took a sip from a bottle of water, and whispered, "Come on, Jenks. Let's do this."

THIRTY-ONE

Now He Knew Why

Turner Bates wore his best phony stage smile as he walked from the Chamber of Commerce meeting. While Jenks was out resolving their problem, he glad-handed local business leaders and made small talk. It was a part he played well. He'd been playing it for years. He smiled pleasantly and chatted with other business representatives. No one would suspect that Entente's development team in Elko was in the midst of a human hunting expedition.

Present at the Chamber meeting were the representatives of two of the largest global mining conglomerates in the world. They were also Entente's primary competition in northern Nevada, although calling them the competition was a stretch. They were the big guys on the block, had been extracting gold, copper, and silver from the Nevada mountains for decades. Despite its international presence, Entente was a relative pipsqueak in Nevada. It couldn't even close a deal to get one small-time operation up and running.

"Making progress with D&B Mines?" Bob Markle asked.

Director of Public Relations for one of the competing mining corporations, Markle approached his job like a good old boy who'd been around Elko all of his life, despite being born in Alberta, Canada. His close friends included the mayor, all the city council members, the sheriff, the chief of police, the local MSHAW and OSHA inspectors, and anybody else he could grease for information with a round of free golf.

"I hear Jake and Ron are being difficult," Janet Chastwell said sympathetically.

She was Markle's counterpart at the other major mine operating in Nevada. Her connections in the community were identical to Markle's, but she approached her job differently. Chastwell took a motherly approach, always interested in who was having a baby or getting married or whose child was graduating from college. She never missed an opportunity to show up at some special family occasion, usually with a cake from her oven and a donation from the company that employed her.

"Working on it," Bates said, forcing the smile a bit wider. "You know how it goes."

"Tough old bastards, those two," Markle chuckled and gave him a friendly slap on the back.

"It must be difficult," Chastwell said, her furrowed brow showing how much she cared and that she understood his predicament and shared his frustration. She patted his arm. "I know you must be under some pressure to get it done."

Bates managed not to flinch at the same phrase that Syndall had used earlier on the call. "You mean to close the deal with Downes and Benson."

"Of course, that's what I mean," Chastwell said, smiling. "What else could I mean?"

Bates was suddenly uncomfortable. "We'll find a way to do the deal and make everyone happy."

"I'll bet you will," Markle threw in a little too effusively to be sincere. "The delays don't seem to be hurting things though."

"Excuse me." Bates' eyes narrowed. "What things?"

"Oh, you know," Chastwell said, continuing the tag-team on him so that he had to swivel back in her direction. "Entente seems to have hit a roadblock here in Nevada. Its development of new markets slowed down to a turtle's pace." She gave a polite laugh and added quickly, "Not your fault, of course, but the financial analysts have put alerts out that failing to move into new markets may be a signal that the company may be in some sort of development crisis, something management related even. They've put out a few red flags that the stock may be about to decline, but …" She smiled and shrugged. "No decline in sight, is there? In fact, the stock just keeps climbing." She raised a hand to simulate the stock's rise. "And climbing. Amazing, isn't it?"

"There's no crisis that I know of," Bates said, forcing himself not to snap back at the bitch playing possum with him. "We have a significant global presence, as you already know. I'm sure the continued rise of our stock price reflects our solid management structure and continued focus on developing new markets around the globe, despite our slow start here in Nevada." Bates felt a slight tic start in his right eyebrow and wondered if they noticed it. "Gaining or losing the D&B deal will not have any substantial effect on our stock or our position globally."

"Interesting." Markle crossed his arms as if he were considering his explanation, then he smiled. "Well, that's not how the analysts see things, but …" He shrugged. "I suppose they've been wrong before."

"They have," Bates said. "More than once."

"That is excellent news!" Chastwell's eyes twinkled with delight. "Well, I've got a meeting over at Great Basin College with the dean to talk about developing a management course to attract more young people into considering the mines after graduation." Chastwell put her hand back on Bates' arm and gave it another motherly pat. "You take care and we'll be seeing you around, Turner."

She turned to leave and Markle followed, calling back over his shoulder, "See you around, Turner. Maybe a round of golf this weekend."

"Maybe so," Bates said and watched them walk away, their heads leaned too close together as they walked, like lovers exchanging whispers. But they weren't lovers, and Bates had a good idea what they were whispering about. He shot one last word at their backs, too low for them to hear. "Assholes."

He waited a few minutes, for appearances' sake, making small talk with several local business owners outside the Chamber building, then he excused himself. "Well, I better get back to work."

He walked the four blocks back to the Entente building. With every step, his prior concerns morphed into certainty. Owen Syndall had seemed worried during their earlier call. Now he knew why.

THIRTY-TWO

Our Boy is Pissed Off

The what-ifs, what-should-have-beens, and what-nows, playing around in his head turned the hour-long drive up the highway to the Turnbridge Road into an ordeal of doubt and second guesses. Usually calm and in control, Peter Jenks was as pissed with himself as he was with Plunkett and Welch. They were idiots. He knew that and yet, he allowed himself to overestimate their capabilities.

He'd hurried things. Violated his own rules. Now he was paying the price. He pounded a fist against the steering wheel in frustration.

The thought occurred to him that he should just keep driving, put as much distance as possible between him and Turner Bates, Entente, and Amelia Downes, and the whole fucking mess. It was only a momentary consideration. Besides the fact that Jenks had never backed away from an assignment, there was money at stake ... a lot of money.

He took the cutoff onto the graveled Turnbridge Road and had to ease back on the accelerator. The frustration and anxiety increased in proportion to the decrease in speed. He inhaled deeply to calm himself and clear his head.

Keep your head straight. Breathe. Think. There is no way Plunkett and Welch can outsmart you. They've been lucky so far, that's all. That luck will run out and you'll get everything back on track.

The teardrop-shaped rock loomed ahead. Jenks slowed and scanned the entry into the adjacent wash. Vehicles passing over it had worn the soft bank down, and he had an uneasy feeling that Yang's rental was not the only one that had traversed it today. At least they hadn't gotten lost, and they could deal with anyone else who decided to follow them up the mountainside.

He turned the wheel, bumped down into the wash, then began the climb out and up along the switchback trail. He hadn't gone far when things changed again.

He was right. Others had found the trail up the mountain. The bodies of Jake Downes and Ron Benson lay on either side of the trail, each shot in the chest and head. Jenks recognized Carl Sink's handiwork. The boy might be crazy as a loon, but he had done his job.

Killing Downes and Benson was not part of the plan, but there was no way to undo it now. In confronting Yang and Sink, the two miners had no idea what they were facing, must have assumed they had the drop on them, and paid the price for that assumption.

Jenks stared at the bodies for a minute, his mind spinning out a new plan. He nodded. This might even be better. This could all work to their benefit.

Downes and Benson murdered by unknown killers in the mountains. Amelia Downes missing, taken by those same killers. He and Bates would report to the sheriff that they were trying to contact Downes and Benson about the mine deal and hadn't heard from them. As concerned citizens, and despite their differences over the mine acquisition, they were worried and felt they should let law enforcement know.

The sheriff would begin a search, get the locals to help, have the National Guard send helicopters. It might take a while, but eventually, the bodies would be located and a murder investigation started. By that time, Yang and Sink would be long gone, and there would be no link back to the concerned citizens, Jenks and Bates.

As for Amelia, she would never be heard from again. He paused. That was the one sticking point. She must never be heard from again.

He left the bodies as they lay, climbed back into the rented Chevy pickup, and continued the climb up the mountain trail. The more he thought as he worked the pickup around boulders and over bumps, the more he liked the new plan.

This could work. It would be even better. It would be fucking perfect.

"Son of a bitch!" His fist hit the steering wheel, and he slammed his foot on the brakes.

Yang's rental pickup loomed in front of him as he rounded a switchback curve. His body lay several yards beyond on the left. Another body lay curled around the duffel near the passenger door, Carl Sink protecting his girlfriend to the last.

Jenks' special operations instincts kicked in. Reaching for the MP5 in the rucksack, he rolled out of the driver's side door to his knees, taking what cover he could behind the open door. He waited, watching and listening for some telltale sign, a sliding rock, a glint of metal, anything that might give away the position of whoever ambushed Yang and Sink.

Crouching in the dirt, taken by surprise once again, he thought about that. Who ambushed his best killing team? It had to be Plunkett and Welch. How could he have so underestimated them?

Or did he? Was someone else doing the thinking for them? Amelia Downes. The name reverberated in his head. One more person he'd underestimated. She had to be pulling their strings, doing the thinking and manipulating them.

The mistakes just kept piling up. If he managed to get out of this quagmire, he was going to seriously consider pulling the pin and heading to that island in the Caribbean. That was for later, though. Now, he had to eliminate his problem.

He turned his head up to the sky, listening. The only sound was the wind in the trees and a squirrel skittering along a branch, stopping, waiting, listening, and then skittering some more. The squirrel stopped at the end of a branch, put its nose up in the air, and then turned and scampered back to the tree to disappear in the foliage, leaving Jenks alone to decide what to do next. He expected any second to hear the crack of gunfire and the metallic thud of bullets punching holes in the Chevy, or to hear nothing at all as a slug went through his brain before the sound could reach him.

He had no intention of waiting for that to happen. Crouching, holding the submachine gun with both hands, he ran along the rocks, past the bodies of Yang and Sink, and moved into the trees. Breathing hard, he knelt behind a large pinyon pine, his head swiveling, eyes scanning for danger.

He pushed forward through the trees, following the bend in the trail toward the cabin, pausing by the edge of the clearing for only a few seconds to scan for threats. Two pickups were parked on one side of the cabin. Did they have help? It didn't matter. He was ending this now.

He moved quickly, making a silent dash to the cabin. Without stopping, he shouldered through the front door on the run, rolled low, and came up with the MP5, searching for targets. There were none.

"Aaahhhh!" It was a howl, primal and enraged. He roared, "You sonsabitches!"

Anger, rage, frustration, anxiety, animal emotions surged to the surface from deep inside. Jenks' finger depressed the trigger, spraying bullets around the cabin's interior, and kept it depressed until the thirty-round magazine emptied and the firing pin gave a resounding metallic click.

Watching from the ledge above, Sole tracked Jenks as he made his way through the trees toward the cabin. The military-style entry into the cabin, followed a second later by the burst of bullets, made Sole smile.

A few seconds after the firing ceased, Jenks stepped back out into the clearing, his rage sated for the moment. He walked around to the pickups. Sole held his breath.

Don't shoot holes in them. Don't disable them. The boys might come back and you'll want to be able to follow them.

Jenks must have had the same thought because, after a minute, he walked back to the center of the clearing to get the strongest signal and pulled out his cell phone. The mountain breeze and distance made it difficult to hear what he said, but Sole picked up a word or two, enough to know that Jenks was calling in reinforcements. Good, that meant he intended to track them down. Sole's plan remained intact—stay on Jenks, let him lead him to Amelia, get her away, and do it all without getting your ass shot off. Simple.

"I want the motherfuckers dead!" Jenks' voice rose above the sound of the breeze just before he disconnected the call.

"Very good." Sole smiled. "Our boy is pissed off."

THIRTY-THREE

Tensions

By three in the afternoon, the sun was setting behind the mountain peaks. Clouds floating in the blue sky above contrasted with the deep shadows below. The fading light was enough to find their way, but Amelia knew that wouldn't last long. In another hour, twilight would descend ahead of the night, and the canyons and ravines would be immersed in darkness.

She'd seen it before. Standing in the dark of a mountain gorge, lighting a campfire with her father, the last rays of sunlight turned a distant peak into a brilliant beacon. A minute later, the sun sank too low for its rays to bathe the peak. The beacon would blink out. The world would turn black.

She shuddered. Things were bad enough. Trapped outside in the dark, unable to move for fear of breaking a leg or tumbling down a mountainside, would only increase the tension between them all. Her control over an already shaky situation could evaporate.

"How much farther," Chester asked.

"Not too far," Amelia said, hoping she was right. "Another mile or so," she added, trying to sound confident.

"You say," Cope snorted from behind.

"That's right, I say," Amelia threw back over her shoulder without turning. "You're welcome to take the lead if you think you can get us out of here."

"Leave her be, Cope." Chester turned to scowl at his partner, plodding behind. "You saw them two back at the cabin. The way they shot at us. If it wasn't for her, we'd a been back there with holes in us now."

Cope snorted again but said nothing.

They pushed along a ridge that circled the shoulder of a mountain summit. Rounding a turn that took them to the western slope, Amelia stopped and held up her hand. The others halted behind her.

They were high enough that the ridge they followed was bare and windswept. The only vegetation was sage and an occasional bent and twisted scrub cedar, clinging to the rocky soil. The mountain ridge they followed was cut by deep ravines that were now immersed in full darkness.

Amelia knew that the old hunt cabin her father had shown her hunkered below in one of the ravines. The question was which one. She studied the landscape for a minute. Chester shuffled his feet behind her. Cope mumbled something indiscernible that might have been the word bullshit, but Amelia couldn't be sure, and at this point, didn't care.

She studied the ridgelines and adjacent ravines. Finally, she nodded, pointed, and said, "There. In that cut right there. That's where the cabin is."

"You sure?" Chester squinted and bent forward, trying to see into the ravine and spot the cabin. "Don't see nothin'."

"You can't see it from here, but it's down there," she

said, with more confidence than she felt. "We better get moving before it's full dark."

They picked their way down the slope to the edge of the ravine. Slipping and sliding in the dim light, they reached the dry wash at the bottom and waited, letting their eyes adjust to the gloom. Amelia breathed a sigh of relief.

Not fifty yards away, the hunt cabin stood against a jumble of fallen boulders under a leaning pine. "There it is." She led the way to the door that hung on one hinge from the post.

"You call this a cabin?" Cope asked with a sneering whine. "Nothin' more than some logs leaned up against the rocks."

He was correct in his assessment. The hunt cabin was in reality a lean-to her father and Ron Benson erected years earlier on one of their hunts. The rocks on one side served as a wall. Logs were laid against them at angles to create the other walls and to form the shelter. Over the years, they'd made improvements, added the post and door, made a tiny stacked stone fire pit at one end with an opening in the ceiling to let the smoke out.

"It's got a roof," Amelia said. "We'll prop the door in place and wedge it closed with some rocks. We can build a fire and stay warm tonight."

"If we don't burn up inside," Cope grumbled. "All those pine logs got sap. They'd go up like a torch."

"Open to suggestions, if you've got a better idea." Amelia was beyond fatigued by his incessant whining and snide remarks. "Remember, it was you boys who got us into this mess, so, if you got a better way to get out of it, I'm all fucking ears. Otherwise, shut up!"

The fire in her voice stunned both men for a moment. Cope's mouth opened, then closed.

The Ghost

Chester recovered first and tried to make peace. "C'mon, Cope. It ain't so bad, and good enough for me. For sure, there ain't nobody around to shoot holes in us." He looked around and started scooping up pine straw and twigs. "I'll pick up some wood to get a fire goin'."

"You do that." Cope pushed past them and went inside, took a lighter from his pocket and gave it a flick to see in the dark, then looked around. After a minute, he grunted, went to a corner, and plopped down with his knees up and his arms and chin resting on top like a petulant child.

Chester came inside with an armful of sticks and kindling, dropped it by the fire pit, threw a look at his partner, and shook his head. "Just wait until I get this fire goin'." He grinned in his simple way. "Won't be so bad with a fire and some pine nuts to munch. I got plenty left."

Chester's exuberance was too much for Cope. He broke his silence. "You really are one dumb shit. You know that?"

"You got no cause to talk to me like that." Chester turned from the fire pit, his usually innocuous expression hard, eyes staring at Cope. "You keep talkin' that way, and I'll …"

"What?" Cope glared at him. "You ain't nothin' without me around to clean up your mess. Like havin' to wipe a baby's ass most of the time."

"Dammit, Cope, I warned you." Chester rose from the fire pit and took a step toward Cope, then stopped. The pistol was in Cope's hand. "You gonna shoot me? That the way you treat a partner? You shoot 'em?"

"Alright." Amelia was on her feet. Things were getting out of hand again. "Settle down. Chester, you get the fire going. I'm cold, aren't you?"

"Yeah." He nodded slowly, his eyes fixed on Cope. "I guess I am cold."

"Good. So, let's have a fire." Amelia turned to Cope. "And you put that gun away. We've already been through this. We'll get an early start in the morning and should make Merchantville before dark. I promise, I'll get you out of here, but you start shooting people and you're on your own. Some hunter might find your bones … in a year or two … maybe."

Cope tucked the pistol back in his waistband and smirked. "Right, you'll get us out and your daddy's gonna give us a big reward and we can head for the hills and everything's gonna be just fine like nothin' ever happened." He shook his head. "You expect me to believe your bullshit?"

"Believe what you want," Amelia snapped back. "But without me …" She nodded at Chester. "Without us, you'll be dead inside a week, lost and wandering around these mountains."

Eyes blazing back at her, but without responding, Cope went back to resting his chin on his knees. Chester busied himself with the fire, humming softly to himself as he worked. Amelia sat with her back against the rock wall, watching them both and thinking. Tensions had risen dramatically through the day. Keeping these two from killing each other or her before they got to Merchantville was becoming a major chore.

THIRTY-FOUR

You Have My Word

"Entente Mining Corporation, Office of the Chairman. How may I help you?" The voice was businesslike, cool, detached, and devoid of any nuance of personal interest in the caller or his business with Entente's boss of bosses.

He was the assistant to Owen Syndall's administrative assistant, one of several, and his official duties were to facilitate access to the Chairman of the Board. Unofficially, he screened calls and did his best to filter out anyone who might disrupt Syndall's day with unpleasant business. Turner Bates had met him on visits to Entente's headquarters, but couldn't remember his name—Calvin or Melvin or something-*in*.

"This is Turner Bates. I'd like to speak to Mr. Syndall, please."

"I'm sorry. Mr. Syndall is not available to take your call at the moment. May I take a message?"

That was new. Bates had always been on the 'put through immediately' list. He paused before saying, "Pardon me?"

"Mr. Syndall is unavailable to take your call at the moment, Mr. Bates." There was just the slightest hint of satisfaction in the voice, the low-level functionary politely telling one of the company's big bosses to fuck off.

"Look ..." The name came to him. Evlyn. Who the hell names a boy Evlyn? "Look, Evlyn. I have critical business to discuss with the Chairman. Put me through to Owen." He added Syndall's first name to emphasize that, in case the little pipsqueak forgot, he was speaking to goddam Turner Bates, a friend and associate of the Chairman, and Turner Bates wanted to speak with goddam Owen Syndall ... now.

"I'm sorry. My instructions are explicit. Mr. Syndall is not available to take any calls at the moment ... from anyone."

Son of a bitch. Bates could almost see the condescending smirk and felt the frustrating need to reach two thousand miles through the phone connection, grab Evlyn by the throat, and shake him until the smirk fell from his lifeless face.

Instead, he said, "Put me through to Barbara Warren." Warren was Syndall's administrative assistant and Evlyn's direct boss.

"Certainly," Evlyn said, and Bates imagined the smirk growing wider. "One moment, please."

He spent two minutes listening to a whiny teenybopper lament her latest lost love on the company's taped music loop. How that tied in with a global mining conglomerate's public image, Bates couldn't begin to fathom. After thirty seconds, the music grated badly on his nerves. After a minute, he considered ending the call, but this was a conversation that couldn't wait. At the minute and a half mark, he decided that Evlyn must have been in charge of selecting

The Ghost

the music, and it was just one more reason to dislike the little bastard.

At two minutes, the teenybopper singer was replaced by a track of avant-garde, dissonant jazz that sounded to Bates like nothing more than a roomful of cats screeching. His frustration was evolving into full-blown rage. He wanted to smash the phone against his desk until nothing remained but a smoldering pile of plastic shards, shattered microchips, and shredded silicone laminate. Did cell phones smolder when destroyed? It seemed doubtful, but at that moment he desperately wanted to find out. He was well into the third minute of waiting when a voice finally came back on the call.

"This is Barbara Warren. How are you, Mr. Bates?"

He ignored the question. "Put Owen on the phone, Barbara."

"Mr. Syndall is unavailable. I will have him call you as soon as …"

"Stop!" Warren's unflappable devotion to her boss was almost as annoying as Evlyn's condescension. Bates took a deep breath. "Look, I know he's in the office today, and I want to fucking talk to him right now."

"I'm afraid that's not possible." Warren's tone stiffened. "And I do not appreciate the profanity, Mr. Bates. If you have a message, I'll be happy to relay it to Mr. Syndall."

"You're right. I apologize for the profanity. That was uncalled for, but I must speak with Owen."

"As I said, I'll be happy to pass on your message."

"Alright, here's the message. Tell him we need to speak about the Remwalt deal."

"Remwalt? I'm not familiar with that deal."

"No, you're not. That's why I have to speak with Owen."

"Fine," Warren said brusquely, clearly annoyed at being stalemated. "I'll give him the message and ask him to call you as soon as he's available."

"No. You give him the message now. I'll wait on the line."

"But …"

"Do it Barbara, or when this deal falls through, I'll make sure we list your name at the top of the list of reasons."

There was no Remwalt deal. Remwalt was a code word the two of them used that meant drop everything, let's talk now, or some very bad shit is about to happen.

"I'll give him the message now. Please hold."

The line went dead, and thankfully there was no taped music loop at this level of the corporate call tree. A few seconds later, Syndall was on the line. Without preliminary, he said, "Call this number." And read off a number for one of the burner phones he kept handy for Remwalt calls.

"Right." Bates disconnected, took one of his burner phones from a desk drawer, and punched in the number Syndall gave him.

"What's the problem, Turner?" Syndall said without preliminaries when he answered.

"That's what I want to ask you?"

"What? Why?"

"Don't bullshit me, Owen. I'm not stupid. I've picked up on the vibes, your unusual concern over what we're doing here. I admit I was a little slow on the uptake, but after a conversation this morning with my counterparts from the other mines, it all clicked."

"What clicked?" Syndall asked, his voice subdued.

"Analysts warning of a devaluation, but Entente's stock price continues to climb. Questions being asked by our competitors, and you suddenly concerned about what we're doing here. It all made sense. Word gets out about what we're doing ... how we're doing it ..." Bates let the unspoken words *kidnapping and murder* hang in the air. "The Feds start asking questions and before you know it, the SEC, FBI ... hell, every alphabet agency in the federal directory will want a piece of your ass."

"Calm down, Turner. You're misreading things."

"No, I've been distracted trying to get this deal closed for you, but I'm seeing them pretty clearly now." Bates leaned forward at his desk as if it helped him look Syndall in the eye. "You'd love to just cut us loose, blame it on the help, and wash your hands of things, but you can't, can you?" Bates answered his own question. "No, you can't because we're all in this together. One goes down and we all go down."

They both knew Bates wasn't speaking about the kidnapping or the efforts to intimidate Downes and Benson into selling their mine. It was an old scheme and not a very original one, but it had worked for years now. Cook the corporate books. Inflate the company's bottom line. The stock price rises at every stock exchange around the globe despite the warnings from financial analysts that Entente was not positioned to compete in the U.S. market and that it could not be as flush as the financial statements made it out to be.

Strategically timed stock purchases, corporate bonuses paid in shares of Entente stock, and stock options as part of compensation combined to increase Syndall's wealth exponentially. By necessity, he had included Bates, a couple of Executive Vice Presidents who oversaw the company's internal audit and accounting divisions, and a lesser but critical member of their team, Peter Jenks.

"One question," Bates said, wrapping things up.

"What?"

"Are we being audited yet?"

"Not yet, but ..." Syndall hesitated.

"Spit it out, Owen."

"A couple of members of the board ... honorary types, but they have a voice." Syndall named a former senator and a big-city mayor who lost a reelection bid for a third term. "They've been asking questions."

"What kind of questions?" Bates asked. "They suspect what we're doing?"

"Maybe, but I'm not sure. Doesn't matter. They ask questions, and smell an opportunity to get in on things with us, or to make a name for themselves, and the next thing you know, they call for an audit. I might be able to hold it off. I think I can, but not if things there take a nosedive and we get sucked into a criminal investigation on U.S. soil." Syndall took a breath. "You can't let that happen, Turner."

"Right," Bates said. "We're working on it. Jenks says things should be handled by the end of the day ... tomorrow at the latest."

"I hope so." Now Syndall leaned forward at his desk, speaking earnestly. "You have to understand that if a whiff of what we're doing there gets out, I won't be able to stop things. Every Fed in the country will try to make a career out of the investigation. It would be bigger than Enron. It'd be like standing on a beach waving my arms to hold back a tsunami."

"I said we're working on it," Bates replied abruptly. "Just one more question."

"Yes?"

"What were you going to do if there was an audit?

Disappear with the millions in your offshore accounts and leave us ... me ... holding the bag?"

"You know I wouldn't do that," Syndall replied.

Bates knew nothing of the kind. "From now on, don't keep me in the dark."

"Sorry about that, Turner. I'll keep you posted on all developments from this point forward."

"You'd better. You leave us hanging, and I'll make sure Jenks' has a new mission ... to find you."

"Th-that sort of talk is uncalled for," Syndall sputtered. "I said you would be in the loop. You have my word."

"Right." Bates disconnected the call.

THIRTY-FIVE

Nothing New

The sun was low in the sky by the time Jenks made it back to Elko. He drove directly to the office, avoiding his house and the curious eyes of Sally Gascon. He'd already let her ask too many questions.

He parked the Chevy pickup in the small asphalt lot adjacent to the Entente office and went inside. There were more plans to make. The problem was that a living Amelia Downes was the weak link in every plan he made. Nothing else could happen until he eliminated that link.

Turner Bates was working late and called out from his office as he passed by. "Everything settled?"

Jenks' shoulders sagged, and he let out a sigh. He did not want to have this conversation now. He stepped into Bates' office, sat across from the desk, crossed his legs, and shook his head. "No, everything is not settled."

Bates' eyes lifted in genuine surprise. He was not accustomed to bad news from Jenks who had been adamant that everything would be resolved today. "What the hell happened?"

The Ghost

"Things didn't work out the way I planned."

"I fucking figured that!" Bates' forehead and cheeks took on a red hue.

Jenks' eyes narrowed. No one spoke to him like that, not even Turner Bates. "Calm down. I'll get it handled."

"You keep saying that, but nothing is getting handled." Bates slammed his palm on the desk. "You have to get this mess cleaned up!"

"I'm working on it." Jenks leaned toward Bates. "But you need to calm your ass down. We're both in this. I'll figure it out, but I don't need your bullshit right now."

Bates sat back, and took a breath. "Okay, you're right. Calm heads … that's what we need." He nodded. "Tell me what happened today."

Jenks reviewed his day's activities, which mostly included the discovery of dead bodies. Usually not one to want the details of Jenks' activities, Bates listened open-mouthed, shaking his head from time to time.

"Downes and Benson dead … your men dead." Bates shook his head. "How? Who?"

"How is the easy part. They were shot. The who part gets more complicated. It looked like Yang and Sink took care of Downes and Benson when they tried to confront them on the way to the cabin."

"And Yang and Sink? You think your men, the ones who kidnapped the girl, figured out what was about to happen and ambushed them."

"I did at first." Jenks shrugged. "Now, the more I think it through, not so much. Yang and Sink were pros and would not be easy to surprise. I can't get my brain around those two dimwits getting the drop on them."

He paused, letting that sink in. Bates' eyes opened wide and the flush in his cheeks brightened.

"You're saying someone else killed them?" Bates' voice was rising. "That means someone else knows about … what we're doing?"

"It's a definite possibility," Jenks nodded calmly. "And so will everyone in Elko if you don't lower your damned voice."

Bates lowered his voice, his eyes widening in direct proportion. "Do you know what this means?"

"I know."

"We not only have to eliminate the girl and your men who botched the whole thing, we have to find this other person and …"

"Or persons," Jenks added in the spirit of full disclosure and understanding.

"Or persons," Bates managed not to shout, instead clenching his teeth, so the words came out in a hiss. "Who?"

"I don't know, but Yang reported that the girl and the other two were gone, running off into the mountains. I have no reason to believe that he was mistaken." He shook his head. "Yang was never mistaken about operational details like that. So, it seems likely that someone else killed him and Sink."

"Who?" Bates repeated.

"Could be anyone. Hunters who stumbled on what was happening, maybe." Jenks shook his head. "But I doubt it. I listened to the radio, driving back. A hunter … some other uninvolved citizen … would have reported the killings to the sheriff. This late in the day, it should be all over the news but it isn't."

"Someone else has inserted themselves into our … situation?" Bates slumped back in his chair, stunned, chin on his chest, staring at his lap.

"It appears that way."

A thought occurred to Bates, and he lifted his eyes. "Who is this phantom person? How can we track him down?"

"My guess is, he or she will be tracking us down. That's why there is nothing on the news. Whoever it is wants to keep things as quiet as we do."

"Stop!" Bates' face paled suddenly. "You think he's coming after us?"

"Can't think of any reason he wouldn't," Jenks said, reasoning things out for Bates. "Whoever it was took care of Yang and Sink. That means he had to see Downes and Benson dead on the trail. For all I know, he was watching when I arrived at the cabin, but whoever it is has reported nothing to the authorities."

"What does that mean?"

"Hard to say, but I can come up with a few scenarios off the top of my head." Jenks lifted his hand and ticked them off on his fingers. "Blackmail ... they want to be cut in on a piece of the action from the mine acquisition or they go to the law. Maybe they want to acquire the D&B mine for themselves and see this as an opportunity to get it by eliminating us now that Downes and Benson are out of the picture. Or, it could be revenge ... someone from our past dealings who has come to get payback." He shrugged. "There could be other reasons, but that's all I have for the moment."

The mercenary nature of his character prevented Jenks from suspecting a fourth possibility—someone trying to find and help Amelia Downes. He was no Boy Scout. Unless it was absolutely necessary, he never made it a practice to do a good deed daily, and his moral compass never pointed toward chivalry and fair play.

"We can't just sit here." Bates looked around the room as if their unseen adversary might be lurking in a corner. "We have to do something."

"We? What exactly would you be able to do, Turner?" Jenks shook his head and gave a sharp, disgusted laugh. "There's nothing for you to do. This is a job for a certain type of man, not your type. I'll take care of it."

Jenks rose and turned for the door. As he stepped into the hall to cross to his office, a thought crossed his mind, and he looked back at Bates. "Your call with Syndall today … any new developments?"

Bates looked him in the eye and decided that it took a *certain type of man* to deal with what he had learned from Owen Syndall that day. He shook his head. "No, nothing new."

THIRTY-SIX

Hunker Down and Wait

What are you doing?

The voice in his head was back, barging in as soon as he started second-guessing himself, and he was second-guessing himself big time right now.

He ignored it for a while, but it was insistent.

What are you doing?

Flying by the seat of my pants. That's what I'm doing.

By the time he climbed down from the ledge, Jenks was long gone. Then Sole waited another fifteen minutes to increase the distance between them. Jenks was a professional. Approaching too closely on the deserted Turnbridge Road could blow his cover, and Sole's plan required him to remain undetected.

While he waited to give Jenks a head start, the second-guessing continued. It went something like this:

Hold on. Tracking Amelia and her kidnappers through the wilderness might be risky and nearly impossible, but was it any riskier than what you're planning?

No, but it is less certain.

Why?
Jenks is a definite target … a bird in hand not the one in the bush.
You're certain about that?
No, but it's all I have.
Well, if it's all you have, I guess it's settled then.
Right. No more second-guessing. Shut up and focus.

After that, Sole did focus on the drive to Elko. Jenks had to be headed there to regroup and meet up with the reinforcements he called from the cabin clearing. He would gather in his troops, give them their orders and send them out on the hunt, and Sole would be watching and waiting and following.

He was playing the odds. Jenks might not be any more able to locate Amelia than he was, but the probability that he would find her was far greater than Sole working alone.

He made the turn from the Turnbridge Road onto the highway back to Elko. Jenks was several miles ahead by now. Sole leaned over the wheel and increased speed. An hour later, he approached the Elko city limits.

Blending in with the evening traffic, he cruised past the house that served as the Entente headquarters and breathed a sigh of relief. Jenks' Chevy pickup was parked in the lot. So far, so good.

He drove to the end of the block, made a right turn, and circled again, pulling into the apartment complex across the street from Entente's office. This was the dicey part. He'd watched Jenks meet with Secret Asian Man and Bag Man from there the day before. Mixing in with the residents' vehicles gave him some cover, but Jenks had seen his truck parked up at the cabin earlier, and if he spotted it here, all his planning would go out the window.

He cruised slowly through the lot and found what he was looking for. A trash dumpster sat in the space between

The Ghost

two buildings, pushed back as far as possible from the front. Several trees overhung the area. Sole cut the headlights and turned, using the emergency brake to stop without the rear brake lights flashing. The pickup rolled to a stop beside the dumpster, deep in the shadows of the trees.

It was as good a spot as he was going to find, and had enough visibility to see what was happening across the street at the Entente building. Jenks had seen his pickup parked nose-out at the cabin. Parked in the shadows nose-in beside the dumpster, it was reasonably well concealed, and if Jenks happened to look that way and notice it at all, hopefully, he wouldn't recognize it from the rear.

Hopefully. He hated that word, a word filled with uncertainty. Right now, he could use a little certainty.

Sole reached up and disconnected the interior dome light, then pushed the door open, exited the pickup, and closed the door silently. Hands in his pockets, he strolled nonchalantly across the parking lot to the street, just a resident out for an evening walk.

He threw a quick glance at the Entente building as he passed on the sidewalk across the street. The window shades in two rooms were lit up, Jenks' and Bates' offices no doubt. He walked to the corner, made a right turn, and circled the block on foot. It was a calculated move. Jenks might leave while he made the circuit, but Sole didn't bother to second guess it this time. Jenks was waiting for his reinforcements, and Sole figured he'd stay put until they arrived.

He made the last turn back along the block toward the apartments, ignoring the Entente building altogether. He stepped from the sidewalk onto the asphalt driveway, squinted, and tried to spot his pickup concealed beside the dumpster. He could just make out the dim outline of the rear bumper in the shadows. The cab was completely in the dark under the trees.

Satisfied that his position was reasonably invisible to anyone who looked his way from across the street, he walked around to the rear of an apartment building and cut across the back toward the dumpster. A bird let out an annoyed squawk from the tree overhanging his pickup, then settled back down for the night. Sole did the same.

He reached through the driver's window to grab his binoculars, then hefted himself over the side to roll into the truck bed. Peering through the binoculars, he spun the focus ring, scanned the parking lot at the Entente building to make sure nothing had changed during his walk, and leaned back against the cab. All he had to do now was hunker down and wait.

THIRTY-SEVEN

Talking Fast

"Where you goin'?" Chester mumbled, his voice thick with sleep. Curled in a ball, arms folded across his chest for warmth, he squinted through one gummy eye at his partner.

"Gotta take a piss," Cope said, moving the rock they had used to wedge the lean-to's rotting door planks in place.

"You goin' out there … in the dark?"

"Yeah, I'm going out in the dark. Unless you want me to piss in the corner."

"Don't get mad. Just askin'." Chester curled up tighter. "Don't get eaten by no bear."

"Ain't no bears around here." Cope pulled at the door planks until the opening was wide enough for him to squeeze through.

"Bears everywhere," Chester muttered and curled himself up tighter. "Just don't always see them."

"Tellin' you, there ain't no bears around here." Cope glared at Chester's form, waiting for a response. All he got was a gurgling snort followed by the buzz of snores as Chester drifted back to sleep.

"Asshole," Cope muttered and looked through the dark at the girl's form, huddled on the opposite side of the lean-to. He sensed she wasn't asleep, her breathing silent and controlled. "So, what do you say? You gonna tell to me watch out for bears out there?"

"No," Amelia said. "Do what you want."

"So, there ain't no bears in these parts. "

"I didn't say that."

"So, there are bears?" Cope crooked his head to peer around the door outside into the dark.

"Didn't say that either."

"Then what the hell are you sayin'?"

"Look, this part of Nevada isn't known for bears, and I've never seen one around here, but we're in the mountains near the Idaho border. There are bears in Idaho, and I don't suppose bears know anything about state lines." She shrugged in the dark. "Could there be a bear out there? Yeah, there could be, but probably not."

"Shit." Cope stood by the door, looking out.

"Oh, for heaven's sake, just go pee. It's a million to one chance you'll run into a bear."

"Million to one, huh?" Cope pulled the pistol from his waistband and racked the slide to chamber a round.

"I wouldn't go shooting any bears with that. It'll just make them mad enough to rip your head off." He couldn't see her grinning in the dark or he'd have known she was enjoying the moment, being in control for just a second, and scaring the shit out of this asshole.

"Make them mad?" Cope glared through the dark in her direction, trying to decide if she was serious. Finally, his bladder decided for him, and he disappeared through the door, mumbling, "You're full of shit."

Amelia couldn't remember the last time she laughed. It

was sometime before this madness started, but she laughed now, long and hard. When she finally caught her breath, she chuckled, "Asshole must really have to pee," and once again convulsed in laughter.

Pistol clenched in his fist pointed out into the dark, Cope stood for a minute, peering into the trees and piles of rock, waiting, listening for sounds, and angry at himself for doing it, but doing it just the same. Chester might be dumb enough to buy into the girl's line of bullshit, but he knew better. Still, being careful hurt nothing, so he listened for a sound that might indicate the presence of a bear, although he wasn't sure what that sound might be—a growl, a roar, a snapping twig ... tearing as claws and fangs ripped him to shreds.

Stop! He shook his head. Enough of this bullshit.

He walked toward a tree, looked around for a second, and tucked the pistol back in his waistband. Then he unzipped and let fly, looking around uneasily as the steaming stream splashed off the tree trunk. It wasn't much of a pee. There hadn't been much to drink along the way, except to sip trickles from a couple of mountain streams they crossed.

It only lasted a few seconds, but he wondered if he'd ever pissed this long before, his head swiveling back and forth to pick up the sound of an approaching bear. Calm down. That bitch got you nervous.

The flow slowed to a dribble. He gave a last squeeze and shake, and shoved everything back in his pants, still dripping.

Then, looking around once more, he turned and moved deeper into the trees. When he was out of sight of the lean-to, he pulled out his cell phone and looked at the screen.

The battery was low, down to twelve percent, and there was no signal. Shit.

He scrambled twenty yards up the slope and checked again. Still no signal.

He climbed higher now. The trees thinned and grew smaller, and his breathing grew heavier with the altitude. Above him, the bald rock summit glowed palely in the moonlight. He checked his phone again.

Cope Plunkett had never been a praying man, had never even said bedtime prayers with his mother when he was a kid. Such a maternal activity would have impeded her visits to the local bar with the latest in the stream of men who passed through their lives.

He looked at the bars on his phone display and uttered a small prayer now. "Thank you, God."

The battery was reading ten percent now. How low would it go and still make a call he wondered? He punched in a number and murmured his second prayer in as many minutes. "Please, God. Someone answer."

Someone did answer and said tersely, "Start talking fast."

He started talking … fast.

THIRTY-EIGHT

Pros and Amateurs

Sometime around midnight, things got interesting. Sole couldn't be sure of the time, couldn't look at his phone, didn't want the screen's glow to attract the attention of the police officer cruising through the apartment complex. Hunkered down in the back of his pickup, all he could do was lower his head behind the tailgate and wait.

The police SUV pulled off the street and crept through the parking lot, the engine idling. There could have been a lot of reasons for its presence. Checking tags on parked cars looking for a stolen vehicle, or a wanted suspect, or because of reports of burglaries in the area, or just because the officer was bored and looking for something to do and a way to make the night pass.

Sole crouched out of sight and tried to control his breathing as if that would prevent the officer from discovering the suspicious person hiding in the back of the old pickup. A slight creak of the brakes and the police cruiser came to a stop. Sole held his breath completely now.

Nothing to see here. Keep moving. No need to check the old pickup beside the dumpster.

The spotlight mounted on the police vehicle flared to life, swinging back and forth. *Do not get out.* Sole tried to send the message from his brain to the officer behind the spotlight and felt as helpless as the Wizard of Oz telling Dorothy and her friends to ignore the man behind the curtain.

The light passed over the back of the pickup and rested for a few seconds on the rear cab window. Sole knew the officer was looking for a head, a startled face, some sign of life, something or someone to check out. The longer the light lingered on the truck's cab, the more he worried the officer might get out to investigate.

If he did, Sole would have no choice. He'd avoid causing the officer any permanent damage, but the poor guy would probably wake up in the morning with a headache. If it came to that, he hoped it was a guy and not a woman behind the badge.

The light flicked off, and the cruiser rolled slowly through the parking lot. Sole breathed a sigh of relief. He heard it make the turn back out onto the street and raised his head to see the cruiser's taillights disappear down the street.

He scanned with the binoculars. Nothing had changed across the street. Jenks' Chevy was still there. Bates was working late too, worried no doubt, or making sure Jenks got things handled.

Sole sat back in the pickup bed, leaning against the cab, concealed deep in the shadows. If the police cruiser came by on another round, he'd have to get down low again, but for now, he could watch the Entente building in relative comfort.

An hour passed with no sign of activity, then headlights approached on the empty street. Sole readied himself to duck if it was the police cruiser again. It wasn't.

A Dodge super-duty-sized pickup pulled into the Entente lot, washing the building in light before the driver killed the headlights. Four men exited the vehicle, silent men, alert, scanning their surroundings and moving deliberately.

They entered the building single file without knocking, the last in line watching for anyone approaching from the rear. He stared across the street to the apartment complex for what seemed an eternity but was probably not more than a few seconds. Sole stayed frozen in place against the wall of the cab, and for a moment, he thought that maybe he was not as well concealed in the darkness by the dumpster as he thought. Seconds passed and then, satisfied, the man turned and followed the others inside.

Sole relaxed. At least now he knew what he was up against—four bad guys plus the boss bad guy, Jenks. That wasn't so bad. He'd heard of worse odds. Audie Murphy, wounded and bleeding, holding off a company of Germans during World War II, came to mind. Murphy survived, won the Medal of Honor too.

Really? Odds not so bad?

How about Custer? Remember him? Now there was a fellow facing some long odds. How'd that work out for old Georgie and his boys?

He pushed that thought away. He wasn't in the mood to argue with himself. He was going through with this, and he needed some positivity in his life.

Oh, it's positivity you want. Well, here's some for you. You are positively fucked.

Whatever. He watched the building and sketched out a

plan in his mind. He would follow Jenks and his thugs to where they were going to get their hands on the kidnappers and Amelia. Then, when they aren't looking, snatch Amelia and hit the road.

Aren't looking? You really are losing it. These guys are pros at looking. That's what they do. Like snakes, they look, wait, watch, and when the moment is right, they strike.

Not if I strike first. That's the key to the plan. Wait, watch, and strike them before they have a chance. Hit them first and hard, and while they're recovering from the first blow, grab Amelia and get out.

He tried to visualize it, think through various scenarios. How he would confront the men and turn their surprise and the natural delay in reaction to his favor. How he could convince Amelia to go with him, a total stranger, and failing that, how he would snatch her and escape.

He had a plan. He might not come out a hero like Audie Murphy, but it might just work.

Then another vehicle showed up across the street, and Sole felt more like Custer. Five men hopped out of a gray van, not pros like the first group. They carried themselves with the strutting, swagger of gangbangers. Street toughs and not the type of professional Sole would have expected Jenks to use.

He thought about that. Jenks was desperate, was under pressure to settle things quickly. Quality manpower must be in short supply or too far away to be of help, so he called in the B-team, knuckle-draggers and bone-breakers. That might work to Sole's advantage. He wasn't sure how, but mixing pros and amateurs on the same playing field was never a good idea. Someone was bound to get hurt.

Sole figured he could anticipate how the pros would

The Ghost

react, but the amateurs were a wild card. There was no way to predict how they would respond when the action started.

THIRTY-NINE

A Helluva Lot Easier

The front door of the old house squeaked open. Turner Bates hated the old building's creaks and groans and found them disruptive to his train of thought. Jenks, a man for whom surprise was anathema, appreciated them as a sort of built-in intrusion alarm system.

Jenks looked up from the map on his desk and called out, "In here."

Habituated to moving quietly as a matter of necessity, the leader of the group that arrived in the Dodge pickup frowned when the floorboards creaked under his feet. He passed down the short hallway from the entry parlor and stopped in the doorway of the room Peter Jenks used as an office. The three men with him followed single file and halted in unison behind him.

Jenks waved them into the room and pointed at a sofa and two chairs. "Sit down."

The leader—he went by the name of Axe, ostensibly short for Axel, but no one knew for certain—sat in the chair closest to Jenks. He was older than the others, including Jenks, and retired from a big-city police department in the northeast. He'd run across Jenks while working a case years earlier and had stayed in touch. The ink wasn't dry on his retirement papers when Jenks offered him a way to supplement his police pension. Axe hesitated at first. Then Jenks scribbled a number on a piece of paper over beers and slid it toward him, just like they do in the movies. Axe looked at it and decided on the spot. He went to work for Jenks on *'special assignments'* the next day.

Over time, Axe recruited the others onto his team. Second in command was Bear. His name required no guessing as to its origin. He was the proverbial mountain of a man, six foot five, two-fifty and solid. Also, a former cop, he'd worked undercover narcotics for years before pulling the pin.

The others—Crew, named for the short flattop haircut he sported and Don, because he was the spitting image of a mafia godfather—sat on the sofa. Both were younger, ex-military types with no actual life skills except for proficiency at killing, an ability not generally transferable to the real world, but perfect for Jenks' purposes.

"What now?" Axe asked when everyone was seated.

"We wait for the others," Jenks said.

"Others?" Axe frowned. "What others? Our fee is set … not negotiable."

"I know that." Jenks nodded. "Not asking you to divide it with anyone. I'll cover it."

"Must be important." Axe crossed his legs and reached for a pack of cigarettes without asking. "Why the extra manpower?" he asked as he lit up.

"It is important, and we need the manpower to cover a fairly wide area." He spun the map around on his desk and pointed so Axe could see. The others stood and gathered around.

"This area here." Jenks pointed at a red line on the map marking a stretch of highway that ran from the Turnbridge Road cutoff up over the Idaho line. "The people we want are in the mountains. I've been over all the routes out. Unless they decide to head deeper into the mountains, the passes and valleys will bring them back to this highway. See here, these fingers coming from the mountains are the natural routes out."

"So, you want us to spread out and snag them when they come out." Axe shook his head. "That must be twenty miles of highway to watch."

"More like fifty," Jenks said.

"Hell, be like finding the old needle in a haystack. How many extra people you got coming?"

"A dozen or so."

"Better than four, I guess, but still a lot of area to cover." Axe sat back and took a long drag from his cigarette, thinking things over before tilting his head and sending a plume of smoke billowing toward the ceiling. "Who did you get?"

"Chino and the boys," Jenks said, knowing what was coming and waiting calmly for it.

"Son of a bitch. Bikers? You got bikers working with us on this?" Axe shook his head. "Not good man ... very unprofessional."

Bear grunted his agreement. Crew and Don exchanged silent looks and shook their heads.

"They have their uses," Jenks replied. "And they're the best I could do on short notice."

"So, who's in charge?" Axe asked. "Us or them?"

The Ghost

"Me," Jenks said. "I'll be in the field with you on this one."

"Shit. This must really be important." Axe's eyes narrowed. "What the hell did you get into?"

Jenks spent the next fifteen minutes bringing them up to speed. He omitted nothing and concluded with the deaths of Yang and Sink.

"You're telling me these two clowns you hired took out Freddy Yang and Carl Sink?" Axe shook his head. "Hardly seems possible. Sink might be crazy as a loon, but he was one of the best, and Yang was as good as they get in this business. Good as me."

"I'm telling you, I don't know who took them out. Maybe the goobers I brought in got lucky, but I doubt it. I think there could be someone else."

"Someone else?" Axe leaned forward. "Who? Someone good enough to take out Yang and Sink ... we need to know about that."

"I just told you about it. You want out?" Jenks nodded at the hallway. "There's the door. Otherwise, focus, get this done and there'll be a bonus in it for you." He leaned across the map, staring into Axe's face, knowing that the others would follow his lead. "We have an advantage. We know this other person is out there, unseen, blending in. Yang and Sink didn't have that information and got careless. We won't let that happen. Until this is done, everyone is a suspect."

Axe thought it over for a few seconds and nodded. "How big a bonus?"

"Half your usual fee added on top."

"Alright, we're in." Axe nodded at the map. "How's this going to work?"

"There are four likely places along the highway they could

head for when they come out of the backcountry." Jenks pointed at the map, thumping his forefinger on it as he spoke. "This campground here … A little town on the reservation here … this settlement, a few houses and a resort here … and this little town up by the Idaho line." He looked up from the map. "We'll station each of you at one of those points. Chino and his boys will patrol the highway, just in case, looking for anyone stumbling out of the mountains in between."

"One question. What if they head into the backcountry instead of out?"

"Then they die and they solve the problem for us, but they won't do that," Jenks said. "I checked the cabin they left from. They didn't take food or water." He nodded to affirm his decision. "They'll come out to the highway because these boys don't want to die."

The front door squeaked open, and the floorboards creaked again. Five more men came down the hall. Their leader, Chino, stood in the doorway eyeing Axe and his men.

"Fucking great," Axe mumbled.

"Not too happy to see you either, *cabrón*." Chino flashed a gold-toothed grin and stepped into the office. "What we got going boss man?"

Jenks reviewed the plan for them, keeping it simpler this time. Spread the bikers out along the highway and keep a lookout for two men and a woman, or two men alone, on foot. Simple. He ended with a warning. "Don't fuck this up."

"Us?" Chino's grin widened. "No way. We got this dicked man. You gonna see."

"Where're your men?"

"Rest area on I-80. Left our rides there with them. We

The Ghost

get done here and I'll go meet them, get them briefed and saddled up, and we'll meet you out on the highway."

Jenks' phone chimed, and he looked down at it on his desk. "Son of a bitch." He grabbed it, punched the call button, and said, "Start talking fast."

Cope Plunkett talked so fast the words came out jumbled and twisted like they were glued to his tongue.

"You gotta understand. We ran from those men ... two of them came to the cabin. Thought they were going to kill us, so we took off. Honest, we don't want no trouble. Just collect our pay and go, you know, like you said. But then Chester and the bitch, they teamed up on me ... didn't have no choice. You see how it is, but I'm calling you now. That should count for something, show you I want to do right by you." Cope took a breath. "Don't it?"

"It does. No harm done," Jenks said, the lie rolling off his tongue like syrup. "We just need to meet somewhere and I'll take the girl and pay you off."

"That's easy," Cope said. "We're walking out of these damned mountains tomorrow. Coming out to some little town or something ... Merchantville, the bitch called it."

"When will you get there?"

"Get there? I don't exactly know that." Cope thought quick. "The bitch says it'll take most of the day to walk out, so I guess sometime in the afternoon."

"That's good. Very good," Jenks said reassuringly. "Just one more question. Did you do anything else?"

"Anything else?" Cope said. "I don't know what you mean?"

"You didn't do any shooting? Didn't shoot anyone?"

"Hell no!" Cope's voice rose in denial. "We heard some shootin', but it wasn't from none of us. And those two men that showed up, they shot up in amongst the rocks where we were hid. That's why we ran."

"Yeah, that was a misunderstanding," Jenks lied. "They got into a tussle with the girl's father and thought that was him up there in the rocks. That's why they were shooting. If they'd known it was you, if you'd stayed in the cabin, it wouldn't have happened and you'd be off spending your pay right now."

"Right." Cope chewed on that for a few seconds. "I suppose that makes sense."

Jenks didn't want him to think on it for very long and said, "Alright, you go back with the others now. Since they already turned on you, I wouldn't let them know we spoke. I'll take care of them when we meet up in Merchantville."

"I ain't sayin' a word to no one. I just called you so you'd understand."

"I do understand and thanks for the call." Jenks ended the call with an innocuous and pleasantly reassuring, "Goodbye, Cope. See you in Merchantville."

"Right ... see you then. Just so you under ..." Cope started to repeat his plea for forgiveness, but the call cut off in midsentence when his battery finally gave up the ghost.

Jenks put the phone down, and Axe spoke up for the group. "What was that all about?"

A bemused smile on his face, Jenks said, "Things just got a helluva lot easier."

"Good." Axe nodded. "I like easy."

"Yeah, we like easy too, man, but we still get paid right?" Chino pointed at the map. "You still need us, right? We come all this way for you."

"You'll get paid," Jenks said. "Everything stays the same until I have them."

The Ghost

"Good, man. That's good." Chino nodded and grinned. "'Cause you don't wanna be jerkin' us around."

"Oh, for fuck's sake," Axe mumbled and turned to look at Chino. "Or what, asshole?"

"Or maybe I cut you a new asshole." Chino touched the hunting knife sheathed on his belt.

Axe started to stand. Jenks beat him to it and stared them both down. "You have something to settle, you settle it after we're done with this job, or I'll make you my next job. Understand?"

There was only a moment's pause, just long enough for each to save face, before they both gave a quick nod. Becoming the focus of one of Peter Jenks' *operations* was a career killer—kill being the operative word.

"Good. Cut the bullshit." Jenks thumped the map on his desk. "This is Merchantville, not on the main highway, but on this side road. The people we want are walking out of these mountains." He made a broad circle with his hand over the area. "That means they could come out ..." He paused, studying the map, then continued, "Anywhere in this area." He made another circle with his hand, smaller than the first. "So, our search area is narrowed down. I figure we should be in position by ten AM, to be safe."

"Your man said afternoon," Chino chimed in.

"We're not taking any chances." Jenks tapped the map again. "Be on station by ten. If they make it out earlier, I want to be ready."

"On station! Yes, sir!" Chino gave a sloppy, exaggerated salute. "Yes, sir ... captain, sir."

"We really need these assholes?" Axe asked, shaking his head in disgust.

Chino's men pushed in closer and Axe's men turned to face them. Jenks let out a sigh and eyed the two leaders.

"Enough! Yes, we need them. I don't care if that girl is Jim Bridger reincarnated, I doubt she can set a course through the mountains directly to Merchantville. She could lead them out anywhere. We have a lot of ground to cover. That's why we need Chino and his men."

"And you." Jenks turned his stare on Chino. "Stop the macho bullshit. You want to get paid, you straighten up and take this shit serious or you're out."

"Okay man, okay. Just havin' a little fun." He held up a hand and his men backed out into the hallway. "We're taking it serious."

"Good." Jenks made a few adjustments to their assignments based on the reduced search area, then said, "Go get some rest, then be in position by ten." He looked at Chino, waiting for another smartass response. Chino smiled, but kept his mouth shut.

Jenks nodded. "Good. Now get the fuck out."

FORTY

Asshole
___

He sat in his leather chair staring out through the louvered blinds at the night, wondering why he was still there. There was nothing for him to do except wait. That was it, and Turner Bates had always been terrible at waiting. He wasn't a man of action in the sense that Jenks was, but he craved activity, to be doing something, to be in control of his future, and right now, he controlled nothing. Everything rested on Jenks.

He wondered if he had let too many things rest on Jenks, relied too heavily on his ability to make issues go away. He'd turned him loose in Nevada without giving enough thought to the fact that Nevada was a part of the good old USA, and making issues disappear in their usual fashion in the USA could raise more problems than it resolved.

At this point, it didn't matter. He was trapped. Jenks would resolve things, or not. Owen Syndall would hold off the audit, or not. All Bates could do was wait in this damned office until the problems disappeared, or the sheriff barged in to haul him off to jail.

Or would it be the sheriff? Maybe the FBI? Or Both? A trial for his complicity in the disappearance and … what—go ahead and say it, and the murder of Amelia Downes, her father, and Ron Benson—or would he be dragged off to a federal court for his involvement in the Entente fraud scheme. Maybe it would happen the other way around. Which would have priority for law enforcement? The fraud or the murder? He decided the feds would be the first to get their pound of flesh. Their need for headlines would override everything else, even murder, or multiple murders.

He reached for the bottle of twenty-five-year-old Macallan scotch on the credenza behind his desk and poured three fingers into a glass. The scotch was a present from Syndall after closing a big deal in southeast Asia, and at $2200 a bottle, Bates never had more than a sip at a time. He gulped down the first glass and poured another.

The warm glow in his belly began to spread, but without its usual effect of calming his worries. There was too much to worry about. Along with Syndall and Jenks, he was in deep shit—hip-high and rising. But he was in the deepest of all of them. Syndall might go down for fraud and Jenks for kidnapping and murder, but he was in the middle, caught up as the middleman and a participant in both. He spent a few minutes considering which sentence would be longer, then shrugged it off. Maybe Nevada executed murderers and their accomplices. That would eliminate any worries about prison time.

He gulped more scotch as the front door opened and Jenks' men tramped down the hall. He swiveled in his chair to watch them pass his door. They ignored him and entered Jenks' office.

The Ghost

The doors were open. Jenks' briefing was plain and simple, and to Bates seemed like more than a longshot. Find the girl and her kidnappers as they stumbled out of the mountain country onto a fifty-mile stretch of highway? That's it? That's the master plan? He reached for the Macallan again.

A while later, the door opened again and five biker-types clomped down the hall, complete with chains attached to wallets, denim vests, heavy boots, and bandannas. This is the team? We're fucked. Bates shook his head and made another dent in the scotch.

The interaction between the groups was noisy and more than a little concerning. They didn't like each other, but clearly, they all respected Jenks, or at least feared him. Fear was good, Bates decided, the scotch finally taking the edge off his worries. Hell yeah, put the fear of God into them Petey-boy, let 'em know you'll hunt them down and rip their balls off if they don't come through on this.

The meeting ended and the two groups headed back out into the night. A few minutes later, Jenks stopped in the doorway. "You heard?"

"Yeah." Bates leaned over his desk and looked up from the glass of scotch gripped between his fists. "Heard it all. Got the fuckin' A-team on the job ... fuckin' great. All gonna work out 'cause ole Petey got everybody scared." Bates nodded and raised the glass. "Yep, heard it all. Here's to you, Peter my friend."

"Are you drunk?" Jenks stepped into the office, towering over Bates' desk.

"Maybe," Bates said and drank more scotch, sipping this time as he looked into Jenks' unamused eyes. "What of it?"

"We have work to do, and we can't fuck it up. You need to be sober in case I need you."

"Need me?" Bates smirked. "For what? Want me to pick up a gun and go do what you were supposed to do?"

Jenks' eyes narrowed. "I'd mind my tongue if I were you, drunk or not."

"What then? So, what if I'm not sober?" Bates lifted the glass and grinned, his eyes red-rimmed and damp. "If I want to get knee-walkin' ... snot-slingin' ... toilet huggin' drunk, why shouldn't I? You got everything under control, right?"

"I have a plan, but all plans have their unforeseen problems. I have no one else to call if one of those problems comes up. So, you need to be sober, because if I need you to do something, and I call and you're inside that bottle, I will come back ... for you."

Jenks stared into Bates' eyes, saying it all in a quiet voice, the kind of voice that made people pay attention. Bates paid attention and put the glass on the desk.

He sat up straight in his leather chair and nodded. "I'll be sober."

Jenks left without another word. The front door hinges squeaked, the door thumped closed. Turner Bates reached for the bottle, poured another drink, leaned back in his chair and muttered, "Asshole."

FORTY-ONE

It Didn't Matter

"Just so you understand. I gotta be sure that we still have an agreement. I'll make sure we turn the bitch over to you, but you just gotta believe I didn't have nothing to do with running off. They ganged up on me is what happened."

The sudden, eerie silence on the line was ominous and terrified the shit out of Cope Plunkett. It would have preferable if Jenks had shouted and threatened to murder him. At least then he would have known what was coming.

"Please, Mr. Jenks. You got to understand."

More silence. Cope pushed the phone hard against his ear, and begged one last time, "Please."

Nothing. He lowered the phone and was about to shove it in his pocket when he remembered the low battery and held it up in front of his face. The screen was dark, the battery dead.

Shit. How much did Jenks hear? The last thing Cope remembered him saying was that he understood, and then Jenks said goodbye, Cope. He called him by name just like that. That was a good thing, wasn't it? Calling him by name meant he wasn't all that mad. Right?

But then the phone died before Cope could renew his plea for forgiveness, one last time, just to be sure Jenks got it. Like a child begging for reassurance that daddy understood why he'd been a bad boy, and please don't spank him, Cope Plunkett was desperate.

He turned to make his way down the mountain back to the lean-to, clinging to trees and rocks, then sliding a ways on his ass until he found another tree to grab. All the while, he worried that Jenks might not have believed his story.

He shook his head. You're so spooked you're not thinking straight. For fuck's sake, you're getting to be as dumb as Chester. Think things through. Jenks said he understood. He didn't sound all that angry, just wanted to know where we were. You told him, so everything is fine now, back on track. This time tomorrow you'll be long gone and Chester will be … well, it didn't much matter what happened to Chester and the bitch anymore. Just as long as you get your ass away … far away.

A cascade of rocks and gravel preceded his descent to the clearing around the lean-to. He came to a rest on his ass near the rocks that supported one wall of the shack and looked up.

Amelia stood there, arms folded over her chest, eyes narrowed. If Jenks was the father figure that Cope wanted to appease, Amelia had become the mother he wanted to fast-talk and avoid.

"Where've you been?" she said, trying to see into his eyes in the dark, but only able to make out his form, sitting on his ass at the bottom of the slope.

"Told you. I had to piss."

"Up there?" She looked up the mountainside. "Plenty of good trees around here to water."

"Okay, so I wanted to take a look around. You know, see what I can see. See if there really is a way out of here, like you say. We been listenin' to you since we left the cabin and all we done is end up out here. You say there's someplace to come out of these mountains, and I wanted to see if I could check your story."

It sounded like a good lie to Cope. He reinforced it by pulling himself up off the ground, standing up straight, and glaring at her. "So, what about that?"

"You think I'm leading you around in circles until everyone is dead, me included?" She shook her head. "You really are dumber than I gave you credit for."

"Listen bitch. You got no cause to talk to me that way, and I don't need to take that shit off you." He took a threatening step toward her. Amelia held her ground but lowered her arms to her side, fists balled, readying herself for a fight if it came.

Cope's voice rose. "You been on my case from the beginning, and I'm fucking tired of listenin' to it."

"On your case? You forgetting why we're here? How you botched a simple thing like threatening a girl on a deserted road?"

Cope remained silent, completely over his head in a verbal match. Amelia changed the subject. "While you were up there checking and seeing what you could see, did you happen to get a signal on your phone? Maybe make a call to someone?"

"I didn't make no calls," Cope said, and he knew she suspected it was a lie.

"If you did, you should tell us ... tell your partner Chester ... because if you told someone where we are, you just put us all in danger. If you want to give yourself up to your boss and see how that goes, I suppose that's your business, but you don't have the right to put Chester in danger. He ought to make that decision for himself."

"How the fuck would I do that? I don't even know where we are." Cope took a step forward, pointed a finger at her face, balled his fist, and cocked his arm as if to throw a punch.

"Don't do it." Chester stood by the lean-to door in the dark. "You got no cause to do that. Besides, she's right, Cope. You want to give yourself up to Jenks, go ahead, but you can't decide that for no one else."

Cope lowered his arm. "She got you all turned around, Chester. I ain't your enemy. We're partners in this … friends, I thought."

"Still are partners." Chester nodded. "And friends if you want it, but we all agreed to let her lead us outta here. Then we let her go and we hit the road."

"You all agreed. I didn't have no choice in the matter." A nasty smirk crossed his face, though no one could make it out in the dark. "She must be givin' you some on the side when I ain't lookin'. That it, Chester. You been tappin' that sweet young ass?"

Chester stepped forward, the movement indistinct in the dark until it was too late for Cope to get out of the way. Chester's hand came up and cuffed him on the side of the head.

"No cause for you to talk like that. You know better than to talk like that."

The blow wasn't hard enough to send Cope to the ground, but he staggered back a couple of paces and went into a semi-crouch, readying himself for a fight.

"I ain't gonna fight you," Chester said. "I shouldn't have

The Ghost

hit you like that, but she asked a question, and I'd like to hear the answer." Chester jerked his head up the slope. "Did you call someone from up there? Did you call Jenks?"

"What do you think?" Cope said, pulling the phone from his pocket. He pushed it into Chester's hand and pushed his way past and into the lean-to.

Chester looked at the phone, tried to bring up the screen, held the power button to turn it on, then he looked at Amelia. "I reckon he didn't call no one. Phone is dead. You wanna see?"

"No, I believe you," Amelia said without adding the obvious. There was no way of knowing when the phone battery gave out and with it dead, no way of knowing if Cope had made a call.

"Okay." Chester pushed the phone down in his pocket. "Sorry about what he said ... about you and me ... you know, doin' it ... on the side like he said."

She stopped him. "I know. It was just Cope, being Cope."

"I like that. *Cope being Cope.* That's about the size of it. Just bein' hisself." He laughed. "You know, he's been a good friend to me, us driftin' around workin' jobs, gettin' drunk, then driftin' on again. Just that things have him on edge and he don't handle that too good, gets nervous about things, but I promise I'll keep an eye on him until we get outta here. He won't bother you."

"Thanks, Chester. We better get some rest now. Come daylight we need to be on the trail."

"Sounds good. On the trail and then outta here by tomorrow night. You go your way and we go ours. Right? Just like we agreed."

"Just like we agreed." Amelia nodded and smiled.

Chester turned toward the lean-to. "You comin?"

"In a minute."

"Okay." He disappeared inside.

Amelia stared into the dark. She was certain Cope had called Jenks. Maybe the battery died after, but he went up there to make a call. With the phone dead, there was no way of knowing if the call went through or if he had spoken to Jenks.

She decided it didn't matter. They had to get out of these mountains. They didn't have any choice about that. If Jenks showed up along the way, she'd find a way to deal with him then. Right now, she needed sleep. She turned toward the lean-to and went inside.

FORTY-TWO

Find the Face

He had to make a decision. Jenks' visitors came piling out the door to the Entente building. First, the B-team biker-types, followed by the A-team pros. Sole watched from the bed of his pickup and scanned both groups through the binoculars.

They moved briskly, with a purpose. Jenks must have given them their orders and some idea where they would pick up Amelia's trail. But that raised questions, the first being which, if either, group would lead him to Amelia Downes.

It was pretty clear what Jenks was doing. A dragnet the old-time TV shows called it. Bring in the reinforcements to corral the bad guys.

So, which group would be the one to find Amelia? Sole thought about that and decided it didn't matter. Calling in the troops meant he was getting desperate. That was good. Desperate people make mistakes. Jenks' boys were the dragnet, but Jenks was the snare. He would want to be there in person and snag her himself. Too many things had gone wrong for him not to want to make sure he had his hands on her.

Decision made. Follow Jenks then and wait for him to make a mistake. Even if he didn't, it seemed the surest path to finding Amelia.

Next question. How was he supposed to follow him without Jenks' dragnet spotting him and alerting him as they searched for Amelia? Sole had to find a way to beat Jenks to the scene and get his hands on Amelia before Jenks did.

So far, he had remained invisible. Jenks might suspect that there was someone else responsible for the deaths of Secret Asian Man and Bag Man, but he didn't know who. He'd have his people looking for anyone suspicious. If they spotted him tailing Jenks, they'd intervene, his cover would be blown, and even if he managed to evade them, his chances of getting to Amelia first would evaporate.

As he pondered the problem, the door opened across the street. Jenks walked out and climbed into the Chevy. Sole rolled over the side of his pickup and got behind the wheel. In the rearview mirror, he watched Jenks pull from the lot and head down the block.

Sole reversed, backed out, and wheeled around to the apartment complex entrance. He waited for Jenks to turn at the end of the block and started to pull onto the street, then jammed on the brakes. There it was, the solution to his problem, staring him in the face.

It was after two AM when Jenks pulled from the Entente parking lot. It had been one hell of a long night, plus the day before. He hadn't slept in almost twenty-four hours, and

The Ghost

it was time to rest if he wanted his head clear for what was coming. Right now, his brain was fried. A couple of hours' sleep would fix that, and he'd be good to go.

Merchantville was two and a half hours away, on the Idaho line. He'd ordered everyone to be on the job by ten. A nap and a shower and he would still be out there before the Axe and Chino and their teams were on the job.

He drove up the hill on Elko's north side and pulled onto his street at two-thirty. Peering toward the end of the block, he half expected to see Sally Gascon spending the night out front on her rocker, ready to ask nosey question. She was nowhere in sight.

He pulled around the circular drive to his front door and hurried inside. Two minutes later, he was standing under a hot shower and five minutes after that, Jenks was in bed, staring at the ceiling.

There was no need to set an alarm. He slept fitfully on a good night. With a world of shit on his mind, he'd be lucky to get three or four good hours. It wasn't conscience that contributed to his chronic insomnia. Conscience was for weaklings like Turner Bates.

What did trouble his sleep, caused him to slumber for only brief snatches at a time, were the details. His mind never stopped working on them, rehearsing them mentally until he could execute one of his plans reflexively, without having to think about what came next.

Now, lying there in the draped blackness of his room, there was one detail that troubled him more than others, one item he could not account for in his plans. Someone had taken out Yang and Sink. It could not have been a random act, a surprise that overtook two of his best operatives.

Someone was watching them, stalking them. Why? The

girl's father and friend were dead. Revenge then? Possibly, but by no means certain.

A competitor sending a team to compete with Entente for the mining rights? Also, a possibility, but it seemed unlikely. Few competitors, if any, would resort to the tactics he used on behalf of Entente.

A good Samaritan trying to save the girl? Good Samaritans were fools, weak and easily overcome by men like Jenks. No good Samaritan could have dispatched Yang and Sink. Whoever it was had a face, and Jenks wanted very badly to know that face and be ready for it when it showed up, as he was certain it would.

So, he stared at the ceiling, and his few hours of badly needed sleep became a handful of fitful minutes. At six AM he dragged himself out of bed, started the coffeemaker, grabbed another shower, a cold one to clear his head, drank the pot of coffee, peed, and left the house.

Sally Gascon sat on the porch across the street as he pulled from his driveway, waving and calling to him. "Morning Mr. Jenks! Still testing out that new truck, I see! Be sure and let me know what you think so I can tell my son!"

Jenks ignored her and accelerated to the end of the street, his mind reviewing the plans for the day. One item kept creeping above the others on his to-do list. Find the face, before he finds you.

FORTY-THREE

A Productive Night

Sole waited for Jenks to leave the Entente lot and disappear around the corner at the end of the street, then backed his pickup beside the dumpster, rear end in this time. He would be leaving in a hurry the next time he pulled out.

After retrieving a few necessary items from the duffel bag and toolbox in the rear crew cab, he stuffed them inside his shirt, put his hands in his pockets, and strolled through the apartment complex out to the sidewalk. He walked to the corner again, but this time, instead of circling the block, he crossed the street and headed back toward the Entente building.

The streetlight a few houses away flickered, creating an eerie strobe effect on the lone man moving silently down the empty street. Sole gave a quick glance up and down the street as he came up even with the building, then walked across the asphalt lot to the front door. He'd watched people come and go through it all night. With any luck, it would still be unlocked, not that a locked door would not have changed his plan, but breaking into the building increased the risk of discovery. He turned the doorknob, gave a satisfied nod, and pushed the door open.

Shit. So much for stealth. The hinges sounded out a loud squeak. Too late to worry about that now. He stepped quickly inside and shut the door.

"Jenks, that you?" Bates called down the hallway. "Didn't expect you back so soon."

Sole reached in his shirt for the ski mask he'd taken from his truck, pulled it tight over his head and face, and took a step toward the hallway. The floorboards creaked almost as loudly as the hinges squeaked. Sole shook his head, annoyed that he was losing the element of surprise.

It turned out he didn't need it. Turner Bates was shit-faced drunk. Sole found him leaning forward with his elbows on the desk, the nearly empty bottle of scotch in front of him, his head wobbling back and forth like a newborn trying to lift himself up for the first time.

"Don't worry. I'm sobering up." That was clearly not the case. Bates managed to raise his chin high enough to see the man standing in the office door. His brow wrinkled. His face contorted as he worked to focus his bloodshot eyes, then he shook his head side to side and said, "You're not Jenks."

"No, I'm not," Sole said.

Stunned, his mouth agape, Bates' head continued to oscillate back and forth in denial as the masked man stepped into the office and took three brisk steps forward until he stood towering over him. A whiz at putting deals together for Entente and making Owen Syndall look good to the Board of Directors, Turner Bates had never looked into the bore of any gun, much less the yawning bore of the .45 in the masked man's hand.

Bates was forced to lean back in the leather chair and

stare down his nose into the muzzle just inches from his face. "Who ... who are you?"

"That's not important," Sole said.

"You're him," Bates whispered. "The one Jenks is worried about ... the one no one has seen. You're the one who killed Jenks' men."

"I am." Sole nodded. There didn't seem to be any reason to hide it at this point. "That should tell you what I am prepared to do to you."

"No. Please, no." Bates was trembling now, and his head shook back and forth faster. "I didn't hurt anyone. It was Jenks. I just handle the business end of things."

"The business end?" Sole smiled, and the smile made Bates shake even more. "The way I see it, the business ... your business ... is behind what's happened."

"No ... I swear ..."

Sole cut him off. "Stop. There's nothing you can say. I know who you are and what you are doing. I know about the threats and intimidation, all to force Downes and Benson to sell you their mining operation." Sole shrugged. "Pretty sure it's just standard operating procedure for you and your man Jenks, but things got out of hand this time, didn't they?"

"No one was supposed to get hurt. Please believe me." Eyes glued to the .45, Bates was pleading, on the verge of tears.

"Someone got hurt, though. Maybe you didn't intend for it to happen, but it did, and now, you're responsible for the deaths of Jake Downes and Ron Benson and whatever they've done to Amelia Downes."

"Not me."

"Yes, you. Jenks works for you. You work for Entente. Your whole operation is rotten from top to bottom, and you're in the middle, and you are most definitely part of it. But it ends today." Sole thumped the bore end of the .45 into Bates' forehead between his eyes.

"Noooo ..." Bates whimpered, and his bladder emptied into his five-hundred-dollar suit.

"This can only go one of two ways," Sole said, leaning forward so that the pistol pressed harder into Bates' forehead. "You tell me what I want to know, and you'll live. If not, you'll die right here, and I'll take my time about making that happen. You'll beg me to kill you before I'm finished with you."

Sole had never tortured anyone in his life, but Bates didn't know that. Tears rolling down his face, he nodded and said, "What do you want to know?"

"Let's start with Amelia Downes. Where is she?"

"I don't know. I swear it."

"Your people took her."

"Not mine. I told you it was Jenks. Nothing was supposed to happen ... just frighten her ... convince her father to sell. No one was supposed to get hurt." Bates was blubbering now, tears and spit spraying with each frantic shake of his head.

"Not good enough." Sole shook his head and pushed the pistol harder into Bate's forehead. "You were here. Jenks has a plan to get her back. That's why he sent those two up the mountain, the ones I ..." He tapped the pistol barrel on Bates' head hard enough to make him wince and leave a bruise. "The ones I took care of. You had to know something or hear something. Start talking."

Bates' eyes rolled in his head, up to the ceiling, down to the floor, wall to wall, as he searched for something, anything, to tell the masked man with the big gun. A thought floated through his alcohol-soaked brain, pulling

The Ghost

along with it the thread of a memory. He nodded rapidly, his head bobbing up and down, his eyes exultant and relieved that he remembered something. Maybe it would be enough to make this man put the gun away.

"There was a meeting tonight."

"I know," Sole said. "What about it?"

"He's sending more people to look for her."

"I know that too. I saw them leave. Do they know where she is?"

"I think so." Bates' brow wrinkled as he tried to remember everything that he'd heard coming down the hall from Jenks' office. He couldn't get it out fast enough. The two groups. The arguing that almost turned violent. Jenks laying down the law to them. His brow furrowed as he tried to pull one more bit of information out of the alcohol fog, then his eyes lit up and he nodded frantically. "That's it. That's it."

Sole leaned forward and Bates recoiled as far back in the chair as he could. "What?"

"A phone call," Bates said excitedly. "I heard a phone call. One of the men who took the girl called Jenks ... gave him a location ... Jenks is going to meet them there."

"Where?"

"It was ..." Bates saw the look in Sole's eyes behind the ski mask and cringed. "I swear I can't remember the name of the place ... I was drunk and all ... some town I think."

"Where?" Sole repeated.

Bates wiped the back of his hand across his sweating brow, thinking hard. Then he said, "It was a town. I'm sure of it." His head bobbed and then shook, trying to force his brain to open up and remember something ... anything that would get the gun's cold steel barrel pointed somewhere else, at someone else. His eyes opened wide as another fragment of memory came to him. "Idaho … up near Idaho, somewhere off the highway."

Sole pulled out his phone and brought up a GPS map. Scrolling the screen looking for towns off the highway north out of Elko. He read off the names of campgrounds, a resort settlement, the Shoshone-Paiute reservation, Wildhorse Reservoir, Mountain City. Bates shook his head at each one. "No, not that."

He enlarged the screen with his thumb and forefinger and moved the map around until he was tracing the line between Idaho and Nevada. Nothing. He enlarged again and a tiny, nameless dot appeared on an out-of-the-way county road. Once more, he enlarged the image, and the name popped into view beside the dot. "Merchantville … is that the town?"

Bates' eyes lit up. "That's it!" The frantic head bob returned. "That's it! I'm sure of it. Merchantville is where they said they were going to meet."

"When?"

"They had to walk out of the mountains, so they said it would be late in the afternoon. Jenks told his people to rest up and then be out there at noon."

"Alright, and how many men does he have? Any besides those I saw."

"I don't know how many, but more biker types were waiting out at a rest stop on the interstate."

"Alright. Stand up."

"Why?" Bates paled and shook his head. "I told you what I could. That should mean something, doesn't it?"

"Stand up." Sole had the pistol in his face again.

Bates pushed himself out of the chair to stand wobbling on his trembling legs.

"Where's the entrance to the basement?" Sole had

The Ghost

noticed the tiny slit windows and the old-fashioned cellar door on the outside when he walked up from the street.

"Th-through the c-closet in the hall." Bates stuttered.

"Move." Sole motioned with the pistol toward the door. "Lead the way down to the basement."

Bates shuffled, his shoulders shaking, sobbing. "Please don't kill me ... please!"

"I'm not going to kill you," Sole said quietly. "Unless you keep wasting my time."

Bates stopped and turned, tears running down his cheeks. "Promise you won't kill me. Please promise."

"I promise," Sole said.

"Okay." Bates nodded his head and turned to lead the way to the hall closet and door to the basement. "You promised, so that means you can't shoot me. Right?"

The question would have been funny if Bates wasn't so pathetically serious, clinging to anything, even a promise from the man holding the gun. Sole felt a slight twinge of pity for the bastard and said, "That's right. I promised. I won't kill you."

Bates made it to the closet and pulled the string to turn on the overhead bulb inside. Then he opened a door that squeaked louder than all the others in the old house. Both men had to crouch to pass under the frame and descend the dozen steps to the damp earthen floor below. Bates found another string, pulled it, and dim yellow light flooded the space.

The basement was empty except for an old mattress and bedsprings leaning on one wall, and an aging, tire-less bicycle turned upside down on its seat beside a workbench. The bench was soaked in motor oil that had leaked from a rusty coffee can, sitting there for twenty years since the previous owner had changed the oil in his wife's car one Saturday.

"Give me your car keys."

"Keys? Sure thing. Here, take them." Bates pulled them from his pocket and held them out, dangling from the end of his trembling hand. "It's a good car. Take it. I swear I won't say anything to anyone."

"Now, put your hands behind your back."

Bates tensed but complied. When Sole pulled the zip-ties from his pocket and bound his hands behind his back, Bates shuddered and began whimpering. "You promised … you promised … please … you promised."

"I promised not to kill you, and I won't unless you give me a reason to." Sole pulled the zip-ties tight and spun Bates around. "But you're staying right here until I get back."

"But what if you don't come back?"

"Chance you'll have to take since I have the gun." Sole sighed and shook his head. "Look, if I wanted you dead, you'd be dead now."

Bates said nothing but relaxed a little. Sole nodded at a spot in the dirt beside one of the support posts, holding up a structural beam. "Sit down there."

Bates complied, and a minute later Sole had zip-tied his hands and feet to the post. Taking a roll of duct tape from inside his shirt, he wound it around Bates' mouth and the back of his head, three complete turns.

He leaned over so Bates could see his eyes. "I'll be back. You had better be here when I get here. Understand?"

Bates nodded.

"If you're not here or if you make noise to attract attention, I'll find you, and you know what I'll do, right?"

Bates nodded again.

Sole turned and left the basement, pulling the string on the switch to kill the light. Upstairs, he removed the ski mask, turned the button on the door lock, and walked outside. It was the middle of the night and not likely that anyone would be around to observe the stranger get into Turner Bates' car and drive away. He didn't go far, just four blocks to a shopping center on Idaho Street.

He parked the car and walked back to the apartment complex. Anyone showing up at the Entente offices today would find them closed for business, the door locked, and no one there.

The police officer who had patrolled through earlier came cruising through the apartment complex lot one last time. It was the end of his shift. He nodded and flipped up his hand in a friendly greeting at the man walking toward his pickup to head off to a day in one of the mines. Sole returned the wave and smiled. "Have a good one, officer."

"You too," the officer said back through his open window, yawned, and drove back out onto the street.

Sole climbed into his pickup beside the dumpster. Ten minutes later, he was headed north out of Elko toward the Idaho line, tired and running on adrenaline but with a sense of satisfaction. It had been a productive night.

FORTY-FOUR

Anybody Want Breakfast?

Thin light filtered down from the peaks, weak and gray in the pre-dawn dusk. The trees and rocks surrounding the lean-to were little more than indistinct shapes, monochromatic and washed-out, without definition or detail, like a sketch on canvass before the artist adds color.

Amelia stood outside the lean-to, waiting. Another few minutes and it would be light enough to navigate along the narrow trails and rocky cliffs. Inside, she could hear Chester snoring in front of the door. She'd stepped over him to come outside. Cope had been sitting with his back against the wall, chin down on his chest, dozing.

This was her chance. If she could put some distance between her and her captors, she might make it down to Merchantville, call for help, and end this insanity.

The branches on a nearby tree began to take shape in the gloom. It was the place that Cope had climbed in the dark during the night, desperate to make his phone call, but going straight up a slope and then back down the same way was far different from trying to navigate a narrow path

The Ghost

along rocky terrain with precipitous drops offs. One misstep and they'd find her at the bottom of some ravine, or they'd never find her at all.

A few more minutes passed. The gray light was a shade brighter now. The world began to take on form. It was time.

She felt a twinge of guilt at leaving Chester behind. He'd become a sort of protector, with a streak of compassion under his dim-witted subservience to Cope. It couldn't be helped, though. She didn't ask to be kidnapped and if there was a chance of getting away, she was going to take it.

She walked toward the tree, careful to lift her feet and not disturb the rocks and limbs on the ground. Peering beyond it, she could see ten yards or so down the trail. It was enough. Things would become clearer as the sun rose, but that would also give Cope and Chester a better chance to pursue. She reached the tree, put a hand out to touch its bark, peered down at the footing, and lifted her leg to move forward.

"Stop!"

It was Cope, standing ten feet away. He must have feigned sleep, listened, and followed her outside. The pistol in his hand was pointed at her chest, too close to miss at this range even in the scant light.

She whirled, scowling to face him. "What? You have to follow and watch me pee on top of everything else."

"I know what you were doing, and it wasn't no piss break," Cope said, shaking his head. "You was trying to get away."

"Think what you want," Amelia snapped back. "I've got to pee, and I was heading for this tree for a little privacy."

"Squat where you're at and pee if you have to, but you ain't disappearin' behind that tree."

"You really are a pig, you know."

"Maybe, but you ain't runnin' off. So squat and get it done."

"What's goin' on?" Chester stepped from the lean-to, rubbing his eyes with the backs of his knuckles.

"She's tryin' to get away," Cope said, waving the pistol toward Amelia. "But I stopped her."

Chester squinted at Amelia, still standing by the tree. "Why you doin' that? I thought we was all walkin' out today to that town ... Merchantville."

"We are. I wasn't running away," Amelia lied. "Just had to pee, so I stepped away for some privacy."

Chester looked from one to the other and then stared at the tree for a minute. "Alright. I'll go stand on the other side of that tree. Cope you stay here. We'll turn our backs while you pee, but you ain't goin' nowhere."

Amelia figured it was the most planning he'd ever done. As it turned out, it was a good plan. There was no way to force herself around him on the narrow trail, and while she was sure she could leave the trail and climb up the mountain slope on that side, she couldn't get away there with them on her heels. Cliff walls bordered the other side of the trail, unscalable even in full daylight. Behind, Cope stood between her and the lean-to, the pistol still raised and pointed at her.

"Okay." She nodded as Chester walked past and blocked her path on the other side of the tree. "Turn your backs." They did, and she dropped her pants, squatted, and let it go. When she was zipped up again, she walked forward, eyes down, following the trail. "Let's go."

"See. She just had to pee," Chester said, falling in behind Amelia and speaking over his shoulder to Cope. He reached in his pocket and pulled out the last of the previous day's pine nut harvest. "Anybody want breakfast?"

FORTY-FIVE

The Rats Were Not Amused

The road to Merchantville ran through the center of a broad valley where the surrounding mountains gave way to rolling foothills covered with low-growing sage and rabbit brush. After passing through part of the Duck Valley Shoshone-Paiute reservation, it continued to the northeast until it crossed over the Idaho state line and took on another name. Sole took his time, driving the backroads carefully in the dark and arrived in town as the eastern skies were graying along the horizon.

He made a slow pass through town to scope things out. There wasn't much. Today it sat in the middle of nowhere, but a hundred years earlier, the town had been a bustling center of activity. The country's westward expansion brought those seeking their fortunes, including those who sought their fortune from the gold in people's pockets and not from the ground. Merchantville sprang up as a place where traders, immigrants, natives, and prospectors could gather and conduct business. The occasional outlaw even passed through. Legend was that Butch Cassidy once spent a night there, but it was only a legend.

Stores and stables, bars and brothels, once lined the half-mile stretch that comprised the town limits, offering their services to miners, wagon trains, and Indians off the reservation. These days, the native Shoshone-Paiute nation had their own stores, nicer ones, and the residents of Merchantville clung to the rocky soil mostly out of habit.

Brandt's grocery store-tavern stood at the center of things. Across the street, two gas pumps in an oil-soaked gravel lot offered the only fuel within fifty miles. An old block-walled building, stained gray from years of exhaust fumes and dust, squatted at the back of the lot. The sign hand-painted on the block read—*Flack's*.

Here and there along the half-mile length of the town, a dirt drive headed off toward a shack or a rusty trailer, some inhabited, most abandoned. The majority of the abandoned ones were nothing more than piles of old timbers fallen down around a foundation of stacked stones.

Sole drove through the town without stopping. Jenks already knew he was being watched, that someone had killed two of his men. Sole didn't want any of the locals to mention the stranger that had come through earlier in the day if Jenks inquired when he showed up, and Sole was certain Jenks would show up. He had to.

On the outskirts of town, Sole found what he was looking for. A rutted dirt trail led off into the surrounding hills. He threw the pickup into four-wheel-drive and bumped along the trail for a half-mile, winding along the backside of a hill. At a spot just below the crest, he reversed, pointed the truck back down the way he had come, cut the engine, and stepped out to survey the area.

Walking below the crest of the hill, hidden from anyone

in Merchantville who might look his way, he scanned the surrounding country. It was too much to hope that he might intercept Amelia coming out of the mountain country to the southeast before she made it to Merchantville, but he hoped anyway. Things would be a lot simpler if he could find her and get away from her inept kidnappers without having to deal with the trap that Jenks was laying.

He knew the general direction they had to come from, based on the location of the cabin they fled, but he had no way of knowing exactly where Amelia would appear. Mountains and hills intertwined and rolled together, forming an immense network of creases and ravines in the landscape, natural paths that people traveling on foot would have to follow to descend into Merchantville. The problem was that there were a thousand possible routes they might follow through the hills. The landscape before him was a three-dimensional topographic puzzle that he was incapable of solving without some communication with Amelia, and at this point, she didn't even know he existed. If he explored the wrong ravine, checked around the back of the wrong hill, he could miss her altogether. The only sure way to find her was to wait for her to emerge from the hills.

Sole made his way back to the pickup, gathered up his bag and weapons, and climbed to the hillcrest. Lying on his belly in the dust behind a sage, he scanned down the slope. Merchantville sat at the foot of the hill. He judged the distance at about three hundred yards. The partially erect tumbled-down remnants of a building sat midway down the slope. It was centrally located along the main road through town, far enough up the slope that Jenks' men would probably ignore it, but close enough for him to take action when the time came.

He scanned the town for movement, then looked at the

sun and checked his watch. A little after six-thirty AM. It would have been better to do this in the dark. Hell, it would have been better if you'd just kept your ass on the main highway and headed on up to Boise, and as soon as he thought it, he regretted it. Jake and Ron had died trying to save Amelia.

Maybe this was fate's way of allowing him to pay the debt he owed for failing to protect his own family. Get Amelia back and make restitution for all the failures.

He smirked. Or maybe it's God's way of sending you directly to hell. Either way, he told himself, this is what you do, the only thing you're half good at.

He took a final look down the slope, wishing there was some sort of cover on the hillside besides the low-growing brush. Gritting his teeth, he muttered, "Get it done."

With the .30-06 slung over his shoulder and the duffle holding his pistols and ammo in one hand, he crouched low, and dashed over the top and down the slope toward the ruins of the old building. The slope steepened at the back of the building, dropping almost vertically to the excavated area that had once been the ground floor. He slid the last ten feet on his backside, landing boots-first against the back wall.

Half the building was standing, leaning precipitously to one side on its foundation but still erect. The other half was a jumble of timbers and stones. He decided to make the erect portion his primary fighting position if it came to that. The wooden plank walls would not provide as much protection against bullets as the piled rocks, but they afforded him hidden firing positions that would be difficult to detect from below. That settled, he went to a front corner and peered through the gaps in the planks at the town below. It was quiet. Apparently, the few residents of Merchantville were not early risers.

He propped the .30-06 against the wall, checked the magazines in the Colt 1911 and the Glock, and sat down in the dirt to wait. At the sound of scrabbling, scurrying feet against the back wall, he offered up a quick prayer. "Please don't let it be a skunk ... anything but a skunk."

He would rather share space with a bobcat or badger than be caught in close quarters with a skunk. He squinted into the gloom and breathed a sigh of relief.

Thank you, God. No skunks. A line of rats scurried along the wall, eyeballing the stranger in their midst, and chattering to one another.

"Chatter away," he muttered. "It's your home."

The chattering grew louder, and the scurrying more frantic. The rats were not amused.

FORTY-SIX

Rituals

It was a little after eight in the morning when Earl Jasso walked down the hill from the small wood-sided shack he called home. Smoke curled from the chimney behind him, wafting the scent of burning shipping pallets down over Merchantville. His wife, Ellen, was cold. She was cold every morning, even now when winter was still a couple of months away. The smoke would hang over the town, close to the ground like a morning fog, until the sun warmed the air and it rose above the surrounding hills.

He chided her about that every day. It was their ritual.

"Again, with the fire," he said, shaking his head as he sat at the tiny kitchen table sipping the strong black coffee Ellen brewed for him.

"What of it?" She knelt with her back to him, feeding oak planks into the stove. Earl cut the planks from the discarded pallets he collected from the dump in Elko when he went in for supplies.

"Everything down below smells of smoke. I smell it all day long in the store."

The Ghost

"Anyone else complain?" Ellen rose, poured a cup of coffee, and sat across from him at the table.

"Who would dare?" Earl gave a sardonic smile.

"You dare … every day."

"The others don't know you as well as I do."

"What's that supposed to mean?"

"It means they're terrified of you." Now his smile widened into a grin.

"And you're not terrified of me?" She leaned back, looking at him over her coffee cup, eyes narrowed.

"Scared to death of you. I've resigned myself to the notion that you will probably murder me in my sleep some night." He shrugged. "But I'd like to go without the smell of smoke in my last breath."

Their morning ritual complete, they laughed softy and drank their coffee in silence. For nearly fifty years, they had lived together in the tiny house overlooking Merchantville, raising a son and daughter there. The children were gone now, but Earl and Ellen remained.

Together, they ran Brandt's Grocery, providing supplies and drinks to the few locals who remained in town or who drove in from one of the outlying ranches. Earl's great-grandparents on his mother's side opened the store. They were German immigrants who crossed an ocean and came to the far west to find their fortune. When their only child, a daughter, married a young Basque sheepherder, they were forced to reconcile themselves to the fact that America was, as friends and family in the old country had warned them, a melting pot of cultures. Holding on to their Germanic traditions would be difficult, they said.

That prophecy came true when Marlene Brandt fell in love with Tomas Jasso. The Brandts accepted it philosophically. The thought of mingling Germanic blood with the wild Basques of Spain and France would have been unthinkable in the old country. In the remote west of the American continent, it no longer mattered. The Brandts had determined to become Americans through and through. This new country required a new way of thinking, and mingling their blood into the great cauldron of people flooding into the land was part of the process of Americanization.

So, Earl finished his coffee, kissed Ellen on the cheek, and walked down the hill to the store he had inherited from his father, who had received it from his father, Tomas Jasso. Out of respect for the Brandts, the store's name was never changed.

The smokey air hovered lower than usual this morning, held close to the ground by the colder air flowing down from the mountains. Earl breathed it in and smiled. Despite his morning complaint to Ellen, he liked the smell. At the store's entry, he turned and looked up and down the road. Smoke curled from a few other chimneys dotting the hills around Merchantville. This time of year, the fires would be out by noon, after the day warmed. When winter descended on the area, they would burn all day and all night. The high desert elevation in Merchantville ensured that temperatures during the deepest part of winter would rarely climb above zero, day or night.

He and Ellen had spoken about moving somewhere warmer, somewhere less remote. Their children encouraged them to make the change. They talked about it over coffee one morning.

"I'm getting old ... past seventy," Earl said. "Maybe we should think about doing what the kids want and move."

"Humph," Ellen said and put down her coffee cup.

The Ghost

"Seventy is not so old. Besides ..." She nodded out the window. "You really want to leave this ... leave our home?"

"No. I suppose not." Earl smiled. "As long as you keep that fire burning, I suppose we're warm enough." They laughed and never spoke of moving again.

He turned the handle on the door that remained unlocked at all hours, stepped in, and flipped on the lights. A voice called to him from behind.

"I was wondering how long it would take you to get down here and open up." Joe Flack walked down the hill from the trailer he occupied on the other side of the road. "Need my coffee."

"You ever think of making your own coffee? They make electric coffee pots these days," Earl said. "Just put the coffee in a basket and some water and bingo ... coffee. Then you wouldn't have to come bothering me first thing every damn morning."

"Hell, why would I do that?" Joe said, crossing the road without looking either way for traffic. "I enjoy bothering you." Both men laughed. It was another ritual.

Earl Jasso and Joe Flack had known each other most of their lives, rode the bus together to the school in Mountain City, worked around town at the same jobs before Merchantville's decline into a backwater. They even dated the same girls. That was before Earl met Ellen at a Basque Day parade in Elko.

After high school, Joe had gone off to the Army when Vietnam was winding down. He came back three years later quieter and gaunter and took over Flack's Garage for his father who died of cancer a year later.

Earl went in and readied the fixings for a pot of coffee. Joe followed him in, pulled a loose cigarillo from a jar on the counter, slapped down quarters, and lit up. "You're gonna get in trouble doing this one day," he said, blowing a plume of smoke toward the ceiling.

"What letting you smoke inside?" Earl said.

"No. Breaking up those packs of smokes and selling them piecemeal like that." He puffed again and nodded. "It's against the law."

"You going to report me?"

"Hell, no! I was just making an editorial comment."

"Well, editorialize this." Earl lifted his middle finger, and Joe laughed.

The coffee maker gurgled and hissed. When it stopped, Joe filled two styrofoam cups and handed one to Earl. He lifted his cup in a toast. "Here's to another day."

"To another day," Earl said with a solemn nod.

They sipped the coffee. Earl's face wrinkled, mouth open, running his tongue in and out a few times as if trying to rid it of a foul taste. "Damn, if you don't serve the worst coffee on the planet."

"Go home and make your own," Earl said, smiling and knowing what was coming.

"Nope. Not gonna happen. Maybe you could invite me up to have coffee with you and Ellen one day."

"Nope. Not gonna happen," Earl said, and they laughed again.

The laughter and comfortable morning rituals signaled all was well with the world, at least the tiny portion of it occupied by the residents of Merchantville.

FORTY-SEVEN

Haunted

From his lookout in the ruins of the partially collapsed building, Sole peered through the smoke haze and watched a man make his way down the opposite hill to the store. As he arrived at the front door, another man came from a trailer on the slope below Sole's position. He could hear him call out to the man at the door, but couldn't make out the conversation. After exchanging a few words, they disappeared inside.

No surprise. He'd expected there to be people in Merchantville. Amelia Downes wouldn't be making her way there if she didn't expect to find help, other people, a telephone, some way of getting away from her kidnappers, but people complicated his plans.

"Stay inside," he muttered, watching the front of the store.

They did. He turned to scan the surrounding hills, hoping that Amelia might come through one of the passes. It was too early for that, he knew, but he hoped anyway.

Timing was critical, and his timing hadn't been the best

lately. His plan to get Amelia away alive had far too many paths to failure and only one to success. The slightest variable, some seemingly insignificant overlooked detail, and things would get ugly and bloody.

He shook his head. Who was he kidding? Things were almost certain to be bloody. The only question was whose blood would be on the ground at the end of the day.

Adapting and improvising to operational variables had been his strength as a Marine and later a police detective, but lately, he felt like he'd lost a step. Too many details slipped through the cracks, and too many people had been hurt.

An hour passed. Overhead, a hawk screeched, then swooped from the sky into the rubble half of the building where the roof had collapsed. A squeal, then the heavy flapping of wings, and the hawk rose again with one of his rat roommates in its talons.

Sole hunkered down in his hiding place. The rat should have stayed out of sight.

He looked through the gaps in the planks, scanning for any activity. If not for the smoke from some of the chimneys and the two men entering the store, he would have thought Merchantville was a ghost town.

Another half-hour passed. The sun was higher now. A few of the old shacks and trailers still had smoke wisping from chimneys. A man came out of one, cranked up an old pickup parked by the door, and drove out of town. Good. One less person to worry about when the shit hit the fan.

A vehicle approached, the sound of its tires on the pavement audible a minute before it came into view around a bend in the road. Sole recognized the Chevy pickup Jenks was driving the day before. It rolled slowly through town until he lost sight of it.

Jenks was checking things out. Sole expected that. A minute later, the Chevy came back, pulled up in front of the store, and stopped.

"Don't get out," Sole whispered. The door opened and Jenks stepped out. "Shit."

Jenks stretched, looked up and down the road, and for a moment seemed to stare through the gap in the boards where Sole watched. Then he turned and went inside the store.

He suspects, but he doesn't know for sure. Sole smiled. "Alright, time to adapt and improvise."

Peter Jenks pondered his dilemma as he drove. Knowing that *the someone* who took out Yang and Sink was still out there haunted him and their dead bodies were proof that he intended to do far more than haunt if he got the chance.

If he knew why the intruder had gotten involved, he might be able to put a face on him and take preemptive action to eliminate him, or at least defend against him. Without knowing, all he could do was wait until he stepped from the shadows into the daylight.

He slowed as he drove down Merchantville's main road, eyes darting from one hillside to the other, searching. Just show yourself one time, and we'll end this now, but he didn't. Jenks knew he wouldn't. Whoever he was, he was too professional to make that mistake.

He drove the length of the town, then turned around and parked in front of the store. The certainty that the haunting eyes must be watching as he stepped from the Chevy sent an uncomfortable tingling up his spine. He lifted his arms over his head, stretching and nonchalantly scanning the hillside opposite the store. There were a thousand places of concealment, the hulks of abandoned buildings, boulders, trees, rusted-out trailers.

He muttered, "Show yourself, you son of a bitch," then walked inside the store.

FORTY-EIGHT

I Guess We All Are

"Morning," Earl Jasso smiled and called out as the door opened.

Jenks entered the store without speaking and turned to check all the visible corners before turning back to Earl. "Got a restroom?"

"Yep." Earl nodded toward the back. "Through that door."

Jenks nodded and walked through the door. Earl and Joe exchanged a look of curiosity. Unfriendly behavior was uncommon in their world.

In the back, Jenks examined the storeroom filled with stacked cases of canned and dry goods. A small aisle between the boxes led to the single restroom and the back door beside it. He checked the restroom, then pushed open the back door and scanned outside. Whoever was watching was not in or around the store. He went back to the front.

"Don't get many strangers around here." Earl regarded the newcomer without attempting to conceal the frank curiosity written all over his face.

"Hell," Joe Flack chimed in. "We don't get *any* strangers around here." He leaned against the counter, watching Jenks with the same intense curiosity.

"I expect not." Jenks nodded at the pot on the counter. "That coffee for sale?"

"You bet." Earl pulled out a styrofoam cup and filled it. "Here you go."

"How much?" Jenks reached for his wallet.

"On the house, if you'll just chat a bit and tell us what brings you to Merchantville." Earl chuckled. "Couple of old-timers like us get tired of looking at each other and talking about the weather. A little fresh blood always refreshes things."

Jenks pulled a dollar bill from his wallet. "This cover the coffee?"

"It does." Earl nodded. "And then some. I'll get some change from the till."

"Keep it." Jenks sipped the coffee and turned to look out the door.

Earl and Joe exchanged a look and raised their eyebrows.

"I get it," Joe said, nodding. "Quiet type. I'm that way myself."

"Really?" Jenks threw a quick sideward glance at him and then turned back to the door.

"Didn't mean to pry into your business," Earl said. "Whatever it is, it's not any of our business. No offense intended."

"Good." Jenks turned back to face them and forced a brief smile across his face as if it were a necessary and unpleasant chore. "I'm waiting for some people. Not sure when they'll get here, so I'll be around here for a while."

"Sure. You're welcome to hang out with us ..." Earl

The Ghost

began and then shut up. The look on Jenks' face made it plain he was not asking for permission.

"Anything to do to kill time around here?" Jenks looked around the store.

"Card table and a deck." Earl nodded at a corner of the store. "We can sit in with you if you want to go a few hands. Not much going on as you can see." He gave a quick smile, but let it fade when there was no reaction from the stranger.

"I'll play alone," Jenks said.

"Solitaire man." Joe grinned. "Me too." Earl shot him a hard look, and the grin faded.

Jenks walked to the table in the corner and positioned it so that he could see out of the window. He shuffled the deck and began dealing out cards one by one.

Earl and Joe huddled by the counter, speaking in low voices.

Joe whispered, "Strange fella."

"You can say that again."

"You gonna be alright here with him?"

"Sure. Seems harmless enough. Just doesn't want to be bothered by two old coots like us."

"I suppose," Joe said, and then in a louder voice added, "I reckon I'll get back to the garage. Promised Emma Caldwell I'd have that old heap of hers running by this afternoon."

"See you later, Joe."

Earl pulled a dog-eared Field and Stream magazine from under the counter. Joe walked across the road and up the hill to his garage. Peter Jenks flipped cards and moved them with one eye on the window and road outside.

In Flack's Garage, Emma Caldwell's fifteen-year-old Mercury sat over the oil and lube pit with the hood up. Joe rolled a multitiered tool carrier to its side, selected a socket, fitted it to the ratchet wrench, and leaned under the hood.

"Don't make a sound," a voice whispered behind him.

Joe jumped up, banging the back of his head under the hood, and whirled to face the intruder. "Who …" He leaned forward, peering at the stranger. "Who are you?"

"I'm not here to hurt you." Sole rested a hand on the butt of the pistol in his waistband and nodded at the wrench in Joe's hand. "Put the wrench down please."

"That's a damn big gun you got stuffed in your pants," Joe said, eyeing the Colt, then laughed and shook his head at the unintended play on words. "What I mean to say is…"

"I know what you mean. Put the wrench down. I have no intention of harming you."

"Well, for someone who doesn't intend to hurt anyone, you got a strange way of communicating that fact. Nearly scared me out of ten years of life, and I don't have that many years to spare." Joe laid the wrench on the Mercury's gray primer-painted fender.

"Step away from it," Sole said.

Joe stepped away and repeated his question. "Who are you?"

"Doesn't matter who I am. I just need to ask you a few questions."

"Well, you got yourself a captive audience. What do you want to know?"

"The man who came into the store while you were there, what did he say?"

"Strange man," Joe said, shaking his head. "Nearly as strange as you. Didn't want to talk. Just said he was waiting

The Ghost

for some people and would be hanging out for a while." Joe jerked his head in the store's direction, visible across the road through the bay door. "He's sitting by the window playing solitaire right now where he can see people come and go."

"He say when his people were coming?"

"Nope. Like I said, he made it clear he didn't want to talk."

"Alright." Sole nodded. "You have a phone here?"

"Not one installed. Just my cell phone."

"Let me have it."

"But …" Joe's eyes narrowed. "This the part where you pull that pistol and put a bullet in me?"

"No." Sole couldn't resist smiling at the old-timer's unintimidated openness. "Told you. I will not hurt you, but you're not making any calls." He put his hand out. "Give me the phone."

Joe pulled it from his pocket, holding it between a grease-covered thumb and forefinger, and dropped it in Sole's palm. "You going to tell me what this is all about, or just keep me guessing."

"The man who came into the store is a killer. You and your friend in the store … anyone else who comes along and sees him … are in danger. He won't leave Merchantville with you alive."

"A killer?" Joe rubbed the back of his hand over his mouth, leaving a grease stain on his chin. "You think he is going to kill Earl … and me? How can you know that?"

"I know the kind of man he is."

"The kind like you?" Joe's gray eyes narrowed, waiting for an answer.

"Fair question." Sole nodded and smiled. "We're different. I don't kill innocent people. He does. He's killed others

... or had them killed. If he thinks you're a threat to what he has planned, he won't hesitate to kill you."

"That doesn't make sense. What kind of threat are we?"

"The witness kind. You've seen him and whatever he plans to do here today. He won't leave anyone behind to tell the story."

"Then you need to give me my damned phoned back so I can call the sheriff and get some deputies out here."

"I can't do that." Sole shook his head. "There are others who will die if I do."

"So, what are we supposed to do? Just sit here and wait for him to do what you said ... kill us."

"No. I'm going to stop that from happening." Sole said it with more confidence than he felt, but he needed Joe to relax.

Joe's brow furrowed, and he shook his head. "Mister, you need to tell me what's going on. I figure I have a right to know, seeing as how there's a fella across the road playing solitaire, and you say he's bent on killing me and my best friend."

He was right. "Okay."

He gave Joe the abbreviated version of everything that had happened over the last three days. Joe listened, incredulous at first, then angry. His eyes narrowed, and he shook his head from time to time. When Sole finished, he asked, "The girl you're trying to save ... she have a name?"

"She does." Sole thought for a second and decided there was no reason not to share it. After today, it wouldn't matter one way or another. "Her name is Amelia."

"Amelia? The only Amelia I know of around here is Jake Downes' daughter." Joe's brow raised in surprise. "Is that who it is? Amelia Downes?"

"Yes." Sole nodded.

"That means to the two fellas you said were killed by that stranger's men on the mountain were Jake Downes and Ron Benson."

"Yes."

"Son of a bitch." Joe sagged back against the Mercury. "I can't believe it."

"Believe it."

Joe nodded. "I don't suppose you have any reason to lie about a thing like that, and I reckon if you planned to do me any harm, you'd have done it by now without all the talking."

"That's right," Sole nodded.

"So that's all you want from me? To know what that stranger said."

"Yes, for now," Sole said. "But I may need your help later."

"What kind of help?"

"I'll let you know when I figure that out." Sole nodded at the old Mercury. "Go back to working on the car like it's a normal day."

"Normal, my ass." Joe shook his head. "This is starting off to be the most un-normal day this town's ever seen." He eyed the pistol in Sole's waistband. "You going to use that to settle things?"

"Maybe. First, I'm just going to sit here in your garage and keep an eye on things."

Miles away in the mountains, the morning sun burned off the chill. By noon, temperatures climbed enough that the tiny group of trekkers struggled to keep their feet moving. Even in the cooler high elevations of northern Nevada, two days hiking through the mountains with scant water and only pine nuts to chew was taking its toll. There was no conversation, not even grumbling from Cope. They focused every bit of their energy on moving one foot after the other.

The descent into the lower hill country that surrounded Merchantville brought them to the bottom of a ravine carved out by a stream. The stream was dry, the bed made up of rocks and loose gravel that made for unsteady footing, but at least they weren't clinging to the side of a mountain anymore.

Amelia raised a hand and plopped down on a large, flat rock. "Only a few more miles, now." She took a deep breath and added. "We can rest here for a bit."

"Good." Chester heaved a sigh and sat in the gravel, leaning back against a scrub pine growing along the bank. "I need a rest."

Cope said nothing and found a spot on the ground away from the others.

"How much longer, you think?" Chester asked.

"Not too far. These ravines coming out of the mountains all lead down to the road running toward Merchantville. With any luck, we'll come out right in town. If not ..." Amelia shrugged. "We'll come to the road and follow it into town. Walking will be a lot easier there."

"Good." Chester nodded and looked at his partner. "That's good, ain't it Cope?"

Cope stood. "Let's get moving." He strode off down the stream bed without looking back.

Amelia raised her head, surprised. "What's got into him?"

The Ghost

"I guess he's ready to be out of these mountains." Chester stood and stretched.

Amelia sighed and pushed herself up from the rock. "I guess we all are."

FORTY-NINE

Helluva Long Way

The Dodge pickup came around the bend into Merchantville and slowed, the faces of the men inside turned outward. As Jenks had before them, they surveyed the town from one end to the other, then rolled to a stop beside Jenks' Chevy at Brandt's Grocery.

Axe exited the passenger side and went into the store. Bear, the driver, stayed with the truck. The others, Crew and Don, headed off in opposite directions along the road, strolling casually, their heads swiveling back and forth, eyes scanning every old building and ruin dotting the hillsides.

"Morning," Earl said as Axe walked through the door. "Can I get you something?"

Axe nodded at the pot on the counter. "Coffee."

"Coming right up." Earl filled a cup and nodded at the men outside. "Anything for your friends?"

"Not now." Axe turned away and walked to the table in the corner where Jenks sat looking down at his solitaire hand. "Nothing happening yet," Axe reported without being asked.

The Ghost

"It's early still," Jenks said without looking up.

"Any sign of the other ... the one who took out Yang and Sink?" Axe stared out the window at the hills across the road.

"No, but I wouldn't expect him to show himself until we get our hands on the others."

"You think that's what he's after ... the girl?"

"I don't know what he's after, but I had the feeling he was watching me up at the cabin ... could have taken me out then, if he wanted." Jenks nodded and looked up. "He'll be here when we have what he wants. You just be ready for him."

"We're ready." Axe nodded. "Feels like he's watching us ... somewhere up there."

"Don't let him spook you. He got the drop on Yang and Sink. We won't let that happen. Just keep your men sharp."

The roar of a dozen chopped motorcycles thundered down the road, and Chino rolled through town with his men. He stopped at the store, gestured to both ends of town, and the bikers dispersed to patrol the road. Then he dismounted and came through the door.

"Morning. Can I get you something?" Earl said for the third time that day, three more times than he said it in the last week.

Chino ignored him and walked to the table in the corner, grinning. "*Hola*! We ready to party?"

"Fucking amateurs." Axe shook his head in disgust.

"Amateur this, motherfucker." Chino's grin widened as he grabbed his crotch and gyrated.

"Enough," Jenks ordered. "Get outside and find them."

Earl Jasso watched the interaction from behind the front counter with the uneasy feeling that he would not want to be the people these men wanted to find.

Sole recognized the four professionals from their meeting at Jenks' office the night before. He stood deep in the shadows of the garage bay, watching the roads. The roar of the bikers coming into town got Joe's attention. He looked up from under the Mercury's hood. "What the hell is that?"

"Reinforcements for the other side." Sole looked at Joe. "You still willing to help?"

"I am." Joe looked beyond him to the bikers separating into groups and roaring off in different directions. "Not much into committing suicide though."

"Me neither," Sole said. "This will all be on me. What I need you to do is get your friend Earl out of the store, and I need to get in, unnoticed, like one of the locals."

"How do you plan to do that?"

"I'm not sure. Thinking maybe you could walk me in, pretend I'm somebody from town just coming in for a Coke. Then you and Earl get out."

"How?"

"That's the tricky part. I'm open to suggestions if you have any."

"I got an idea."

Joe explained. When he finished, Sole shook his head. "I don't know. It's dangerous and there will be shooting. I'm trying to keep everyone else out of the line of fire, including you."

"Nothing I want more than to stay out of the line of fire. Let me do this, and I'll have me and Earl out of the way so you can do what you need to do to get Amelia away from those assholes."

"Okay." Sole nodded. There didn't seem to be any other options. "Does Earl have any weapons in the store?"

The Ghost

"Twelve-gauge pump under the counter. He keeps it loaded with 00 buck."

Sole raised his eyes, surprised. "Got a robbery problem way out here?"

"Nope ... a coyote problem. They come into town and kill chickens, cats, dogs. Makes an easy meal for them instead of chasing down a jackrabbit like they ought to. Earl uses the shotgun to shoot at them." He laughed. "Gets lucky and even hits one now and then. He's kind of looked on as the local varmint control officer."

"Okay. That helps knowing it's there. Now, I need to get close to them, inside where I can do what I have to ... find out what's going on without them knowing who I am. Sure you can you handle that?"

"That's the easy part." Joe nodded, thinking things over. "First thing is for me to get over there," Joe said and held out his hand. "But I'll need my phone."

"Why?"

"Way I see it, there's three things got to happen. First, I need to get over there. Then Earl needs to leave. Then you come over and I get my ass out of there, and then you can go to work."

"That's four things, but yeah ..." Sole nodded. "Sums things up pretty well."

"Earl's wife is up there in that little house above the store," Joe said. "If she calls and tells him to come up, he will. She won't do that for you, but she will for me if I explain things to her. I'll tell her to wait a few minutes until I get over there, then call and tell him to get his ass up the hill. Then you come over, and I wander out back and head for cover too."

"She can't call the sheriff," Sole said. "Later, when

everything's settled one way or the other, you can call all the law you want, but not before."

"I got that. No sheriff." Joe nodded confidently. "If I tell her not to, she won't. She'll be annoyed as hell, but she'll wait for me to get up there and explain."

Sole stared hard at Joe. He'd been on his own for so long he had a hard time trusting anyone and a harder time asking for help, but Jenks had him outnumbered and outgunned. A little help from someone he trusted could make a difference. The question was, could he trust a man when he didn't even know his name.

"What's your name?" Sole asked.

"Joe Flack. What's yours."

"John," Sole said without adding his last name. "I didn't kill you, Joe Flack, and you know I could have, so you know you can trust me. Can I trust you?"

"There's all kinds of trust. I suppose I can trust you not to kill me … for now. Later, who knows?" Joe said and grinned. "As for anything else … time will tell. But if all that you told me about Amelia Downes is true, you can trust that I'll do what I can to get things clear so you can get her free of those men."

"It's true." Sole reached in his pocket and pulled out Joe's phone. "I'll be listening."

"I expected you would." Joe took the phone. "One question."

"What?"

"You some kind of law?"

"No." Sole shook his head. "Not anymore."

"Then what are you doing all this for?"

"I made a promise."

"Well, you sure go a helluva long way to keep a promise."

FIFTY

At the Alamo

"Joe Flack, you better start explaining to me what the hell is going on."

"I told you I will, Ellen, but right now I need you to trust me," Joe said, speaking in a low voice as if the men in the store across the road might hear.

"Why are you whispering? Something's wrong."

"Nothing is wrong ... not right now at least, but it's important that you do what I say. Watch from your window. When you see me go across to the store, wait ten minutes, then call Earl and tell him you need him up there. Don't make it sound like an emergency, just something you need him to help with, and make sure he stays with you."

"And when he gets up here, what'll I tell him?"

"Let him know it has to do with his customers this morning, and he'll understand. Tell him to wait a little while and then call me to come up and help with something. I'll come up explain everything then. Remember ..."

"I heard you the first time, Joe. Don't tell anyone ... no call to the sheriff or anybody else."

"That's right."

"You know, saying that … all this mystery … just makes me think I should call in the law."

"I know, Ellen. That's why I need you to trust me. Lives are at stake."

"And that only makes me worry more," she said. "You mean Earl's life … your life."

"Yes, but others too, and when I tell you, you'll understand."

"Alright," she said, sighing. "I don't like it, but I'll do it, and when you get up here, you better have a damned good explanation."

"I do." Earl ended the call and looked at Sole. "She'll do it."

"I heard." Sole nodded, and his conscience forced him to add, "She has a right to be worried. So do you."

"Believe me, I am worried," Joe said and nodded his head emphatically. "Scared as shit right now, but these men are already in town … that first strange fella, then the others, and then the bikers. Something is up … something bad, and you being on the other side of whatever they got planned means I have to trust you … to a point at least."

"Fair enough," Sole said and asked, "Does Earl have any other weapons up in his house?"

"Sure," Joe said. "This part of the country, everyone has guns. Earl and Ellen have several that I know of."

"Good. When you get up there, load them up and be ready." Sole saw the apprehension on Joe's face. He owed him the truth. "I'm going to do what I can to handle things, but there are a lot of them and one of me. They won't want witnesses and you and Earl are witnesses."

"I understand." Joe gave a solemn nod.

"Good. If they come, barricade yourselves in the house,

find a good firing position, and don't try to get fancy. When they show themselves, shoot for center mass. Hit them hard and make them go down, then look for more targets." He stared into Joe's eyes. "Have you ever shot anyone, Joe?"

"Long time ago," Joe said quietly. "I was a young man, younger than you, in Vietnam." His eyes hardened, and he nodded. "Don't worry. If it's kill or be killed, I'll pull the trigger."

"Alright then. You take the lead with Earl and Ellen. Tell them what to do. Keep them calm."

"I'll do the best I can."

"I believe you will." Sole nodded. "Anything you want to talk about before we do this?"

Joe thought for a second and shook his head. "Nope. Seems we've covered everything." He forced a grin and said, "Let's get this show on the road, but first we need to get you looking the part." He reached in his back pocket and pulled out a greasy rag. "Here, take this. Wipe it over your hands."

Sole took the rag and smeared black grease over the backs of his hands.

"Now here," Joe said and pointed at his chin and face. "Looks like you got in a fight with a porcupine."

Sole had forgotten about the broken glass peppering the side of his face when Lola's boyfriend shot at him. He nodded and wiped the rag over this face and chin, leaving a dark streak.

"One more thing." Joe pointed to a rack where several grease-stained shirts hung. "Grab one of those and put it on."

Sole eyed the shirts and shook his head. "I don't think that's necessary."

"I expect you're planning to carry that big cannon when

you come over to the store." Joe eyed the bulge of the .45 under Sole's shirt.

"What of it?" Sole eyed the shirts on hooks, smelling of old oil and grease.

"Unless I miss my guess," Joe continued. "Those men over there are sharp. You won't be able to sneak up on them like you did me. They're liable to spot that gun. Those shirts there belonged to a fella that used to work for me, Randy Gooden. He was a biggun, tipped the scale at close to three hundred. His shirt ought to be big enough to cover that Colt without showing the bulge."

"You're right." Sole reached for one of the shirts. "What happened to Randy?"

"Up and died of a heart attack one day." Joe nodded at the floor. "Right about where you're standing."

"Great." Sole slipped into the shirt and noted the name *Randy* stitched over the left breast pocket.

"Good. I just hate throwing anything away, and I knew those shirts would come in handy one day." Joe grinned. "Now you look like a regular grease monkey."

With that, Joe Flack turned and left the garage he'd inherited from his father and wondered if he'd ever see the inside of it again. Don't think like that, he thought as he descended the hill and crossed the road to the store. Sure, you'll see it again. Who's going to fix Emma Caldwell's old heap?

He crossed the road. One of the strangers leaned against the Dodge pickup, watching him. Two others had taken up positions along the road at opposite ends of town. Joe ignored them all and walked through the door.

"Coffee still on?" he called out to Earl.

"Hang on. I'll put a fresh pot on." He nodded at the

men in the corner, one seated at the card table, one standing. "Poured a few more cups than usual today."

Ellen Jasso watched through the parted curtains until she saw Joe head from the garage to the store. Then she went back to the kitchen table, picked up her coffee cup, and glanced at the clock on the wall. "Ten minutes," she grumbled. "You better have a good explanation, Joe Flack."

She had half a mind to march down the hill and find out what kind of foolishness her husband and Joe had gotten into. She didn't, though. Joe might be a silly old fool at times, but she'd never known him to be a practical joker. He meant what he said, so, when exactly ten minutes had passed, she put down the coffee cup, picked up her phone, and punched in Earl's number.

The two men in the corner, the solitaire hand in progress, turned their heads at the loud beeping coming from the phone on the counter. Earl ignored them and picked up the cell and answered. "What's up Emma?"

"I need you up here."

"Why? What's the matter?"

Jenks and Axe exchanged glances. Leaning against the counter, sipping a fresh cup of coffee, Joe saw their eyes narrow, suspicious. Make it good, Ellen, nothing too dramatic.

"I was trying to move that damned old sofa your mother left us, the one in the extra room, and threw my back out."

"I've told you before not to try and move anything heavy," Earl said, genuinely annoyed.

"Well, I did, and your damned preaching isn't going to

change that. I need you to come up here and give me a hand."

"Alright," Earl sighed. "I'll be up in a minute." He ended the call and looked at Joe. "You mind watching things for a few minutes while I run up the hill and check on Ellen?"

"Don't mind at all," Joe said, and asked as casually as he could, "What's up."

"The woman decided to move that old sofa in the extra room by herself and threw out her back."

"Now why in the world would she try to do a thing like that?" Joe shook his head, hoping the show he was putting on for the men in the corner was believable.

"Because she's Ellen," Earl said, shaking his head. "Headstrong as ever."

"That she is," Joe said, chuckling.

Earl headed through the store to the rear, turned the bolt in the lock, and pushed the back door open. "I'll be back in a few."

"I'll be here," Joe called after him. He walked around behind the counter and plopped down on Earl's stool. "Anything I can get you boys?" he called to the men in the corner. "There's a fresh pot of coffee on."

"We're fine," Jenks said.

Sole watched from the garage bay. He allowed another ten minutes to pass, then headed outside and down the hill to the store, wiping his hands on the greasy rag and shoving it in his jeans pocket for show.

The man by the Dodge stared at him without speaking.

The Ghost

Sole smiled and said, "How ya doin'," then pulled the door open and went inside.

"Friendly sort," he said, walking up to the counter nodding at the man outside by the truck.

"Don't mind him, Randy. Lot of fresh faces in town this morning," Joe said, making sure to use the name stitched on Sole's shirt. "You get Emma Caldwell's car running?"

"Yep," Sole said, making things up on the fly. "Had to adjust the timing and replace the tensioner, then changed the oil and plugs. Running pretty good now." He walked to the cooler along the back wall, retrieved a Coke, and looked around. "Where's Earl?"

"Went up to the house to help Ellen move a sofa or something. Asked me to watch the place."

Sole held up the Coke. "Well, have him put this on my tab."

"Right." Joe nodded and made a note on a pad by the cash register.

Sole leaned on the counter and sipped the Coke. "Got anything else this afternoon? I'm thinking of heading over to Wildhorse and do some fishing before dark."

"Just an oil change and rotate the tires on Buddy Galt's pickup. After that, you're free to go."

"Sounds good." Sole nodded, and for the first time since entering the store, glanced back to the corner where Jenks sat playing solitaire while the leader of the group in the Dodge watched the road through the store's plate glass window. Both men seemed unaware of his presence. Sole knew they had listened to everything he and Joe said.

"Gonna hang out here and take a lunch break. Then I'll get on Galt's pickup," he said.

"Suit yourself," Joe answered.

They played their parts perfectly, he hoped. Sole walked

back to the cooler and grabbed a plastic-wrapped ham sandwich and another Coke. Joe picked up Earl's Field and Stream, leaned back on the stool, and began flipping pages.

Minutes dragged by. Sole leaned nonchalantly against the counter, just a normal day in Merchantville. He chewed down the last bite of cardboard tasting sandwich and washed it down with Coke. He was considering going back and grabbing another to kill time and justify his presence in the store when Joe's cell phone finally chimed.

"When you gonna get back down here?" Joe answered it with no other greeting. "I've got my own business to run."

"Sorry," Earl said loudly enough that, even without the speaker on, they could hear his side of the conversation. "I need your help."

"What's the matter?" Joe asked, leaning forward, feigning concern. "Is Ellen okay?" It was a masterful performance. If there was an award for undercover supporting actor, Sole would have nominated him.

"She's alright," Earl said. "Threw out her back though, and she is mad as a hornet. That's why I need your help."

"What is it?"

"That sofa she tried to move. She wants it out today … now. I'm supposed to take it out to the shed, but I can't lift it and get it through the door without help."

Joe sighed. "Alright. I'll be up in a minute."

"Thanks."

Joe ended the call and looked at Sole, shaking his head. "Sorry, Randy. You might have to go fishing another time. I have to give Earl a hand and need you to hang out here for a while. Hand out coffee or drinks or whatever anyone wants, just note it on the pad here."

"Son of a bitch," Sole said, shaking his head, then

The Ghost

added, "That Ellen ... when she expects something done, she can be a hard woman to please."

"You can say that again."

"Well, I reckon the fish'll be biting tomorrow good as today."

"I expect so." Joe walked toward the back door.

"Stop." Axe stared at them from the corner and shook his head. "Stay here."

"Say what?" Joe turned, eyes narrowed. "You got no cause telling me what to do."

"Stay here," Axe repeated. "No one leaves."

"I'm free to go wherever I choose," Joe snapped back. "And I'm going to help my friend."

"I said ..." Axe began.

"Let him go." Jenks looked up from the solitaire hand and eyed the two men at the counter. "We know where he's at ... if we need him."

Axe shrugged and turned back to the window.

For the first time, Jenks' eyes met Sole's, and for an instant Sole wondered if he was on to their game. If he suspected who the man wearing Randy's oversized shirt really was, he didn't let on.

Jenks looked back down and flipped a card. Joe walked out the back door. Sole breathed a sigh of relief, walked behind the counter, and sat on the stool. Everything was coming together.

An uneasy thought crept into his mind. That's right. You got them right where you want them, just like Travis and Crockett and Bowie did ... at the Alamo.

FIFTY-ONE

Someone's Looking for You

They were making good time. The traveling became easier as they descended from the mountains, the dry stream bed widened, and the uneven, rocky footing changed to smooth gravel. As they approached the road to Merchantville, the ground leveled. After two days of trekking up and down mountain ridges, the easier walking was a relief. Like a horse that knows it's nearing the barn after a long ride, their pace increased.

It was mid-afternoon when Amelia stopped and pointed. "There!"

Cope, still leading the way, raised his eyes and gazed ahead. "What?" It was the first word he'd spoken since their rest break.

"The road," Amelia said. "I'd say about a quarter-mile ahead."

"I don't see nothin'." Cope stood up straight, scanning the horizon.

"Hard to make out, but see how the hills come down on the other side of the valley and the way this stream bed leads down to where they end. That'll be where the road is, right in the middle of the valley on the flattest land."

"I see it," Chester said, standing on tiptoes and looking in the direction she pointed. "Kind of just a thin line in the middle where the hills end."

"That's it," Alice said.

Cope forged ahead again, moving more briskly than before. Walking beside Amelia, Chester shook his head. "He's in one all-fired hurry."

"Yes, he is." Amelia had been worrying all day about Cope's suspected phone call the night before. Now, as they neared the road, her concern increased. Cope was heading out like a man on a mission.

"He seems eager to get to the road ... like someone's waiting for him," she said and slowed, scanning the valley from one end to the other.

"Out here?" Chester looked at her from the side and gave a reassuring smile. "Who would he be meeting?"

"Whoever he called last night."

"Yeah, but he said he never called 'cause his battery was dead."

"That's what he said," Amelia muttered.

"But you don't believe him." Chester looked at his partner's back up ahead, hunched forward as he quickened his pace.

"I don't know what to believe." Amelia stopped and looked at Chester. He turned to face her. "Just be ready, Chester. Just in case ..."

"In case of Cope trying to do something? Trying to hurt us?" He shook his head. "Naw, we're partners. He won't try to do nothin' to me, and I'm not gonna let him do nothin' to you."

"I hope you're right.," Amelia said and started walking again.

It took another ten minutes to make the last quarter mile to the road. Cope was standing on the shoulder, waiting as they caught up with him. "Which way?"

Amelia searched the surrounding hills and mountains for a landmark, recognized a rock pinnacle on the opposite side of the valley, and nodded to the right. "That way. Probably another three miles or so."

Without another word, Cope started walking. Amelia and Chester fell in behind. They hadn't gone a hundred yards when the rumbling of motorcycles approached from behind. Two men rode by, their motorcycle club colors emblazoned on the backs of their denim vests. One lifted a cell phone to his ear, spoke briefly, then both bikes stopped on the shoulder a half-mile ahead.

"What you reckon they're doing?" Chester said, squinting.

"I don't know." Amelia stopped. Bikers on these back roads were not uncommon, but two bikers passing by and then stopping on the side of the road seemed more ominous than just a couple of retired easy-riders enjoying the fresh air and mountain vistas.

Cope kept moving. If anything, he increased speed toward the motorcycles.

"I think we should get off the …." She started and then turned, mouth open in mid-sentence. Four more bikers roared up around the bend, circling them, pistols in their hands.

"What the hell is going on?" Chester said. He pointed at the nearest biker. "You fellas get out of the way. We're not botherin' anyone. Just let us be. Go on now! Move!"

The biker dismounted and walked up to Chester. He

smiled and shook his head. "Naw, man. You not goin' nowhere." His right arm came up in a backhanded swing, The pistol barrel crashed into Chester's face, and his mouth erupted in a torrent of blood and teeth. He sank to his knees, hands holding his face.

"Stop it!" Amelia shouted. "He didn't do anything to you." She knelt beside Chester and put an arm protectively around his shoulders.

Cope walked up, herded back by the first two bikers. He nodded and grinned.

"You did this, didn't you!" Amelia rose and rushed toward him, hands extended as if she would grab him by the throat and strangle him. Two bikers reached out, grabbed her, and threw her to the ground beside Chester.

"You son of a bitch!" Amelia spat the words at him. "You gave us up ... betrayed your partner ... your friend."

"I did what I had to do," Cope said. "You two been against me from the start." He shook his head. "Not no more. I'm settin' things right with Mr. Jenks." He nodded at Chester. "He shoulda' stood by me."

Another motorcycle rolled around the bend. The rider dismounted, and the group parted for their leader. Chino looked down and grinned at Amelia. "Someone's looking for you, girl." He pulled out his cell phone, punched in a number, and said, "We got her. On the road couple of miles south of town. What you want us to do?" There was a pause, then Chino nodded and said, "Right."

FIFTY-TWO

You Drive

Sole flipped the pages of the Field and Stream absently. The phone's sudden loud chiming reverberated inside the store. Jenks lifted it from the card table and answered. Sole listened to the instructions Jenks gave the caller. In the next few minutes, Sole's plan was either going to come together or unravel completely.

"Wait there," Jenks said. "Keep the girl safe. I'll come get her. You know what to do with the others."

He ended the call, looked at Axe, and motioned to Sole sitting behind the counter, the magazine spread open on his lap. "Take care of him."

Axe nodded, turned, and moved toward the front of the store, pulling a compact pistol from the belly holster under his shirt. Sole recognized the Walther PPK, .380 caliber, a good undercover weapon, a professional's gun.

Axe raised his arm. The magazine fell from Sole's lap, and Axe was looking into the barrel of Earl Jasso's coyote-killing shotgun.

The Ghost

Sole lifted the twelve gauge and shook his head. "Don't do it."

To Axe's credit and misfortune, he never hesitated. It wasn't the first time he'd looked into the muzzle of an enemy's weapon. His arm rose in a smooth, practiced motion to bring the pistol bear on his target. Most people flinch, hesitate for just an instant, freeze, or just back down when confronted by a determined adversary. Axe was counting on the man with the shotgun to react like most people.

Sole wasn't most people. He pulled the trigger at a range of ten feet, close enough that nine 00 buckshot pellets struck Axe in the chest. He went down hard before the roar finished echoing off the walls.

Behind him, Jenks stood exposed, pistol in hand, but he was wiser than Axe and lowered his arm. "It's you," he said.

"It's me." Sole nodded and motioned with the shotgun. "Put the gun on the floor and step toward me."

Outside, the one called Bear ran from the Dodge pickup to the door, pistol in hand. Crew and Don came running from their positions along the road. Bear took the time to gauge what was happening inside, saw Axe dead on the floor, the pool of blood, and the shotgun pointed at Jenks from a few feet away.

There were no good options. Rush in and Jenks would probably die before they could take out the shooter, who seemed to know what he was doing. Axe's bloody body was testimony to his ability. If Jenks went down too, their paycheck disappeared. The situation assessment lasted only a few seconds, and Bear motioned to the others to hold tight and not do anything rash.

Sole kept the shotgun pointed at Jenks and said, "Tell your men to go back to the truck, get in and drive north out of town, and do not come back. They have two minutes to disappear. If I see them after that, you'll join your friend there." He nodded at Axe's body.

Jenks shouted toward the door. "All three of you. Get in your truck and leave. Head north."

"And don't come back," Sole said, the shotgun barrel waving back and forth to emphasize the point.

"Don't come back!" Jenks added.

Leaning against the doorpost, peering through the window, Bear called back, "You sure?"

"I'm sure," Jenks said. "If you want to get paid, do what I said."

The three men exchanged glances. Bear led the way toward the truck. Crew hesitated as if he might attempt to rescue his boss and his paycheck. Jenks shouted, "Get the hell out of here! Now!"

Crew joined the others at the Dodge. Bear cranked the engine, backed into the road, and headed north.

"What now?" Jenks said. "You could have killed me, so you must want something else."

"Now we go get the girl, just like you told your man on the phone."

"That's it? You want the girl?" Jenks' brow wrinkled, then lifted in curiosity. "She means something to you ... girlfriend ... sister ... something?"

"Never met her," Sole said.

"Then why?"

Sole studied the puzzled look on Jenks' face and decided he didn't deserve an answer. Let him go on wondering. With one hand, he pulled the Colt from under his shirt, then laid the shotgun on the shelf under the counter and motioned to the door with the pistol. "Let's go."

"You know, I could use a man with your skills." Jenks

gave an appreciative nod. "You had me fooled, and I don't fool all that easily. Just one of the locals hanging out at the store. The shirt was a nice touch, grease on your chin, the other guy calling you Randy, the phone calls." Jenks paused and nodded. "How'd you get them to play along with you? That took some persuasive skill."

"Not so much. A mysterious stranger shows up in town, then his steely-eyed killers, followed by a gang of biker thugs. Didn't take much convincing at all. You already had them spooked. Once I explained things, helping me was the only logical alternative to get you out of town."

"Well, they're going to pay for that ... helping you."

Sole shook his head. "What makes you think you'll be around to make anyone pay?"

"Those men you just ran off, they know what to do. They'll come back, even if I told them not to. No witnesses, that's our first rule. They all know what to do, whether or not I'm here, and there are others."

"You mean your biker buddies?"

"You've been watching ... paying attention."

"I try to." Sole came from behind the counter. "That's where we're going now. I expect those bikers have the girl, so let's move it."

Sole motioned him outside with the pistol and checked up and down the road. The Dodge was nowhere in sight. He pointed at the Chevy. "You drive."

FIFTY-THREE

Something Ain't Right

Jenks disconnected. Chino shoved the phone back in his pocket, grinned at Chester and Cope, and shrugged. "Sorry, boys."

He nodded at two of the bikers. "Drag them out in the brush and do 'em."

"No!" Cope tried to push his way past the men toward Chino. One landed a fist on his jaw and he went down. He pulled himself up, tears streaming down his face. "You can't do it ... that wasn't the deal! Me and Jenks, we had a deal!"

"Don't know what to say, bro." Chino shrugged and grinned. "Deal's off."

"But ..." Cope's eyes darted around the circle of men, to Chester, to Amelia, his head swiveling back and forth in panic.

The bikers watched, grinning at the show. The terror in his eyes, the tears, the sweat dripping from his forehead. His panic had the circled gang members laughing and jeering.

"Grow some balls, cabrón!"

"Look at him ... like he gonna piss himself."

The Ghost

"Fuck, I think he did piss himself."

Cope made a dash through the ring of laughing men, running toward the mountains. He didn't get far.

Chino pulled his pistol. The bikers parted to give him a clear field of fire. Sighting along his arm to the end of the barrel, he aimed carefully and squeezed the trigger three times.

Cope went down writhing and screaming, but that didn't last long. Blood fountained from his left leg, saturating the ground around him, turning it into red muck. One of the bullets had punched through the back of his thigh and exited his groin, cutting the femoral artery. His heart spent the last few seconds of its existence pumping his life out into a crimson puddle.

Chester gaped and turned wide-eyed to Amelia. "Why'd they do that? Cope ain't such a bad guy. Gets grumpy, sure he does, but he don't mean nothin' by it. He's still my friend. They didn't have to do that."

Amelia reached a hand to touch his arm before the men jerked him up from the ground and led him away. Chester looked over his shoulder at Amelia, blood dripping from his battered face as he shuffled and stumbled along between them, the confusion in his eyes turning to fear.

She looked up at Chino, her face wet with tears. "Please, you don't have to do this. He's harmless."

"Maybe he is, maybe he isn't. Not my call." Chino shrugged. "Anyway, it's done." He nodded to the two men standing with Chester ten yards away, near a clump of sage.

Terrified, Chester looked at Amelia pleading as if she could change anything. She could only put her hands to her face and sob.

"Amelia, why they doin' this? Tell 'em they don't ..."

The bullet plowed through Chester's brain before he

finished the sentence. The crack of the pistol echoed up the canyon, and his body hit the ground like a two-hundred-pound sack of meat.

Amelia doubled over on her knees, her shoulders shaking with her sobs. "You didn't have to … you didn't have to do it. He was harmless."

Chino and his men stared at her with the mean curiosity of bullies, watching the suffering of a dog run over in the street, dying but not dead … yet. They looked up at the sound of a vehicle approaching. It was Jenks' Chevy.

"Stop here," Sole said, the pistol's muzzle inches away from Jenks' ribs.

Jenks stopped the pickup a hundred yards short of the bikers gathered on the side of the road. They were standing around a woman on her knees in the dirt.

It was Sole's first glimpse of Amelia Downes since this nightmare had begun. Her head shook as she rocked back and forth, as if in pain.

"If she's hurt," Sole warned, thumping Jenks in the ribs with the pistol barrel. "You won't like what comes next."

"She's not," Jenks said, rubbing his side. "I told them I was coming to get her. I need her." He shrugged and looked at the pistol. "*Needed* her anyway."

"I counted on that. Couldn't trust your thugs to make her disappear," Sole said. "Too many mistakes and you had to take care of that yourself. Make sure of things."

Jenks shrugged. "I pay attention to details."

"Here's a detail you missed," Sole said, thumping the gun into his ribs again. "You stand there by the side of the pickup, in the open door where I can see you, and tell the

The Ghost

leader of that group to bring her to you, alone. Then you tell them to leave, and that you'll settle up with them later."

"You really think this is going to work?" Jenks shook his head, chuckling.

"Up to you to sell it. They better buy it or you're the first one who goes down." Sole nodded at the door. "Now get it done."

Jenks pushed the door open and stepped out. He lifted an arm and waved.

"What the hell's going on?" Chino muttered.

"Bring her here to me!" Jenks called out. "Just you, Chino. No one else."

"Why's he doin' that?" one biker said. "Why don't he just come up here and get her?"

"Damned if I know." Chino shook his head. "This whole thing's been fucked up since the beginning." He looked around at the others and shrugged. "He got crazy-ass-white-dude-syndrome, is all."

They laughed. Chino grabbed Amelia by an arm, pulled her off her knees, and shouted back to Jenks, "Headed your way!"

The walk to the Chevy took less than a minute. As he approached, Chino could make out the silhouette of a man in the passenger seat. "Who's that with you?"

"Don't worry about him. He's with me," Jenks said. "Bring the girl here."

Chino walked forward, pulling Amelia by the arm. When they were ten feet from the front of the Chevy, Sole said. "Tell him to stop and the girl to keep coming."

"Stop there, Jenks said." He nodded at Amelia. "You come here."

"Where's my father?" she said, wiping the tears from her eyes. "What did you do to him?"

"I didn't do anything to him. If you want to see him, come here."

Jenks told the lie easily, the words slipping off his tongue like water off a duck's back. Sole listened, knowing that Amelia was going to find out the truth soon enough, but right now, she needed to get in the pickup, and if it took a lie, so be it.

Amelia stepped forward and Chino took a step with her. "Go back to your men now, Chino," Jenks said. "Meet me in Elko later today and we'll settle up." He gave a nod. "Good job."

Chino's eyes went from Jenks to the man in the passenger seat to the girl and back to Jenks. Something was up. Jenks was cool and calm as usual, but the dude in the passenger seat was saying something low enough that he couldn't hear it. Chino squinted, trying to see through the sun glare on the windshield. The passenger turned his head to look into Chino's face.

"I said get back to your men," Jenks ordered. "Everything's fine. I have business with this man ... loose ends to tie up. After that, I'll meet you in Elko at the office."

Chino stood there sizing things up for a few more seconds, then made up his mind and nodded his head. "Alright, *jefe*. We'll see you later. Have our money ready."

"I'll have it," Jenks said.

Chino turned and walked away, with the uneasy feeling the passenger's eyes were focused on the center of his back. Amelia took another step forward. "I don't care what you do to me. I just want to know about my father."

"Get in the back seat," Sole said loud enough for her to hear.

She came even with the open driver's door, looked in,

and saw the gun in the stranger's hand pointing at Jenks. "Who are you?"

"Your father sent me," Sole said. It was true enough for the moment. "Get in so we can get out of here. I'll explain everything when we're away and you're safe."

Amelia brushed past Jenks and pulled open the back crew door.

"Get in and drive," Sole said, the pistol barrel still leveled at Jenks.

"Where to?" Jenks said as he slid behind the wheel.

"Back to town … fast."

Jenks flipped a U-turn and stomped on the accelerator. Behind them, Chino and his gang watched the Chevy disappear around a bend in the road.

"Something ain't right," Chino said.

FIFTY-FOUR

It's Going to Get Loud

"What are you doing?" Crew looked at Bear behind the wheel of the Dodge super-duty.

"Going back," Bear said as he slowed and pulled the truck onto the shoulder.

"You ordered me in the truck." Crew's brow wrinkled. "We could have taken care of things while we were there like I wanted."

"That asshole had a gun on Jenks and he knew how to use it. You saw what he did to Axe." Bear turned to Crew, looked at Don in the back seat. "We want to get paid, we get Jenks back."

"So how do we do that?" Crew asked. "What's changed?"

"We go back, find Jenks, and take that asshole by surprise."

Bear turned the wheel, pulled forward, reversed, and pulled forward again to get the long-bed truck turned around on the narrow road and headed back toward Merchantville.

"Good." Crew nodded. "Didn't sit right with me leaving Axe like that."

Don said the first words he'd spoken since they left Merchantville. "We left witnesses behind."

"Where's my father?" Amelia asked, leaning forward in the back of the Chevy, overwhelmed with questions. "Why didn't he come? Where's Uncle Ron? How did they know where to send you? Why didn't they come with you?"

"I'll answer all your questions," Sole said, one eye watching Jenks and scanning the road ahead with the other. "First, there are some things I have to do, and I need you to come along ... just to keep you safe."

"I'm coming along," Amelia smirked. "Don't seem to have much choice about that. I traded one kidnapper for another."

"You're not kidnapped," Sole said over the seat, his voice sharper than he intended. "And I promise to tell you everything. Things are moving too fast right now for me to slow down and bring you up to speed. Just be patient for a little while longer," he added more gently.

"You got me away from those men," Amelia said, studying Sole's profile for some clue, some sign that he wasn't being honest with her. "I suppose I can trust you. I have no choice really."

"There's always a choice. You're not a prisoner, but if we want to get out of this alive, I need you to work with me."

Amelia nodded, deciding. "Alright. I'll be patient ... for a while." She turned her head to glare at Jenks. "They killed the others … Chester and Cope. They didn't deserve that. You ordered it, didn't you?"

Jenks kept his eyes on the road and said nothing. Sole gave him credit for not trying to make excuses. Engaging in conversation with Amelia was a dead-end road, with him likely being the one dead at the end of it.

They came into the Merchantville town limits, and Jenks took his foot off the accelerator. Sole shook his head and motioned with the Colt. "Don't slow down. Drive through town and I'll show you where to turn."

Jenks steered the Chevy past the store and garage and the houses and shacks dotting the hillsides. They came to the far end of the town limits, and Sole said, "There. That dirt road to the right. Turn there."

Jenks made the turn and slowed to survey the creviced road and steep slope. "What's up there?"

"Drive." Sole motioned with the pistol barrel, and Jenks drove.

They followed the trail Sole had driven up earlier, staying just below the hillcrest that overlooked Merchantville. He pointed ahead. "Park beside that pickup ahead, there near the top."

The Chevy rocked to a stop. Sole pushed his door open and stepped out, keeping the pistol's muzzle centered on Jenks. "Get out … here on my side."

Jenks complied without comment, climbing over the console and sliding out on the passenger side. As hostages went, he was turning out to be unusually cooperative, no doubt a consequence of his experience in being on the other side of the hostage equation. He had a pretty good understanding of the penalty for non-compliance.

Sole knew that made him more dangerous, not less. He could anticipate Sole's next moves, know what was coming.

The Ghost

There would come a moment when Jenks would know it was now or never, and he would do whatever he could to escape.

Amelia got out and came around the truck to stand beside Sole. He motioned to his pickup. "In the back, there's a bag. Inside are a bundle of zip ties. You know what they are.

"Yes."

"Grab a handful and bring them here."

She nodded and walked to the pickup, opened the crew cab door, and rummaged around in the back for a minute. Her head disappeared when she bent over to open the bag and popped back up a few seconds later. She slammed the door and came around the pickup holding a fistful of plastic zip ties. Sole kept them handy in case the cartel boys ever got on his trail again and he needed to cinch one up without putting a bullet in him.

"You know how to use those?"

"I do." She nodded.

"I'll cover him. You bind up his hands ... in front. Make them tight."

"In front?"

"Yes."

"What about his feet?"

"I'd like to, but no." Sole shook his head. "We've got to get over this hill, and he needs to be able to walk."

"Alright."

"Extend your arms," Sole said to Jenks. "All the way."

Jenks thrust his arms out in front. Amelia stood at the very limit of his reach, while Sole kept the pistol pointed at him. She looped a zip-tie around each wrist and tightened them down until they dug into the flesh. Then she joined the two zip-ties together with a third. With his hands secured together, she took a fourth tie as an extra measure and looped it around both wrists, and pulled it hard, tightening until Jenks winced.

She stepped back to admire her work and looked at Sole. "I'd still feel better if we could tie up his feet. I want the bastard helpless."

"Maybe later," Sole said. "Right now, we have to move."

"Mind if I ask what's over the hill? Why don't we just get in your truck and get the hell out of here?"

"Some people down there helped us. They're in danger."

"Because of me," Amelia said.

"Not you," Sole corrected and nodded at Jenks. "Because of him."

"But they were trying to help me, so, let's go." Amelia started toward the hillcrest.

"Wait," Sole said. He motioned Jenks up the hill ahead of them. At the crest, he knelt to survey the scene below, then pointed. "That ruins there, the one partially collapsed. That's where we're going." He looked at Jenks. "You first. Get moving."

Sole understood the look in his eyes, wondering if now was his chance. Jenks looked at the pistol, then into Sole's eyes and decided not yet. He nodded and started down the hill toward the ruins Sole had selected as his fallback position.

They scrambled down the slope to the back of the building, sliding the last few feet on their rumps. Sole waved them inside. He pointed to a corner inside the portion of leaning walls that were still upright and motioned Jenks in that direction. "Sit there."

Jenks walked over, turned his back to the wall, and slid down until he sat in the dirt, giving the ruins a quick assessment as he moved. Good fields of fire down to the road and across to the opposite hillside. No close cover for anyone trying to flank the position. Concealed firing positions behind the still-standing part of the building. It all confirmed that the man pointing the .45 at him was a professional.

Sole nodded at Amelia and motioned to the duffel he'd left in the corner earlier. "Get the pistol out of the duffel."

She retrieved it, holding it down, finger off the trigger. Another good sign. She had some familiarity with firearms. She looked at Sole and cast a glance in Jenks' direction. "What do you want me to do?"

Sole had the feeling she hoped he would tell her to put the pistol barrel against Jenks' forehead and pull the trigger. He hadn't decided what to do with Jenks just yet, but they might need him still, and now was not the time to satisfy her need for revenge.

"That's a Glock 22, .40 caliber. Whoever you hit with it will go down. Hit them in the right spot, and they won't get up again. You keep it pointed at him."

He turned to Jenks. "You see the look in her eye. She would like nothing more than to empty that magazine into your worthless carcass. Sit there and don't cause problems or I'll give her the nod and let her do it."

Jenks smirked but said nothing. His eyes moved around the space like an animal searching for an escape from the hunter's trap.

"My father," Amelia said, her eyes never leaving Jenks. "What about my father and Uncle Ron? You said you would tell me where they are."

"I will, I promise," Sole said and then added truthfully, "but right now the shit's about to hit the fan, and I need you to focus on him while I take care of business."

He lifted the .30-06 and moved to a sagging window in the still-upright part of the structure. Standing a couple of feet inside, where he would be invisible to anyone outside in the sun, he scanned the town below. He had cut the timing too close.

Below, a man descended the hillside and walked along the road to the Brandt's Store. He disappeared inside for a few seconds, then emerged to scan up and down the road, looking for Earl. He went to the side of the store and shouted something up the hill toward the Jasso house, then went back inside. A couple of minutes later, he reappeared with a sack of items.

"Hurry up," Sole whispered. "Get out."

The man ambled along the road casually. He stopped once to lean back and watch a passing hawk, then he knelt and picked up something interesting from the dirt. All the while, the sack swung from his fingers in a carefree way, like a boy walking home from school dangling his book bag.

The man reached the path up the hillside to his trailer, when the sound of a roaring engine caught his attention. He turned to see what the commotion was. The Dodge was back. It skidded to a stop in front of the store. The driver and one of the men jumped out and went into the store, guns in their hands.

The man with the sack saw the guns, dropped his sack, and started to run up the hill toward his trailer, but he was older and not making good time. The third man from the super-duty truck trotted down the road after him. He'd be in pistol range in seconds.

"Shit." Sole lifted the rifle to his shoulder and said to Amelia, "Keep the gun on Jenks. It's going to get loud."

FIFTY-FIVE

Battle of Merchantville

Earl and Ellen Jasso watched from the front windows of their house on the hill behind the store. Joe Flack had taken up position outside behind the six cords of firewood Earl kept stacked to feed the wood burner during the winter.

They watched the Chevy pull through town and keep going. Joe wondered about that until he spotted three people making their way down from the opposite hillcrest. One was a woman. He nodded, good. Amelia Downes was safe. One of the others was the man who had come into the store to wait and play solitaire. The third was the man he only knew as John.

A few minutes later, the oversized Dodge super-duty pickup cruised back into town from the north. Three men got out. Two went into the store. One followed old Tom Stocks who had come into the store, probably to pick up something for dinner, bologna and a couple of beers. Tom saw the guns and started running, but Joe could tell it was too late.

"Tom, run!" he shouted, mostly because he didn't know

what else to do, but Tom was already running from the man with the gun. Joe stepped from behind the woodpile to do what he could to help with Winchester .30-30 he'd borrowed from Earl, but he knew the distance was too great for him to be much help. He raised the rifle to his shoulder and then lowered it, muttering, "Holy shit."

It was not a shot Sole wanted to take. The man below was moving laterally, across his field of vision, making the shot more difficult, and with every step he took, it became more difficult. He relaxed, found his target in the scope, calculated the distance to lead him, exhaled, and squeezed the trigger.

The hundred-and-sixty-five grain bullet smacked into his side just as he raised the pistol to fire at the old man running toward his trailer. He went down but was still moving, trying to bring the pistol up again. Sole put another round in him and he lay still.

The old man stopped and fell to the ground when the .30-06 thundered down the valley. He squirmed over on his side and saw his pursuer lying motionless, the pistol still in his hand, then looked up at the hillsides, trying to find the shooter. Whoever it was, wasn't shooting at him, so he pushed himself up, half crawling, half running the rest of the way to his trailer.

"Good," Sole said and swung the rifle back toward the store.

The men with the pistols came out from the store and saw their man down and not moving. Knowing his unseen assailant outgunned them, they turned back-to-back, providing cover for each other, scanning the hills and buildings, moving toward the super-duty pickup to make their escape.

Sole couldn't let that happen. It was only a matter of time before they returned with more firepower to finish what they had started, eliminating anyone who saw them. He put the scope's crosshairs on the one facing his direction. A roar of engines filled the air and a second later, the view of his target was blocked. Trigger discipline kicked in, and he didn't take the shot. Then he wished he had.

The bikers were back, pulling up around the men from the super-duty, blocking Sole's shot. He'd hoped to avoid taking on the bikers. Three to one were reasonably acceptable odds. Fifteen to one was stretching things.

Below, Chino pulled up beside Bear, crouching back-to-back with Don beside the super-duty. "What you boys doin'?" He smirked at the two men, eyeing the surrounding hills. "Look like you seen a ghost."

"Axe is dead," Bear said. "Inside the store. Crew is lying in the dirt up the road with two bullets in him."

The grin left Chino's face, and he was off his bike, crouching beside Bear and Don. "Who did the shooting?"

"Don't know who, but it came from up there somewhere." Bear nodded at the hills across from the store.

Chino's men were off their motorcycles now, pistols out, all crouching behind their bikes and watching the hillsides. "We need to get the fuck out of here."

"We were about to do that when you showed up." Bear looked at Chino's men. "But we have enough manpower now to take on whoever it is. You know how it goes ... no witnesses. We eliminate the shooter and everyone else who saw anything today."

"That could be the whole fucking town," Chino said and turned to look at the scattered shacks on the hillsides.

"Everyone who saw anything," Bear repeated.

"Where's Jenks?" Chino squinted through the plate-glass window into the store. "He came and got the girl from us." He shook his head in disgust. "Dammit, I knew something wasn't right ... had some dude in the pickup with him. That's why we came back ... to check things out."

"Probably the shooter," Bear said, putting things together. "There was a guy in the store, the one who killed Axe ... had a gun on Jenks and he told us to get out of town. We get him and we'll find Jenks ... and get paid."

"Right." Chino nodded. He looked at the bikers crouching around him, eyeing the hillsides. "Spread out. We're goin' up that hill and find the motherfucker."

There were no heroes in the crowd. The men looked at each other but stayed down.

"Extra thousand to the man who kills him. Move!" Chino shouted. "We all go at the same time and he won't know where to take a shot. Get your asses up!"

"C'mon boys. Hop on those bikes and get the hell out of Dodge," Sole muttered, watching from above, then a second later said, "Damnit." Their leader had them up and moving across the road toward the hill. He looked over his shoulder at Amelia. "Get ready. Whatever happens, keep that gun on Jenks."

Amelia nodded without speaking. She flinched when the .30-06 thundered and reverberated off the old plank walls, but never took her eyes off Jenks.

They were spread out in a line moving up the hillside. Sole picked off the one closest to his hiding place. The biker went down face first. Another grabbed the pistol from his hand, tucked it in his belt, and continued up the hillside. Sole put him down ten feet from his comrade and then swung the barrel to the next man to the left. The battle plan was simple. Take out the greatest threats first. Bikers who were closest to the ramshackle building were the most likely to reach the ruins and overrun them, so he picked them off in that order, closest first, then next closest, and so on.

Three were down when one jumped up and began running down the hill to escape. Sole centered the crosshair on his back, but before he could squeeze the trigger, the leader of the group was up and firing at him, emptying his pistol until the biker stumbled and slid down the slope like a sack of dirty laundry.

"Fucking *pendejo!*" Chino shouted below. "Anybody runs, I'll kill him." He pointed up the hill. "You want to live, get that motherfucker!"

No one else ran. The bikers began moving up the hill again. They were amateurs at this kind of fighting, but they were smart enough to use the sound of the rifle fire to triangulate their attacker's location. The men on either end of their advance turned to the sound of gunfire as they heard it, effectively pinpointing Sole's position. The leader pointed at the old ruins. Sole sent a round his way, but too late. The bandanna-wearing biker ducked into a crease in the hillside.

They began sending pistol rounds through the walls of the ruins, forcing Sole to take cover. The range was too great for the fire to be effective, and the uphill angle of attack sent most of the rounds high. But enough came through the planks to force him to keep his head down.

Sole moved from one shooting point to another inside the ruins, exposing himself briefly, searching for targets. With the odds stacked heavily against him, every shot had to count. A roar and five were down. Another roar, the sixth went down.

The leader below motioned for the remainder of his men to move out and converge on the ruins from opposite sides. It took a while for them to figure that out, but they were flanking him.

Sole swung the rifle from one side to the other, sending rounds downhill to keep their heads down until he found a target. Two bikers crouched behind a sage, well-concealed but vulnerable. Sole sent a round through the center of the bush and one biker dropped. The other scrambled away on his knees. Sole worked the bolt and threw a snap shot after him, but it kicked up dirt without hitting flesh. The biker disappeared, rolling into a gully. Sole waited for him to put his head up, but he was smart enough not to expose himself again. Sole swung, looking for another target.

Jenks watched the action from the corner, staring into the Glock's barrel. If he was going to make a move, it would have to be soon. He had no faith that Chino and his men were going to overrun the shooter.

"You know, he killed your father," Jenks said, looking into Amelia's eyes behind the pistol barrel.

Her brow furrowed. "What?"

That got her attention. Jenks nodded at Sole across the space, peering into the scope, searching for a target. "You wanted to know what happened to your father. Why do you think he hasn't said anything?" He nodded. "Because he killed him ... and the other, Ron Benson."

"You're lying." Amelia put another hand on the Glock's grip to steady herself. "You're the one trying to get the mine."

"I'm not lying." Jenks shook his head. "We want the mine, that's true, but there are limits to what we'll do to get it. He has no limits. Look at him. He'll kill anyone who gets in his way, and he's using you to get the mine. He killed your father and his partner so that the mine will go to you, and then ..." He shrugged. "Figures you'll think he's your savior, but once you have the mine, and he has your trust, what do you think will happen to you?" Jenks shrugged. "Believe what you will, but he killed your father. That's the truth."

It was just a fleeting moment, an instant of doubt. Even knowing that Jenks' men had killed Chester and Cope, Amelia wavered for the briefest of moments, but it was enough. Her eyes shifted away from Jenks toward Sole as the rifle roared again and another biker went down. Jenks sprang up and hit her low with his shoulder, bowling her over, and then continued through a gap in the planks.

"Dammit," Sole muttered through gritted teeth and swiveled to send a round after Jenks.

Hands bound in front, Jenks only made it twenty feet down the slope before he stumbled and fell. That saved his life. Behind him, the .30-06 roared, kicking up dirt near his head. It didn't stop him. His forward momentum carried him into a roll, tumbling down the hill.

Chino and his men saw what was happening and intensified their firing at the ruins. Sole turned to find Amelia staring at him, the Glock pointed in his direction.

"He said you killed my father," she said.

"I didn't. He lied to get away." He'd wanted to wait for a better time to tell her everything, but the way things were going, there might not be any more time for either of them. He nodded at the pistol in her hand. "Make up your mind. Your father is dead, but he sent me to find you before he died. That's the truth. Now, you can use that pistol on me or get ready. They are going to flank us." Sole swung the rifle back to the opening in the walls, looking for a target as a volley of pistol rounds tore through the planks. "

She stared at him for a moment and brushed the tears from her eyes with the back of her hand. She'd known her father was dead ... suspected it at least ... had suspected it since the shooting they heard up on the mountain. "Alright," she said, deciding. "What do you want me to do?"

Sole spoke without taking his eyes off the hillside below. "Put your back against the rocks over there and stay out of sight. If you see one of them come over the side or around the back, put a round in him, then look for another and do the same. I'll try to take out as many as I can with the rifle."

"Are we going to die here?"

"Maybe." The rifle roared, and a bullet zipped down the slope, just missing a biker as he flattened himself behind a rock. Sole worked the bolt, loaded another round, and a second later the rifle roared again. This time, the biker went down. Sole swung, searching for more targets.

They were closer now, advancing in rushes, taking cover, and rushing forward again. As they closed in, he lost his advantage. At a distance, he could track multiple targets in his peripheral vision as he dealt with the most immediate threat, but with each shot, the survivors came closer. He lost sight of those to the far right and left, and the closer they came, the more his field of vision narrowed, forcing him to expose himself to find the next threat and eliminate it.

A sudden flurry of lead buzzed through the ruins. He crouched behind the foundation and glanced at Amelia. She followed his example, pushing herself lower behind the rocks. Across from her, a head appeared above the rocks. She waited, pistol steady in her hand. The biker's torso rose above the rocks now. Sole reached for the .45 in his belt, thinking she might freeze.

She didn't. The Glock bucked in her hand, and the biker went down, dead or dying. She swung toward another target coming around the back of one of the standing walls and sent three cracking rounds in his direction. The biker disappeared, condition unknown but no longer an immediate threat.

A bullet slammed into the rocks beside Sole's head, kicking up splinters that stung his eyes. The next instant, white-hot fire seared his right arm. He tried to transfer the .45 to his left hand and turn to face his attacker, but it was too late. The biker leader, the one who had delivered Amelia to Jenks, came around the back of the ruins.

Chino saw the man on the ground, his right arm bleeding and useless, struggling to get a grip on the .45 with his left. Chino grinned and raised his pistol. "You mine now, motherfucker. Gonna be a bonus for taking you out, *cabrón*."

Two sharp cracks echoed through the ruins, followed by the metallic click of the hammer striking an empty chamber. Amelia was out of ammo, but not before Chino fell, two bullets through his chest. Her arm remained frozen in position, the pistol still pointing to the place where the biker leader had been standing.

"Reload," Sole said to bring her out of it. He nodded at the duffel. "There's another magazine."

Amelia crawled to the duffel.

Holding the .45 in his left hand, Sole chanced a look through the planks, searching for the other bikers. The three survivors were kicking up dust as they scrambled and tumbled down the slope. They climbed onto their motorcycles and roared out of town.

Sole relaxed, peering through the gaps in the planks. The first battle of Merchantville had ended. Gunfire signaled that the second had begun.

FIFTY-SIX

Second Battle of Merchantville

Things were tense in the house on the hill. In the few hours since coffee, Merchantville had become a scene out of an old B-Movie, complete with a motorcycle gang raiding the town and gangsters trying to murder the residents.

Ellen and Earl were not easily convinced to go along with the plan and not call in the sheriff. After leaving the store, Joe had barged into the house without knocking. He nodded at the closet by the hall to the bedrooms. "That's where you keep your guns, isn't it?"

"You know it is," Earl Jasso replied. "Why do we need them? Start talking."

"Don't know why for sure, but there's a fella who came to the garage and seems pretty certain of it."

"What in holy hell is going on?" Ellen demanded. "Start explaining yourself Joe Flack, or get your ass back down the hill."

Joe walked past them to the closet and jerked the door open. He rummaged around inside for a second and handed a rifle back to Earl while he felt around for another

The Ghost

gun. "Here, take the .270. I'll handle the .30-30." He turned and held out a Remington twelve-gauge to Ellen. "You take care of anyone who gets close."

"Give me that." Ellen snatched the rifle from Earl. "With your eyes the way they are, I'm a better shot at a distance. You take the shotgun." She turned to Joe. "Dammit. Start talking before I turn this rifle on you for getting us all stirred up."

"Alright." Joe took a breath. "Here's how it is."

A few minutes later, Earl shook his head. "Jake Downes and Ron Benson dead ... murdered. I can't believe it."

"And Amelia kidnapped," Joe said.

"You think we can trust this John fella who came to the garage?" Ellen asked. "What if he's part of it all?"

"I think we have to trust him," Joe said. He looked at Earl. "That stranger who came in, the one playing solitaire and then the others in that big pickup, they seemed kind of dark don't you think?"

"I suppose so." Earl nodded, thinking over his interaction with the stranger.

"What do you mean, dark?" Ellen said.

"I don't know ... you probably know a better word for it ... you know, some people just make you kind of worry, scared even without saying or doing anything outright threatening."

"Ominous," Ellen said. "You're saying he was ominous."

"That's it!" Joe smiled. "That man was ominous, that's what he was for sure."

"But the one who came to the garage and took you by surprise, this John fella, he wasn't ominous." Ellen shook her head, sending a doubtful look in his direction.

"Well, I won't deny, he gave me a start, but no ..." Joe

shook his head. "He wasn't ominous ... more like ..." He looked up, thinking, and then said, "Business-like. That's what he was. A man with a job to do but not a threat to anyone who didn't get in the way of that job."

"Seems awful strange," Ellen muttered. "Business-like, but he doesn't want us to call the law."

"No law," Joe said, shaking his head for emphasis. "He said we could call the sheriff in when this was settled, but to have a chance to get Amelia back alive, we had to keep the law out of the way. He believes these men will kill her if they get a whiff of any kind of law."

"They might kill her anyway," Earl interjected. "Might already have."

"True." Joe nodded. "But this John, he said he couldn't be sure of that and that he thought she was probably still alive because the guy in charge would want to do it himself and make sure no one could find her body, and he didn't trust the people he'd sent out to do his dirty work because they'd already fu ..." He shot an apologetic look at Ellen. "Already screwed things up pretty bad."

"Alright then." Earl nodded and looked at Ellen. "I say let's wait and see what happens. We're safe enough up here where we can keep an eye on things. If we need to, we can call the sheriff."

"If they've got Amelia, I'd like to see her back safe," Ellen said, nodding. "But the first sign that things aren't what this John fella said, we call the sheriff."

"Fair enough," Earl said.

Things happened quickly after that. They took up positions at the windows and Joe went out by the woodpile. A few minutes later, the shotgun blast echoed up the hill from the store. Then the three men left in the super-duty truck, followed by the stranger and John taking the Chevy and heading in the opposite direction.

"What do you make of that?" Earl called from the window to Joe.

"Don't know, but four men came in that truck and three left."

"You think that's it? It's over now?"

"Let's wait a spell and see what happens," Joe called back.

They didn't have long to wait. A few minutes later, the Chevy cruised back through town. After that, they spotted three people come over the opposite hill and down to the ruins of the old Merchantville Hotel. Then, the big Dodge truck rolled back into town from the north, moving slow, cautious-like, Joe thought.

The shot that saved the life of old Tom Stock and killed the man with the pistol who was bearing down on him awed all three. At the same time that Joe exclaimed, "Holy shit!", Earl gave out an admiring proclamation. "That son of a bitch can shoot."

Then the bikers arrived, and all hell broke loose on the opposite slope.

The two survivors from the Dodge seemed content to let the bikers take on the man with the rifle. They focused on the house up the hill. Separating, they wisely avoided a direct approach, circling around opposite sides of the hill.

"Get ready," Joe called. "They're trying to flank us and come up on the sides so we won't see them until the last second."

"We're ready," Earl replied and looked at Ellen. "You watch the front. I'll watch the side and back. Joe's got the other side."

"Right," she nodded and slid the rifle's bolt back and

pushed it forward, sending a round into the chamber. "You be careful, Earl Jasso."

"You too, Ellen Jasso." He looked at her, peering out the window, holding the rifle at port arms and smiled, then he found a spot near a side window where he could see anyone circling to the rear. The shotgun didn't have much range, but it would do some permanent damage if they got close enough.

Joe moved along the woodpile, trying to keep an eye on the one circling to his side of the house. When the man was about a hundred yards off, Joe raised quickly and fired a round, but missed. "Shit, you're getting old," he grumbled as he ducked back behind the pile.

An instant later, a flurry of bullets zipped and snapped into the stacked wood, sending splinters into the air to cascade down on him. Joe knew it was suppressing fire, intended to force him to stay down while the man from the Dodge advanced closer. Armed with a pistol and up against the .30-30, the man was outgunned, and knew it but, but he was a killer and not about to leave. If got closer, within pistol range, the advantage would be his.

It was time to move. Joe crawled along the woodpile and then, shielded by it, made a dash to the corner of the house, where he could watch the woodpile and the slope to the side. He prayed the man from the Dodge had not seen him move, levered a round into the .30-30, and waited.

It took a few minutes. The man with the pistol moved toward his target cautiously, dashing forward and then taking cover, then dashing forward again. He reached the woodpile and came around the end, holding his pistol in front in a two-handed combat posture. There was only the briefest flutter of surprise on his face to find no one there.

Then he swiveled to find Joe staring at him over the Winchester's sights.

Joe gave him no time to react. He squeezed the trigger. The man went down, but Joe was taking no chances. He levered another round into the chamber and sent a second bullet into the body crumpled on the ground by the woodpile.

Then he crouched again by the corner of the house, feeling exposed, his position given away by the gunfire. There was another attacker somewhere on the hill, and Joe hadn't seen him since they separated to flank the house.

Peering out the side window, Earl glimpsed movement, a man running in a crouch through the sage and then kneeling out of sight. He waited for the man to come closer, but the attacker was taking his time, waiting for the right opportunity to approach.

It seemed to be a standoff for several minutes. When the shooting started by the woodpile, the man popped his head up for an instant, then ducked back down, unwilling to leave his concealment without knowing what was happening inside the house.

"Ellen, fire some rounds," Earl whispered.

"What?" She looked over her shoulder, eyes narrowed.

"Fire four or five shots out the window down the hill, then take cover."

"What am I firing at?"

"Nothing. Just shoot down the hill real fast, one after the other, then get over behind the sofa."

"I don't …"

"Just do it!" Earl said sharply.

"I'll do it, but don't be talking to me in that tone, Earl Jasso."

She stood in the window and fired off a round, worked

the bolt and fired again until she'd sent five rounds down the slope. Then she moved behind the sofa in the corner. Earl nodded, a grim smile on his face. "Good."

Outside, the man with the gun rose at the sound of the rapid firing and charged across the last twenty yards to the back door. A second later, the door crashed open, and he rushed in, his pistol in front and ready, searching for a target. His eyes widened with sudden understanding—he'd made a serious mistake.

Standing ten feet away, Earl held the shotgun to his shoulder and pulled the trigger. Thunder filled the small house. Bear fell backward against the wall, his chest a bloody pulp, the pistol still clenched in his dead hand. The second battle of Merchantville had ended.

FIFTY-SEVEN

One More Thing to Do

It was a debacle. Jenks was fuming. In all his years of conducting *special operations* for employers, never had one fallen apart so completely, unraveling like a ball of twine tossed over a cliff.

Peter Jenks rolled down the hill from the ruins and landed hard in the ditch by the road. He lay low while the gunfire roared around him, letting the realization sink in. His days as the go-to person for companies like Entente were finished. It was time to cut bait and get the hell out.

He poked his head above the ditch. Chino and his men were advancing up the hill, but he knew they were outmatched by the man with the rifle. They were thugs. He was a killer.

He turned. The Dodge super-duty was still parked near the store. Axe's surviving men, Bear and Don, were making their way up the opposite slope. They were soldiers, following orders to the end, and also aware that their paycheck depended on getting Jenks out of the line of fire. So be it.

He waited for the firing to increase up the hill, his signal that Amelia Downes' rescuer was occupied. He made a dash from the ditch to the Dodge, scurried around the side away from the shooting, and lay on his back. It only required a minute of hard scraping against the truck's exposed sheet metal edges on the underside to cut through the zip-ties binding his hands together.

Pulling open the passenger door, he stayed low and looked at the dash. The keys were still there, as he knew they would be. It was an operational protocol in the event escape was necessary and the driver was incapacitated, and at the moment, escape was a definite necessity.

Jenks climbed behind the wheel, started the engine, backed away from the store, and sped north out of Merchantville. Behind him, the gunfire faded. If he felt any guilt about abandoning the men he'd thrown into harm's way, the relief that he would survive overshadowed it.

Sole watched from above. With his right arm injured, the .30-06 was useless at any distance. Damnit. He'd wanted to end this today, here in Merchantville.

He slumped back against the rock foundation, exhausted. He'd been going almost non-stop since meeting Jake and Ron on the Turnbridge Road.

"Here, let me see that." Amelia reached for his arm and lifted it gently to examine the wound. "Bend your elbow and move your fingers," she said.

Sole nodded and winced as he moved his arm.

"Good," she said. "I don't think anything is broken. Bleeding pretty good, but we can stop that."

"Hurts like hell," he said.

"I expect it does." Amelia worked efficiently, tearing a strip of cloth from the bottom of her shirt and removing the duffel's shoulder strap to wrap over the wound and staunch the bleeding.

She gave the strap a tug, tightening it down. Sole winced but said, "Thanks. Good field dressing."

She ignored the compliment. Eyes narrowed and her voice hard, she said, "Start talking."

Sole talked, walking her through his encounter with her father and Ron Benson. Their efforts to find her. Finding them on the trail to the cabin, her father dead and Ron dying. He went through all of it, watching her eyes, not certain she believed it, not sure he would believe it if he were in her place. When he finished, he waited for her to say something.

Amelia remained silent for a long while, tears sliding down her cheeks. She'd known that her father and Ron must be dead or they would have been here with this man. She looked at him, her brow furrowed. "I don't even know your name."

"John," he said.

"That's it? Just John."

"That's it."

"Alright, John. We need to get you to a doctor. I suppose they'll pry more out of you there."

"No doctor." He shook his head. "They'll ask questions … want to know things about me … things I don't want them to know. They'll get the law involved." He shook his head again. "No doctor."

"You've been shot."

"Not the first time, and like you said, nothing is broken. It'll heal up."

"Fine. If that's the way you want it. I guess we're done here." She stood. "Can I get a ride with you back to Elko?"

"Why?"

"Because I'm going to the sheriff and tell him everything. They murdered my father and Uncle Ron. Someone is going to pay."

"Someone will pay." Sole nodded. "Help me up. There's one more thing to do."

Turner Bates was still on the basement floor, the air around him pungent with the odor of stale urine. Entente's Senior VP and Head of Business Development had pissed himself. He started sobbing when Sole and Amelia came down the stairs.

"Thank, God. I didn't think you were coming back!"

Sole stood over him, the ski mask pulled down over his face, his injured right arm hanging at his side, and the Colt in his left hand. "Do you want to live?"

"Oh, God ... yes! Please! I don't want to die!" Bates' eyes moved beyond Sole and saw Amelia. He started shaking his head rapidly. "I had nothing to do with it. I swear to God, I had nothing to do with it!"

"With what?" Amelia said quietly.

"With killing your father, with kidnapping you ... with any of it."

"But you knew what happened to my father," she said, her voice quieter still and threatening. "You knew and you let it happen ... said nothing about it ... didn't try to stop it." A new thought occurred to her and her eyebrows lifted in curiosity. "Or maybe you ordered it and Jenks was the one you gave the orders to."

"No! No! I swear it!" His head nearly swung off his

The Ghost

shoulders, shaking back and forth in denial. "It was Jenks. It was always Jenks! I could never do anything like that."

"But as long as you got the mine for your bosses, you were content to let him do what he thought it took to intimidate my father and Uncle Ron."

"No one was supposed to be hurt." Bates' lips trembled as he spoke. "Intimidate, yes. But not murder ... not kidnapping." His pleading eyes moved to the Glock in her hand. "Please ... I'm begging you. Don't kill me."

"Whether or not you live depends on you."

"What do you want me to do?" Bates was sobbing again. "I'll do anything. Just say it."

"This all ends," Amelia said. "Threats, intimidation, dirty dealings." She shook her head. "The whole rotten, corrupt empire that Entente has built is coming down, and you're going to bring it down ... if you want to live."

"I do! I'll do anything! Just tell me what to do."

Amelia took a cell phone from her pocket, turned on the voice recorder, and said, "This is Amelia Downes. I am with Turner Bates of Entente Mining Corporation. Mr. Bates has agreed to make a statement." She extended the hand holding the phone toward Bates. "Is that right, Mr. Bates?"

"Yes ... yes, that is correct. I want to tell everything."

"Alright then." Amelia nodded. "Then why don't you start at the beginning. Tell me about the methods Entente has used against my father and Ron Benson to acquire their mine."

Bates started talking and didn't stop for an hour. He told it all. Jenks sending men to intimidate and threaten ... the kidnapping ... the murders of Jake Downes and Ron Benson ... the bikers and killers sent to find Amelia ... what would have happened to her if Jenks got his hands on her ... all of it.

When he finished, Amelia turned off the recorder and looked at Sole, who had listened silently. He stepped forward, the pistol still in his left hand, but raised now.

"Nooo!" Bates' voice rose to a terrified shriek. "You said if I talked, you wouldn't kill me!"

"I have one more question for you," Sole said.

Epilogue

They left Bates on the basement floor of the Entente building, still bound, still sobbing, and begging for his life. When they got back to the pickup, Sole had to stop to lean against the side, breathing heavily. He reached out his hand. "Give me the key."

"Nope," Amelia said, shaking her head. "I drove us here from Merchantville, and I'll drive us away."

"No," he shook his head weakly. "I need to go away, and you have things to do." He nodded at the cell phone still in her hand.

"That will keep for a couple of hours. Right now, you are in shock and in no shape to be driving. That was a good show you put on for Bates, but you can barely stand up."

She was right, and he was in no condition to argue about it. He nodded and climbed into the passenger seat.

She drove them back to Turnbridge and up to her cabin on a mountainside overlooking the town. Once inside, she got him stretched out on a bed, and said, "Alright, now I have some business to tend to."

Amelia left him and hiked down the trail to the D&B mine office. From the phone there, she called the sheriff's direct number. His assistant answered and let her know the sheriff was out on a major incident up in Merchantville. Amelia thanked her, went outside, and climbed into one of the mine's service trucks.

When she arrived on the outskirts of Merchantville, deputies had the road blocked. One held up his hand and stood in front of her truck. "Sorry. Road closed. No one in or out."

"I need to see the sheriff," Amelia said.

"Sorry." The deputy shook his head. "Can't let you in. We have a major crime scene here."

"I know that." Amelia smiled.

"Then you know I can't let …"

She interrupted and said, "I killed two men up there … maybe three. I'm not certain about one. Biker types who came riding into town."

The deputy's mouth hung open in mid-sentence. He leaned forward. "Who are you?"

"Amelia Downes." She motioned with her head back up the road in the direction where the bikers gunned down Chester and Cope. "You'll find two more bodies up the road in the brush. I drove by them on the way here. You didn't see them in the dark, but they're there."

The deputy spoke into the microphone hanging from his uniform shirt epaulet. "Sheriff, there's someone here you need to speak to."

The interview lasted for hours. They sat on folding chairs in Earl Jasso's store, sipping soft drinks from the cooler and leaving money to pay on the counter. By the time Amelia finished telling her story and playing the recording of Bates' confession, the investigators from the Nevada Department of Public Safety arrived and joined in on the questioning, and there were a lot of questions.

At first, most were about the fight in Merchantville, then they focused on the murders of Jake Downes and Ron Benson. Finally, the questioning turned to Entente's tactics. That's when the Feds showed up, and she repeated it. Once again, she gave her account of the kidnapping, murders of her father and Ron Benson, the fight with the bikers and killers in Merchantville, the recording of Bates' confession.

It had been dark for hours when she finally said, "I need to leave, now."

"That's understandable." The FBI special agent nodded. "You've had a trying day … several trying days. It's late. We'll put you in a hotel room in Elko. Tomorrow we'll have some more questions for you."

"No, I'll drive myself home to Turnbridge."

"That's probably not a good idea," the agent said sympathetically. "You shouldn't be alone right now after the trauma you've experienced."

"Am I under arrest?"

"No, no." The agent shook her head. "There doesn't seem to be any reason to bring charges against you. You shot those bikers in self-defense. That was corroborated by the residents in Merchantville. So, no, you're not under arrest. It's just protocol that when someone has suffered a trauma like …"

"I don't give a shit about your protocol." Amelia stood up. "I want to be alone. I want to sleep in my own bed with nobody to tell me what to do or where I can go, or watch me take a pee." She stepped around the table. "I'm leaving."

"Alright," the agent said mildly. "I can understand that."

"Doesn't matter to me whether you understand or not." Amelia pulled open the store's front door.

"Where can we find you if we have more questions?"

"My father and I have a house in Turnbridge next door to the mine offices. You can find me there."

The sheriff insisted on providing an escort back to Turnbridge, and Amelia accepted. When the deputies left her at the house beside the mine, she waited until they had disappeared around the bend and hiked back up to the cabin.

She'd been gone almost twelve hours by the time she got back to the cabin. Sole was still on the bed, but he was awake. He smiled when she walked in. "Thought you abandoned me."

"Not a chance," she said and sat on the edge of the bed. "You look better … relatively speaking."

He smiled. "I feel better … relatively speaking."

The investigation lasted for weeks. Sometimes Amelia would go into Elko to meet with the sheriff, or the state investigators, or the Feds. Sometimes they would meet with her at the house in Turnbridge or at the mine office, where she was trying to get things up and running again. She kept them away from her cabin up on the mountainside.

Lots of questions were asked about the mysterious man who rescued her and took on the bikers in Merchantville. He was a key witness, and every law enforcement agency involved was desperate to speak with him. It seemed fairly certain that he killed the men who killed Jake Downes and Ron Benson. As for his whereabouts, Amelia said he disappeared after taking her to record Turner Bates' account of things. They couldn't break her story.

"So, you want us to believe that this complete stranger rescued you, tied everything up in a package with the recording of Bates, then disappeared ... a phantom in the night." The special agent's lips turned down in a skeptical frown. "And you have no idea where he is."

"He said my father sent him," Amelia said and looked hard into the agent's eyes. "He was there for me ... didn't give up until he found me, saved me from what they were going to do. Then he left. That's all I know."

In the end, they had no reason to disbelieve her. Except for her rescuer's identity, every aspect of her story was verified. Being held captive in the cabin, the escape through the mountains on foot, the murders of Chester and Cope, the attack by the bikers in Merchantville.

The investigation turned its focus on Entente's involvement, and questions about the unknown rescuer were put aside. Investigators from more alphabet agencies joined the FBI team. SEC, Federal Reserve, CFTC, FDIC, Comptroller of the Currency. Everyone wanted a piece of the action and the publicity attached to bringing down one of the biggest stock and banking frauds in history.

Entente's Elko offices were shuttered and searched ... repeatedly. Entente's stock plummeted, and its operations folded up around the globe as the investigation spread internationally.

Turner Bates cut a deal in exchange for information on Entente's fraudulent bookkeeping practices and his testimony in the series of trials that would follow. His lawyer made a lame attempt to object to the use of the coerced confession, but it didn't matter. There was enough information for the Feds to follow leads and develop their own case.

In the end, he confessed again, having been officially read his rights and with his lawyer present. He pled guilty to lesser charges and received a reduced sentence. There would be a stint in prison for him, but not as long as Owen Syndall's.

Sole spent a month recovering in Amelia's cabin in the mountains overlooking Turnbridge. It was an ideal place to recuperate. Amelia was an excellent nurse, attentive to his needs, making sure the wound was clean, that he ate properly, and when he was able, that he exercised, walking the trails into the mountains as his strength increased.

One morning he looked across the wooden kitchen table at her and said, "I'll be leaving tomorrow." He flexed his arm for her. "See. You fixed me up good as new."

"Do you have to?" She put her cup down, her brow furrowed. "I mean you could stay … if you want."

Their relationship had been strictly platonic. Sole slept in the guest room, waited until she was out of the house each day to shower and take care of his personal necessities. He went to lengths to ensure the friendship that developed between them remained just that—a friendship.

She'd known this day would come but had hoped somehow she could convince him that there could be a life there in Turnbridge for him … with her. He'd explained his past, some of it at least, and he reminded her now. "I meant what I said. I can't become close to anyone … not in that way."

She'd smiled, "But we already are close, aren't we?"

"Yes, we are," he answered, returning the smile, then

shook his head. "But not in that way. Besides, I'm too old for you."

"Not so old." She smiled and looked into his eyes. "And I'm not as young as you may think. There are lots of ways of being old ... things that make you old."

"I know." He shook his head, and she detected a trace of sadness in the motion. "I can't stay."

"Alright." She nodded, picked up her cup, and sipped her coffee, forcing herself to stop talking.

Later that night, after supper and after they'd done the dishes together, and sat on the porch for a while watching the stars come out, and then gone to their separate bedrooms, the door to the guest room opened in the dark. Amelia entered and stood looking at him for a few moments, not sure if he was awake. Not sure if she was going to do what she had planned to do. He lay motionless. She couldn't even hear his breathing in the dead silence of the cabin.

She made up her mind and lay down on the bed beside him, close but careful not to touch him. A minute passed, and still, close to him like that, she couldn't hear his breath. Then, without speaking, he reached out an arm, put it under her shoulders, and pulled her to him.

They lay like that for a while, not talking, not moving, then he said, "Like this, but that's all."

"It's enough," she whispered and turned on her side to put her cheek on his shoulder.

They lay like that through the night. In the morning, she rose from the bed and left the room, closing the door behind her. When he had cleaned up and gathered his things in the duffel, he came from the room. She had his coffee ready. They sat at the wooden table drinking it like they had every morning for the last month.

The time passed for her to head down to the mine office, but she stayed at the table with him. "Aren't you going to be late for work?" he asked.

"I'm the boss," she said, smiling. "They can't fire me."

They laughed and drank more coffee, neither wanting the moment to end. In the end, he stood and picked up the duffel. "I need to be going now."

"Alright," she said, resigned not to ask him to stay. She followed him through the cabin to the front door.

He opened the door and stepped out into a cold, sunlit morning. She followed him onto the porch, afraid to say anything that might shatter the moment and hasten his departure. He turned, a smile on his face but his eyes serious. "You know, I would if I could … stay, I mean."

"I know." She stood up on her toes and gave him a brief kiss on the cheek.

"Goodbye, Amelia." He turned, stepped from the porch, and walked to his pickup parked at the side of the cabin.

"Goodbye, John," she said as he backed the pickup away and started down the drive. She brushed the back of her hand across her eyes, fighting back the tears, a forced smile on her face and whispered, "I don't even know your last name."

It was the slightest of sounds, a muffled creak, nothing more, but it was enough. Peter Jenks' eyes opened, immediately alert. He reached for the pistol on the nightstand.

"Don't."

Jenks' hand froze. He recognized the voice. "How did you find me?"

"Guess."

"Bates," Jenks said between clenched teeth. "I should have killed the son of a bitch before leaving."

"You wouldn't have had time."

Jenks looked at the man standing in the shadows at the foot of the bed, pointing a pistol at his head. He nodded at the bags he'd packed and left in the corner before going to bed. "This isn't necessary. I have money. I'll pay you whatever you want. I'll disappear. In fact, I'm leaving in the morning. Saw the report today that the Feds are tracking down the bank accounts, coming after everyone involved. Just a matter of time before they find my little island sanctuary."

"You should have already gone."

"I know." Jenks pushed himself up on the pillows, speaking almost casually. "It's just that I love this place … island paradise and all. The work keeps me from enjoying life the way others do. I wanted to savor this place until the last moment. You know how it is for men like us."

"I'm not like you."

"Really?" Jenks smiled. "I think you are more like me than you know."

"Think what you will."

"So that's it, then." Jenks sat up straight, defiant. "Get it over with! You could have killed me in my sleep. What are you waiting for?"

"You need to see it coming … understand the justice."

"Justice!" Jenks spit the word back at him. "Don't talk to me about justice. It's a word without meaning. What matters are the results … who wins … who loses. That's why we do what we do … men like you and me. We win."

"I told you, I'm not like you."

"Look, you don't have to do this," Jenks said, changing

tack. "You have your justice. I admit it. What happened was wrong, but it was a mistake. But now, there is money to be made ... a lot of money ... the kind of money that brings justice and evens things out. I have contacts. We could be partners." Jenks was speaking fast, the words tumbling out, hoping to distract the man with the gun as he reached for the pistol on the nightstand. "Don't you see we could ..."

He wasn't nearly fast enough. The .45 bucked and roared. The slug punched through Peter Jenks' skull and lodged in the wall behind the bed.

A few days later, when the FBI would enter the house on the island with the Belizean authorities, they would examine the spatter of blood and brain matter circling the hole in the wall and retrieve the bullet. In time, they would match it to the bullets taken from the bodies of Freddy Yang and Carl Sink. The investigation would end there.

John Sole lowered the pistol and walked from the house. Outside, the stars blazed over the Caribbean in a moonless sky. He took out a cell phone and punched in a number.

Amelia Downes answered, "Yes?"

"It's done."

"Oh." She let out a long breath. "Are you coming back now?"

"No." The word sounded harsher than he intended. He wanted to say something to soften it but could think of nothing that would change things or make it easier for either of them.

"Alright, then." Amelia's voice broke a little, then she gained control. "Take care of yourself, John."

"And you, Amelia."

"I'll miss you," she offered, hoping against hope that the open admission might change his mind.

Voice thick with emotion, he said, "I have to go now."

The call ended. Separated by three thousand miles, they stood under the same moonless sky, staring into the night, wishing it didn't have to end this way. But it did. Sole knew it, and in her heart of hearts, Amelia knew it too.

Next in the Sole Justice series

vinci-books.com/darkwinter

Trapped by a blizzard in a small South Dakota town, a drifter with a haunted past confronts the secrets lurking beneath the idyllic surface

John Sole, seeking escape from his troubled history, finds himself stranded in a tight-knit Midwestern community. As he envisions a fresh start, a murder and a dead cop shatter his hopes, and a truck harboring a terrible secret threatens to unravel the town's fabric.

Turn the page for a free preview…

Dark Winter: Chapter One

NO CHOICE

Don't stop. Keep moving. Eyes straight ahead, foot on the gas.

John Sole watched the rearview mirror, willing the car behind to follow him through the intersection. It was an older model sedan, stopped for the traffic signal. The driver hesitated too long. Several young men, some in their early teens, the oldest in their twenties, surrounded the sedan, street thugs looking for easy targets.

A few had been standing on the corner as Sole pulled up and stopped for the red light. They eyeballed him. He eyeballed them back. One standing on the curb lifted his shirt just enough to expose the butt of a pistol tucked in his waistband. He gave Sole his best narrow-eyed gang stare. Sole reached under the seat and pulled the Colt 1911, his go-to weapon. He held it up, then laid it on the seat beside him in easy reach. He locked eyes with gun-thug for a moment until he moved on to examine the car behind, looking for easier pickings, someone more vulnerable and less aware.

When the light changed to green and Sole moved forward into the intersection, more young men came from the alleys and shadows of the buildings. They surrounded the sedan behind him, pounding on the hood with their fists, kicking dents in the sides. The driver panicked and froze.

"Keep moving," Sole watched and muttered. "Put a foot on the gas. Run them over if you have to."

The driver didn't. He was older, staring wide-eyed, hands on the steering wheel in a white-knuckled death grip, his head swiveling from window to window as the mob moved around the car.

His wife beside him sobbed and whispered, "Oh God, no." She put a hand on the side window to cover the face of one of the gangbangers pressed against the glass, laughing wildly at her.

Two more emerged from a nearby alley and jumped up on the hood, using it as a trampoline. The old sedan's worn suspension bounced like a souped-up lowrider, tossing the occupants around inside.

Sole made it across the intersection, still watching the rearview mirror. *It's not your problem. You've got enough problems. Keep moving.*

They were trying to open the sedan's doors now, pulling at the handles and pounding on the glass, taunting and shrieking at the old couple inside. One grinned and leaned close to the driver's window. "Open the door, motherfucker, or you dead." His face was close enough to the window that drops of spit ran down the glass where he'd leaned in to shout.

Start driving. Get away from them. Sole tried to will the old couple forward. He looked up and down the street for signs of a police response. There was none.

The crowd around the sedan was growing. Traffic in the street swerved to miss it, cars and trucks sped up to get away and not be caught up in whatever happened next. What had started as a carjacking was growing into a small riot. Passersby went into self-preservation mode, avoiding the commotion in the street. No one was inclined to intervene and become the new target of the mob.

A heavyset young man, no more than sixteen years old, came around the back of the sedan with a baseball bat. He swung it over his head like an ax pounding on the trunk. Then he lifted it to his shoulder in a batter's stance, ready to swing for the stands.

"Shit," Sole growled. He spun the pickup's steering wheel and turned down a side street a block from the intersection. Pulling to the curb, he jumped out, holding the Colt down along the side of his leg, and ran the block back to the intersection.

The bat connected with the glass, and the side window exploded in a shower of glass. Two others pulled the door open and jerked the old man from the driver's seat onto the ground. They held him down while another pummeled him with his fists.

The teen with the bat moved to the passenger side. The old woman shrieked in terror, then the passenger window shattered in her face. Blood poured from lacerations where the glass fragments lodged in her paper-thin skin. She covered her face with her hands as more assailants reached in and dragged her onto the ground.

Fists raised high above her head, then froze. The Colt's thunder reverberated between the buildings. Sole had fired one round into the asphalt. He lifted his weapon and held it in a combat stance, ready to engage any threat that presented itself.

The Ghost

"Back away." Sole motioned with the pistol toward the curb. "Get away from them, and you might live through the next few seconds."

"Shit. You think you can take us all on, motherfucker?" Gun-thug put his hand on the pistol butt to pull it out.

Some of the mob backed away. Others moved toward their comrade to provide support. Several were armed, but they weren't professionals. They bunched together, providing easy targets if things went badly in the next few seconds.

"I said back away." Sole held the pistol on gun-thug who seemed to be the leader.

"Naw, man. We ain't backing away. We just about to …" Gun-thug jerked his pistol from his waistband. Before he could bring it up to bear on the stranger who had mixed himself up in their business, another roar thundered, and he dropped to the ground.

There was no Hollywood reaction to being shot. No dramatic stagger backward. No arms flung up in surprised agony. Gun-thug simply crumpled, his head smacking into the sidewalk with a thud and a forty-five-caliber hole punched through his sternum.

The round cut through his aorta and a pool of blood spread rapidly around him on the pavement. His partners in crime never saw it. They were running for the alleys as Sole swiveled to target the next attacker, but they were gone. Their leader gone, lying in a pool of blood, no one wanted to join him.

Sole went to the sedan. The old woman sat on the curb sobbing, incoherent, and unable to speak. It would take her a while to recover from the emotional trauma of the attack, but physically, she was in reasonably good shape … considering.

Her husband wasn't so lucky. Sole found him sprawled on the street by the driver's door. They had beaten him with something hard. Sole recognized the marks of brass knuckles in the contusions on the side of his face and wished he'd been able to put a round through the one who beat an old man senseless. Facial bones were fractured and the old man's right eye protruded from the orbital socket as if it might fall to the ground, hanging suspended from the optic nerve.

A man came from a store at the corner. Sole motioned him over. "Stay with him."

"Right." The man nodded excitedly. "I saw it all … I mean, the way you took care of those assholes." He nodded at the old man on the ground. "You saved his life … and the old woman's too." He shook his head. "I mean, that was some shit."

Sirens sounded a few blocks away, and the man added. "I called the cops. They'll be here in a minute. Don't worry, I'll be your witness."

Sole stood. "Stay with the old man. Don't move him until the paramedics get here unless he starts choking. If he does, roll him on his side and make sure nothing is blocking his airway."

"Airway?" The man from the store knelt by the old man.

"His throat. Make sure nothing is choking him."

"Oh, right." The man looked up, surprised to see Sole walking briskly away toward the intersection. "Where are you going? The cops will be here in a minute." He shouted at Sole's back. "You're gonna be a hero! I'll make sure of it. My wife got the whole thing on video."

Sole was trotting now, the Colt tucked in his waistband. He crossed the intersection and picked up speed, heading down the block to the side street. By the time he was in the pickup and pulling from the curb, the first police units were arriving at the intersection, followed by paramedics and a news crew that picked up the police call on their scanner.

People emerged from the surrounding buildings where they'd taken cover from the gang in the intersection. They milled around gun-thug's body until the police pushed them back to secure the crime scene.

Sole drove a dozen blocks along the side street, then turned onto a major highway that crossed through the city. A half-hour later, he made his way onto an interstate.

The city could have been any sprawling metropolis where the inner-city streets were largely controlled by gangs and street thugs. By sunset, he'd put a hundred miles between him and the intersection.

The man from the store said he'd saved the old couple's lives. Sole knew that was probably true, but something else the man said haunted him.

My wife got the whole thing on video.

When are you going to learn to walk away, John-boy? The voice inside was nagging again.

He shook his head. And do what? Let the gang terrorize, maybe kill, an old couple?

For once, the voice inside understood and shut up. He'd had no choice.

Dark Winter: Chapter Two

BALANCING ACCOUNTS

"*Jefa*, excuse the interruption, but you should see this." Reynaldo Gutierrez stood in the office doorway in the hacienda high on a mountainside above the Mexican port of Lázaro Cárdenas. Beyond the plate-glass window, the distant swells of the Pacific reflected the sunlight into glittering points blinking in and out of existence with the movement of the ocean.

Juana Elizondo looked up from the cluster of papers scattered across the desk that had once been her father's. "Yes, Reynaldo. What is it?"

"This." Gutierrez entered and placed a tablet on the desk in front of her, touched the screen, and brought up a video. "It is a recording of a news report in the States."

"A news report? We have news reports here."

"This one is of special interest, *Jefa*."

Elizondo touched play on the video then stared at the screen for several minutes while an American reporter in a city two thousand miles away stood before the camera, microphone in hand interviewing witnesses interspersed with long shots of a heavily damaged older car and a blood-stained sheet covering a body sprawled on the sidewalk.

The reporter continued speaking off-camera while a series of low quality, but viewable videos taken by cell phone users appeared. One video, in particular, caught Elizondo's attention. Her eyes narrowed, and her body tensed, hands gripping the sides of the tablet as if she might crush it with her bare hands.

When the report concluded, she looked at Reynaldo. "Find him."

"*Si, Jefa*. I already have men searching now that we have a location."

"Keep me advised."

"*Si, Jefa*." Gutierrez turned and left the office, leaving the tablet on the desk.

Elizondo played the video again, freezing the image that appeared during the segment taken from cell phones. She stared at the screen and the face frozen there. Finding that face had consumed her since her father's death in the Mexican desert.

Since that day, there had been no sign of the man who orchestrated the ambush that killed Bebé Elizondo, and his deputy, Alejandro Garza. Bebé might have headed up the deadliest cartel on the continent, but to her he was *Papi*, and Garza, her father's right hand and a merciless killer, was simply *Tio* Alejandro to the Elizondo family.

She had taken over the family business, running the *Los Salvajes* cartel's operations with ruthless efficiency, but never had she forgotten the man who took her father away. Others, including Reynaldo, suggested that the gringo must have died alone in the desert after the shooting ended. He may have been wounded, they said, or perhaps he ran out of water. Despite the cartel's efforts to find him, they were unable to recover a body, but there was no sign that he had escaped and his survival alone in the desert without transportation seemed unlikely. Others suggested that scavengers had eaten and disposed of the gringo's body. They laughed and joked that what was left of him was probably coyote shit scattered across the desert. It was only fitting that he should end that way, they said.

Juana never believed it. Somewhere the man who killed her father lived, and that was unacceptable. Before his death, she kept the accounts for her father, balancing debits and credits to perfection. She remembered his round, smiling face and the gentle pat on the head when she pleased him.

"Such a good little accountant," he would say. "Tell me, *mi estrellita*, my little star. Is everything in order?"

"Yes, *Papi*. The accounts balance perfectly."

But there was one account that had not balanced since her father's death, and she promised herself that she would find the man responsible. He would pay, and only then would the accounts be balanced.

In a motel room far from the intersection in the city, Sole watched the same news report, shook his head, and sighed. The reporter interviewed the witnesses standing nearby … a crime scene the police were calling it.

When she asked a police captain with the homicide investigation unit why they were calling it a crime scene when the person who intervened saved the life of the old couple, he said, "We have a zero-tolerance policy for murder, regardless of who does it or why. A vigilante killing is still a murder and we intend to investigate and find the killer."

The reporter moved on to the witnesses who had kept their distance but saw what happened. Isaiah Selander and his wife Doreen stood beside her, recounting what they'd seen through the store window as the gang of young men terrorized the old couple in the sedan. The reporter had the studio play the video from Doreen's cell phone as they told their story.

"It was terrible what they were doing to those people. I mean, we called the police, but you know how long they take to get to this part of town these days, what with everything happening and all."

"It must have been terrifying," the reporter said, "seeing all of this transpire just outside your window." She held the microphone in front of Doreen to get the human-interest angle of the story. "A forgotten neighborhood where this kind of violence takes place." She shook her head sympathetically. "Tell me, how did it make you feel to know that such violence could occur here?"

"I was frightened. I admit it," Doreen said. "This used to be a quiet neighborhood, but not anymore."

"And you?" The reporter shifted to Isaiah. "I can't imagine the helplessness you must have felt."

"Well, we were helpless, I admit it. I mean, I don't have any experience dealing with this sort of thing, but ..." Isaiah leaned close to the microphone to make sure it picked up his words. "But he's a hero ... the one who took care of him." He nodded at the sheet-draped body on the sidewalk. "He's a hero."

"The police are calling him a vigilante ... a killer," the reporter said. "How do you feel about that?"

"If he's a vigilante, in my book he's a vigilante hero. He

did what had to be done, and if he hadn't, there's no telling what would have happened to the people in the car. I say he's a hero and I don't care what the police call it."

Sole turned off the television. He didn't feel like a hero. He had done what needed to be done at the exact moment it needed to be done. Gun-thug had the chance to make a different choice, to leave the couple alone and call things even. When he didn't, Sole did what he had to do. Nothing more.

He pulled up a map on his phone, looking for out-of-the-way places, the sort of places where people paid little attention to the news out of a big city back east. Tracing a route west, he made up his mind.

Grab your copy…
vinci-books.com/darkwinter

About the Author

Glenn Trust is the author of the bestselling *Hunters, Sole Justice, and Journey Series* of mystery/thriller/suspense novels. He has also written standalone works, including *Dying Embers, Mojave Sun, and short stories*.

There are no superheroes or knights in shining armor in his stories. According to Trust, knights are for fairy tales. His books are gritty and based in the real world, with characters who face their frailties while dealing with their roles in the story. The heroes are average people doing the best they can.

The villains, as real villains often do, look like us. Trust's monsters hide behind the smiling faces that pass us on the street. They look like us, and this makes them more frightening.

He is a Georgia native but has lived in most regions of the country at one time or another. Varied experiences, from construction worker to police officer, corporate executive to city manager, color and provide insight into the characters he creates. His stories are known for detailed plots, solid research, and realism.

Today, he writes full-time and lives quietly with his wife and two dogs, Gunner and Charlie.